JET BLACK JUSTICE
A TRIED & TRUE NOVEL
BOOK TWO

CHARLI RAHE

TRIED AND TRUE PUBLISHING

Copyright © 2014 by Charli Rahe
All rights reserved.
No part of this book may be reproduced in any form or by any electronic or mechanical means, including information storage and retrieval systems, without written permission from the author, except for the use of brief quotations in a book review.
First paperback edition March 2023
First hardcover edition March 2023
Cover Art by Miblart
Chapter Art by Etheric Designs
Edited by Dana Mohn
ISBN (ebook) 978-1-958055-03-8
ISBN (paperback) 978-1-958055-04-5
ISBN (hardcover) 978-1-958055-05-2

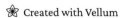 Created with Vellum

NOTE FROM THE AUTHOR

Scarlet's fantastical story follows a woman's journey through her magical heritage in which she encounters several dark scenarios. It is not intended for readers under 18 years of age and includes adult content.

While I'd prefer you to experience it as you go, your mental health matters. Please refer to www.charlirahe.com for a detailed list of possible triggers.

PROLOGUE

It started after Wren disappeared on Beltane. She returned home in the wee hours. A completely uncharacteristic occurrence from the otherwise dutiful daughter. She had apologized and explained that she'd gotten lost in the dangerous jungles of Ostara before she found her way back.

Wren seemed to have changed overnight. Matured. Flowered.

Lark had been with Hawk searching for her. He worried that his attention to Sea may have been the cause for her flight, but he'd been wrong.

She'd met someone.

Someone special if her monthly visits to Ostara were any indication. It had started at as monthly. Every fifth of the month, then it was fifth and fifteenth, it progressed to Thursday night visits after the family went to sleep, Hawk had confided to Lark.

Although she was the same age, there was a youthful, innocent quality to Wren.

Since Beltane, there had been no more chases in Lark's family woods. No more sleepovers with Lark's sister, Robin, only to and stay up daring one another to do ridiculous things. Robin had secretly married her son's father and had returned after a lengthy stay with the

Valkyries. Lark couldn't speak to her maturity, but Robin wanted to seem as if she had.

Wren had been smiling and laughing all night as her family entertained the Haust and Dagr families. The wine flowed freely, and Hawk and Lark noticed Wren, Sparrow, and Robin stealing swigs of a skin they had filled under the table. The three girls could have been sisters for all their physical similarities.

Peak hadn't come. He was still sore about Lark stealing Sea from him, though he courted the beautiful Willow Natt. She bore a slight resemblance to Sea.

"I see you two conspiring. Leave her be, Lark. She is not your ward anymore, and she is not your sister," her full lips curled knowingly at Lark who sighed.

He should not have confessed to her that Wren was his first kiss. Sea was his second, as he was for her. He was waiting until he turned eighteen before asking his father to come with him to the Dagr's and ask for her hand. It would be a long two years.

Hawk ran his hand over his black hair as he typically did when deep in thought, "She is my sister and I want to know whom she has been sneaking off to meet. How has she met anyone? Her only friends are in this room."

That was true for each of them except Robin and Sea. Robin's husband wasn't invited, no one was supposed to know about him.

Wren stood and bent down to whisper to Sparrow and Robin who teased her under their breath as she walked to kiss Pearl and Flint goodnight.

Wren walked behind their chairs and kissed the top of Hawk's head. "Goodnight, brother," she waved to Sea and Lark before she strolled from the dining hall.

Hawk gestured to the hall she disappeared into, "I do not even know that girl. She is floating on air. If you do not help me, I will do it on my own."

Hawk glanced to Sparrow and made a detour before following Wren.

"Go then. I can feel you thrumming with the thrill of the hunt. Do not spoil her fun, Lark. She is in love. You can certainly empathize," Sea whispered.

Lark stole a peek at their parents before stealing her kiss, "How right you are. I love you, Sea. I will be back before you know it."

"Ostara. I should have known. Can you track them?"

Lark nodded as they followed the arches of white and purple blooms deeper into the jungle. Her scent was fresh. Jasmine and roses. No scent of a male, yet.

"She came through alone," Lark informed him.

Wren had to be running to be so far ahead of them that they couldn't spot her. Lark was feeling guilty about their covert mission when he heard the deep voice of a man followed by Wren's purr.

"This way. Keep low," Lark told Hawk as they crossed into the flower beds.

He heard a spring and followed its trail until it cleared into a large pond. He spun and faced Hawk.

"We should go. She is with a man. We were right," he said more stiffly than he should have.

Hawk narrowed his eyes at his friend before pushing past him. The greenery opened so the moonlight could beam down giving an illuminated view of the patch of moss that smoothed the ground near the pond.

Lark shut his eyes and followed his friend whose eyesight wasn't as good as his own. Hawk jerked to a standstill and Lark came to stand by his side.

He could never look at Wren the same way again.

The little girl who'd stripped down to her skin when they dared her to swim the castle's moat was a scrawny little thing, not the woman on her knees with a man's hands intimately holding her fair share of curves while she moved.

Lark wished his heightened senses weren't quite so heightened. Her wet hair curved around her chest and over his fingers as he kissed along her throat.

"By the Mother, what is she thinking? Who is that with her? He is most certainly older," Hawk cursed.

Lark realized Hawk couldn't make out the details of the man's face or see the gold tree of life buckles on his boots where they rested haphazardly against the wet stones.

"Does it really matter? I hope we sated your curiosity, my friend," Lark patted Hawk shoulder and they left the clearing.

"I suppose not," Hawk grumbled, "She has always been wild with no sense of self-awareness. She is a woman; men have noticed her. She needs to safeguard her reputation."

"She is, Hawk. She is not flaunting her relationship. If we had not followed her, we would have no clue," he reassured Hawk and told him he was going to head straight home so he would take the portal separately.

Instead, he went back to the jungle to wait for Wren.

Wren twirled the white peony in front of her nose as she skipped back to the portal. Her and Tree always parted ways at the arches well before the town roads even though they were heading in the same direction.

Tree, as in the year of the Tree. He called her Little Bird because she was born the year of the bird. She hadn't wanted to know his name or give her own though he hadn't stopped asking. She was a Tio and a Sumar. If her family knew she was cavorting with a commoner, they would be disappointed. For once, she was just a girl, not a greater family daughter with expectations and responsibilities. Tree liked her for her.

"Wren."

She felt as though lightning struck the way her body jolted when Lark stepped from the arches. Her brow drew down in defiance.

"You followed me! Where is Hawk? Did he put you up to this? I am not doing anything wrong. All of you do it. I choose to do it with someone who does not have lands or an island to run. I refuse to be judged for it. Did you see us?" her eyes widened at her last thought, but Lark's mouth had fallen open.

"Do you not know who that is? What did he tell you his name was?"

Lark was suddenly angry, and Wren started. She could count on one finger how many times she'd seen Lark angry, and it was after he started seeing Sea when he got into an altercation with Peak. His eyes reflected the moonlight and Wren wasn't entirely sure she was looking at the boy she knew all her life.

"Knowing his means he will want to know mine. I do not want to be Wren Tio with him. I just want to be me," she hugged herself and Lark seemed to shrink.

His posture changing abruptly as he hurried to her and embraced her, "I did not mean to frighten you. I thought he lied and took advantage of you."

She shook her head letting it rest against the familiar chest of the boy she knew who was rapidly becoming a man. He had to be at least three inches taller than the last time he held her.

"No one takes advantage of me, Lark. No one," she emphasized, and Lark sighed.

"I hear you, fair Wren. Your—scent is strange," he told her.

"Are you politely informing me I need a shower?" she asked with a wry tone.

"No—I... May I?" Lark stepped back and held up his hand. She nodded for him to delve, and his warmth unfurled in her belly. "Oh, Wren," he said sounding pained.

She knit her brows, "Lark?"

"You are with child. Two months or so. You have only—"

"What do you think of me? Of course, it has only been him!"

Her intake of air stuttered as she skirted Lark. She needed time to think. Her last monthly had been nearly three months ago. She'd been so preoccupied with lovemaking she hadn't taken care of what happened after.

"Wren, wait! What are you going to do? You can tell him. He cares about you."

Wren sniffed, "Because he tells me he loves me after we lay together? All men do."

"No, Wren. They do not. Do you know how to reach him?"

He sounded so sincere; she wanted believed him.

"We plan our next meeting at the prior one. I have no way to get in touch. The whole point is to not have any strings. If we do not want to see one another again, we do not show. I wanted to keep it simple."

"What are you thinking?" Lark grabbed her wrist, so she had to face him.

Wren shook her head with a shrug, and tears gleamed in her eyes, "I do not know. I do not want to burden a man I barely know. What did Robin do?"

Lark sighed and slung his arm over her shoulders, "Come. We will tell your mother together and form a plan."

The Valkyrie with the big green eyes gestured to the bed at the very back of the long room. Lark thanked her and held fast to the two bouquets of flowers as he crossed the nearly empty room. A white divider separated the beds from one another and he stopped at the first and smiled.

Robin nursed another dark-haired baby boy and gave her brother a broad smile. Coyote's intense gaze swept over him until Lark winked and the boy giggled.

"Regn," he inclined his head to the golden eyed man who apparently couldn't wait until publicly wed to Lark's sister before getting her with child.

My sincerest gratitude to everyone who left a kind word after my first novel. It gave me the courage to chase bigger dreams. Thanks to Dana for working through rough drafts with me and asking the hard questions which, hopefully, has created a fuller experience for you readers. A special thanks to my "fit fam" for coaching me through that pesky imposter syndrome, and the members of the "dream team" who helped me give myself permission to show up for myself.
Finally, and always, to my husband and children — I love you.

"She is not well," Robin told him furrowing her brow, her green eyes worried.

That was what Lark feared. He handed Robin one bouquet which she passed off to Regn before crossing to the next bed behind its divider.

"Knock, knock," he said as he looked in on Wren.

She laid under the white sheets on her side with her hand hanging in the bassinet beside the bed, "My mother is going to claim him. She has been careful about who has seen her the last few months and…"

She trailed off. Pearl had told his mother she was pregnant and gone through great lengths to hide that she wasn't. They told everyone Wren was studying in the States which was common for Guardians to do once proven tried and true, but not before. Still, Hawk had no clue where his twin sister had gone.

"It is better this way. He will have a mother and father. Stability and a safe, reputable family. I will care for him like a mother until he no longer needs me, and my mother can raise him," she said as if to herself as Lark found an empty vase in a cupboard behind her bed. He filled it with water before putting in the flowers.

"You have not heard from him?" he asked sitting behind her.

"I already told you; I do not wish to burden him."

"A man should know if he has a child.", he breathed as he peeked into the bassinet at the blue clad bundle with dirty blonde feathery hair, "He is a good mix of his father and your grandmother."

"I thought the same thing," she murmured.

"You can be his very impressive, overprotective sister. You can let yourself love him, Wren," Lark whispered resting his chin on her head.

"I am in shock. Yesterday, I gave birth and once I lose a little of the baby weight, I go back to the academy as if nothing ever happened. I should be happy it has all worked out, but I feel strangely empty. There was a peek behind the curtain and found nothing extraordinary," she said as the baby grasped her finger.

"Are you in love with him?" Lark asked.

Wren swallowed hard and nodded, "I think maybe I was. *Am*. I do not know anymore."

Lark and Sea ate breakfast on the covered walkway of the Dagr palace.

"It is not proper to eavesdrop even if you have the ability," Sea chastened as she rubbed her pregnant belly.

Lark couldn't help it. Orion Vetr had gone into the room with his son, the eligible Ridge and heir to all Elivagar. Lark was a second son and couldn't fault the Dagr's for wanting the most advantageous match for their youngest daughter.

"I must admit. I did not know you were interested in my daughter."

"I have seen her at festivals over the years," Ridge told him.

"When I heard Hawk Sumar had not yet approached you for his marriage contract with her, I knew time was of the essence. Thank you for agreeing to meet with us," Orion stated.

Lark could hear the creak of leather as if Sea's father sat forward in his chair, "It has been a foregone conclusion that Hawk, and Sparrow would wed. They have grown up together, they have dated for years, and only one another. I can only assume Hawk has waited until they are both at the university."

"Assumptions only. We are prepared to sign a blood contract today," Orion continued, "Sparrow would be mother to the future Patriarch Vetr whom have the richest lands of the islands."

"Patriarch Dagr, I have not entertained courting another greater family daughter because none have interested me the way your Sparrow has. She would have my total loyalty. There is no other," Ridge reassured him and Lark ran a hand over his face.

Hawk was waiting until the induction ceremony. He had planned out the whole thing. He wanted to do it on the stage in front of everyone. Lark had thought it a fine idea. Sparrow didn't always like tradition and a big gesture after years of dating would please her immensely.

The door opened, and Patriarch Dagr called over one of his staff members to retrieve Sparrow. Lark fought the overwhelming urge to run to his friend so he could fight for his love.

Sea set her hand on his hand. Few knew she was a prophet, "The Norns are cruel today."

Time heals all wounds they say. Whomever *they* are. Wren knew they didn't heal but were out of sight and so out of mind.

Years went by and the baby boy grew into a toddler. Tan and a darker blonde than his sire, but the resemblance was there.

"You look pretty, Wen," Steel said peeking into the bathroom as they readied her for her first masquerade.

Wen not Wren. She loved that nickname.

She smiled indulgently at him, "I got you something. Check on my table. The blue box with the silver ribbon."

His green-blue almond eyes went wide as he smiled gleefully and wandered over to the table in the other room.

"You spoil him," Hawk grumbled.

"You look pretty too," Wren teased hoping to coax a smile from Hawk.

After the devastating news that Ridge and Sparrow had signed a marriage contract, Hawk had fallen into a deep melancholy. It only grew worse when they received the public notice at breakfast.

When Sparrow signed that contract, she signed away Hawk's love. His every happiness for his future, gone with the press of her thumb in her own blood. Wren hadn't spoken to Sparrow probably because Sparrow knew how upset she would be over breaking her brother's heart. It made little sense. Ridge never spent time with her once. She would've told Wren.

"Will you be my date tonight?" Wren asked him and he forced a smile as he pushed off the bathroom door frame.

"Certainly," he said before he disappeared into the bedroom.

"Have fun, darling," Pearl said not directing her comment specifically for Hawk, but Wren knew whom she meant to hear it.

Hawk wore a mask of his namesake and to match him, Wren dressed as a snow owl. She spotted Lark and pregnant Sea straight off who stood closely to Ridge and Sparrow. Lark gave a little wave and Wren returned it. Their wedding had been the Guardian event of the summer.

"You can be the bigger man," she whispered to Hawk.

"When you must watch the person you love wed another, I will say the same to you and see how well you do. I plan on drowning in wassail tonight. Are you going to be a good date and join me?" Hawk asked looking miserable.

Wren gave him her brightest smile, "I would not be a very good twin if I did not."

Drunk and dancing and probably embarrassing themselves and their parents, Hawk finally smiled. They had avoided the two couples and eventually they had disappeared.

"Come. It is time we find you a husband," Hawk said pulling Wren off the dance floor, so she had to pick up her skirts.

She giggled as she followed him, and he stopped still, "I have missed your laughter."

She elbowed him in the ribs playfully, "Come. Let us find you a wife. We are the Sumar/Tio twins, totally insatiable and unmarriable. Is that a word?"

Hawk smiled lazily, his dark eyes glassy, "I prefer the term unattainable."

Wren laughed again, "I am going to have to use that when people ask me why I am always alone."

"Little Bird?" came a guttural voice that made Wren's stomach drop and her laughter died.

"You mean Wren? The unattainable Wren Tio?" Hawk chuckled, "Alder Var, yes?"

Wren slowly turned around, mouth agape and came face to face with Tree.

"Alder Var? As in, the heir to Ostara?"

Wren felt the heat rush to her face and her stomach roiled. The wassail was no longer sitting as well as it was.

"Do not worry, Wren. I am not embarrassing you in front of a potential suitor. His betrothed is Delta Natt."

Powder blue eyes peered out from a black leather mask. Wren had to crane her head back to meet them. He had to be six and a half feet tall, even bigger than he had been three years past.

He inclined his head to Hawk, but his eyes never left Wren. "And you are?" he reached for Hawk's hand, and they shook.

"Hawk Sumar."

"The Sumar heir, I did not recognize you with your mask. My apologies. Where are your dates?" Alder asked.

"We do not date. Unattainable, remember?" Hawk gave a lopsided drunken grin and slung his arm heavily across Wren's feather collar.

"So, neither of you have betrotheds?" he asked.

"You would have received a notice. We are greater family after all. Ah, Ms. Blomi is looking lovely tonight. You are on your own. Lera!"

Hawk flagged down the sultry Blomi heir, daughter of the illustrious Spinel Regn. Everyone knew the Regn were trouble.

"Hawk, do nothing foolish!" Wren shouted, cupping her hand to her mouth.

Alder's hand clasped hers and she went rigid, but it was follow him or he was going to drag her. She could hardly see where he was taking her because he blocked her entire line of sight.

He yanked her sideways, and they were in a darkened alcove of the hall. Alder pushed the mask over her face and sucked in sharply.

"Did you need to speak to me in private?" she asked folding her arms under her chest hoping she looked surer of herself because she had never been less sure than in that moment.

"You did not show. I went every week for two months and then every fifth of the month. I went the last three Beltane."

The alcove seemed to shrink with him towering over her.

"We agreed. If we did not show, it was over., Wren said weakly.

Where was her moxie? She used to have spirit.

"I thought perhaps an unforeseen circumstance occurred, and it detained you," Alder said searching her dark eyes.

"What did you think the second time I did not show?" she asked dryly.

"I thought perhaps you left a note. Some explanation."

"The third?" she asked knitting her brows.

He pushed his leather mask over his face, and she suppressed a sigh, "I hoped you had changed your mind."

"Perhaps I found out you had a betrothed." Wren said, giving herself a mental shake.

She had seen Delta. Beautiful beyond reason, blonde and statuesque. His perfect match.

"We were not betrothed. Why did you stop coming? Had I wronged you?"

Wren knit her brows and shook her head causing the curls the stylists had pinned up to catch on the flair of white feathers. "No, Tree — Alder. It was an unforeseen occurrence, as you said. Nothing you did. I did not know who you were. You worked at the Var castle because of your sigils, I thought. I did not know you would keep going or I would have sent a message. It was a difficult time for me."

"If I had known what island you were on, I would have sought you out. I did not mind going to our pond. It holds my most precious memories. I carved my name, my real name, in the stone at the ledge in case you came, and I was not there. I understand now why you did not want to tell me your name, Wren Tio. Do you regret our time together?"

"No. Of course not. I have had a hard time finding a suitor who measures up to those nights. Alas, my date tonight is my brother who may be even more lonesome than I am," she gave him a rueful grin and watched his eyes drop to her lips.

"I have missed you, Little Bird. Not Delta. I kept coming back to the pond because I hoped you felt as I did."

"I do. I mean, I did," Wren's mind was adrift without a lifeline.

Alder closed the distance between them and picked her slight form off the floor crushing her to him as he kissed her. Wren was breathless. She'd dreamed about Alder almost every night, but things had grown infinitely more complicated since they had last seen one another.

"Your betrothed," Wren breathed when he hoisted her up, carrying her through the open door.

Alder kicked the door closed with his heel. "I love you, Wren. Since the moment Jackal attacked you and you let me clean your beautiful face. There was never another woman here for me."

He took her hand and placed it over his heart.

CHAPTER ONE

PRIDE COMES BEFORE THE FALL

Shadow Breakers, marriage, the Wild Hunt, and everything in between. After years of extra courses trying to get through first high school and then college at breakneck speed, it had accustomed me to having little to no life.

Steel and Tawny were doing wedding planning when I reached her rooms. It was going to be quite the extravaganza. Papers, fabric swatches, and an enormous binder sat atop her glass octagon table. They sat side by side on her silver chaise huddled together that implied an intimacy past the physical. I watched them for a moment as his hand rubbed her back absently while she jotted notes down and said something too low for me to hear, but it made him laugh and kiss her fair cheek. That was what love was.

I had had doubts about Ash and me, but I could make anything work. A fixer. I set myself on a problem and worked it out. Watching Tawny and Steel told me we needed more than smoothing. I wasn't in love with Ash. I liked him, sure, but could he be the father of my children? Could I spend the rest of my life, which if Pearl was right would be something like another one hundred and twenty years, with him?

If not Ash, then was there anyone I felt that way about? Would I ever? I wanted my heart to skip when I saw him, for him to make me melt whenever he touched me, for me not to feel the need to conform to what he wanted, but for him to bring out the best in me.

Brass Regn. Mrs. Scarlett Regn — I wondered if I was going through my boy crazy phase later in life because I never had a chance.

"Knock. Knock," I said, entering the room and Tawny and Steel turned as one to smile at me.

The two could not be more different. She had long dark brown hair, while his was short and dark blonde, her skin was fair, his tanned, her eyes were wide and hazel, his almond and turquoise like mine.

I crossed the room and sat on the carpeted floor across from them and looked at their plans. It was going to be a huge wedding at the Vetr castle. I hadn't known that little tidbit.

Tawny held up two swatches, "Scarlet red and alabaster white. The colors of the Vetr sigil coincidentally, what do you think?"

"Stunning. When's the date?" I asked, checking the invites.

"The autumnal equinox in late September," Steel replied with a poster boy smile at Tawny.

"So then, I don't suppose you have plans for the first autumnal equinox in August?" I beamed my best smile at Steel.

"I know that look. What do you want?" Tawny asked, arching a thick brow at me.

"I can read emotions well now. I know you're getting a lot of flak for not finding the Jorogumo nests after the attack and the Wemic said they thought the Merfolk might be involved. I think I might get a read on whether there's a traitor in the Merfolk or not. If you're willing to take me there. I figured you're going to have to investigate them anyway, bring me along, let me help you."

I felt surprise and then consent in Steel while Tawny was wary.

"That might be a good idea. It will be hard to talk to everyone without a Merfolk escort," Steel said running his hand through his short, tousled hair.

I held out my hands, "I have a plan for that. Don't worry, I've got it handled. I met Cordillera... and Brass."

Steel's cheeks reddened, and I knit my brows. I hadn't expected that reaction, "Who are they?" Tawny asked not having seen Steel's shameful expression.

"Cordillera was the trainer who Pearl brought in from Valla to teach Slate, Jett, and I along with her nephews. Brass is one of her nephews. We grew up together. He was one of my roommates at Valla U along with Solder," Steel informed her.

I tried not to look too interested. "The guy from the Armored Armoire?" I asked.

"The same. They don't get along anymore, but we all used to be close. How'd you find out about Brass?" Steel spared me a glance, his full lips pursed wryly.

"He ran into me," I said and internally smiled at my private joke since he had, in fact, tackled me, "I forced him to introduce me to Cordillera and his friends."

"Don't let Jett hear that. Jett stopped training with her the year he met Amethyst and Cherry. He hasn't spoken to her since."

Tawny looked at Steel through narrowed eyes, "Right so — by train you mean slept with. When did you stop 'training' with this cougar?"

Steel gave me a desperate look, and I leaned back and gave him a look. He got himself into that mess.

"I never trained the way Jett and Slate trained with her," Steel told her.

Tawny sniffed. "Just don't bring this Cordillera around," she told me and Steel winced.

"She is Matriarch Blomi."

Tawny looked down at her seating chart and scowled, "Great. We will have a table filled with all your old lovers and one for mine as well... Oh wait, I don't have any."

"Your old lovers can sit with all my lovers, Tawns." I said smirking, and I saw her mouth quirk.

Steel offered me a grateful smile at diffusing a little of Tawny's ire then held up a drawing of an elaborate ice sculpture, "What do you think of this one?"

Wedding talk further cooled her temper and she was back to making moon eyes at Steel. Tawny always cooled as quick as she heated.

I was humming to myself as I shut Tawny's bedroom door, proud I persuaded Steel to go along with my plan when I noticed Pearl and my mother coming from my room. I cocked my head in question.

My mom beamed at me, "We were looking for you."

"I got caught up in Tawny and Steel's wedding planning," I gestured with my thumb back at her door.

You couldn't beat the smile off my mom's face. First Jett's wedding, now Tawny and Steel's. I'd never ever seen her happier.

Her big brown eyes twinkled as she looked at me.

"I spoke with your father," my mom started. Pearl looked like she had heard whatever she had to say her emerald cat eyes watching my reaction, "He wants to meet you — officially. I warned him that Jett might not be open to a meeting, but I thought if you spoke to him, he might be more amenable."

I couldn't hide my excitement; it was the first step. First, we would meet, then we become a family, all that was left then was our happily ever after.

"When did he want to arrange it? It might be hard with classes. Did he tell you I asked him if Steel was really my brother?" I groaned remembering the first time I'd had a conversation with my father. "I felt like such an idiot. He cleared it up," I gave her a pained smiled, but she was busy looking at Pearl whose big coppery brown curls slid over her dusky purple silk clad shoulders as she returned her gaze to me.

"First things first," Pearl said out loud either to her or to me, I wasn't sure.

My mother shook herself out of her stare, her wide mouth returning to her constant smile. "The first day of your harvest break, we'll meet at the cottage in Valla. Before you visit the Wemic would be the best time. Slate said he planned to take you for your birthday. Who knows, maybe it will go well, and you could spend a few days together before your trip," she said smiling.

Slate said that? It sounded thoughtful and even romantic for him to plan a trip for us. I had a hard time acknowledging that things blurred horribly between us. No — I wouldn't read too much into it.

Pearl pursed her full lips and wrapped her draped sleeved arm around my shoulder, so we walked down the hall together. They were both several inches shorter than I was even in their heels and I was only average height.

"It is very exciting but consider the tribal concerns and general disarray of things. Best to keep it quiet for a time, darling."

I nodded. Alder's wife looked like she could chew me up and spit me out. I wouldn't want to cross that woman. My mom was nodding making her long dark waves slide over her bare shoulders at what Pearl was saying about the tribes.

"How are the Aves, mom? Have you made contact yet?"

I knew she was having a hard time with the Ostara tribe, but I also knew my father was with her while she was attempting to contact them.

My mom glanced at Pearl. Pearl made some gesture, and I could sense the air rushing around us muffling our voices to anyone outside the three of us.

My mom looked nervous, her big dark eyes serious, "I have. Scarlett, this is ambassador business for now. But just so you're careful. They're telling me things that are concerning. I don't mean to scare you, only don't go wandering off alone like you did in the red hills."

I nodded. Her grave tone frightened me, but also curious. There was no way I would do something so foolish like get myself attacked again as I had in the red hills. I would've been killed if Slate hadn't saved me... but, I wanted to be a part of the conspiracy.

"What things are they telling you?" I whispered, I didn't know why. It felt like it needed to be whispered.

My mom looked reluctant to tell me.

Pearl interjected, "It is best that we confirm what they have said before repeating it." She gave me a smile willing me to understand. I did. I still wanted to know everything though.

"So, tell me anyway, what are they like?"

My mom made contact with a tribe no one had dealt with in fifteen years. It was too bad it was overshadowed by information I couldn't know about yet. I didn't think my mom was even telling people she had made contact; it must not have been very good.

She told me about their floating land and the tree that they lived in. How many different Aves existed, she confirmed my wildest dreams. — there were Aves that resembled peacocks.

I was feeling productive finally doing something, other than the dodging of a wedding I no longer thought I wanted. Slate and I hadn't spoken outside of the rare times I'd trained with him on the weekends I was at the Sumar palace.

I had sent a message with Quick for Brass to let him know once Tawny's wedding was over next month, I'd start coming regularly to train with him. Quick said it wasn't a big deal and to come whenever I could. It had proved harder than I thought between helping Tawny plan her wedding and time I spent with Ash.

I packed light for the trip to the Merfolk. Steel had told me we'd spend most of our time in bathing suits anyway since the Merfolk didn't really wear clothes. I strapped my weapons over my bathing suit and pulled on a thin pair of pants and a snug white shirt for the trip there and back and slipped into a pair of slouchy suede boots.

Tawny wasn't going, I knew she couldn't. Steel told me I'd see why soon enough. The girls didn't want Jett going either, so he let it drop. Steel told Gypsum he'd take him when he another time which I suspected had to do with something Jett had told me about Merfolk really liking their ambassador. I hoped our lack of traveling companions meant we were safe; I'd never seen Steel fight, and I was hoping I wouldn't have to.

We were meeting in the portal room in the Sumar palace. Tawny, Jett, and the girls had gone home while I got ready, so I walked through the portal room alone from Valla U. Blue faux starry lights greeted me as the bright white light be- hind me faded and I shut the door. My eyes adjusted to the room slowly, and I realized there were three men in the room.

"Good, Scarlett. You're here. All set?" Steel asked. He held his pronged spear like a walking stick as he approached.

"Yes. Solder. How's it going?"

Solder's luscious lips parted in a bright, sexy smile, the blue light making his cobalt eyes seem to glow. He swaggered over to me and lifted my hand to those lips. Oh. They were as soft as they looked.

"Much better now. Ready to get to know me better?"

I blushed right on cue.

"Alright. Alright. My niece is being courted by the impetuous Ash Straumr. The famous upcoming Tio and Straumr wedding," Steel said pushing us apart.

Solder looked me over. "That is you? I had not realized. Well, you are not married yet." He said with a quirk of his eyebrow.

I grumbled. "Technically, I'm being courted, but not exclusively." I said trying to make myself feel better as I touched the amethyst teardrop on the ring that hung from my Yggdrasil necklace.

Slate brushed past my shoulder ignoring me. Steel pressed his lips together suddenly realizing his mistake inviting Solder to join us.

I expected a six-hour hike through the desert, what I got was completely different. Steel guided us around a path at the back of the palace that brought us to a stone bridge that crossed the River Sols. It emptied into the waterfalls. A large sturdily build raft waited at a small dock that looked reserved for palace use only.

We all climbed onto the raft with Steel steering after he waved to a dock master who beamed at him. The man obviously liked him and knew him well. He called water to push us downstream. I sat against one of the four short sides of the raft, that came up to my shoulders, high enough to keep a random breeze from sending water spilling over the raft.

Solder sat next to me, so our sides touched. I liked Solder, he'd be harmless if I didn't let him think he stood a chance. Steel was trying to keep his disapproval at Solder's attention to himself, but I could feel it. Slate sat against the back behind Steel and out of side. He blended in with the small shadow the raft gave from the falling light.

Solder had a broad smile and twinkling blue eyes, but it was his lips that you couldn't help, but stare at. Big, pink, and luscious. He kept licking them or sucking them into his mouth, it was incredibly distracting.

"How did you meet this suitor of yours?" he asked, making small talk.

I told him about the night of the masquerade and how Ash was the first person in Tidings to introduce himself to me and the rest was history.

"Lucky man. The first man you met here? I knew it had to be something like that. It is only because you had not met me yet," he winked and pulled a giggle from me.

Rage assailed my empath abilities and it stopped my laugh short. I recovered at a snail's pace thinking I must have misread it.

"I take it you are very single. How long have you been working at the Armored Armoire?" I asked.

Solder's smile deepened, "I own the shop. It is mine and my family's. I like more than my fair share of wiggle room."

"Seems like that is the consensus of men around Tidings," I said unable to disguise my bitter tone.

Solder eyed me, "Ah. I see. The disapproving sort. A simple way to fix that is for you to sample all that Tidings offers. Decline the Straumr's proposal and spend a year finding out what you like in a man. You may surprise yourself."

I hoped it was too dark for him to see my blanch. That hit way too close to home. I'd sampled a bit more than I had meant to in the eight months I'd been there.

"I have never seen the Merfolk. Should be fun. Jett, my brother told me they're jealous, —emotional. He wasn't entirely clear, even so, I haven't met a tribe I didn't like."

Except the Jorogumo, but I tried not to pigeonhole the entire tribe because of the ones who had tried to kill me.

Steel's body moved with the ship. He looked so natural out on the water. I wondered if Tawny had seen him like this. He saw me watching his steering abilities and beamed a bright perfect smile at me. I wondered if all the guys in his year had brilliant smiles. Solder certainly did and come to think of it, Brass's smile was perfect too.

"I'm just going to jump in and tell you how it's going to be," Steel said suddenly.

I looked questioningly at Solder who gave me a shrug. "Okay?" I asked hesitantly.

Little apples of red burst onto Steel's cheeks, "They don't wear clothes. Ever. I wanted to prepare you for that. They can shift to have legs out of the water too. Where we'll see them, they'll mostly be on land."

A bunch of nudists didn't have the same effect it used to. I could deal with nudists; I would spend a great deal of time looking up. No problem.

"Solder is our gift to them. They crave humans, something to do with how warm we are," Steel shrugged toned broad shoulders.

I stood so quick the raft rocked, "What! You want to give your friend to them?" I emphatically shook my head.

Slate narrowed his eyes at me.

Solder laughed, "You are very spirited. They will not sacrifice me or anything along those lines. They just want to borrow me until Steel leaves."

I sank back down to the floor. My face must have been one of confusion because he felt the need to elaborate.

Solder's big lips parted to reveal his broad smile, "It is enjoyable. Good thing Steel went and got himself a wife so I could join him on these trips."

Solder's hand rested on my knee like a hot coal. He had done it to comfort me, but now I was keenly aware of his warmth. That, and Slate's searing gaze on top of Solder's hand.

Steel blanched. I remembered how Jett had laughed about Steel and mermaids and how Tawny could never go there. I shot Steel a death stare.

"Tawny knows," he said with a grimace.

"I am usually on the other side of that stare," Slate said suddenly. I gaped at him.

Steel laughed, "She's terrifying."

They were making fun of me. That was my best glare!

The land sped by the six-hour hike would be over in no time with our calling powered raft. Small adobe houses in creams and browns lined one side of the river. Fishing villages, Steel had said.

Canyons sprang up shortly after, red rocks that looked like they erupted from the earth. Scattered greenery sprouted along the river; it was the greenest I'd seen in all Thrimilci.

I passed the time giving in to Solder and telling him about my life back in Chicago and he told me about his life in Thrimilci. It was very much like Jett's stories, full of mischief and hard training.

Solder's hand was still on my knee. Men in Tidings had this way about them where you felt simultaneously intimidated and protected by them. Most of them had a prickly sense of honor and considered themselves to be chivalrous, taking care of their women — however many that might've been.

Funny thing was, they also had this innate possessiveness. One step above cavemen. Slate and Ash had both acted that way with me to different degrees, so did Jett. Even stranger, I liked it. Even the way Solder's had innocuously rested on my knee was a form of possessiveness. All the times Slate had lounged in my bed or rubbed his body over mine. He was marking his territory like a dog. I thanked the gods he hadn't peed on me.

We slowed down when we spotted round huts and docks. There was an actual beach! I could just make out the coastline beyond. We pulled into a dock where several other rafts were and Steel handed a man a rope to tie it off. Steel made pleasantries with the man, and we grabbed our few items before walking onto the sand.

Rounded huts were everywhere trading with humans and Merfolk alike. I knew they were Merfolk because they had strategically placed shells, scales, star fish, kelp, etc. Otherwise, they were completely nude.

I tried not to gawk; they were surreal. Aside from their purple, green, and even blue tinged skin, they had gills under their chins and angled features. Their ears were pointed, eyes tilted up, and jaws angular. Their eyes were all iris and pupil, no white to speak off. If I hadn't known they were Merfolk, I would've thought they were elves. Not Santa's elves, but the kind fans imitated at conventions.

Steel led us to the round topped huts so we could change, we were going into the water. I felt like a Bond girl in my gold bikini, my belt of daggers with its golden Daymark buckle around my waist and my seax strapped to my thigh.

We checked in the rest of our items in with a human woman running the changing huts. Solder, Steel, and Slate came up behind me. Steel had throwing darts strapped to his back and held his pronged spear in hand like a walking stick and blue swim shorts made of the same material as my bathing suit. It left little to the imagination, and I realized this trip just got awkward. Solder had two double-bladed axes strapped to his back and a pair of grey swim shorts on, he was stocky with thick corded muscles. I kept my eyes fixed on faces. I was pretty sure I was moving like a robot, my blushing luckily hidden by the moonlight.

Then I saw Slate. Quads flexed as he walked towards us, his tiny black swim shorts were even smaller than the underwear that I was used to seeing him in. Something about the bright moonlight shining on his bronze skin, his body ripped with muscles that I knew could be gentle when they needed to be, lit my world on fire. He belonged above a pedestal in some majestic pose, not walking with us mere mortals.

Slate had belts of knives crossing over his chest, his usual weapons. It was the least number of weapons I had seen on him outside of Thrimilci, not including when we were with the Wemic.

Solder made an appreciative noise at my tiny bikini, and I blushed to my toes. Solder laughed.,"I apologize. You look even better with your clothes off."

My skin tingled from the compliment, "Thanks. You should really pay Slate the compliment, he's the one who whipped me into shape when I got here."

"I doubt he bestowed those curves on you. Whipping, you say? Now there is an idea. Thank you, Slate," Solder teased.

"Do not mention it," he growled and Solder laughed.

"We're going to head into the water. Follow me. We're going to the palace, it isn't too far, but you're going to have to call some air so you can breathe. It wouldn't hurt to use air or water to help push yourself along either," Steel interrupted and gave us one of his All-American poster boy smiles you couldn't help but smile back at.

I walked behind Steel and Solder, Slate took up the rear. Merfolk were gawking at us. Some looked like they were going to molest us or maybe I just felt that, either way, lust was heavy in the air. They made no secret of it.

Steel dove into the clear cool shimmering water and we followed. He was an amazing swimmer, which explained his body shape.

In the water it was just as active as on land. The second they were knee deep they shifted into whatever their true form was. For some that meant iridescent fish tails, others it was tentacles. There was something androgynous about them. They all had long flowing hair in the water, or tentacles that curled from their scalps. It was miraculous; I was in awe of them and couldn't stop staring at their lack of noses. Where there should have been a nose was a flat mound like a cheek that blended along with the bone.

We were the only humans heading towards a huge coral palace.

The palace was deep in the water, its spires wound high above the ocean floor. We swam parallel with the surface and then straight down. The coral palace was alive with creatures, fish swam in and out of little coves, its colors brilliant. Merfolk where swimming in and out of what appeared to be an entranceway. How the Merfolk could create the palace out of living coral, I'd never know, but it was beautiful.

We hit the ocean floor and before we could swim to the entrance, a Merfolk with red and black tentacles swam up to us. Steel immediately formed a giant bubble that encompassed me with him.

She was obviously female.

"Steel," Was all I understood before she caressed him with her tentacles as he tried to pry her away while she cooed to him in Merfolk just outside the bubble. I was hopeless in Merfolk.

"English, Vanna'ra. I've brought guests. This is a leisurely visit, and please, I've told you I'm betrothed now," Steel was still pushing her tentacles away, but it was futile, they outnumbered him.

I expected her to pout like most of the girls would have done, instead she sneered and continued to speak in Merfolk.

"Vanna'ra, English please. No, my niece. Not wife."

Her sneer disappeared and instead she appraised me. I thought she would check my teeth.

"She will do."

The octopus woman arched her high black brows and stared at us with big black pupils and brown irises. A tentacled arm broke through the bubble and swept around my waist. I resisted the urge to stab her. Her red lips gave a flash of teeth.

"She is not the gift, Vanna'ra. Solder has volunteered."

Steel gave Solder's back a pat as he popped in from the watery barrier. Solder gave his best smile, and it was so very good.

Vanna'ra looked to me and back to Solder. She let go of our waists reluctantly and swam to Solder.

"Dion're will be disappointed, but Larn'ra will be pleased. I may be as well."

She cocked an eyebrow at Solder, his big lips pulled back into a smile. I didn't watch where her tentacled arms went. She swam away, pulling Solder along, he gave us a wave before being taken into the entranceway. Steel released the bubble, and we were right behind them when she shifted.

Vanna'ra's other form was a peach tone, but with black ribbons of curls that went past her backside. Her eyes remained the same, and her tentacles changed into hands and arms; only two of each. Solder held her hand as she guided him down a coral filled hall. Red and black mottled scales stretched over her breasts and below her belt to offer some sort of covering, it wasn't much, but at least she wasn't completely nude.

Magic was involved in the construction of the coral palace. There was a standing wall of ocean water where the entrance met it like a window, you could stand with one foot in the ocean depths and the other dry inside the palace.

"Sorry about that. They're very possessive, prone to jealousy. You get used to it. Now you can see why Tawny coming would be a terrible idea," Steel said looking for some vindication.

I wasn't giving any, I'd just watched an octopus lady feel up my betrothed uncle and take a Guardian into what I can only assume will be in her sex dungeon. I wondered how many times Steel had been wherever Solder was going.

Then I had a spike of jealousy like nothing I had ever known.

I looked at Slate. "How many times have you been here?" I demanded.

My tone was much harsher than I intended it to be. I could feel my face flame up, for once it wasn't in embarrassment.

Steel looked shocked I'd spoken that way to Slate, I was too to be honest. Slate looked like he was fighting back a smile. I wanted to throw a dagger at him.

"Twice," he stated.

I couldn't help but notice the glistening drops of water on his lashes or the way his long, wet hair clung to the sculpted shape of his pecs where it fell over his shoulders.

I tried to suppress a sigh, twice; he was probably in their creepy sex dungeon both times. I knew if I were an exotic elfish mermaid, I'd bring him there. Steel gave me a funny look as he walked ahead. I glanced back in time to see a shark swimming right for the entrance, and consequently directly at me. I screamed and braced for impact. What I heard instead was laughter.

What was a shark on one side, was a man as tall as Steel on the other. He had long black hair peppered with silver streaks, his skin had a blue tinge and around his large pupils was a bright blue twinkle. He was laughing inches from my face.

"I think I scared your woman," he laughed.

It was a full throaty sound that came from his belly. His well-muscled belly, I noted. His cool hands were on my shoulders to balance me. I had crouched down when I thought he was going to crash into me.

Steel liked everyone, so I didn't put any stock into the fact that he gave this shark man a big smile, "Sear're, how are you? Where were you coming from? Thank you for speaking English," Steel added and gestured to me.

Sear're puffed up. I didn't know how he breathed outside of the water, but the gills on the sides of his neck slit open as if he sighed.

"Perimeter check, you understand., Steel nodded grimly. "Is she for me?" he gave a smile that better suited his shark half.

I took a step back. He held his hands up.

"Sorry, we do not get many women down here. One can dream," when he smiled at me, I noticed he kept his sharkish rows of teeth.

Steel laughed, "Sear're this is my niece, Scarlett. She is here on a vacation of sorts. You know my brother."

The shark man nodded a greeting to Slate but sized him up at the same time with a hint of a smile as if the two hadn't seen each other in some time.

I almost gagged when Steel called Slate his brother after introducing me as his niece. Not the sort of thing I wanted popping up in my mind on later dates. I'd always thought it was awkward that both Jett and Steel called Slate their brother, though my mom and Lark adopted him.

"Dion're will be happy," he elbowed Steel.

Steel gave a small knowing smile; he had expected this. Slate had too since there was a lack of jaw clenching. I had asked to come to the Merfolk for a reason. I had an idea; it wasn't foolproof, but it could work. How the others would react to such a risky venture was unknown, but I knew who could help me. If Sear're was an enforcer, he'd be just what I was looking for.

Before Steel could answer I asked, "What is it you do here?"

He looked surprised I addressed him.

He was appraising me just like Vanna'ra. "Advisor to the king and Merfolk warden," he said carefully.

He let his eyes linger over my legs; no one looked that intensely at my legs before, I almost fidgeted. I knew there was a king; I remembered that much from Butterfly's tribal affairs class.

"I have a proposition for you. I think you might be the right — man for the job."

I wasn't sure if man was the right term for him, maybe male would've been more accurate. Either way, my hesitation loaded the comment full of innuendo. I heard Steel shuffle in the sand behind me.

Sear're sucked his teeth and stepped close to me again, I put a hand up to prevent him from coming closer, but he stopped so my hand rested on his blue tinged pecs.

"Maybe we should speak alone."

I would eventually have to get Steel involved, but the less he knew now, the better. If he acted strangely or if Slate did it might not work.

Sear're liked this idea a lot. He had a kelp skirt that worked like a loincloth, but it didn't hide nearly enough.

"Follow me," he pushed past me and started down the hall.

Steel gaped at me; Slate had smoothed his face. I wanted to roll my eyes, but I didn't.

"I'll be right back. Don't worry, trust me," I whispered to Steel as I passed him.

Sear're turned to see if I was following. I jogged to catch up, which he enjoyed immensely as I momentarily forgot I had on a bikini top. I blushed, and he may have enjoyed that even more. Steel wasn't kidding about being attracted to our warmth.

I didn't want him to get the wrong idea, "I'm not a gift, by the way."

He cocked a dark pointed eyebrow, "Dion're will be disappointed."

"Dion're is your king?"

Sear're nodded, "What is it you want to talk about, little woman, if you don't want to please me? Or would you like to do that too?" He smiled with his rows of teeth but kept walking.

"I didn't want the others to know what I was up to because I don't want them acting differently or jeopardizing them."

He nodded and walked up porous rock stairs. The floors were sand, the walls the same porous rock as the stairs. Enormous pearls hung in strands along the walls. He turned to one door; it was a huge clam shell. He pushed it open and turned-on globes of light that reminded me of the ones at home that we used energy plates to activate. I wondered if the Merfolk had magic. They could obviously shift, but maybe they could use energy too.

We were in a bedroom. I stopped at the threshold. He grabbed me by the wrist and pulled me through the door. Not roughly, but insistently, like, I annoyed him.

"I would not take you unless you wished it.", he said, "Explain." He sunk onto his bed, a waterbed of course.

"I can feel emotions. I was hoping you could mention your perimeter search to Merfolk, and I can keep close so I can pick up their emotions. We could see who reacts differently and question them."

He looked at me again, lips curling into a smile, "You can pick up emotions? What am I feeling right now?"

I blushed, which only made what I felt more intense. "Desire." I breathed. His smile deepened. "It works even if it was not obvious. How do you plan to stay close?"

"I'm open to ideas. I must be close enough to be sure who the emotion is coming from. You can tell them you found nothing, and I can tell if they're relieved. Or you can say you found something, and I can tell if they get nervous."

"How do you know I am not the one who transported the door?"

He stood then and walked to where I stood; I pressed against his clam door. He looked down at me.

I put my hands out again and he let them rest on his blue chest, his skin was chilled to the touch, "Because you're angry, but not at me."

His big pupils narrowed, "They would have the Guardians come here and threaten us. Ruin what we have built here, cause tensions within our people. Yes, I am angry." He turned and sat back down on his bed.

I stepped away from the door. He was in. He wanted this Merfolk traitor caught as much as I did.

"You understand we probably won't have time to go through everyone, but at least you'll know that the ones close to you aren't guilty."

He nodded, "I know how to keep you close to me." He smiled his shark smile.

I had been trying to ignore the fact that he was good looking, I'd hoped he was married or whatever they did for commitment here.

"You will be my gift, at least act like you are," he smiled again, "They will not trust you if you are not convincing."

"You don't think I can be convincing?" I asked him while cocking an eyebrow.

I hoped I looked cooler than I felt. I strutted over to the bed swaying my hips and knocked his legs apart. Kneeling between them, I leaned over him arching my hips.

"Convinced?" I asked in a deliberately breathless voice.

He had laid back on the bed, looking down the length of me smiling his shark like smile. Quick as a whip, he grabbed the back of my neck and pressed his lips to mine.

Sear're let go of my neck, my seax was at his throat.

He was smiling as if I'd just confirmed something, "Your lover will not like it. Is he going to be a problem?"

"I don't have a lover. I have a suitor and he isn't here."

"And I am a dolphin. Is he going to be a problem or not?"

I sheathed my blade, "I don't think so, I can handle him. What else do we need to do?"

Sear're grabbed me again and kissed me more deeply, I felt his teeth scrape my lip.

He let me go, and I shifted away to sit between his legs on the bed. "I would hate to have to stab you," I told him.

He laughed and sat up, "You better get used to it, we will need to do it at court."

"Done. What else?" I asked, steeling my resolve.

It was why I'd left Steel in the dark. He knew I'd planned to root out the traitor, but if he hadn't looked thunderstruck at my actions, the Merfolk might have suspected something. I knew my plan could work.

"Change," he said as he pulled on a bikini string. I was too fast for a free show, thanks again to my trainers.

"Okay, let's get started before they wonder what we're up to," I said standing up.

"That is why we should take our time," Sear're said curling his lips.

It took twenty minutes to doll me until Sear're was satisfied. I looked like a mermaid sex worker. He brought in a woman with blonde hair that went to her fanny pack and huge green tilted eyes. She wore shells on a skirt and mottled orange scales covered her breasts.

Sear're and I agreed to vet her first. Sear're started talking about the portal doors and I paid close attention. There was overwhelming disinterest on her part. She didn't know anything; she didn't even care. I gave my head a shake, and he understood.

I would walk into the Merfolk court on Sear're's arm, my breasts pushed up in a seashell bra, strands of pearls hung in loops from the front to the back in graduating lengths.

My skirt, if it could even be called that, was strands of pearls and seashells... and nothing underneath. I'd never been more concerned my lady bits would show in all my life. I was never gladder that I'd kept up regular appointments with Bronze the beautician. The blonde had even done my hair, she teased it to the ceiling and pinned back locks of it with starfish, they threaded my jade canine fetish into my hair at my nape.

Pillars ran from floor to ceiling, the floor looked like marble in the court. I didn't know how they would've done it; it had a Roman pantheon feel to it. The king was blonde with a long matching beard. Like the rest of the Merfolk, he was powerfully built. I'd seen. He had on a skirt of sapphires and pearls and couldn't have been a day past forty, his skin had a peach look to it like Vanna'ra's had. I wondered if he was an octopus too. He sat between two other blondes; a young man, and a young woman, the princess, and the prince.

The princess had long blonde hair like her father with strands of pearls that dangled down the length of it. They even made her top of pearls, her skirt though shimmered with diamonds.

The prince stiffened when he saw me walk in on Sear're's arm. He had hair like his father without the facial hair. His skin was blue tinged, but lighter than Sear're's dusky blue. He had a skirt made of kelp and pearls that swayed as he got up, striding straight for us.

"Be convincing, do not embarrass me."

He looked down at me and smiled. I licked my lips and gave an imperceptible nod as I let him pull me to his cool chest and slant his mouth over mine.

My count was up to eight men, human and otherwise. I was no longer keeping track.

Then he placed me back down, because he had lifted me off my toes.

The prince was standing in front of us. I had my empath powers turned way up, and I felt jealousy. The prince started speaking in warbling Merfolk, Sear're held up a hand.

"Please, in English for my gift," Sear're smiled smugly.

I tried to look sexy; I hoped it was working. Awkward and uncomfortable I was my bread and butter.

My guess was yes since with all that jealousy, I could feel lust coming from him. The prince had big green irises; he leveled them at me then brought them back to Sear're.

"Steel said there were no female gifts, and yet you appear to have one. What luck."

I was nervous the prince was going to demand me. It would blow our plan right out of the water.

Sear're gave him a cocky smile, "There were no female gifts, but then she saw me and could not resist."

He gave my bottom a firm squeeze. I tried to keep the alluring look on my face while wanting to shove a knife in his eye.

The prince laughed, I still felt jealousy and lust, but admiration trickled in. It was working.

"How did today go?" He asked but kept a keen eye on me.

I couldn't believe how easy it had been, he was asking us. I supposed it made sense since it was Sear're's job.

"Ah, fruitless. No news is not good news in this case."

The prince nodded, he felt eager. He wanted to catch whoever it was, but he wanted it to be him to do it. One down — who knew how many others left. The prince looked at me and smiled. It wasn't a pleasant smile. He was handsome enough, but there was something unkind about it.

"If you decide you prefer royal blood, I will be on my throne," he walked back to the dais drawing the attention of the other Merfolk at court.

"Non're would have you bound to his bed in the time it takes a goldfish to forget. Stay away from him, you may prove too much temptation. He is not an evil man, but he is not a good one. What was your read?" Sear're asked.

"Aside from the fact that he is kind of jerky, he isn't the one moving the portal door, but he would prefer to be the one to find the traitor," I told him. I hoped he didn't see my shiver at his warning.

Sear're nodded, and I glanced around the room. Amongst the Merfolk men and women, most of whom had their eyes focused on me, there was a second group the ethereal people were paying close attention to.

Steel and Slate drinking and speaking with several of Merfolk. Except they weren't speaking, they were watching Sear're and me. I was conflicted; I wanted to go explain what was going on, but if they started acting suspicious or defensive of me it would ruin my plan. They needed to believe I wanted to be with Sear're, their surprise would work with it.

My plan was going to work, I just knew it, but looking at Slate's smooth expression I wondered at what cost.

"Introduce me to your king."

The Merfolk King was the one we wanted to eliminate right away, if he knew what was going on, we'd have major problems. The blonde king sat atop his throne next to Non're, the princess had wandered off. Lust, a boatload of lust, wafted from the king. I put it out of my mind as I swung my hips while we walked to him.

"Sear're, Non're has informed me of your gift. I fear she only chose you because she had not met Dion're, king of the Merfolk."

He extended a hand to me and Sear're gently urged me forward. The marble steps were cool under my feet, but I doubted the Merfolk felt it. Dion're grabbed my hand in his cool one and spun me, sending my dangling strands twirling. He grunted appreciatively, and I stepped back down.

Never having been so objectified in all my life, I prayed Slate and Steel had not seen that.

"Sear're, I do not believe I have ever been envious of you. This is a first," the Merfolk king said amusedly.

Sear're held me to him possessively, "Wait until after tonight, then you will have something to envy."

The three men laughed. I was trying to look tempting — apparently it was working too well.

Sear're continued, "I swam the perimeter today." His tone turning serious, "No sign of the traitors."

Dion're spiked with anger and vengeance. I would not want to be the person who moved the portal door when he got his hands on them, "Very well, we will find them eventually."

Sear're and Dion're spoke at length, but I had all I needed from the conversation, and Non're's eyes roaming all over my body was making me keenly aware that I was all but naked.

Sear're handed me drink after drink of something sweet and alcoholic. One of those drinks that snuck upon you, and *BAM*, you're three sheets to the wind. I needed my wits about me to catch the traitor. I didn't eat, the food there didn't look all that appetizing. Seafood, of course, most of it raw. There was no way that would stay down after all those drinks.

We walked through the court as Sear're kissed and squeezed me. I didn't see Solder all night or the Vanna'ra woman, I assumed they were making good use of his "gifting". It turned out the Larn'ra she'd mentioned was the princess and the fact she had disappeared made sense.

We avoided Steel and Slate — all night — but I knew eventually I'd have to face them.

I hadn't gotten the emotions I'd been looking for, or anything close. The longer it went on, the drunker I got. We turned to talk to more people, and Steel and Slate were in front of us. If I started acting weird after we'd come so far, it would spoil my mission.

Luckily, I was too drunk to be anything other than drunk.

I smiled slowly when I saw them; it caused Steel's eyes to widen. A chuckle burst from me like the bubbles I laughed. Slate kept his face smooth, his eyes on Sear're. His face was unreadable. Sear're wasn't the kind of man/Merfolk to be intimidated easily. He pulled me against him, so my hot skin pressed against his cool.

"Sear're, I... Scarlett, how are you feeling?" Steel asked obviously at a loss for words. He was looking at Slate out of the corner of his eye.

My eyes were heavy, I pressed my lips together and puckered them. "Fine, why?" my amiable smile slid back onto my face.

Steel took a deep breath, "Okay. Having fun? Thanks for showing my niece around Sear're, I —don't mean to be rude," Steel said apologetically.

Steel was ambassador, he'd have to deal with them again.

"Not a problem, she has been showing me a thing or two," Sear're gloated.

Steel was dumbfounded. Slate's smooth exterior cracked, but he quickly pulled it back up. Slate stood watching our brief scene, luckily no one was paying any attention.

"Enjoy your night," Slate looked me up and down and pulled Steel away.

I was fuming. If I was going to let myself indulge in sin, I certainly wouldn't advertise it. He acted as if I was promiscuous. As if he didn't know that I had never been with a man.

I grabbed another sweet drink.

The night was over, Merfolk were leaving and it had been a complete bust. I had drunk so much, but I knew they wouldn't have plumbing, so I'd held it the entire night. I was fit to burst.

"Tell me you have something like toilets."

"Garderobe," he said with a small smile.

He gave me directions, and I found it without a problem, except for a little stumbling. I left the room on wobbly legs and headed back to the court trying not to think about where that pipe let out.

Sear're found me right away and led me out of the room.

I was irritated and confused, "Well — that was a bust."

"I disagree. We eliminated much of my people," Sear're told me seemingly happy.

I nodded, "Yes, you're right. I'm glad they cleared, but there's still a traitor on the loose."

Sear're nodded, "We will look around more in the morning. You will need a good night's rest."

He was half carrying me, I really had drunk too much. His body was cool, but it felt good against my booze warmed skin. I rested my forehead against his shoulder as we walked.

Sear're looked down at me feeling the flush of my skin. "Change your mind about being my gift," he shot me a lascivious look.

"I've thought about it, but I couldn't. Slate would kill us both is my first time was with a Merfolk," I sighed gustily.

Sear're opened the door to his bedroom and let me fall to the satiny bed. The strands of my skirt fell haphazardly, giving him a good show.

"Where is my room?" I asked him with every intention of leaving.

"You are in it; you are spending the night. Do not argue. I did not spend all night acting like I was sleeping with you to have them find out you slept in the Guardian quarters."

I was too drunk to gape. He had a point.

"What do you have for pajamas?" I asked him.

He scoffed and let his kelp skirt fall to the sandy floor before crawling in bed next to me. Not too drunk for my eyes to bulge. I sat up so fast my head swam.

"Okay, what about a towel — or a robe? Something?" I asked, facing away from him.

"You can wrap yourself in the sheet. I do not recommend sleeping in all those beads," he said with entirely too much smugness.

I nodded, and he rolled off the sheet. I threw it over my back while I took off the hard-shelled bra with all its complicated strands and pearl skirt. Sear're hummed behind me. It was extremely annoying.

When I firmly wrapped myself, I laid down on the bed as far away from him as I could get. He laughed and rolled onto his stomach.

"What did he say?"

"Who say?" I asked, blushing.

"Your lover. Assuming he caught up with you like he was planning to do."

"He didn't," I said, irritated, "He probably found a nice pair of some-time-legs to crawl between."

"I may not read emotions as you do, but I know men. He must have missed you," he chuckled. "Did we give him a good show?"

I sighed, "It's not like that."

"I remember when he came before. Quiet, introspective, a deep sadness dwells in that boy. Then Larn'ra took him and something fundamental changed in him. He was angry, full of rage.... unpredictable. It is better, but he struggles with it."

I turned towards him. He looked invisible in the dark. No light skin to reflect, there was no white to his eyes. All I could see was teeth.

"He's better? What do you mean Larn'ra took him?" I asked in disbelief.

I felt rather than heard Sear're nod, "Made a man out of him. Steel was young, he lost track of the boy. He found him the next day. Luckily, he had only been with Larn'ra."

Jealousy spiked through me unfounded. "How old was he?" I asked.

"Just a guppy, perhaps fourteen."

"How old was she?"

I was seeing red. There was no way Slate had been with a woman before that.

Sear're thought for a moment, "Fifty at most."

I spluttered, "The princess? Fifty? Impossible." She couldn't have been much older than I was.

"We are long lived. I am one hundred and two," He boasted.

I'd been kissing a geriatric all night. Wonderful.

"Breakfast?"

A plate of something delicious smelling was being held inches away from my face. My head pounded, and it took a minute for my eyes to focus. It was Non're and my sheet had fallen around my waist. I quickly pulled it up and pushed myself into a seated position.

"Where's Sear're?" I asked, noticing the shark man was gone leaving me alone with the prince.

He pretended to pout, "Am I not good company?"

"You are, I just..." think Scarlett think! "What did you bring me?" eating would postpone any added awkwardness until Sear're returned.

Non're smiled, those bright blue eyes gleamed. He held his cornflower blue hand higher to reveal a kelp, shrimp concoction that caused my belly to rumble.

"And a drink," I reached for the drink, and he lifted a vial, "You drank quite a bit. This will make you feel good. Do you accept?"

I nodded, "thank you."

I took the goblet as he emptied the vial of purple into it. It would save me from having to ask for healing from Slate or Steel.

Non're licked his lips. It drew my eyes to where his nose would have been if he were human, just flat powder blue tinged skin, gills just beneath the sides of his neck sucked in air like nostrils. Non're shifted on the bed as he handed me the plate and his long blonde hair fell over his shoulder. He was handsome and a hint of a smile played on his lips, but there was something I couldn't put my finger on that got my hackles up.

I could feel his over large pupils sliding over the bare skin of my back, "We have a relic. You may have heard of it. It is ancient, few who live know we have it."

"Never heard of it," I said flatly between bites.

His smug smile faltered, "I believe it was one piece of the project Natt worked on before Dagr died."

I knit my brows. I knew that was what the stained glass above our room at Valla U depicted, Storm and Wind and their tragic romance.

"I am not familiar with that tale," I said warily.

His huge pupils dilated, so it almost swallowed the bright blue around it, "We have a piece that would allow you to access untold power. I would give it to you for a price."

There it was. His whole reason for being there.

"Some prices are too high," I said carefully.

I'd crossed my legs on the bed with the sheet pushed under my arms to hide my chest and wrapped around my hips, but he leaned back on the bed now slightly behind me to look at my bare back.

"Two nights with me. That is all," he said so nonchalantly it seemed like such a reasonable request, "You would leave after with the piece — price paid."

The door swung open, in walked Sear're leading Steel and Slate. I sat in Sear're's bed with a single sheet wrapped around me. My hair probably looked shamefully tousled with the prince of the Merfolk leaning back on the bed seemingly quite at home.

I handed Non're my empty tray.

"Thank you, Prince Non're," I told him hoping he'd get the hint.

Slate menaced in the doorway, Steel's body physically in the way was the only thing that stopped him from attacking the prince.

"Non're, come to take away my gift? How kind of you to bring breakfast."

Sear're sat on my other side and pushed my hair away from my shoulders letting his fingers trail along my collarbone as I shifted the sheet higher under my arms.

Non're smiled wickedly, "You should not leave such precious gifts unattended; someone might seek to take better care of them."

He left. I wasn't sure if he noted the raw anger in Slate's eyes even though he kept his face smooth, but I did.

Steel looked like he wanted to slap my hands for touching something I shouldn't have. I rolled my eyes and held out my hand.

"Sear're, please hand me my suit." He was leaning against me, testing Slate. I knew it, he was pushing it. "Sear're."

He chuckled and gave me the gold suit I'd been wearing. I hid under the sheet as I wiggled back into it.

"Did you tell them?" I asked, grunting as my bottoms slid over my fanny pack.

He hadn't gotten off the bed as I'd gotten dressed; he was enjoying torturing Slate.

"Maybe I had too much fun last night and mean to keep you."

My head popped up from under the sheets and I gave him a look. Optics were bad, granted, since Steel and Slate didn't know that nothing had happened, Sear're's statement was full of innuendo pushed Slate over the edge. I saw it happen in slow motion. Slate, always full of dark primitive violence kept tightly in line, snapped.

His body seemed to swell and shrink before my eyes as he lunged forward gripping Sear're's throat. Sear're didn't look the least bit intimidated. Maybe he knew something I didn't, because I could feel the emotions coming off Slate and he was more dangerous than I'd ever suspected. I wasn't even sure if he was a man now. If he wasn't standing in front of my eyes, I would have registered him as an animal. Not a squirrel either, more like a rabid panther that starved for weeks and had scented blood.

We were in the middle of a tribal relations nightmare. We'd never leave alive if Slate murdered the king's advisor.

I rose from the bed. Sitting next to Sear're on the bed wasn't helping matters, so I came to stand beside Slate. I knew it only took me a few precious seconds, but it felt like an eternity. Slate didn't even notice me there. I reached to Slate's powerful jaw and ran the pads of my fingers along it; he shivered and blinked.

"Slate," I whispered, and I saw his fingers unclench from around Sear're's thick throat.

Steel pushed past us and healed Sear're who wasn't looking very concerned, if I didn't know any better, I'd say he was looking amused. I pulled Slate by his arm and to my surprise; he followed. I cupped his face and peered into his eyes. They were back to normal. His walls were back up around his emotions, and he was a man again. I called delving into him.

"Are you alright?" I asked, trying to mask just how concerned I was about what I'd just seen from him.

"Yes," he took a deep steadying breath, "I am sorry, Sear're."

Sear're stood and clasped Slate's forearm, "Think nothing of it."

There was some dynamic I didn't understand there.

"It was a ruse. I needed to stick to Sear're so I could use my empath abilities to feel out the traitor. That's it, that's all. Right?"

I faced Slate trying to process what just happened. It was deeper than him being jealous about another man who might have been with me. The rage I'd felt was unhinged.

"We kissed," Sear're told them.

"Sear're you're not helping," I scolded.

He smiled, "Yes, it was all planned. We thought your outrage looked authentic enough. It worked splendidly, and she only ended up naked in my bed — no others."

"Okay, stop helping. Good news, no one I spoke to was the traitor," I said shifting my feet.

"I'm glad everyone's fine. So, no one there was the traitor?" Steel asked thoughtfully.

I shook my head, "I'm positive."

Steel dry washed his face, "I don't know if I feel better or worse. You can't risk yourself like that, Scarlett. You said you had a plan. I thought you were sewing your oats or something before you settled down with Ash. You seemed to like Keen when we visited the Wemic."

I shut my eyes. That drew me away from Slate in a heartbeat. I moved to where I'd placed my knives on a beautifully crafted shell stand and buckled them on.

"No. Just acting. Keen was different," I said as I blushed.

"Your suitor, is that this Ash?" Sear're asked.

"Yes. And before you mention us sleeping naked together, there. It's out now. No one here cares," I said coolly and noticed both Steel and Slate stiffen.

"To be young and foolish again. Come. Let us see if we can visit some of the other Merfolk you did not meet last night," Sear're offered me his elbow, and I took it without looking at Slate.

A wave of heat splashed over me, and I staggered. "You okay, Scar? Do you need some healing?" Steel asked.

His tan brow furrowed, his dirty blonde hair disheveled charmingly that reminded me of Hawk. "Yeah, hot flash. Should be too young for that though, huh?" I laughed it off, but my cheeks were still flushed.

The three men looked at one another and back at me. Slate moved to stand next to me and Sear're moved forward so our four bodies made an arrow formation. I gave them a curious look, but Sear're just smiled his rows of shark-like teeth at me.

As I walked, I noticed how close fitting my bikini bottoms were and how they rubbed between my legs as I walked. Another wave of heat rolled over me and I let out a low moan. The men stopped, and I blushed.

I cleared my throat, "It's sweltering in here."

The three men looked at one another again and I grew irritated. I had to ball my fists to keep them from tearing off my bottoms, that or walking too quickly so I could appease the aching build between my legs. We passed under strands of pearls that hung from the coral ceiling and I purposely caught one in my mouth letting it slide between my lips and bump along my tongue until we were past.

By the Mother, what was wrong with me?

Steel stopped, "Slate, please look at my niece. What is she doing?"

Me? Nothing.

I looked down and realized I was kneading my own breasts beneath my top. I gasped and pulled my hands out of my top. The pressure of the thin material was excruciating. It teased what needed satisfaction. No, demanded it. I raised my hands and shook my head at Slate.

"Um, sorry?" I offered.

Slate narrowed his eyes at me but kept walking.

We reached a dining area, long thin emerald marble tables made an open-ended rectangular shape along the porous walls, Dion're sat at the short end between his son and daughter. Solder sat along the table eating happily but rose to join us when we entered the room.

Another wave of heat washed over me, and I froze while panting. My bikini strangled my aching skin. I looked to Slate who had stopped a few paces away as Steel and Sear're continued forth. I parted my lips to catch my breath.

Had Slate always been so irresistible? I stood with purpose, and he continued forth. I followed with only one thing on my mind.

He strode down the length of the hall until we reached the kin and my eyes fixated on Slate's backside as he took each step — every flex. The muscles in his lower back seemed to point like an arrow to his thin black shorts.

Dion're smiled flashing white teeth, "Good night?"

Sear're smiled in return and nodded.

"Checking the perimeter again today?" Dion're asked.

I could feel his confusion and something else. Someone felt apprehension.

I stood next to Slate panting from the exertion of not touching him. I fought the feeling. Temporarily, I could think clearer through my all-consuming lust.

"We are going with Sear're, we think we have a better chance to catch the culprit with our abilities," my nails were biting into my palms as I rounded on Slate. "I need you, Slate Sumar," I said breathlessly. I hoped he'd put me out of my misery and just touched me.

Slate could blush. I took a step forward, my skin tingling and charged. I had to be touched, or I'd probably die.

I touched my fingers to his lips, his grey eyes watching me. "I want these. Here. Now," I touched myself between my legs and I heard Steel suck in a deep breath at the same time as Slate did.

Slate's eyes flared silver, and I threw myself at him, parting his lips my tongue and wrapping my arms around his neck so I could get my legs around his waist. Slate pulled me off him roughly and I panted and squirmed in his arms.

"Get ahold of yourself," he growled.

"I'll get ahold of you," I thrust my hand down his teeny tiny black shorts and found him there waiting.

Slate cursed and peeled my hand off him one finger at a time. Apprehension turned into terror, it was terror, not anger. Sear're and I had worked out a signal if I felt something, but I was a little distracted.

"Sear're, I'd scratch your back right now, but I have my hands full," I breathed and Slate gaped at me.

I laughed full and throaty and watched as his eyes lit with carnal want and need.

"You are sure?" Sear're asked, bringing me back again.

I nodded, irritated, and turned around releasing Slate and rubbing my body all over the front of him like a cat trying to get its back scratched.

"Slate, what the hell is going on!" Steel shouted.

Slate raised his hands, and I grabbed them and place them over my breasts as I arched my back. Slate cursed again.

"She knows something," I breathed; my eyes focused on the princess.

The princess's eyes widened.

Everything happened at once. I felt someone panic, and I threw up a wall of solid air and heard thumps of something hitting my wall. Slate pushed me forward face first into the sand and guarded my body with his. I heard screams and a scuffle as I rubbed my backside against him. I was slipping deeper into a pool of penetrating lust that seemed to bring the surface of my skin awake with delicious searing purpose.

"Scarlett, drop the damn wall. Don't let her out of your sight!" Steel shouted.

"I do not know what has gotten into you, Torch, but you cannot pull out a man's cock and attempt to ride it in a room full of people," Slate growled in my ear.

I was barely registering words. "Please. Now. I need you," I breathed, struggling against his weight.

"Why now? Why not last night? You slept with Sear're. The man is a hundred years old," Slate whispered. I could tell all my wriggling was getting to him.

"A hundred and two. You slept with the princess," I retorted.

"Sear're told you that?" he whispered in disbelief.

Oh, my gods, why was he still talking when a perfectly willing woman was under him?

"Turn me around. I need to touch you."

I felt Slate sigh against my back.

He moved and I whimpered a protest before he pulled me to my feet. I turned on a dime and pulled his head to mine to close my mouth over his. Slate pushed at me, but I kept coming. He laughed at my persistence and finally spun me around to clamp his arms around me, pinning my arms to my sides. I rubbed my backside hard against his hips searching for hard friction.

Steel held up something looked like sand dollars but with razor-sharp edges, someone had thrown them like ninja stars at us. Whoever had thrown them was in a rush to get out, so they hadn't made sure they'd hit their targets.

The princess had paled in her seat. She hadn't moved. Sear're was bellowing out orders, Dion're was trying to talk to Larn'ra, but she had retreated into herself. The prince was gone.

My eyes met princess Larn'ra's, "You know who is involved."

I didn't know where the words came from, somewhere deep down buried beneath my need to be filled was a sliver of logic.

Dion're eyes flashed angrily at me. Steel stepped up alongside Sear're.

"Your daughter stands accused of aiding the traitors. She needs to answer our questions," Steel said, his tone was cool as ice.

Dion're raged, "On what grounds does this girl accuse my daughter?"

Sear're spoke up, "She can read people's emotions. The princess was guilty. Larn'ra, you must tell me everything you know for the Merfolk. If your role was minimal, I will see what I can do to help with the Guardians," he looked to Steel who gave him a grim nod.

Dion're's brow knit, his sharp eyebrows drawing together, "Larn'ra, tell them it is not true."

Larn'ra shook her blonde head and looked to her father's blue eyes, "She said no one would find out. That once Guardians are out of power, you would be free to rule as you wish."

Dion're shook his head. "Guardians do not rule us Larn'ra. They are annoying at times." He looked to Steel who hadn't blinked. "They are here for our benefit, the rest of the world would not understand, our race wouldn't survive. They are necessary," he added gently.

A necessary evil. I hoped that wasn't how the rest of the tribes thought of us.

Larn'ra spilled her guts. The tentacled woman we'd met first approached her a year ago and asked her to turn a blind eye to what she was doing, keeping her informed of what the Guardians were up to so they could remain a step ahead.

"I informed her of what I heard, that is all." Green tinged tears leaked from her blue iris eyes.

"You spied." Non're spat at her, his tone dripped with disgust.

The prince had returned shortly after Slate pulled me up to my feet. I would never want my brother to look at me like that.

"I thought I was helping our people. Vanna'ra assured, it would hurt none of our own," she sobbed, "I know nothing else. I did not ask."

Sear're was stone faced. He finally had the answers he wanted, but it was at a cost. The princess was involved and there was no way to fix that.

"Were they caught?" Sear're asked Non're.

Non're had chased after Vanna'ra and the fleeing traitors.

"I caught two of the four. Vanna'ra escaped."

Vanna'ra had been the one to throw the razored sand dollars, it caused just enough distraction for them to escape.

I moaned as I felt a reaction from inside Slate's shorts. Finally!

Steel walked over to me. The blooms of red on his tanned face, his turquoise eyes wide as I never stopped my wriggling. I couldn't help myself. If not Slate, I would've found someone else.

Larn'ra was crying again. Steel turned let out a long exhale.

"I will have to collect the traitors. Since Larn'ra is cooperating and she had no direct involvement with the transportation of the portal doors, I will plead her case to the council. What she did was betray her people, I believe you may handle her in your own way," Steel was in ambassador mode.

Solder walked up behind us, "The traitors are ready to transport."

His face was smooth. I wondered if all guys did that when they were upset. If I had slept with a bunch of traitors, I would have been distraught. Except in that moment, it impossibly aroused me. Solder finally noticed me, and his eyes widened.

Sear're walked up to me and cupped my face. I leaned my head back and opened my mouth, sliding my tongue out to receive whatever he wished to give me. Sear're's lips curled in his dusky blue face and glanced past me to a growling Slate. Sear're pulled back my eyelids.

"Did you have something to drink today?" Sear're asked, suddenly serious.

"What?" Steel asked and pressed against Sear're who was showing him my eyes.

Steel spun around to a smirking Non're.

Heat flared around me, but it wasn't my heat, it was Slate's. "You gave her rousen?" Slate ground out.

Non're held up his hands, "Half a dose. I offered it to her, and she accepted. Leave her here if you cannot handle her."

I nodded at that idea. Non're would do what need doing. Me. Slate growled in a way that vibrated my body. Dion're was looking at me speculatively, but I could feel his lust as well. I pulled away from Slate to go to them and Slate held me all the tighter.

"She wants to stay," Non're said as if it was obvious.

"She didn't know what she was taking. My niece is not from Tidings;

she isn't even a Guardian yet," Steel said trying to reign in his anger, "The Prime's nephew vies for her hand. You want Moon to know you seduced his nephew's future wife?" Steel voice rose steadily and Non're narrowed his eyes.

"So young," Dion're breathed, "the Prime's nephew courts her, you say?" The Merfolk king's desire for me only increased.

"Dion're, I believe the Merfolk may be in enough trouble with the traitors without adding this to the tally," Sear're said sensibly, turning to the king.

"As always, you are correct. She cannot stay now."

Something in the way he said now implied that there would be a later.

"We need to get going," Steel told them.

Dion're nodded and Sear're guided us to our captives.

Sear're brought us to two shackled Merfolk. A female with pink tinged skin and red waist length hair, and a male with green tinged skin and long brown hair. They were each shackled hand to hand and foot together, another chain led from their hands to their feet.

"It keeps them from shifting," Sear're informed us.

Steel took hold of the female, and Solder grabbed the male. Slate was stuck with me.

Sear're stood before me, "I know you cannot understand me now, but your memories will remain when the rousen wears off. When you told me your plan, I thought it was a good way to get you into my bed. I did not completely believe you. I am sorry for underestimating you. If your lover does not wise up, know that you look good in my sheets."

He gave me a wink. He said it for Slate, but he meant it too and since Slate was behind me holding me still, he growled at Sear're making him laugh.

When we got to shore, I had thoroughly irritated Slate. He'd had to call for both of us so we could breathe, and I had not cooperated in the least. Slate picked up our clothing and pulled me into the hut to dress me, but I took it as an opportunity to have him to myself.

"Damn it, Torch. I regret ever training you."

I was stronger than I'd ever been, and he had gone through great lengths to keep my hands off him as he pulled my clothes on. Unfortunately for him, I finally figured out I could call.

"No. Scarlett. No. Stop. Now."

I wrapped Slate up with air and yanked his shorts down to his ankles and dropped to my knees.

"If I have to shout for Steel, this is going to be very embarrassing for you," his words said one thing, but his body said another.

I grinned wickedly at him and started forward. Slate cursed and shouted for Steel who must have been waiting for such a circumstance just outside of the hut. He grabbed me kicking and screaming and I dropped my air ropes. My calling temporary lost to me again once I spotted Solder.

"Hurry, Slate!" Steel wrapped me in air ropes, and I screamed and thrashed in the sand against them.

People skirted by us, locals, and Merfolk alike as I fought against Steel who sat on my chest to keep me from remembering I could call again and breaking from my bonds. I was stronger than all of them at calling, just less practiced. More than one person mumbled the word 'khoraz', the name Cordillera had called me.

"I will take her if you are sick of holding her," Solder offered, and I nodded.

"No!" Slate roared as he came out of the hut pulling a shirt over his head.

Steel scrambled off me and I jumped up and into Slate who caught me effortlessly as I wrapped my legs around his waist and kissed all over his face.

"Maybe she'll wear herself out? She screams every time I use air ropes. If you think you can handle her on the raft, that might be better. I don't want her to have to scream for hours as we get back," Steel asked thoughtfully to Slate.

I could hear just how much he loathed to let me scream, he might've even let Solder hold me.

"I will take care of her. I do not want her screaming either," Slate said roughly from between my frenzied kisses.

"I could take care of her," Solder offered again as Slate passed by him with me clinging to him like a monkey.

"She is my—"

I covered Slate's open mouth with mine and pulled his tongue into my mouth sucking hard. A stirring below his belt rewarded me.

Slate carried me to the back of the raft where he sat with me straddling his lap. Steel helped bring on the Merfolk traitors and sat them down opposite Solder, and Steel took hold of the tiller and used air to push us off. We started back towards the Sumar palace.

It was a long trip back. The Merfolk couldn't or wouldn't stop staring at me. Once or twice I tried to claw my way over to the green tinged merman who had shown me with a shift of his kelp skirt just what I would get if I came closer.

The merman had laughed when Slate grew enraged and had finally started kissing me back to keep me in his lap. Steel was studiously ignoring me and everything that concerned me. He especially tried to ignore that whenever Slate grew lax, I tore at his pants, and succeeded at gripping him a time or two. Or that I'd thrown my shirt off the raft and Slate had to grip my wrists to the point of bruising to stop me from tearing off many other articles of my clothing or his.

My hands slid under Slate's shirt as I rocked in his lap, my body begging for friction. I kissed along his neck, and jaw and pulled on his long hair. I took his hands and placed them all over my body and shouted in frustration incoherent gibberish when he refused me what I needed.

I jumped off his lap and darted to Solder. I knocked him back so hard his head whacked on the bottom of the raft and straddled him as he blinked dazedly before Slate caught me with a growl and dragged me back to our little corner. The Merfolk laughed all the while. Steel's face had taken on a permanent red tinge.

Solder sat up rubbing the back of his head. "Feisty, that one. I admire her vigor," he joked and Slate shot him a murderous glare as he tried to keep me on his lap again.

"Send her over. You obviously cannot handle her," the merman taunted Slate.

"Shut it," Solder snapped, turning serious.

Slate breathed deep and cupped my face and I nuzzled his hands, "Torch, you have put me in a bit of a conundrum. On one hand, I know you will be mad at me and embarrassed of how many people around, but on the other I think you will calm down, maybe even fall asleep until the rousen is mostly out of your system."

"Don't even think about it. For the same reasons I told the Merfolk they couldn't," Steel interjected.

Slate kissed me deeply behind Steel's back and I moaned against his mouth. I pressed my breasts firmly against his chest rubbing and freeing them from the fabric that confined them.

"Did you sleep with her, Slate? Tell me honestly," Steel asked, "You didn't gift yourself last night. Were you hoping she would come to your bed?"

"Never. She does not let me get close. She is going to be very upset after this., Slate rumbled and I slipped my index finger into his mouth.

He arched an eyebrow suppressing a smile and sucked on it gently running his teeth along it until I panted. I placed my hand between us and ran my fingers along his hard outline over his pants.

Steel mulled over this information, "You cannot hope to keep her, even if you bed her."

Slate rubbed his thumb between my legs against the seam of my pants as I shoved my chest into his mouth. I sucked in a sharp breath at the skill his thumb had between my legs. He created an epicenter of pleasure so intense my sight blurred as tension coiled inside me making me squeeze my thighs tight around his waist.

His mouth broke away from my heavy breasts. "I know," he agreed roughly, and I smiled bringing his face back down against my chest. "Slow, Torch," Slate whispered.

My fingers were greedy for him.

"The Straumrs are one of the few families who don't hate us. They have too much power to betray. Ash is their golden boy; he'll be Prime one day. Scarlett could be wife to the Prime," Steel continued.

His reminder seemed to incite Slate, he stroked between my legs more intensely seeking to please me instead of placating me. Swirling his tongue against the swell of my breast to bruise the skin instead of pleasuring me. He clamped a hand over my mouth as soft, ragged moans escaped me and I licked his palm with the promise of what'd I'd do to his skin if he'd only let me.

"I know, Steel. She knows what is good for her," Slate said, slipping his hand beneath the fabric of my pants and rubbed against the dampness between my legs.

I gasped sharply against his hand, and he slanted his mouth over mine absorbing my noises, swallowing them with his mouth. I saw his neck strain as I unbuttoned his pants to run my fingers along his smooth hard skin.

"Ash can never know," Steel said sternly, addressing Solder.

"I am a lockbox of secrets," Solder told him as he stared directly across at the Merfolk and away from us.

"About this either," Steel said.

The Merfolk laughed watching what Slate and I were doing to one another. Slate's thighs flexed under me as if he was holding back and didn't trust himself to relax while I rubbed myself against his hand. I closed my eyes as I gripped him as best and pulled him from his pants and stroked the length of him. He sucked a deep breath in.

I pulled Slate's finger into my mouth and simulated what I'd rather be doing to him and opened my eyes as he threw back his head and felt him spill into my hand in complete silence other than his heavy controlled breaths.

Watching Slate receive the pleasure I gave him sent me over the edge. I had none of his restraint. I threw my head back and cried.

"Ah!"

Slate bit back a smile and closed his lips over my mouth to buffer the sound as I dwindled down to a moan. He tucked himself back into his pants after he pulled his hand out of mine and rinsed off my hand with his calling.

"What the fuck, Slate!" Steel shouted without turning around.

Slate tucked my breasts into my bra and pulled his shirt over his head then slid it on onto me before I fell against his chest, "She is going to go to sleep now and stop chafing my cock."

He pulled me up, so I curled in his lap, and swept my hair over my shoulder holding me tight to his chest. I blinked slowly as he gazed down at me. His grey narrow eyes framed by his dark lashes as he gently kissed my lips. My eyes closed, and I dozed listening to the steady beat of his heart.

I slept maybe a half hour and woke up again. I called water into my mouth and swallowed.

"Why haven't I fiddlesticked yet?"

They were the first words out of my mouth.

Laughs rang out all around me except for Steel, who, when I turned around, was sporting his new red color. "Good to see you are speaking again. It will not be much longer now," Slate said with glittering grey eyes.

"You talk too much. Shut up and kiss me."

He obliged.

Slate kept me from molesting him for the next twenty minutes and then I wondered why I was sitting on his lap and moved to sit next to him but held his hand. Then I no longer felt the need to have him touch me every nanosecond, and I scooted a little further dropping his hand.

About a half hour from home, I had completely come down off the rousen and had moved to sit at the far end of the raft. I faced out at the water letting the light spray of the river dampen my face and warmth of the hot Thrimilci sun heat my skin. I sat there with my knees pulled up and my eyes closed willing the raft to go faster so I could escape how terribly I'd embarrassed myself.

. . .

I heard the telltale sound of boots over wood and Solder sat down next to me, careful not to contact my skin. I appreciated his sensitivity to my humiliation.

I spoke without looking at him.

"I'm sorry I knocked your head against the raft," I told him and heard the Merfolk titter.

"Worse things happened to me today besides a gorgeous girl wanting to jump my bones. I found out I had been having sex with three of the five Merfolk traitors. Her included," I opened my eyes, and he pointed a thumb to the woman chained on the raft.

"I am sorry about that too. You didn't know though. It's not your fault," I said, trying to soothe him.

"Right back at you, gorgeous," A corner of Solder's big, lush lips curled up, and I smiled.

"I should have researched the Merfolk better; I would have known what Non're gave me. Have you ever had it before? The rousen?" I asked Solder, unable to face my uncle yet.

What he must've thought of me, and I was certainly not on speaking terms with Slate. He knew I'd remember everything. As if I could forget when he decided suddenly to succumb to my whims when Steel started mentioning Ash. That was what probably had excited him more than anything. I was certainly giving it my best effort, and he had Steel drag me out of that hut when I tried to — internally, I groaned.

"I have. No lie, I would have fucked anything with a hole. I still take it when I first get there and then very little to maintain that buzz. Humans can not drink much of it, a couple ounces and you will not eat or sleep, only try to get as much pleasure as possible. Any more than that and you risk brain damage — the permanent kind."

"So, it's an incredibly potent aphrodisiac. Good to know."

I shook my head and felt the added weight of something in my hair. My fingers reached for my jade piece I'd stolen from Slate and found with it a single ivory pearl bead. Slate must have threaded it through my braid when I'd fallen asleep. I didn't understand him in the slightest.

I planned on ignoring Slate for the duration of his life.

I napped for a few hours when we got to the palace and woke up feeling refreshed but determined to apologize to Steel and then figure out what happened with the Merfolk.

"The council is trusting the Merfolk to take care of their princess at Steel's behest. The two captives told them they had delivered portals to every island, including Valla. We have dispatched guardians to comb the areas they delivered them," Hawk explained. He'd sat through the meetings that had lasted hours.

"They did not know who had asked to transport the portals, and they did not know to what end. They were told when and where — that is all. The portal would show up just outside of Merfolk's perimeter underwater and they would transport it," Pearl added.

I bet Vanna'ra knew who it was. I was furious she got away. Steel was back, Solder had gone home. Steel said he was in better spirits after delivering the traitors to justice. They'd go to Karkinos for their roles in betraying their people and jeopardizing the precious balance of the islands. I was feeling good. We had finally solved one of our many problems.

Steel had told only Tawny about the rousen, and I wanted it kept that way. I cornered Steel after dinner and apologized. He kissed the top of my head and told me that our family was well versed in scandals. He was no one to judge if word got out about me and my adopted brother.

He actually thought that would make me feel better.

CHAPTER
TWO

 I went to a hearing of the council and received the same medal Slate had received for saving my life in the red hills from the Jorogumo. Moon pinned the little gold Mjolnir to my dress while Ash beamed with pride at my side. Pride and jealousy radiated from him.

I was glad the council acknowledged my good deed since I'd gotten so much sugarfoot for endangering myself from my mom, Sparrow, and Pearl. You'd think they had known about being slipped the rousen from how they reacted. I thought it was progress, the only time I'd needed healing was from Slate's love bites he'd left over my breasts on purpose and Tawny had done that for me discreetly after I'd woken up from my nap. That was a gigantic step up from being gutted or having my throat slit.

Progress people.

Ash hadn't known about my trip to the Merfolk. When he found out he was less than pleased. Then he discovered Slate had gone with, and he made a point of being glued to my side. Even coming back and spending the night on the weekends. Ash and I trained separately from everyone else, even though we were all in the same room. We were in our own little Ash and Scarlett bubble — the future Prime and his future wife.

The colors of my stained-glass windows lit Ash's face as he watched me doing classwork. I set down my pencil and gave him a flat look.

He laughed, "Studying."

"Yes," I poked my fountain pen at his arithmetic page.

He was fast. His hand caught my wrist, and he pulled me to him for a kiss. "You are adorable when you concentrate," he grinned with heavy lids.

I puckered my lips to his again and then withdrew, "There's a reason I was an English major." I chuckled to myself.

"Do not be modest. You are incredibly intelligent. I admire it," he looked disinterested in his own work.

My eyes slid over the flawless lines of his face. The way he sat was so proper it made me smile. His stunning eyes drifted up to mine and his brow quirked.

"You're fairytale handsome," I blushed, but kept his gaze.

"As are you," he began to smile, "What urged you to speak your thoughts out loud?"

"The sudden need," I shrugged with my face still hot.

"I have the sudden need to tell you that I care deeply for you, Scarlet," Ash murmured.

For the first time since we met, he sounded unsure of himself.

"I do, too," I whispered.

His expression smoothed and his lips lifted a bit. It was such an innocent expression; it made my heart hurt.

"I'm sorry — again. I didn't think it would become the thing it did when I asked to see the Merfolk. I should've offered," I gave him a hopeful smile.

Ash drew in a deep breath, " I believe you. Your uncle would protect you, but not as I would."

Again, I felt the sentiment laced with jealousy.

"Well, I'm finished," I leaned to the nightstand slightly behind me. I set the papers and book atop it.

I saw Ash's supplies slide off the bed and straightened before he leaned to kiss me. I chuckled against his lips and his hand scooted me down the bed while he climbed over me.

Ash was so patient with me. I felt as though I should've rewarded him with more affection.

He did kiss me until my toes curled. I liked how close our bodies were and could imagine how much better it would be undressed.

I gently pushed his shoulders. It was a gesture he was used to. He rolled off me and laid beside me catching his breath. I slid my eyes shut and flexed my fingers.

Slowly, his trousers unbuttoned from a bit of called air. He moaned in expectation, and I felt my own thrill. My lips popped as I drew in a sharp breath.

I'd been chasing that thrill ever since Slate unleashed my orgasm.

Ash seemed to sense it. He didn't reach out with a hand. It was his warm thread of air slithering up my leg.

My hand gripped his wrist. There was no stopping it.

I inhaled sharply and contorted. Ash rolled back over me and kissed my lips. He moaned and dropped his head beside mine. His chest rose and fell until he rolled over.

My eyes slowly opened and disbelief flooded me, "I can't believe I just did that."

"There is more to do," Ash purred and I laughed.

I chuckled again and looked to him. His eyes ran over my face in that innocent way from before. I cupped his cheek and kissed him.

"I *do* care deeply for you, Ash. I'm just nervous."

He leaned and kissed my lips again, "I believe you." He withdrew and looked down my caftan, "I apologize."

I wrinkled my nose and he smiled, "I'm going to go change."

"I could join you."

I chuckled knowingly and slipped from the bed, "Staying the night?"

"If Pearl does not mind."

I smiled at him before I went into my closet, "She doesn't."

Aside from the calling we could've been a coming-of-age movie. I enjoyed every second of it. Especially when he was in a good mood. Lately, he had been in a great mood.

The month flew by. I blinked at it was Tawny and Steel's wedding.

The Vetrs were the wealthiest of all the greater families. It disappointed Sparrow that all we had to do was wait around in one of the pristine rooms while hairdressers ran around pampering us. I sat next to Tawny, Sparrow, and my mom while our hair and makeup was done.

I'd peeked into the hall when I arrived, it being my first time in the Vetr castle, and castle it was. One word to describe the entire castle was cold. It was undoubtedly beautiful, but bitterly cold, and not just the temperature.

They did not introduce color into any aspect of the castle's design or furniture except for the scarlet red of its sigil and the bedrooms. Otherwise, everything was uniformly black and white. That didn't keep it from being ornate enough to rival the Sumar palace. The castle's plaster and wood carvings were its point of pride and it was admittedly arresting. It would hold the reception in the ballroom where with pillars that made larger columns topped with carved leaves that reminded me of a blooming flower that led to the ceiling.

Red ambient light lit around the white walls and reflected off the white marble floors with glittering black skein. Towering crystal vases held bouquets of red roses and strands of crystals hung from the vases. It was what I imagined a vampire banquet would look like; old money and lots of red.

When I'd imagined our weddings growing up, it was never so lavish. Tawny hadn't needed the big wedding; Orion had all but begged her for it. He wanted her to use his castle, wanted her to marry and take his name. He was making Tawny his heir. The sole heir to the Vetr castle and fortune to rule Elivagar after he passed away or until he stepped down.

Orion had invited everyone, and people were too afraid of old man Vetr to decline. Everyone that is except for his wife and daughters.

Cassiopeia, Delta, and her older sister Willow who was Sterling's mother, had not shown, nor would they have any part in Tawny's wedding. It had nothing to do with Tawny or her becoming heir, and everything to do with Sparrow and who her best friend was, my mother.

Gossip was the number one currency at Valla University and the rumor mill had caught wind of an unhappy marriage between Alder and Delta. It snowballed from there. I'd heard rumors of my mother and father's exploits through Ostara. They may have hidden it from the world before, but it appeared Alder was done with secrets.

"Wren, that color looks great on you," Sparrow told my mother.

"Good thing since you picked it out," my mom replied.

Her warm smile took the bitter out of the cold castle.

Sparrow was wearing an identical dress in a deep burgundy taffeta; the floor length gowns went well with their dark hair and eyes. Tawny smiled over at them. I kept feeling a burn in my nose. Tears threatens to assault me. She was breathtaking. Her smile could melt the ice off Elivagar. If her grandmother and aunts had got their sugarfoot together and had come, even they couldn't have denied Tawny.

I must have told her half a hundred times already, but I said it again, "You look so beautiful." Tears pricked my eyes, and I fanned at them with Sparrow and my mom laughing at me.

"Thank you. Again," Tawny said, smirking.

Her lips matched the scarlet of our strapless dresses. Amethyst, Cherry, and Indigo sat in chairs in the room with us with more women doing their makeup. Tawny had made Indigo a bridesmaid. Indigo was every bit a part of our little group. I wished we had known her in high school so we would have had one more friend, and it would've been hard for girls to hate Indigo. No one hated Indigo, the girl was just too nice.

My mom and Sparrow had gone to talk to her at every chance, getting to know our only friend that wasn't bound to us by family. I glanced over at Indigo, her hair pinned so it spilled down her back in a cascade of bouncy champagne curls. She cast a smile over her shoulder, the beauty mark over her right cheek lifted as she beamed. Tawny's good cheer infected the entire room.

"There you go, hun. All set," Bronze said, shoving another bobby pin in to style my hair identical to Indigo's, with the same red lips as Tawny had.

"Bronze, you know you're the best."

I always went to Bronze for my beauty needs. The brunette's skills were unparalleled.

"Sure. Sure. For the tears because you will need it," Bronze pressed a handkerchief into my hand, and I tucked it into the bosom of my dress.

My mother was back by Indigo, I might have to save her soon. Tawny stood and Sparrow helped her into her gown, the tulle fabric overlapped in folds over her bodice and flared out just below her knees. Sparrow cinched the back of her corset as I pulled on my dress and slipped into my shoes. Bronze tied the back of the dress for me giving my already hourglass figure a teeny tiny waist.

"Five more minutes."

The woman Orion hired to handle the details poked her head in with a plastered smile. I had a feeling Sparrow very much wanted to strangle the woman.

Tawny and Hawk stood behind me ready for their turn to walk down the aisle. I stood behind my brother and the girls, in front of them was Gypsum and Indigo. My bouquet of snow-white roses in hand, I my arm through Slate's. It made more sense that they would pair me with Gypsum, but there was no way Tawny would have intentionally put me with Slate knowing our history.

No, that would be way too sneaky.

The men all looked handsome in their red waistcoats over their long sleeve white shirts, red and black brocade ascots at their throats. Slate's hair had oil in it that brought out its natural waves, it hung loose down his back with a dozen thin braids threaded through with silver beads and white fetishes that stood out against his midnight mane. We didn't talk about my stolen jade carving, or the pearl bead that had magically shown up in my hair. I caught myself gazing up at him and averted my eyes.

We hadn't come into physical contact since that day on the raft a month ago. Shale had made a reappearance into his life, and I'd kept my distance even when Ash wasn't breathing down my neck.

I was self-conscious around him. Remembering to apply some gloss to my lips before going down to dinner or curling my hair instead of letting it air dry when I knew we'd both be at the palace together. I didn't know it was possible to be utterly aggravated with oneself.

My only explanation was that I had touched Slate in a way I'd touched no man and he hadn't said a single word about it. Not so much as 'That was terrible, I'll never do it again', or 'Fiddlesticking fantastic, Rabbit!'.

Nothing.

What was worse was that he had touched me. Didn't he realize I didn't do those things casually? That I had no experience with it and so I'd be extra sensitive after- wards? Couldn't he have apologized, or sent flowers? A note slipped under the door. It could have said, 'You're very welcome for your first orgasm ever, sorry they drugged you while it happened.'

I sighed.

Hawk and Tawny were right behind us, and I knew they would hear what we said. Slate looked down at me making me feel like he was taking my measure.

The music started, and I watched as our mothers exited into the room. Steel would lead them to the front row where Pearl had sat instead of being led down the aisle. The rest followed out until it was Slate and my turn.

We walked on a red runner scattered with white petals under garlands crammed full of matching roses that hung across the ceiling. Hundreds of people, possibly a thousand, faced us in their white seats tied with red tulle. I walked down the aisle with Slate, his steady presence quelling my nervousness. I scanned the faces as we went being sure to smile broadly at Ash or face his ire afterwards, but as we passed the Straumrs, I noticed he wasn't there.

I had seen him before I'd gone to get ready, we'd greeted each other briefly be- fore he had gone to hang out with Sterling. Sage hadn't come either, not caring to if his mother wouldn't I supposed.

"Looks like lover boy had something better to do." Slate murmured.

"Maybe he thought the sight of us together would hurt too much." I whispered harshly trying to keep my lips still.

"Does he know?" It piqued his curiosity.

"There's nothing to know." I muttered curtly.

Slate sniffed, and we parted ways before Steel and gave him a big smile.

Steel looked as handsome as ever. His poster boy smile was at full wattage as he awaited his bride. The crowd stood as the music changed and Tawny and Hawk entered. I watched as Steel's face changed. I didn't think he could smile any brighter, and I was wrong.

My eyes met Slate's just past Steel and my world faded in a blur of background noise. Sometimes it felt like he could read my mind. He knew how I felt before I knew it. He anticipated my reactions.

I moved to take a step towards him, drawn to him by some inexplicable force and received a bouquet. I looked down at them and the world came back into focus.

Tawny was in front of me. Sugarfoot! What was I doing? I bent over and fixed the train of her dress and took a step back holding her bouquet.

That was a close one.

I avoided Slate's eyes afraid whatever vortex I'd found might draw me in again. There was no officiant, in the eyes of the Guardians, once Hawk gave up Tawny and they said the blood vow, they were married. Steel took her hand and slid on the ruby ring he'd already given her. I handed Tawny the ring she picked for him, and she slid on his satin finished ring. They chanted the blood oath in unison.

"By the name gifted to me by my ancestors, I give my word May I never stain it. From my blood, I vow with the voice of my forbearers. On my honor, and on the honor of my descendants, I hereby swear to keep it."

They kissed and turned to the crowd who cheered up at their rapturous faces.

I took a deep breath as I looped my arm through Slate's, and we followed Tawny and Steel whose emotions bolstered my own until I was nearly as happy as they were. We filed into the hall where Steel and Tawny stood greeting people and I took my chance to go find Ash. They'd be there awhile.

"Looking for lover boy? I think I saw him upstairs. I can show you if you like?" Slate offered, and I narrowed my eyes at him.

"Okay," I said slowly and told Indigo where we were off to.

Slate strode purposefully through the halls, and I followed slightly behind him brimming with suspicion. If it was some ruse to get me alone, I was going to be seriously pissed.

"Down here. He was —" Slate stopped short and pulled me into an alcove as I heard another door shut.

"We missed the ceremony. My mother will be furious." A girl said.

"I suppose we could have stayed., Ash said sounding cocky as ever.

"No, that is not what I meant. Oh, Ash. I love being with you, I would not give it up for the world," The girl said hurriedly followed by sounds that could only be them kissing.

I was standing pressed against Slate in an alcove of a doorway during Tawny's wedding listening to the man who proposed marriage to me make-out with another girl. I should have felt something, but I had the habit of going numb when my feelings were too much for me to process or bare.

I risked a peek, Slate's arms loosened enough so part of my face made it past the alcove. Ash stood with the pretty redhead from our course. She was my distant cousin, Crimson Rot. My stomach turned, and I moved back to press my face against Slate's chest wishing I could disappear.

"I love you; you know," Crimson told him sounding breathy.

"I know you do, kitten."

I imagined Ash running his fingers through her hair like he so often did me.

Something surfaced inside me, and I thought about how I'd been holding myself back since I'd arrived there. While it was all my fault, I did it because I thought Ash and I had a future. I moved away from Slate and stepped into the hall tearing the Yggdrasil necklace from around my throat.

"We are so over," I said, throwing the ring Ash had given me at his chest which he caught easily in one hand.

His expression was cool, hers not so much. Crimson's cheeks blushed the color of her namesake under her smattering of freckles as her hand covered her mouth.

"Scarlett. Do not be hasty. You have never asked me to be exclusive," Ash said pointedly, he was right.

I didn't feel cheated on. I felt disrespected that he seduced my distant cousin on my uncle's wedding day and had missed the ceremony.

"You're right. I didn't expect you to wait around for me, but this is disrespectful. We had fun, but now that fun is over. Enjoy the rest of your night, Ash. Crim- son." I turned around in the expansive hall and listened to the satisfying click of my heels on the marble.

"Scarlett! We will discuss this once you have time to reflect. You know there is no better husband than I for you." Ash shouted after me.

I didn't bother responding and passed where Slate hid in an alcove listening to Ash and Crimson talk as they walked the opposite way. She was crying; I hated making people cry. It made me feel like a monster.

Slate caught up to me quickly once they'd turned a corner. He pulled me to him, so my arms were up between us, his wrapped around my waist tightly and I bent away from him just wanting to be free.

"Torch?" he asked.

"Just because I broke things off with Ash ten seconds ago doesn't mean I'll leap into your bed now," I said stiffly, wanting to be anywhere but in his arms.

Slate pulled me closer ignoring my vehemence. "Ah, Torch. I have been waiting months for you to end things with Ash. I understand you have been single all of ten seconds, but I do not mean to let some other man sweep you off your feet tonight. If it happens again, I may have to forgo my room and move my things into yours," his tone was soft and coaxing.

My mouth opened and closed. "You're insane. You can't even keep your hands off women for a single day, and you want to... what?" my astonished reflection was almost visible in his silver eyes.

"Gods, Scarlett. You are a stubborn woman. I want you. I want you in my bed right now if you will come with me," Slate purred pressing his palm to my upper back to rest my chest against him.

My mind was reeling. "Your bed? Just your bed?" I asked feeling the swift beat of my heart pump adrenaline through me. I needed Slate to spell it out for me.

His full lips curled as he gazed down at me through thick long lashes, "Torch, you are an all-or-nothing kind of woman. I cannot give you everything you deserve, but you can have —"

"Scarlett? Slate? What are you doing?"

My mom's voice was inquisitive, not harsh, or accusatory at all. Somehow it made it worse. As if she wasn't surprised we were embracing in the hall, but simply curious what we were discussing.

I squeezed my eyes shut and hoped when I opened them, I had been in a dream, and it was still the morning of Tawny's wedding. I'd wake up and everything would be fine. My mother would not have caught me pressed up against her adopted son while I was being courted by Ash at my cousin/uncle's wedding.

Nope. It was really happening. I could barely keep up with all the *happening*.

Slate released me reluctantly as my mother approached as I tried to get a feel for her emotions.

"Mother, I persuaded Scarlett here to have a private conversation. I am sorry," Slate said straight away.

I gave him a side glance. He never acted like my brother. He spoke to my mom it was like he was speaking to *his* mother, and worse yet, he sounded almost proper when he spoke to her.

My mom raised a hand and nodded, "Yes. I heard. You've missed them cutting the cake, and the dancing is about to start so I suggest you get down there."

I hung my head feeling like I was five years old getting caught stealing cookies.

"Scar?" she let it hang there leaving the rest unsaid.

I turned around and they were both looking at me. I couldn't hide the horror I felt, and I couldn't lie to my mom.

"Mom. *Please*," I begged her not to say anything to him.

"I thought so," my tiny mom turned to the giant that was Slate, "It would appear we have a minor situation."

I was shaking my head emphatically, "Everything's fine."

I did the only logical thing I could think of; I grabbed my mom's arm and started tugging her away. All I needed was for her not to tell Slate something crazy — worse — him tell her about his plans for me and his bed.

"Please, mom. Not now," I begged.

She pressed her lips together and looked between the two us again. Slate was looking like he wanted to talk to my mom. Had she heard what he was saying about his bed? Oh Gods!

She relented, "I won't let you two make the same mistakes —"

"Mom, please stop talking!" I shouted over her.

We left Slate standing there as I dragged my mom back downstairs to the ballroom.

"Scar. What have I done?" my mom said, absently looping her arm through mine once I stopped pulling her.

"I ended things with Ash, but Slate isn't the man for me. I need some time to be alone."

My mom sighed, "If you don't fight for what you want, no one else is going to fight for you, Scar. Do you want to be with Slate? Think about it before you answer."

Some things you didn't delve into because of the fear of what you might find. I'd let the rushing waters of my heart trail around my fingers never allowing myself to dive in — to submerge myself. The waters might've been too strong and pulled me under. The waters were a rushing river, and I might be the only one drowning.

"Slate isn't the settling down type," I told her fueling my words with images of Slate and the other women I'd seen him with *so* many times.

My mom squeezed me closer. "There's still time," she said cryptically as we entered the ballroom in time to see Hawk and Tawny dancing together, "I want to tell you a short story."

"Mom..." I said just wanting the talking to stop.

"It's a short story. I met your father when I was sixteen. If I hadn't been so afraid to risk my heart, I might have been able to marry your father the Guardian way. I left him for years until my first masquerade. He told me he waited for me and that he never stopped loving me — but it was too late. Eventually, I married Lark. It was probably the best decision I made concerning my love life."

I felt like I was holding my breath. Maybe I was. My mother never volunteered information about her life before Chicago. Most of what I'd learned was from tidbits Hawk and Sparrow let slide.

She was smiling wistfully, but her eyes were gleaming. "I could have fallen in love with Lark. Never tell your father," she chuckled to herself, "Not that you would have that discussion with him. Lark wanted another child. I could never have denied him, he was an excellent father."

I watched as a tear rolled over her cheek.

"Don't let love slip through your fingers. Sometimes it scorches as often as it melts. I have lost love twice, but I'm lucky. Your father is too stubborn to let me go again. I love your father. I'm sure you've heard the rumors. Scar, things are going to change. He wants to be a part of your life — our lives. A family. You don't want to wait. Life doesn't wait," she turned to me and hugged me, "I love you. I love Slate, too. We should sit with Silver Regn. His mother and I were best of friends along with Sparrow."

Ash was in prime charm mode; it almost made me forget what I'd seen. It didn't let me forget my mom's sudden outpouring of truths. She had left me in a stupor after she brought me over to Silver, whom I knew, and told me she was his aunt through marriage. Lark was his uncle. It was the second time I hadn't seen 'Quick' Silver hit on a woman.

Brass wandered up to us as we spoke to Quick, and he greeted my mother with a hug. He remembered my mother. He said she helped save Silver during the Red King Massacre, which she modestly denied. She looked at them with the un- abashed affection I'd seen her give Jett, and Steel, or even Slate. I felt like I hardly knew her. Brass asked to escort her onto the dance floor which she happily accepted, and I moved my trance along to another table.

I couldn't understand how Ash could look at me so adoring and devoted when he was seeing other women. He was casting glances my way all night while avoiding a confrontation. He was careful about whom he took onto the dance floor, making sure none of them were younger women, or if they were, that they were related.

I'd allowed him to guide me onto the dance floor without so much as a peep. He was hard to say no to when he was like that even knowing what I did. We'd have to let people know about our breakup slowly or it would make us both look bad.

Tawny hadn't left the dance floor since dinner, Steel had joined the other guys at the bar, ascots misplaced, waistcoats unbuttoned, and sleeves rolled up while getting sloshed to the gills. Slate cast Ash and I a glance as we danced looking homicidal.

I lost track of my parents and the Regn brothers during my dance with Ash but knew that neither party would be up to any good. Orion had hardly moved since sitting content to watch Tawny and her all-consuming joy. He had raised his goblet to me when our eyes met, and I made a note to ask him to dance even if he was tremendously intimidating.

Sterling was with the rest of the men in the wedding party. Ash joined the men laughing and drinking and released me after pressing a kiss to my hand. I resisted the urge to roll my eyes. I had been divesting the bowl at the center of the table of its wassail and decided it was the perfect time to find a bathroom and get some air.

It muffled the music to a dull roar as I walked the halls of the Vetr castle looking for a way to get onto a balcony. I headed higher; I knew there was one in the bedroom we'd readied in, so I followed the marble stairs until I found the floor we'd been on.

A woman's scream filled the air and my chest constricted in excruciating pain.

I knew that voice. That scream.

The feeling that something was terribly wrong and the fear of seeing what made me hesitate. Suddenly, I was floating as if in a dream.

I walked to the room we readied in and before I could open the white intricately carved door, another scream sounded. Closer — I knew that scream, too.

Heat joined with my fear, and I turned the knob. I glided into the room. My eyes searched it and found French doors wide open, the strong winds buffeted thick red curtains. I drifted towards the doors knowing what I'd see there. I could feel it mingling with the heat and the fear.

Indigo hung half over the balcony screaming. Her long blonde hair whipped around her strained face as the wind pulled tight against her body her scarlet dress. I hadn't realized she was still screaming. Instead of questioning her, or pulling her away from the edge, I moved beside her and bent to see what she saw.

I'd jumped from three stories before, or so they told me. I was nearly five stories over the ground floor, but the only thing on my mind was getting down there as quickly as possible. Gravity, physics, logic be damned.

I pulled as much calling as I could to my body and saw that I had stripped the breeze from the air, harnessing the cold to use it. I stole the surrounding energy, sucking Mother Earth's elements from existence without thinking of the repercussions and threw myself over the balcony in a swan dive.

Indigo's blood-curdling scream followed me down. Several people were slowing my impact with the mountain. I felt my ankles give with mirrored barbs of sharp pain. I couldn't get to my feet, something else may have been broken as well, but all I knew is I had to get there.

A dark figure placed a hand on the body, and I felt irrepressible anguish.

"NO!" I howled and clawed my way to the body.

The balcony was so cold it hurt my palms as I tried to drag my useless legs behind me. The wind slapped at my cheeks and the tears that fell over them.

Abruptly, I was scooped off the ground as people filed out onto the downstairs balcony. The body laid across the rocks of the mountain on the other side of the white balustrade and people were shouting and crying all around me. I saw a few women faint and another fall to her knees. I fought the arms that held me with everything I had, but they clamped down tight.

"I want that man arrested for questioning!"

It couldn't be happening. This wasn't real. I couldn't feel the fluffy snowflakes falling around us, or the bite of the wind, so it must be a dream, a nightmare.

Ash drew on his calling and faced off against the dark figure who had hopped back over the balustrade, but the figure was heedless of Ash, his eyes were only for me. Guardians clasped a nix torque around his muscled neck and my brother and uncles shouted at the Guardians, resulting in Brass and Quick having to drag Jett away.

The Guardians pushed the man past me, his hands were bound behind him in smaller versions of the torque around his neck. I stole the Earth's elements. Pulling them into my body in a way I didn't know was possible. The wind died on the mountain as I screamed pouring myself into a single word.

"NO!"

People ducked and held their ears.

No, for Slate being arrested. No, for the utter disbelief of what was becoming my reality, and no for my mother's broken body on the rocks of Elivagar.

A puddle of crimson on the stark snow. Her delicate fingers curled as if she'd hope to sprout wings like the Aves and found herself without feathers. I hadn't seen her face. Her thick hair had shrouded her flawless skin.

I needed to see. I had to be sure.

The surrounding arms flooded me with warmth, and they forced me to sleep.

My mother died three days ago.

Whenever I woke up three words replayed cruelly in my mind. My mother died.

I rolled back over in her bed. My father healed and carried me from the Vetr castle when he brought me to my grandmother's palace, but as soon as I awoke, I'd numbly found my way to her room.

Alder had cradled me like a baby until we had reached my bedroom in the Sumar palace. I hadn't fought him when I woke up and as he stood there for a time. His light blue eyes were bloodshot from unshed tears, his short corn silk hair, normally not a strand out of place, matted to his scalp from the melted snowflakes that had fallen outside of the Vetr castle after we'd found my mother's body.

My mother died.

It was no more believable than it had been when I'd tried to claw my way over to her broken body that had laid on the rocky mountainside outside of rooms filled with laughter and joy celebrating the union of Tawny and Steel.

I would have wondered if Slate was still in custody for my mother's murder, or how my family was doing since the death of my mother, or why Indigo had been in the upstairs room, the same room that let out to the balcony my mother had fallen or pushed off. I would have, but I didn't.

I pulled at my nightdress. Tawny, Amethyst, and Cerise had forced me into a shower last night and helped dress me. I didn't care about showering. Who cared if my hair was greasy? Not me. I didn't stink or anything at that was where my bar was set these days. Even then, I supposed it would depend on how bad I smelled.

My mother died.

I held my breath until the need to cry and scream, to break things passed. Jett had spent every night with me in our mother's bed. Since arriving to Tidings, Jett and our mother had grown close, he wasn't taking her death well. I vaguely remembered him getting in the guardian's face escorting Slate to be questioned.

He had nothing to do with my mother's death even though he'd been standing over her body. It looked bad if you hadn't heard her scream on the way down.

I had.

I swallowed hard. I'd known before even going into that bedroom that it had been my mother's scream that had trailed as she fell. She was pushed. The question was, by who? The Guardians were so consumed with my mother's body and Slate that I was willing to bet they hadn't searched the floors of the castle to see if the true culprit was hiding somewhere. There had been nearly a thousand people at Tawny and Steel's wedding, it could have been anyone.

My mother's broken body was seared into my eyelids. I'd never forget that image. I'd never see her brown eyes soften when she knew I was lying to myself, or doing something childish, or her wide warm smile that reminded me of why I could tell her anything, why we had no secrets from one another, or so I thought. Since coming to Tidings, I realized I'd barely known her. My mother had a whole other life, and it was full of secrets. But she was still my mother, and I didn't keep secrets from her.

They might've murdered her for one of those secrets.

I rolled onto my back and stared about the room. My mother hadn't updated it. It was her old room because come to find out, she'd had a wing there because she'd been married and had adopted a son with that man. The son they arrested.

I ran my hands over my face and slid them over my hair. It was good that Tawny and my brother's wives had forced me to bathe, my hair didn't feel nearly as dry as it had yesterday. All the hairspray from the up-do I'd worn as Tawny's maid of honor had still been in my hair.

Poor Tawny. I hoped she didn't blame her wedding on my mother's death. Tawny's mother would be a complete wreck. I groaned. Sparrow and my mother had been best friends since—well, forever. I couldn't imagine losing Tawny, it'd be just as hard as losing my mom. Sparrow hadn't come to visit me in my mother's room yet, I didn't expect her too. I didn't want her too. I didn't want anyone to.

My mother died.

I squeezed my eyes shut and pressed my palms to their lids. I didn't need a mirror to know my eyes were bloodshot and puffy, or that my tan skin was blotchy, my already full lips swollen from crying. My mother's perfume made its way into my nostrils. Jasmine and a subtle hint of roses.

An impossible ache ripped through my chest making me curl into the fetal position on my mother's massive bed.

Someone was knocking on the door. I didn't so much as make a noise. They would come in on their own. I hadn't spoken since I screamed on the balcony as they arrested Slate.

The arched wood door creaked open to reveal a dark shadow that nearly blocked all the hall's light from spilling into the dark room. As soon as I got to my mother's room, I closed the shades. I didn't want to see sunshine. I couldn't understand how the world had kept going as if nothing was wrong, when nothing was right.

My mother died.

The bed bowed beneath his weight as he climbed into bed facing me.

"Morning, Torch," Slate rumbled with a voice so deep it sounded like it growled out from his stomach.

I looked at him numbly as his eyes peered out at me from their thick black lashes.

"Have you eaten?" He asked lifting his hand to push strands of my hair out of my face.

No talking. No appetite. I hadn't eaten since my mother died. Savoring food when my mother was dead felt wrong. Anything other than nothing felt like a betrayal of her memory.

"You must eat, Torch. I will ask someone to bring up some oatmeal. Apple cinnamon?" his lips curled.

He'd told me I smelled like vanilla and spiced apples.

I sighed and turned over in the enormous bed. Slate moved closer so his body curled around mine and wrapped his arm around me holding me tight.

"You are going to make yourself sick if you do not eat or drink," he murmured into my hair.

Inside, I was glad Slate was out. He must have just gotten home; he was still wearing the waistcoat from Tawny and Steel's wedding.

"We are going to put your mother's ashes to rest today. I need you to get up so I can help you get ready," he said gently and my chest tightened.

I thought my heart must be trying to physically fill the gaping hole left by my mother's absence and the blinding pain a part of the healing process. Either that or I was dying. I swallowed against the lump in my throat.

"Bronze and the other beauticians are going to come and help you get ready after I feed you. Then we must go outside, I will be right by your side if you wish it," he said and paused for a moment awaiting my response.

He sighed and rolled away from me, and I listened as he found a staffer. His footsteps were deceptively light as he walked back to the bed. Slate climbed back in and wrapped his arm around me again. I felt the warmth of his calling delve into me and he sighed again. He saw how dehydrated I was, and how my body was half starved. I didn't care. I had no appetite.

"Food is here. You can sit up and eat it, or I can hold your nose until your mouth opens and dump it in. Your choice," Slate was doing his best trainer's voice and my knee-jerk reflex was to obey.

I sat up and slid my feet off the bed but stayed seated. I had spent my energy for the day with the motion. He showered and wore black as usual. His black pants tucked into shining leather boots, which meant he dressed up, and his satin waistcoat fastened with gold sunbursts, so he was really dressed up.

I looked at the dress he'd brought for me. Long sleeve but made so it would cling to my curves until it hung off my hips in a small train. It was a beautiful slinky material, but I should have worn a garbage bag.

Those were black too.

It would be just as effective to cover me up, I shouldn't wear anything pretty, my mother couldn't.

Slate shoved the bowl at me, but I didn't have the energy to lift my arms to take it from him. Instead of glowering like he normally would have, he took the spoon and dipped it into the oatmeal, then raised it to my lips. I gazed at him over the spoon. What did he care if I ate? The hairdressers would come in and get me ready then someone would force me into the dress.

He reached up with his free hand after balancing the oatmeal on his thigh and arched an eyebrow at me. I opened my mouth, and he slid the spoon into it.

Once I finished the bowl of oatmeal, he handed me a thick green liquid and leveled his grey eyes at me, daring me not to drink it. I took the cup weakly and lifted it to my lips to sip on it. His fingers met the cups bottom and tipped it back until the entire cup's contents was in my stomach. I wanted to have the energy to scowl.

I lifted my arms up obediently before he bothered to ask. He sat on the edge of the bed and furrowed his bronze forehead at my gesture until I scooted off the back of my nightdress. I didn't care who dressed me, one person was just the same as another. Besides, Slate had seen me only in my underwear before and he'd been with enough women that what I had wouldn't be an enormous shock for him.

Realization dawned on him, and for once, I thought, he was nervous. Maybe not nervous, but he hesitated before taking the silky orchid hem and raising it up over my arms. My hair fell around me in a shower of golden waves, and I watched blankly as Slate twisted away to grab the black dress off the bed. I couldn't wear a bra with the dress. The back was a sheer panel of black from my shoulders to the small of my back. Not appropriate funeral wear, but it barely registered.

He turned back around and hesitated again when he saw me sitting there with my arms outstretched for my funereal garb in nothing but a pair of lacy orchid boy shorts. I didn't look away when his eyes flashed silver and he quickly yanked the black dress over me, then stood placing a pair of black pumps on the floor. His gigantic hands lifted me effortlessly from the bed and I slid my feet into the shoes as he pulled my hair from the back of the dress.

"Now I am certain you are not feeling well. The only time you let me see you in such a state of undress was when you were drugged," he rumbled and lowered me back into a seated position on the bed.

Slate sat down next to me and wrapped an arm around my shoulders making me lean into his chest. "I dislike seeing you this way, Torch. I keep waiting for you to slap me or say something scathing. I would welcome it," he confessed.

Whatever he saw in my eyes made him press his lips together and wrap his muscular arms around me and pull me on top of him as he laid back against the pillows. Somewhere deep beneath the anguish, it incensed me he would be so arrogant to assume I'd need his comfort, but for now my cheek rested against his heart as I listened to its beat in a steady soothing rhythm blocking out all other thoughts. I dozed off again.

My three favorite hairdressers, Bronze, Katydid, and Cricket came and went. Bronze, the busty brunette, had teared the entire time she did my hair in my mother's bathroom. Tawny and Pearl had come into my mother's room to find me napping on Slate. He woke me so my grandmother and cousin/aunt could bring me into the bathroom to prepare for the hairdressers.

I stared at my reflection next to Slate's powerful frame that sat on the bathroom counter watching the women work with his corded muscled arms crossed over his broad chest. Even in satin, the man looked deadly.

If Pearl or Tawny thought it was peculiar that my adopted brother was taking such a keen interest in me, they kept it to themselves. If I was in my right mind, I would have shooed him away, or at the very least wondered what his motives were.

Dark circles had ringed my almond eyes before Bronze had worked her magic. Something still swelled my full lips, likely from my bouts of crying, and my high cheek bones border lined on gaunt from not having eaten for days. Bronze had contoured my face, so my cheekbones had the little round apples that appeared when I smiled, were outlines even with my blank expression.

Cricket, the serious blonde with meticulously curled hair, had clipped a black veiled fascinator at the back of my hair that was piled atop my head in cascading curls and lowered the birdcage veil over my face. I was grateful for anything that would obscure it. It felt wrong to be primped when I was grieving.

The pyre was lit, and my mother's body was burning. Valkyries descended the stone steps erected for the pyre; the women's bald heads gleamed under the bright Thrimilci sun. They were the only organized spiritual group in Tidings. An all-female group like nuns who worshipped Mother Nature and were the ones who helped with funerals. They wore plain flowing robes of cream that covered their bodies loosely synched at the waist by a brown silken rope.

When the whoosh of the flames engulfed her body, my fingers curled reflexively and my nails bit into Slate's forearm. He gently uncurled my fingers and interlaced them with his own. I could almost feel Ash's fury behind me where he sat with the other Straumr family members.

When I came out onto the balcony at the back of the Sumar palace where my mother's funeral was being held, Ash had ignored Slate and placed a kiss on my lips before offering his condolences. Slate had coolly told him I hadn't spoken in four days.

Ash had appeared with Diamond, his mother, and his father Basil. Basil looked just like his brother, but with lighter coloring and narrower shoulders.

They all looked empathetic, apart from my future mother-in-law. Dahlia's fair face had a permanent pinched expression to her once beautiful face. Her strawberry blonde hair fell to her shoulders, pinned back to reveal her fair skin and green eyes. Dahlia Natt, sister to Cassiopeia Natt and Tawny's grandmother who had refused to be present at her wedding.

My mother died.

Aside from the soul-crushing anguish I felt occasionally, I was utterly empty. I didn't care about anything either way, had no opinion.

I spared a glance, hours after my mother's body had burned, for the Straumr family behind us. The handsome youngest brother of the Straumrs looked uncharacteristically somber. His sky-blue eyes in his caramel skinned face didn't glitter as they normally did. Fox's tight dark curls and goatee looked recently trimmed, probably for Tawny's wedding.

Amethyst's brother was my favorite instructor at Valla U aside from my uncle Jackal who was my father's brother and taught my worst subject, languages. The two older Straumr brother's, Crag, and River, were also battle trainers at Valla U.

Crag looked like his father Moon whose ebony skinned face was just as somber as Fox's. Moon had aged like a person outside of Tidings would have. He had the face of a person who had seen too much and had barely survived through it. River's wife and kids were sitting alongside him looking terribly bored, he looked the most like his sister with his mocha skin and obvious good looks. A goatee framed his well sculpted lips that resembled Ash's. They gave me forced smiles before I turned back around.

Anguish assailed me. I could not fall apart. I'd managed not to cry in front of anyone so far except for Jett at night.

Steel, Gypsum, and Pearl had reached us just before we went onto the balcony that overlooked the two rivers Mani and Sol that created the waterfall behind the palace. They had constructed a stairway that led to nowhere but the open sky above the waterfall where my mother's body burned. It was possibly the worst honeymoon ever; poor Steel and Tawny were sitting further down my row. They comforted one another, but it was futile.

Gypsum had a crush on Ash's little sister, Diamond. His long sable hair was pulled back in a leather strap away from his olive skin and threaded through with a dozen narrow braids like Slates, and little copper beads caught the sun. His thick brows were drawn down over his dark eyes, and not a single sign of his trademark dimples were to be seen. Diamond had squeezed his hand as they parted. Her light green eyes that matched Ash's gleamed with unshed tears as she'd pushed her thick chestnut hair away from her soft features.

When we took our seats and I had scanned the crowd unabashed. Pearl sat on the far end of the aisle, her coppery brown hair in loose curls to her shoulders, her emerald cat eyes straight ahead. She too wore a veil so I couldn't see if her deep tanned skin betrayed her emotions, or if her wide mouth my mother inherited pulled down at the corners.

My uncle's silver hair swung into view as he sat down beside his mother.

Hawk.

My mother's twin brother. He must feel the pain as bad as Sparrow and my grandmother. Maybe as bad as I did. Jett's big hand interlaced his fingers into mine and I felt his callouses from weapon training for years on his palms. The girls, my brother's wives, sat on his other side. Steel and Tawny sat on the other side of the girls; Tawny's dark tresses hid her fair face from me. Steel's cheeks had red blooms in his tan cheeks, and despite his put together look, I knew he was upset. He only had those red blooms when he was very emotional. His eyes met mine over Tawny's head and I looked away.

I knew Sparrow would be a wreck. I couldn't fathom how right I'd be. She must have had her hair and makeup done by the three hairdressers as well, yet she looked haggard. Her veil was crumpled from where she'd pushed it aside drying her tears countless times that morning. It hurt looking at Sparrow. Her long wavy dark hair and chocolate brown eyes were so like my mother's.

When I was little and we had been neighbors in Chicago, there had been many times that I had mistook Sparrow with my mother from behind. Now, she was a reminder of everything I'd lost. I missed Chicago and wondered why we'd ever moved to Tidings almost ten months ago. My mother had been safe in Chicago, and that was really saying something. Safe and Tidings were two words you'd never find in the same sentence.

I nearly staggered when I saw my father and Indigo sitting in the front row side by side. Indigo looked worse than I did. Her long corn silk hair hung limply, and her powder blue eyes were watery and red, her tan skin even blotchier than Jett's. My father looked no better. His heavily muscled arm rested across Indigo's slim shoulders as she dried her eyes with a kerchief.

Grief hung heavy in the hot perpetual summer air, and I lost track of the hours as I watched my mother's body burn on the stone dais above the stairs. Her body covered in roses and jasmine on the pyre.

It was the worst day of my life.

CHAPTER THREE
JETT

Jett sat at Scarlett's side with his wives, Amethyst, the mocha silk daughter of Moon Straumr, and Cerise, nicknamed Cherry with her fair milky skin, wide blue eyes, and raven hair, sat on his other side. The girls had shaved his square jaw that morning and gave his dark blonde hair a close trim since he hadn't cared to do it.

He had spent the last few nights in Wren's room with Scarlett, holding her hand and stroking her long caramel waves as she either stared blankly or sobbed uncontrollably, he never knew what to expect when he entered the room. He wasn't sleeping himself, there was too much anger and frustration at his mother's death to do anything — but rage.

When he'd left Scarlett in the mornings, he'd made love fiercely with his wives just to feel anything other than what was rotting him from the inside out. It wasn't fair, he'd hardly known her, and now she was gone. She'd left behind Scarlett who didn't seem to know how to function without her, and Jett felt helpless to know how to soothe her.

When Scarlett had entered the balcony, he had disentangled himself from his wives, strode purposefully to her and Slate. She had run into his arms, and they collided as he caught her effortlessly. He squeezed her tight and heard her whimper trying not to cry. Jett had not known how easy it would be to let his little sister into his heart, but it had happened in an instant.

"Baby sis. How are you?" Jett choked out.

He'd placed her back down, not waiting for her response. He had lifted her right out of her shoes, and he let out a strangled chuckle as he knelt to guide her feet back into her pumps.

"They want us to spread mother's ashes. Do you want to release her ashes with me?" he nodded towards the stairs.

Scarlett looked at Jett from beneath the dark veil and he saw acceptance there. She hadn't spoken in days, the only noises she emitted being ones of sorrow and heartache. Jett nodded in understanding. She started and seemed suddenly aware that it wasn't just the two of them on the stone balcony. Row upon row of seats lined the pillared edge and filled with hundreds of people.

Slate met Jett's eyes over Scarlett's head and Jett saw all he needed to see in the big man's eyes. Slate may not have been his blood brother, but he was still his brother no matter what and he knew Scarlett would be taken care of in his hands. What's more, Slate would let himself grieve for Wren with Scarlett. They needed each other to get through it.

Jett gave him a slight nod, and they walked with the girls to the front row of seats before they'd lit the pyre.

Jett glimpsed the Regn brothers, Brass and Quick, in the shadows of the tall white columns that lined the balcony. Their family members were seated in the rows before the pyre. Slate had likely asked them to be extra observant for the time being. Jett owed them for holding him back after discovering his mother's body and Slate had been arrested. If it wasn't for the Regn, Jett would have been spending the last few nights in the cell next to Slate's instead of comforting Scarlett.

The five men had trained together for a decade, the brothers were only a few inches shorter than Slate and Jett, but just as powerfully built. A build like his father. Alder Var was six and a half feet of rock-solid muscles with a deeper chest, the kind that came with age. His father didn't look a day past his mid-thirties, all Guardians aged slower once they hit twenty years old.

Jett controlled his tan brow making sure it didn't furrow when he saw Slate lace his fingers through Scarlett's. The Straumrs were right behind them, Ash hadn't been visiting the Sumar palace to check on Scarlett's well-being though flowers by the boatload were being brought to her rooms.

He'd never get used to seeing Slate acting like he cared, it'd gone past trying to get into her bed. Scarlett was unconscious when he'd been kind in the past. Jett had only seen her return his attention once aside from their current hand holding. That one time though, it had spoken volumes.

Hawk's lean frame moved to the stone stairs that led over the waterfall and called air collecting Wren's ashes and deposited them into a bronze hammered urn. Hawk tore the petals of the white roses and jasmine as he descended the stairs and walked to where Jett and Scarlett sat. With Wren's death he had been distraught, coupled with Sparrow's breakdown, the man who normally looked ever the polished patriarch of the Sumar family was despairing.

Jett took the cool urn from Hawk's hands and pulled Scarlett up to her feet. Jett wrapped his free arm around her waist and held her steady as they ascended the stairs to stand over the roaring waterfall. He lifted the top of the bronze urn with the blazing sun embossed on the side and passed it to Scarlett. She lifted it up to the sky, standing on the small dais above the falls.

Jett began to speak and call, lifting their mother's ashes from the urn.

"Lo, There do I see my father. Lo, there do I see my mother. My sisters and my brothers. Lo, There do I see my people. Back to the beginning. Lo, there do they call to me and ask me to take my place in the halls where the brave may live forever."

The urn finally emptied, and the roar of the waterfall washed out the tears of the people gathered.

Jett turned to Scarlett and recognized the tortured agony she'd been repressing; it reflected in his own face. Alarm flooded Jett when she swayed hundreds of feet above the bottom of the falls. There was a collective gasp as her heeled foot took a step back and hovered over the abyss. Jett caught her with the practiced ease of someone reacting on instinct and steadied her as they watched her shoe fall into the crashing waves below.

"This was a bad idea," Jett said as he clutched her in a death grip and his alarm rang anew when she seemed disappointed not to be following down after the shoe.

Jett pulled off her other shoe at the bottom of the stairs and led her back inside the palace while she clutched the empty urn to her chest until her knuckles were white. The gathered Guardians filed out after them.

CHAPTER
FOUR

I sat with my mother's urn in the drawing room of the Sumar palace. I'd never been in the drawing room before. There were so many rooms to explore in the enormous palace. They did not vividly decorate it in the Moroccan style. White, gold, and walnut decorated the drawing room, sheer panels of white draped in front of each mosaic column that divided platform seated section around the circular room Food was served around the small fountain in the center. It was softly lit by long multilayered metal lanterns that hung in a ring at the center of the room and on each column decorated in intricate filigree.

We crammed in one of the alcove sections with Jett, Steel, and the girls on one side and Tawny, Diamond, and Gypsum sitting next to me. Slate had turned over my care to Jett and Tawny once we'd reached the room and disappeared. I assumed he went to speak to the Regn brothers I'd seen lurking about. The Regn family were one of the prominent families in Tidings, but not a greater family and the younger brothers were friends of our family.

Ash was moving around to mingle, leaving me alone for the time being. I was second guessing everything. I'd broken things off mere hours before my mother plummeted to her death. She told me to find love but when I searched my heart, I only found ashes.

My mother died.

I ran my thumbs along the sun embossed on the urn. How could I still be alive and feel this much heartache? People had been coming in and out of our section for two hours and I wondered how much longer the torture would continue. I wanted to crawl back into my mother's bed and disappear. It was a bad idea to come back to Tidings.

I had nowhere else to go though. When we moved from Chicago last December my mother and I came with our only known family members. Hawk, Sparrow, Gypsum, and Tawny would never leave Tidings again. Tawny was heir to the land of perpetual winter, Elivagar, where my mother died. Hawk was the patriarch, Gypsum was the heir, to the Sumar palace and Thrimilci the land of perpetual summer. Sparrow was the last Dagr now that old man Vetr had taken Tawny as his. She alone could fill the seat on the council of nine that ran the five islands that made up Tidings. There were the Tios that lived on the central island, Valla, and the only island that had all four seasons. Since Ash had been sleeping with Crimson Rot and she was a Tio like I was, I didn't think the two of us living in same place would be a good idea even if it was a palace.

That left Mabon where the Haust's lived on the island of perpetual autumn or Ostara, the land of perpetual spring, where my stepmother lived with the Var and my father's family. No way I was going there. I hardly knew the Haust. I was stuck.

"She can stay with us. We will have our staff come and retrieve her things later today. Whether it be now or in a few months makes no actual difference, she might as well get used to it," Dahlia said behind me.

Jett stared over my shoulder through the white gauzy fabric, his eyes held a light of rage.

I couldn't imagine leaving the Sumar palace forever. I was just getting to know my family and I was supposed to leave and start one of my own. Every fiber of my being rebelled against it.

"Of course, Dahlia, but during this time we feel it is best that our family surrounds her," Pearl said, reining in her temper.

"Ash is her family. He is as good as her husband and will make sure she is taken care of," Dahlia said defensively with a sniff.

"Why do we not ask her what she wishes?" Hawk asked, sounding exasperated.

My uncle was one of the most even keeled men there ever was so it spoke volumes that he would sound peevish speaking to Dahlia.

"The girl has not spoken. She will not eat. She does not know what is good for her," Dahlia noted.

I cringed. Did that really need to be public knowledge? I kept my eyes on the urn, so I didn't have to face the looks of concern on my family's faces around me.

"Dahlia, my daughter is staying. Until I give her to Ash, she is my responsibility. The boy will understand. I will speak to him now," My father's guttural voice sent the first emotions through me other than soul crushing sorrow since it happened.

My head shot up and Jett looked as astonished as I did.

"Your daughter?" Dahlia stammered, and I imagined her thinking of how I was a direct descendant of not only the Tio and Sumar but also the Var.

"Yes. I have four children. I believe you are familiar with all of them. Excuse me," Alder excused himself and I felt determination.

I couldn't help, but peek past Tawny and Steel through the sheer panels of white to watch my father speak to Ash. He turned around to face where I sat. Ash nodded and shook Alder's hand. Ash seemed pleased. He strode over to where I sat and passed under the curtains to stand before us.

"You are full of surprises. Did you know who your father was?" Ash's green eyes danced as he looked down at me.

"She knew," Tawny answered.

Ash appraised me after a flicker of hurt passed through his eyes. "A Var, Tio, and Sumar. Our children will have a heritage so rich they will be the envy of all others. Come along Diamond, we will go soon."

Jett glared at his back and Amethyst nudged him. Ash was her cousin.

People said their goodbyes, and I sat there waiting for them all to leave. Indigo and my father were staying at the palace. Indigo was taking the room next to mine and she briefly stopped by. She was too consumed with tears to stay long before going to her new room.

Night had fallen when Slate returned. The guests had departed, namely Ash to avoid a confrontation, I'd noted. I was appreciative, or would have been, that we didn't instigate an argument or altercation on the day. It must have taken a great effort from him since he was the only one who knew apart from Crimson Rot and Ash that knew we were over.

"Are you hungry, baby sis? I know you are, even if you don't think you are. You want me to run to the kitchens?" Jett offered.

I still hadn't found my words. What could I possibly say that would express what I felt?

"Dinner time, Torch. Then bed. I have got her, Jett," Slate said, getting to his feet.

Jett got to his feet as well, his usual jutted smug expression was nowhere to be found. I reached up and ran my slim hand along his chiseled features. Jett closed his eyes and shivered. I knew I reminded him of our mother, and it hurt him just to look at me.

I felt reluctance in my brother with my empath abilities. I gave his hand a squeeze and lifted my arms to Slate. He didn't hesitate for a nanosecond before scooping me up to his chest making me feel safe. For all his womanizing and all the times he'd tried to seduce me, he cared and tonight I wanted to be held in a way my brother couldn't hold me.

"I'll have some food sent up. What room?" Jett asked as Tawny got to her feet looking shocked.

"My room. My thanks," Slate said and carried me from the room.

I was walking through carnage. I felt her; I heard her; she was standing in a white dress arms held out, her face is my mother's. She told me I could fix this. I tried not to look at the bodies, the battleground alongside a castle. Not everyone was dead. frozen angry faces stare up at angry faces on the castle, I couldn't even tell if the faces were human. They all looked like monsters to me. The wind was whipping at me; I looked up at the sky, even the sky was angry. Black clouds, lightening without rain. She was all around me, "You are night".

I stood in the middle of a circle, people around the edges, Slate laid on the ground in a pool of blood. Light and gushing wind blasts from my body, my hair, my hands, shoot up. My mouth opened in a silent scream.

I woke up in a panic. The woman had a face. She never did before, and I'd been having the dream all my life.

I sat up raked with sobs. A hand rubbed at my back, and I whimpered before I could stop it. Slate sat up next to me, the black sheets pooling in his lap as he peeled my hair from my sweating face.

"Nightmare?" he asked, voice thick with sleep.

Slate handed me a kerchief, and I blew my nose in an unladylike manner.

After I ate smothered steak tips and garlic mashed potatoes, Slate had helped me change into one of his oversized shirts and tucked me into his bed.

It was quite the bed. It reflected the owner, that was for certain. A tufted black leather headboard that towered over the bed piled with a black fur blanket and satin sheets. The bed had been barely visible through the arched opening of the wall. The walls were light grey with a high glossed Moroccan lantern pattern. I had expected them to be red and plain, maybe a few dripping candles, but no, narrow wrought iron lantern sconces hung at intervals on the walls. Tufted black leather couches sat across from one another on a dark grey Persian carpet. A low modern glass table sat between the couches of his sitting room with no adornments on it.

Slate took the used kerchief and called it to some place unseen then pulled me to his bare chest, kissing the top of my head. A cynical part of me kept waiting for when he'd make a pass at me, the part of me that felt empty and broken was counting on it.

Everything about the man radiated a raw savage power that extended to his sexuality. You couldn't look at the man's graceful fluid movements and not wonder if his hips would move that smoothly into you, that the countless sculpted bronze muscles that covered his upper body would be softer than they looked when he held you. If he would hold you afterwards.

Slate was holding me now, and it solved one mystery; his skin was silk over steel and unbelievably warm. His midnight waves were tousled and fell over his shoulders. When my cheek pressed against his chest, my nostrils filled with the scent of him. Fresh fallen leaves, earthy, and spicy cloves. No manufactured scents there. The urge to hold him back was worse now than it was before he had tucked me in.

He had told me he didn't spend the night with women, that they weren't allowed in his bed. I hadn't asked to come; he had taken me and called so I would rest in a deeper sleep.

"Want to tell me about it, Torch?" he murmured into my hair.

If I started nuzzling against him or touching him, I'd have to leave. Nothing good would come from paying Slate affection. He scooted down and propped another pillow behind him as he pulled me on top of him. I wasn't holding him, my hands hand fallen to either side of him and I wasn't nuzzling — it was gravity.

His leg slid between mine when I settled against his chest. He pulled my hair over my shoulder to touch the single narrow braid behind my ear that he'd had Bronze thread a jade canine carved fetish into with an ivory pearl just below it, both from Slate. One I'd taken when he'd saved my life, the other he'd given when he'd taken care of me after we visited the Merfolk.

"We are going to headquarters tomorrow. I spoke with Brass; he is expecting you to come in for training. Laying in beds all day will make you weak, you need to be stronger," he whispered as he slid his hand into the gaping sleeve to stroke my back.

His calloused palms scratched at my skin, but I didn't mind just another reminder of how dangerous he was in case I became too comfortable. There was only one way he'd gotten those callouses, and that was from handling weapons for years.

His fingers massaged along my sides, and my cynical voice spoke up. Now he would try something.

When he didn't and I felt him call instead. I mentally chastised myself for being disappointed.

Slate brought me clothes to train in with breakfast the next morning. I ate scrambled eggs and bacon and washed it down with the thick green liquid he'd brought me the day before. My guess was that it contained a bunch of fruits and veggies juiced into one convenient glass so I would get my necessary vitamins.

When he pulled his shirt over my head, I turned around so he would only see my back. I was thinking he liked it when my hair tumbled down making my skin prickle. He took a step back as I put on a bra for the first time since the day my mother died and changed the rest of my clothes. I heard him turn around when I slid my fingers beneath the lace of my underwear to replace them with the black nylon boy shorts that he'd picked out.

I sat down on the bed to put my boots on, and Slate turned back around to tug on the supple black leather boots Hawk had given me. He knelt, tucking my knives in my boots, then strapped my short seax to my thigh. Its black handle carved into a woman and etched in gold, the black hand stitched scabbard had gold embossed wings and gold buckles. Slate had bought it for me our second day in Tidings. He meant it as a peace offering for having come on so strongly the night before, or maybe he just thought it suited me like he said.

He turned over my wrists and buckled on the wrist blades. It had solid gold lace work over the bracer so it would deflect, three blades that angled away from the outside of the wrist as the blade shot out giving me three added blades on the sides of them that sprung with a gesture of my pinky fingers, elegant and deadly. Another one of Slate's gifts. Maybe he was sick of saving me so instead he'd kept me well armed.

Slate leaned towards me as he pulled my belt of knives with the golden daymark buckle around my waist, so his waves toppled to one side, beads clicking and glanced my cheek. I held my breath and the desire to inhale deeply, otherwise I would have to leave his room for good.

"I have already sent a messenger to the Headmaster; they know I will not be in the rest of the week. I took the liberty of sending one to Dahlia as well, written as you are of course," he said with his head angled down to fasten my belt.

Even this view of him didn't diminish his ferocity and when he lifted his eyes to mine and when I met by his penetrating steely gaze, I remembered there were soft parts to him too.

Those long thick black lashes framed his silver eyes...I stared at him.

"There are two others who you will train regularly aside from Brass and Quick. Amalgam and Shale," he continued in his kneeling position even though all my knives were fastened, his arms placed on my legs with his hands resting on the sides of my thighs. "You will like Ama, Shale is a gained taste, but she is fiercely loyal. I know the two of you will get along, eventually," he rumbled, his grey eyes glittering.

I wanted to snort. Shale was the only girl he'd ever brought to the Sumar palace. The petite woman was just as arrogant as Slate, with her little saunter and glittering up tilted eyes that always seemed to mock everyone. I could admit, she was striking. She had a curtain of black sheen that fell past her shoulders and a smoky voice that she spoke confidently with, but I had long suspected she was one of Slate's many lovers.

"Scarlett?" I listened intently; he almost never used my name,

"While you share my bed, I ask that you refrain from being intimate with any other men, and I will reciprocate the concession."

The look he gave me almost made me smile. There was the Slate that I knew. He managed to say something that could have been sweet in a way that made it an order and his eyes promised very dark things if I should disobey that order.

S<small>LATE INFORMED</small> the family that he was taking me out to get some fresh air and not to expect us for lunch. Sparrow hadn't been at breakfast, and neither had Jett nor the girls. My mother's death was taking its toll on us all. Pearl had forced a smile; her emerald cat eyes were bloodshot and her coppery mane flat. Gypsum had looked like he wanted to join us, but let it go when Slate wrapped a big arm around my shoulder, a certain sign he wasn't inviting anyone else. Steel had then offered to train Tawny and Gypsum after breakfast though he hardly looked to have slept in days. Indigo and Alder weren't at breakfast either, though Slate said they were around.

Shadow Breaker headquarters were in Valla, the central island of the five that comprised Tidings, the home of the Guardians. They built Valla in a star formation, its portal was a freestanding stone gate with sculptured tree branches twisting up it, a sculpture of a woman, hands extended forming into branches crested the top. It sat at the center of a hexagon devoid of anyone, but others moving into and out of the gate. Guardians wearing black tunics with silver interlocked triangles on the back guarded the gate and the three gates that led outside of the town's heart. They named each gate after a Norn, or fate. Past, present, and future for Urd, Verdandi, and Skuld. Urd gate led to Straumr palace, Verdandi to beyond the city, and Skuld led to the Tio's palace. Urd and Skuld both had paths that lead around the mountains and up to Valla U. Six roads extended from the hexagon.

Slate took one of the cobbled roads that led towards the Verdandi gate and started towards the little shops with wavy tiled roofs to either side of the road in all fashions of storefronts, brick being the most prominent and all of them having big glass windows so you could see their wares. Vendors stood with little carts adding to the cacophony of noise.

Slate's arm around my shoulders never eased, it maintained a level of pressure that both guided and kept our bodies in constant contact.

I wondered if people thought maybe he was holding me against my will by all the looks we got before arriving at the dead-end street that housed the stone-dead end that grated back to reveal the entrance to Shadow Breaker headquarters. Slate had laid his hand atop the stone slab and watched as it rolled back into the building before stepping through.

Slate kept me tucked close as we walked down dimly lit polished wood steps with pewter sconces. We reached the hall, and I saw low hanging lamps from the ceiling and smelled leather even before we reached the room. No sound of pool balls cracking against one another so early in the morning, no card games at the little round tables, but there were many black clad guardians eating breakfast. The large loft like room's lamps lit it so spots of bright light existed between spots of darkness. The bar complete with bottles with tender, and stools was open, but no one was drinking. They scattered two pool tables and four couches around the expansive room. Dark walnut floors spanned the room from purple wall to wall. They randomly splayed scattered expensive looking rugs in the long room. You could almost smell how lethal all the gathered people were, like metal. Cold shiny metal and leather.

The door directly across from the hall was closed. I wondered if Cordillera was behind it and what she would think about her longtime lover holding me so protectively, part of me hoped spitefully that she would see us. The last time I'd seen her, she's bombarded me with images of her and Slate in intimate situations, she could transmit images into other's minds.

There were stairwells on either side of the long room, one that led up, and one that led down. We'd be going down today to use the Crash Course.

I caught sight of our destination right away. Soft amber eyes spotted us the second we came in under the lights. Brass didn't rise, he sat with three others at a table. I recognized the notorious playboy, Brass's younger brother, Quick, with his short dark hair stylishly combed like a gentleman and the peek of black Celtic tattoos at his collar. His dark eyes glittered when he followed Brass's gaze, that dazzling smile of his that woman had no defense against flashed. Shale was there with a girl with short blonde curls that looked like an angel with a rosy bud for a mouth and wide chocolate brown eyes.

Brass could read minds, not intentionally, but we transmitted thoughts to him in a constant flow as if he had another set of eyes that picked up what those around him thought. He offered a smile with his plump defined lips when we grew close. A lock of darkest brown hair fell from behind his ear to graze his dark honey cheek, his hair brushed his shoulders and was threaded through with bronze and ebony beads on a dozen braids scattered through his hair. Brass was both muscular and soft but most of his warmth came from those thickly lashed amber eyes that didn't miss a thing.

It became apparent that they were not used to seeing Slate with women, at least not upright. The girl I took for Amalgam smiled warmly at me tossing her bouncy chin length curls out of her face.

"Scarlett, this is Ama. I am going to take her downstairs, whenever you are done with your meal, she will be ready," Slate told us.

"Hi! I have heard so much about you! Mostly from Quick so I will ignore it, but Shale has said some nice things. I look forward to training with you. Sorry about your mother," She gave me an apologetic smile with her pouty mouth.

A wave of pain made my chest tighten, and I suddenly wanted to be anywhere, but there. I wanted Slate to take me back to his bed, back to the dark.

I couldn't stop myself from turning my face into his side like a child in their mother's skirts. He cooed softly by my ear letting me know it would be okay, but I thought he must want to be rid of me. He needed a break from my clinging and crying. I loosened my grip on the back of his shirt that I hadn't even realized I'd grasped and turned back sucking in a deep breath.

"I am finished. I will go down with you. Silver, come down with the girls in a few," Brass said before his brother joined us.

Slate gave a curt nod, and the three of us started towards the stairway. We walked down several flights of stone stairs with wrought-iron balustrades until we came to a set of metal double doors. Brass pushed them open, and we were in a modern preparation room with black metal cubbies and gray marble tiles with white and black marble skein benches.

Brass led us to the aisle and opened the cubbies, "Do you have anything to leave?"

I looked up at Slate but thought not.

Brass nodded, and I realized Brass would be the only person who would still hear me.

He smiled warmly; the corner of his mouth pulled up. "Yes, I can still hear you. It will make training easier. Do not worry, we will start out with something easy today," his amber gaze lifted to Slate, "Anything you wish to ask her?"

Slate turned his cool silver eyes on me, he was jealous that Brass could communicate with me while Slate couldn't get a single word from me.

"Not at the moment."

I would have been amused or even irritated, instead my anxiety was flourishing at the thought of being with people I hardly knew no matter how comforting they'd been in the past.

"Do you have something for her to wear in the studio?" Brass asked in his usual deep smooth tone, as if he spent most of his time whispering sweet nothings.

"No. Torch, do you mind doing some stretching in your undergarments?" Slate rumbled.

He was jealous. There was no doubt in my mind. I cared little about anything now. The underwear Slate had picked out covered me just as much as a swimsuit, so it wasn't a huge deal.

"She does not mind. Looks like we are all set," Brass said smoothly.

My energy levels were better now that I was eating again, whatever Slate had in those green drinks gave me an extra boost, "I would not have brought you here if I did not believe you could handle it."

I let out a long sigh. Part of me hated that Slate had somehow made me dependent on him. How did it happen so quickly? Was it because he had been training me and wasn't as polite and careful as the rest of my family had been?

Slate wrapped his big arms around me and pulled me close letting me listen to his steady heartbeat that soothed me in any situation. I allowed myself to close my eyes and just be held without holding him back, if I did, then I couldn't spend to- night in his room. Brass looked anywhere else, but at us.

"Slate," Cordillera's mature feminine voice rang through the prep room and Slate sighed.

"I will stick to my promise, Torch. You have my word," Slate murmured into my hair, "Brass will take care of you. I will meet you here once your training is finished." He kissed the top of my head and drew back without looking at my face which was good, or he would have seen the plea in my eyes.

"Lera," Slate rumbled in response before he strode purposefully to her.

Cordillera, Grand Mistress of the Shadow Breakers, and Slate's long time, on again, off again lover had caught the plea in my eyes and narrowed her dark narrow eyes drawing down her thick high arched brows. I knew it would be bad, so I closed my eyes when she hit me with the images.

Slate leading her into the women's bathroom at Valla U, him sitting back on the couch in the powder room as she unbuttons his pants. The two of them laughing and smiling as she lowers her mouth to him.

It was the longest glimpse she'd shown me, and it took my breath away. They had seen me and gone in moments later. Slate and Cordillera had known I was in there.

The back of my knees hit the marble bench, and I sat down sucking in a breath. Slate had purposely waited for me once Cordillera had finished with him. She had left knowing that we would be alone in the bathroom. To what end? I knew the petite older woman had some method to her mayhem; she wasn't the type of woman who didn't calculate everything. I was just another calculated move.

Brass cursed and sat down next to me.

Slate had noticed my movement and whirled back around. "Torch?" he asked, concern lacing his deep voice.

"Come Slate, the girl is fine. It is only grief; Brass will comfort her," her tone was not lost on Slate, and he stiffened.

"I have her," Brass murmured, getting me to my feet.

Brass gave me a serene smile and wrapped his arm around my

shoulders in the same manner of which Slate did and he guided me easily, he had a soothing presence I'd nearly forgotten about.

The level above the prep room led to a cavernous studio with walnut wood floors and a wall of solid mirrors. Brass opened a little box that rested on the wall and when he shut it, I immediately felt the temperature change. It was a hot studio.

The door opened behind me and Quick strutted in with Shale and Ama. Ama was a hair taller than Shale, maybe five foot three at most. The bouncy blonde had ample curves despite her teeny tiny waist and smiling seemed to be the way her mouth naturally rested.

Ama pulled her shirt over her head as she walked to reveal a barely opaque white bra and I dropped my eyes. I would never get used to the Guardians being so comfortable with their bodies. Nudity didn't make them blink an eye unless it was someone's body they hadn't seen before.

Shale's body was just as hard as I thought it would be. She really was tiny but ripped. She had washboard abs that didn't surprise me. Even Ama in her barely there bra and panties, had a firm body, her breasts looked almost comical on her petite frame.

I pulled off my boots and socks resigned that there was nowhere to hide. I wanted to be more flexible; I wanted to be faster. I would do a lot to make my mother proud.

Quick had shucked his clothes in a blink and I finally saw the bottom half of his tattoo. It covered the entire left side of his body in black jagged Celtic tattoos, it even wrapped around to his back and extended done to his ankle. He stood barefoot now with a knowing smirk on his face. He'd tricked me into dropping his pants when I wanted a glimpse of the bottom half of his tattoo to reveal that he did not wear underwear. Quick was wearing them now, a pair of red boxer briefs that fit snugly on his powerfully muscled body barely covered him.

"Knock it off," Brass said as he pushed his pants down off his hips.

I had almost forgotten about Brass. He had the same build as Quick and Slate. His dark honey body didn't have the tattoos that Quick's did, and Quick's body was slightly thinner. He had the type of body you could easily imagine wrapped in white sheets stretching in your bed, body hard and full of sculpted muscles, but soft enough to fall asleep atop. Dark hair dusted his sculpted pecs that led to forest green boxer briefs and the dark happy trail that disappeared beneath the waistband. His powerfully built legs weren't bare like some men's who lifted weights religiously and dusted with silky dark hair down to his ankles.

"Are you blushing?"

Quick was as fast as his namesake to point out Brass's dark honey cheeks reddening as he dropped his head, and I realized it was my fault.

Brass had heard all my perverse thoughts, and I turned my back to the others to pull my shirt over my head and pulled off my pants.

"If you guys will not behave, you can leave," Brass said with a hint of amusement.

Quick chuckled and Ama giggled, when I turned around Shale was smirking, her dark up tilted eyes always glittering. "I did not figure you for a black underwear kind of girl," Shale noted.

"Slate chose them," Brass answered and angled towards the mirrors.

It was nearly a hundred degrees in the room; I walked to Brass's other side hoping his body would grant me a little discretion.

"Curious and curiouser." Quick mused.

After an hour and a half of stretching in a room, in what was essentially a hot box, I wanted to take a cool shower and take a nap. We grabbed our clothes and trudged downstairs to the prep room in our underwear. Brass kept me close, simultaneously offering me the comfort of his body and a modicum of modesty.

"You do not have to shower here if you do not want to. You can wait until you go home. We do plan on eating lunch after if you would like to join us," Brass said as we walked the aisles.

...I'll shower...

It was the first time I'd addressed him with my mind directly. He took my clothes from my arms placing them on the bench with his own before leading me towards the showers. Across from the showers, were massage tables and just outside the shower room were towels neatly rolled for everyone's use. Soaps dispensed within each shower stall, except there weren't really stalls. There were frosted glass partisans that retracted in an otherwise big wet room.

"You can take the very last stall in the corner if you do not wish to be seen," Brass said, trying to bolster my spirits but getting naked in front of everyone was the least of my worries even though it was not something I would have normally done.

I undressed with my back to Brass in the aisle. With the towel around me, Brass took me to the showers where Ama, Quick, and Shale were unabashedly nude and showering within a foot from one another. I kept my eyes on the floor in front of me trying not to raise my hand to cover my eyes. Brass guided me to the furthest stall and pulled out the frosted partisan before hitting the plate to turn on the water. He walked down a few stalls before pulling his own partisan and showering.

I hadn't showered since the bath Tawny and the girls had forced. The warm water ran down my body as I leaned my forehead against the marble tiles blowing water from my lips occasionally. I had needed the shower, but it had left me alone with my thoughts with nothing to distract me.

Grief snuck up on me, and I swallowed hard against the tears that threatened to overflow. A whimper escaped me, and I slapped a hand to my mouth. I couldn't hear if the others were done with their showers or not. I hoped they were so I would be left alone; I was sure they thought I was weak enough already without having to add breaking down in the prep room to their opinions.

"Torch, are you done?" Slate's deep voice rumbled from nearby.

"I do not think she has done anything yet," Brass murmured barely audible over the stream of water, and I heard his bare feet walk away on the tiles.

"Thank you, Brass," Slate sounded like he was thanking him for more than his answer. "What do you want me to do? Do you need time to yourself?" he asked, and I felt the rise of panic of being left alone with my thoughts again.

"That would be a no," Brass shouted from wherever he was deep in the prep room.

I turned around under the stream and tried to take fortifying breaths, but my sudden anguish was demanding, and I couldn't stop the sobbing. The sound of footsteps retreating, and Slate curse was what I heard. I whimpered again; he'd left me. He'd really left me all alone. I sunk back against the wall and slid down against the tiles to rest my head on my knees. Lethargy claimed the little energy I'd had left.

A deluge of tears fell as my shoulders shook there in the shower. I had enjoyed my session with Brass and the others, but left alone, even for the moment with nothing to occupy my mind caused it to go down a dark path. It'd been five days since my mother died, and it could have been five minutes before.

A hand stroked my wet hair back from my face, and I lifted my head up. It was Slate, grey eyes full of concern and gloriously nude, "I do not have swim shorts here. If you wish me to put on my undergarment, I will."

I must have looked like a mess. I could already feel the puffiness around my eyes and lips from crying. My face must've been red, but I didn't care. His eyes, the color of a winter storm scanned my face for a hint of disapproval. When he didn't find it, he took my hands and lifted me up to my feet before embracing me. I'd never held a naked man, much less had a man hold me while I was undressed. If it was up to me, it would have been when I was feeling very sexy and confident without tears and all sorts of disgustingness on my face, but that wasn't the case.

Breaking my rule, I slid my arms around Slate's lower back. I pressed my face hard into him as if I somehow attach myself and never have to be alone again.

"By the Mother, Torch. You have got some grip on you," Slate said in a playful tone, and I almost laughed, instead I sucked in a shuddering breath, and he ran his hand down my hair.

"Come. Let us get you washed so we can eat and go home," Slate said, and I didn't think a better plan had been hatched.

Slate shampooed and conditioned my hair for me as I leaned against his chest and moved me into the stream to rinse me. I summoned enough strength to wash my body and Slate moved aside. I thought I heard a sharp intake of breath, and when I looked behind me, Slate quickly turned around.

I'd seen Slate nude; it wasn't something you ever forgot. He had a magnificent backside. One day, I'd tell my grandkids about the man with the buns of steel when they were old enough to hear such stories.

Every inch of Slate was hard packed sculpted muscle. I could understand Lera's jealousy that he was taking such good care of me, but if she knew he was only being tender, not sexual in the slightest, it would put her mind at ease.

"All done?" he asked turning his head to the side, so I saw his profile, his glossy black hair curled when wet and it trailed little rivers along his bronze body.

I hit the plate and grabbed the towel I'd placed there before taking a step towards Slate.

"Go ahead without me, Torch. I will be there in a moment.", he rumbled, and I stood there watching him. "Please.", he said, and it shocked me.

Slate didn't say please, he said *now* and *do it*. I couldn't disobey his request after he'd taken care of me, so I walked away without a glance back and found the bench that held my clothes.

I didn't want to wear my dirty underwear after sweating in it, so I pulled my pants on and tucked them in my pocket. I'd have to remember to bring spare clothes tomorrow if Slate brought me again.

He walked up a little while later with a towel wrapped around his waist and glistening with water droplets. If I had been looking to lose myself in the throes of passion instead of dealing with the pain of my mother's death, now would've been an excellent time. He didn't bother to hide himself as he dressed with purpose. If my eyes bothered him, he didn't say a word. When he was done, he dried my hair without having to be asked and then his own before tying back the front in a leather strap.

Slate saw my bra sitting on the bench and looked at my chest. "Torch, from now on, you must always wear underwear or something to cover yourself. No more showers here until you can do them yourself, or we wait until we go home. I am no Brother of Paragon," he said cryptically before sitting down on the bench next to me and helping me buckle on my weapons before doing his own.

The Brothers of Paragon were all but a distant nightmare. Between discovering Slate's secret life as Cordillera's longtime lover and the Shadow Breakers and our trip to the Merfolk was the Brothers. Similar to the Valkyries, they were a male sect devoted to The

Mother. Their leader, a friend of Pearl's, was murdered by one of their own and those involved were awaiting trial in Karkinos, the underwater prison. The remaining Brothers were leaderless and had disbanded, as far as we knew. They hadn't been a large group to begin with and the incident toppled what had started as a group with an admirable mission.

As with most things, evil began with the best of intentions.

He picked up my bra and tucked it into his pocket shaking his head. "My ego is taking a serious blow," he murmured as he wrapped his arm around my shoulders.

We had the same routine for the next two days; I ate lunch feeling grimy and Slate hurried us home. Cordillera showed up every day to request Slate and I never once asked if he was going back on his promise.

My family was slowly healing. We had breakfast and dinners with everyone except for Sparrow who was still deep in her grieving, not that I wasn't, I wasn't even making noises much less speaking unless you count my crying. Alder and Indigo had moved into the palace, I wasn't ready to address it. Seeing him made it harder and easier at the same time.

No one commented on where I was sleeping at night, or why Ash wasn't visiting. They were all wrapped up in their own anguish; they were trying to get a semblance of routine back. I was functioning; I brushed my teeth and washed my face, my showers were still long and painful, but Slate waited outside them talking about random things until I finished, and he left me again only to return once I dressed.

I decided he must have bought me nightdresses because I'd never seen the ones, he's given me to wear, blush pink, white, ivory, all lace, and satins. I didn't think it wasn't another woman's, Lera would wear nothing so bright, but I couldn't imagine him out there buying me lingerie. It was a mystery for another time.

When I'd laid down under Slate's fur piled bed, he'd climbed up between my legs to rest his head against my chest like I'd always done to him. I hadn't held him since the day in the shower. Again, I broke my rules as his glossy waves spilled over my satin clad breasts. His hair was silken, and my fingers glided through it as we laid in silence.

"The day after tomorrow, we will go to the Wemic. You like it there and they have a ritual for grieving It will be beneficial. I spoke to Jett and Steel, Tawny, Gypsum are going to come. Jett said he would ask Indigo, so there will be a sizeable group to keep you company."

My heart skipped. I missed the Wemic and more specifically, Keen, the chief's youngest brother. The big cat/human hybrids had humbled me, and made me wish I lived more simply, or less complicated.

Slate lifted his head and smirked, his full sensual mouth quirking. "I thought you would like that," he dropped his gaze and moved his hand under the blankets, "Scarlett."

I arched an eyebrow. It was probably the most expression I'd made, besides when I cried, in a week. He scooted up and rested his weight on his elbows, so our faces were only a few inches apart.

"You do not have to go back to your room," his hand sought mine under the blankets and I felt a ring slip over my finger.

My breath caught. What was he doing? He was ruining everything! We both knew Slate wouldn't marry, that he didn't want kids.

I wanted both. Not to mention that Slate would grow tired of me in weeks, maybe months if I was lucky, and then he'd leave me heart broken and empty. That was the best-case scenario. I never wanted to experience the pain Slate would inflict on me. Tawny had once said that a man like Slate would leave me tied in knots, well knots untied, Slate would leave me in tatters and throw the remains into the four winds.

No! No! No! This couldn't be happening! My heart was thundering in my chest as my hand balled into a fist. How could he do this? Everything was going so well!

His grey eyes peered at me, his long lashes almost tangling with his straight black brows. Then I realized he was going to kiss me. Oh Gods, no!

His full mouth hovered just above mine, so close I could smell the cloves on his breath. He was waiting for me to come the rest of the way, but I couldn't. My brief time being under his wing was at an end. He sighed and pressed his forehead to mine.

"The ring is yours, Torch," he whispered as if he could read my thoughts.

"*To the garden, the world, anew ascending, Potent mates, daughters, sons, preluding,*

The love, the life of their bodies, meaning and being, Curious, here behold my resurrection, after slumber.

The revolving cycles, in their wide sweep, have brought me again, Amorous, mature — all beautiful to me — all wondrous.

My limbs, and the quivering fire that ever plays through them, for reasons, most wondrous.

Existing, I peer and penetrate still,

Content with the present — content with the past,

By my side, or back of me, Eve following, Or in front, and I following her just the same."

I loved when Slate quoted Walt Whitman, not only was he ridiculously good looking and built like a brick house, but he had a big sexy brain too. He rolled off and turned his back to me. It was over. I felt bereft without his touch, but I didn't dare try to cuddle up to him, not after that.

I snuck out of Slate's room once he fell asleep. I wandered around the mosaic designed halls in the gold and royal blue colors of the Sumar sigil. They did the entire palace in Moroccan designs.

The palace was warm as I walked up the white stone steps to the next floor where the girls' rooms were. When I climbed into my royal blue satin covered bed, my heart broke anew, and I didn't sleep until the light of dawn shone through my stained-glass windows.

When I woke up, I didn't know where I was. My heart thudded in my chest as my head swiveled taking in my surroundings. I laid in my enormous bed intricately carved and big enough for five people. Through the archway that separated my bedroom from my sitting room was a royal blue and gold upholstered love seat and matching chaise lounge were in the seating area directly in front of me. There was an octagonal table and end table around the seats resting atop a large blue and beige fringed rug. When you walked up to the couches to either side was a door.

I swung my legs over my bed looked behind me at the little bench nook and the stained-glass windows and decided not to check outside. I crossed the room to the door on my right, the bathroom I would now share with Indigo since Tawny had moved into the family wing with Steel since their wedding.

The bathroom was just as elaborate as the bedrooms. A huge bathtub sat in the middle of the room all done in pearl and iridescent tiles. The bathtub was two split sides so one person could sit facing the other in two separate baths. Two low tiled walls hid a huge shower. Water sprayed from every direction, there was even a waterfall of sorts at the entrance that fell across the low wall so no one could see you if you were showering past it. It was all controlled by the energy plates you called to activate from the outside wall. The opposite side was a wall-to-wall mirror with double sinks trimmed is swirling champagne and silver mosaic. The bathrooms were the most modern part of the palace, but then I'd rarely visited the kitchens.

I stripped off the ivory nightie Slate had bought me and went into the shower.

I lost track of time as I numbly took my first glance at the ring Slate had slipped on my finger. He must not have been paying attention to which finger he'd slipped it on, the ring finger on my left hand had to be a mistake of epic proportions. A more addled girl would have read into that gesture, but I knew better. Slate wasn't the commitment type, that much I knew beyond a doubt.

The bright lights of the bathroom shone on an oval-shaped emerald in an antique setting covered in little diamond arches. I couldn't dream of a better ring. I shook my head in disbelief. Slate had lost his mind; he had almost kissed me last night!

Eventually, I made my way downstairs after donning a long black sleeve scoop neck and snug black pants and all my weapons. It was lunchtime, and I wound my way through the halls until I made it to the portal room. If I hurried, I'd catch everyone at headquarters eating and persuade Brass to train some with me so I wouldn't sit around doing nothing all day.

Blue starry light filled the portal room in the Sumar palace with faux blue star light that made the room look cavernous with its reflective floors and tiny bits of mirror in the walls. Huge double doors that were mirrored with spokes radiating from a gold center circle, with white ovals around each one that looked like a blazing sun led the way to travel between islands. I stepped into the bright light thinking of Valla's town center.

I stepped into the rumpus room at headquarters twenty minutes after I left my home and found everyone eating at the round tables by the bar. Brass stood looking alarmed, his amber eyes wide as he pushed away from the table and headed towards me.

"I did not expect to see you today when you did not show up with Slate. He did not know you were coming, did he? We can train now if you wish," Brass said in a tone that got my hackles up.

He was rushing me. I scanned the people seated at the tables and didn't see Slate, but I saw Ama, Shale and Quick must have been back at Valla University. He said Slate had come there, so where was he? Only one answer stood out in my mind. With her.

I was a woman possessed. I went into my numb place as my mind cancelled out all else around me and I floated towards the carved walnut door directly across from me. It loomed in my mind, and I was vaguely aware of Brass tugging at me. I was deaf to his words as I reached for the filigree doorknob.

I watched as the pattern twisted before the door opened and I came face to face with my betrayer. Slate had red lipstick smeared on the corner of his mouth looking impossibly wide eyed at me and I shifted to see past him to see Cordillera's wavy raven hair looking down as she laced her black blouse. Her head shot up because one man was speaking, and she smirked with smeared red lips It was as good as a blow to my stomach.

I staggered back and Brass caught me under my arms. Slate knelt to help me up, but I blew him back hard with my calling. He slammed against the dark red love seat, smashing it into the desk.

I whimpered pathetically and freed myself from Brass's arms. My vision grew blurry while I stumbled away from the Breakers eating their lunches. The sensation grew until I fell to my knees inside the stairwell that led upstairs and tore at my clothes. Heat from my core burned in me.

Brass's face hovered into view, "Calm down, you are burning up. You must relax." It creased his dark honey face with worry, and I pulled off my weapons, the metal burned at my skin.

I was breathing shallow, quick breaths laying on my back, unable to move — paralyzed with pain. Slate came into view, and I cried out until I saw another set of arms pull him back. Brass cursed and fell back.

That's when the screaming began.

"Get out before she wakes and burns my room down. You are lucky Lera let me bring her up here, she thinks she is going to incinerate headquarters. You could not wait even a day?" Brass sounded as angry as the day I met him and Styg.

"If I had known she would have come —" Slate started, but Brass cut him off.

"Go back to Lera, you do not deserve her if you cannot wait for her," Brass barked and for a moment I thought Slate was going to say something equally scathing, but the door shut loudly, and they left me alone with silence.

Silence was my enemy. It was when my thoughts turned dark and threatened to suffocate me with my grief.

"I am here, Scarlett. How are you feeling?" Brass asked in his deep smooth tone.

I was on a bed, and it bowed as he sat down next to me. I tried to sit up, but he cradled me and held a sheet over my body, my eyes popped open and see him give me a warm smile.

"Best you stay put, you burned off all your clothes. Do you know what you are?" he asked, kicking off his boots.

I shook my head, and he chuckled. "Up to head shaking, are we? You, my dear Scarlett Tio, are an elemental. The likes of which have not been born in hundreds of years. A fire elemental at that. I suspect the skill has long lain dormant and the series of emotional events triggered it. How are you feeling otherwise?" he asked as he swung his legs up on the bed to lie beside me.

I sighed and rubbed my palms to my eyes. The room wasn't as fancy as the palace, but it wasn't bare thread either. I laid in a wood four-poster bed that was against the far wall. He wallpapered the walls with grey and brown stripes, the carpet chocolate brown. A small sitting area with a big grey colored couch rested towards the front of the room with a rectangular coffee table. There was a smaller table against the hall's wall and a mirror that hung above it. The only door led to a closet; they probably shared a bathroom at the end of the hall.

I tucked the grey cotton sheets under my arms and sat up against the headboard trying to process all this new information.

... *I've been better...*

Brass laughed as he scooted to sit next to me crossing his legs in front of him. "That is an understatement. Do you plan on going to classes this week? I can send a note to Dahlia Natt if you like," he said casually as if a naked woman wasn't in his bed.

Dahlia. Ash's mother. I sighed and nodded.

... *Please send a note, or I can write one if you don't mind sending it for me...*

He smiled brightly flashing perfect white teeth, "Writing and nodding. My, my, you are progressing well today. Are you still going to the Wemic tomorrow? Slate wanted to know."

I bit down on my lip and nodded. I didn't have any right to be mad at Slate, but I couldn't help my hurt. It was inexplicable to me, mad I could understand, but hurt? What for? I wasn't his girlfriend or wife, or anything really. His adopted sister — that's it. Friends on a wonderful day. The last five nights with him had been a fluke, a momentary lapse in his womanizing, but things seemed to be back on track. I was glad for it. I had almost forgotten when he put that ring on my finger.

My fingers were twisting, and I realized I hadn't taken it off. I could always do it later, there was no rush. Besides, I'd burned off my pockets. I looked around for my weapons and sighed in relief when I saw them on top of the table. I patted my silver Yggdrasil necklace I'd gotten as an inductee into Valla University; it was still there, so were the pearl and jade fetishes in my hair.

I must have been in shock at being an elemental, it made me feel anything either way. What I'd learned at Valla University for Guardian Mastery in my quest to become tried and true, was exactly as what Brass had said. Elementals were extinct.

"I will go get that paper and pen so you can write that message," Brass said, sliding off the bed and went into his closet bringing back a shirt and pants.

He tossed them to me, and I quickly slid the shirt over my head. It smelled like Brass, cinnamon, and spring rain. He handed me a folder and a pen then placed a sheet of paper atop it. I scribbled out a note and handed it over.

"I will run this down and bring back lunch?" he asked with a gorgeous smile.

I nodded and slid back down in his bed.

... Brass. Thanks, for taking care of me and everything. You don't even know me; I appreciate it...

His lips curled. "No need to thank me. It has been some time since I have had a beautiful woman in my bed. Try not to burn it down," he chided and left.

Brass woke me with lunch and my limbs felt thick and clumsy. He said it was because of the amount of energy I'd used to shift into an elemental. He suspected it would get easier every time I did it.

I hadn't meant to spend the night. So, when I woke up curled around Brass's sleeping form, at first, I thought it was Slate, then I realized I had nearly climbed on top of Brass and had fallen asleep on his chest like I'd done with Slate.

I blinked several times to be sure I was seeing things right until Brass stretched beneath me and I scooted back from him. He was shirtless and flexed his arms high above his head in a superb display of corded dark honey muscles.

"Good morning, Scarlett. You should get a move on it if you are going to go see the Wemic this morning. I believe Slate said you would leave early," Brass purred with self-satisfaction.

I arched an eyebrow at him, and he chuckled so richly it made my skin prickle.

"I suppose I let you sleep in so he would wonder where you were. It is some well-deserved revenge," Brass rolled onto his side, the sheet gathering at his hip.

Mrs. Scarlett Regn…

I'd slept next to him, practically on top of him and nothing had happened. He swung his legs over the side of the bed, and I saw he had a pair of low-slung drawstring pants on that hung off his hips to reveal the dreaded 'V' muscle that made my knees go weak on my most resolute days.

"I have a pair of slippers you can borrow so you do not have to wake any of the women. You might keep an extra change of clothes in case of emergencies here. You can keep it in my room if you wish," he said with a smirk and his dark hair fell from behind his ear to graze his cheek in a click of bronze and ebony beads.

I narrowed my eyes at him playfully and caught myself. I had no right being playful. He sighed, and I scooted to the end of the bed to pull on the pants he'd thrown to me last night thought I had to roll them up nearly ten times. My ensemble was complete when I slipped into a pair of loafer like slippers and gave him a slow spin.

"Yes, now he will be properly irritated," Brass chuckled and got to his feet.

Brass led me down the steps to the rumpus room and I got my first taste of the walk of shame. I glared at Brass who had not bothered to wear a shirt as he walked me out and noticed more than one head turn at Brass walking out a girl in his clothes first thing in the morning. Ama and Shale were eating breakfast and so was Quick. Quick gaped unabashedly as Brass walked me all the way to the hall where he stopped to face me.

... Thanks again...

He waved a dismissive hand. His amber eyes glittered as he looked from my eyes to my lips. He wrapped an arm around my hips and brushed his lips against mine, gently, sweetly and I heard someone drop their silverware.

"You look like you could use a kiss," Brass breathed against my lips and when I fumbled for thoughts, he pressed his well-formed lips to mine in a chaste kiss that left mine tasting like cinnamon.

I blinked at him — blushing — when he released me and caught sight of Lera standing in her doorway after having spotted us.

"Have fun with the Wemic and try not to overthink that kiss. You looked like you needed one is all," he said with a dazzling smile that rivaled Quick's and I realized where Quick had learned it.

I turned away forgetting to say goodbye and shuffled from the Shadow Breakers' headquarters in a man's pajamas and slippers carrying my weapons in my hands. I was a hot mess.

The blue starry light of the portal room greeted me when I reached the Sumar palace, so did my family.

"By the Mother, Scarlett. Where have you been? Is that men's clothing? What man did you spend the night with? He left beard burn on your face!"

Jett was all riled up. He had just cause, since my mother's death, Jett became overprotective in the extreme. He wanted to know where I was every second, the only exception was when I had been with Slate. I gaped at his questions and then rubbed at my face as if I could wipe away the red scratches from Brass's trim stubble.

Slate crossed his arms across his expansive chest and looked down his nose at me.

Tawny stared openmouthed at me, "What guy, Scarlett? Wait let me guess. Not Quick."

I shook my head.

"Not Ash? I know you guys are on the outs."

Slate growled. I shook my head.

"Hmm. Solder, the guy from the armor shop!" Tawny squealed, and I shook my head.

"Gods, Tawny, try to look less disappointed," Steel murmured.

"It was Brass," Slate said through clenched teeth, and I blushed.

"Quick's brother!" Tawny was bouncing on the balls of her feet.

I nodded, and she clapped her hands.

"He is so dreamy! Are you going to see him again? I mean, it wasn't like a one-night thing, right?"

My eyes bugged out. I shook my head emphatically, and she clapped her hands.

"Wait! You're sort of communicating! Did he do that? I suppose all you would need was grunting," she waggled her eyebrows at me, and I smiled for the first time since her wedding. Tawny covered her wide mouth with a hand and stifled a sob. "Oh Gods, you smiled. If he made you smile, keep him. He's a lesser family middle son, he's a good match! Maybe we should ask him to come with?" Tawny asked looking at Steel and Jett.

"There is not enough time. It is bad enough we must wait for her to change out of those clothes. We are not going into Valla to wait for him to get ready as well," Slate barked.

Jett closed the space between us and gave me a big squeeze.

"Whatever the cause, I am glad you are getting better. Hurry and change, Indigo isn't down yet, and I need to have a talk with our resident asshole," Jett's turquoise eyes drifted over my head to where Slate stood like a petulant child.

I pressed a kiss to everyone's cheeks and skirted Slate since he was sending glowers my way. Tawny had sniffed me deeply as I hugged her.

"Mmm. He smells like cinnamon, doesn't he? It's positively delicious," Tawny said, lifting his collar to her nose.

I blushed again and Slate growled, "I will wait in Thrimilci for whenever you feel like starting this trip."

I didn't think I'd ever seen Slate stomp, but he did now, or I fancied he did. It was more of a stalk.

Twenty minutes later Indigo, Gypsum, and I joined the others waiting patiently in the portal room. I hadn't had time to shower and when I stopped walking, I could smell Brass on my skin. It was a wonderful scent that lightened my mood significantly as we crossed through the bright white light and into Thrimilci's town heart.

A fifteen-foot gate with a high mosaic arch, done in whites and blues, spiraling ironwork below it radiating from a blazing sun and below that an iron patch work door. There was a door for people in the middle of the gate, but during the day it stayed open all the time. Further behind us was the sloping cliff-side the Sumar palace rested on top of. Several pointed domes and turrets in metallic blue and golds glittered in the sunlight, the palace was reminiscent of the Taj Mahal in both its style and size. It's arched hundreds of windowless windows sculpted into the face of the palace. You could see the two rivers, Mani, and Sol, that flowed around the palace that led to the waterfall behind it. White pueblo styled houses spanned the slopping cliff-side each with a blue roof and the occasional garden. Every spare inch had decorative mosaics, on walls between homes, the fences around gardens. It was a glittering flow of colors amidst the blue and white.

The shops at the town level were white stucco with large glass windows and pillars, each with their own blue and gold embossed sign. We found Slate leaning against one of the many white pillars that decorated the store fronts looking as smooth as ever.

He pushed away from it in one fluid move and strode over to us like an oversized panther. Whenever we went on these long treks through the desert, he donned whites and creams making his bronze skin look darker. Even Jett who favored black was wearing chocolate brown pants tucked into suede boots and a white linen shirt.

Without preamble, Slate started out down the white shimmering road that was made using magic to be compacted so smoothly it was like asphalt.

It wasn't long before we made it to the end of the white roads and pulled our loose scarves around our heads and continued the flat compacted sand. Tawny trotted up to walk with Indigo and I while the four men fell back. I had a good idea of the direction we needed to go, walking straight into the sunset helped as a navigational beacon.

Random trees around small oases and varieties of cacti, but overall, not much for vegetation scattered across the desert terrain. There was some red dirt and clay sections around the watering holes, otherwise it was one big desert.

It was early evening when we came to red and orange sandstone striped hills. The red hills — where the Jorogumo had attacked me. Formations that seemed to roll and swell like waves frozen in time. The sun was going down; the hills cast long shadows over us, and I took down my scarf. The temperature was dropping and the breeze that flowed through the hills lifted the damp hair off the back of my neck.

When we came to the end of the undulating forms, we checked the perimeter for dangers. I wouldn't be caught with my pants down again. Slate and Steel gave their approval to let us light a fire while we ate our packed dinners.

I sat between Indigo and Tawny as I spread out my roll. Gypsum was across the fire between Jett and Slate and Steel was to Tawny's right. The men spoke in deep rumbling murmurs, and I sat in silence listening to them as they chatted on.

"Have your dream lately?" Tawny asked, making conversation.

I had it a few nights ago in Slate's bed. I nodded, and she pursed her lips to the side.

"What is this dream? Is this the same one from the other night, Torch?" Slate asked.

It shocked me he was speaking to me, but he was using his trainer's voice and I nodded immediately, and he looked at Tawny for explanation. Tawny rolled her wide hazel eyes and pushed her long dark tresses over her shoulders before starting.

"It's Scarlett walking through dead bodies outside some old castle in the middle of a war with monsters and people during a dark storm. A woman all in white guides her and tells Scarlett she can stop it and that she is night. The dream shifts and she stands in a circle with people around the edges, a body that's dead or dying lays within the circle and then Scarlett starts on fire," Tawny said in a bored tone.

Slate and Tawny would bump heads if they ever took the time to spend time with one another. They were too much alike, her too short-tempered and he not liking anyone disobeying his commands. He had trained her too though, and I noticed she grudgingly conceded to him.

I had always thought it was light, but now I wondered if Tawny was right, that it was fire. It struck a little too close to home, and I shifted uncomfortably on my roll.

"That was creepy. Are you murdering him or something?" Jett asked. Tawny didn't say it was him, it had to be a coincidence.

I looked at him ruefully and shook my head.

"You've been paying too much attention in history class," he said gesturing with a piece of jerky.

"What do you mean?" Gypsum asked.

My cousin had his long hair pulled pack in a low ponytail and his scarf gathered around his neck. His thick winged brows drew down.

"It sounds like where Dagr died," Jett noted, "Don't worry — it disappeared. The place doesn't exist anymore."

I squirmed again and Slate watched. "Do you know the body on the ground?" he rumbled.

The firelight made Slate's hard planes look harsh and his silver eyes reflected like a cat's in the dark. I dropped my head and nodded avoiding his intense stare.

"Who is it, Torch?" he pressed.

How do you tell someone you dreamt about them dying? It's beyond creepy. I shook my head not wanting to answer him and feeling like I was on the verge of tears. Why did he always push? Couldn't he be happy with what I would give?

"Was it me?" he asked in a low tone, and my head shot up in disbelief.

Out of all the people on the planet, how could he have guessed it was him on the first try? Steel sucked in a sharp breath, and I realized there was more to this than I was seeing. Slate looked at the firelight as he finished chewing and lifted his eyes to mine with a lip curl.

"Are you psychic or something?" Tawny teased, but Slate didn't meet her eyes. Those were for me.

"I am a prophet. I remember everything. My forefathers had prophecies and I inherit them," he tapped his temple. "That is why I can quote Whitman better than anyone," he said with an arrogant grin.

My mouth hung open as I tried to process this new information. "Is it a secret?" Gypsum asked, and I saw Steel shift in the corner of my eye.

"I would rather no one knows about it," he said ruefully, and Gypsum nodded. "Do you believe in destiny? Fate?" he asked in a soft reverent tone.

"No. Every action is a reaction to our own special kind of stupidity that even we can't predict," Tawny said pertly.

"My mother was a prophet; it is an inherited trait like your empath abilities. We passed the prophecies down with each birth. With my birth, I received my ancestors' prophecies. I told you about my perfect memory, I remember everything. They do not dull over time; I do not forget. I will always remember..." Slate trailed off, but his fingers curled covetously, and I vainly wondered if he was thinking about the nights I'd slept in his arms.

"As much as we love knowing that you will never forget even one of your incalculable one-night stands, you have yet to tell us what this has to do with Scarlett's dream," Tawny said with a sardonic grin.

I broke his gaze. I hadn't thought of that, and it made my stomach turn. Slate inhaled sharply and for another man it was a shout. Tawny had pissed him off.

"It is fate, but fate is a cruel mistress. My dream corresponds with yours. It would appear we have different parts of the same dream. A prophet's dream. Are you sure you do not have a prophet in your ancestry?" Slate said, still only addressing me.

"No. No prophets," Jett answered with confidence.

"Dad can fold shadows," Gypsum offered, "He says it's useless unless you're hiding." He broke into a smile, "he told me he used it to play hide and seek with us as kids."

"What about Alder?" Jett asked.

Indigo who had been silently looking down at her slim fingers the whole time finally spoke. "I know that he does, but he doesn't speak on it. You have the same dream?" she asked, tucking her hair behind her ears.

Indigo looked as bad as I did, it almost made me feel better. Misery did like company. She'd been as quiet as I had during our day long hike.

Slate nodded. "I dreamed of a golden-haired girl since I was born, it was my mother's prophecy. You dreamed of watching me die? I have dreamed of dying while you watch. When I saw you at the masquerade that first night, I recognized you... when you were with Ash," he finished, and I lifted my gaze to him.

He had been as aware of me as I was of him. He had guided Lera into that bathroom so I would notice him, as if I hadn't already. What an idiot.

I laid back on my roll and tried to digest the new information. My brain wasn't running on all cylinders, and while I knew you had to have a talent to be a Shadow Breaker, I hadn't stopped to think what Slate's could be. He was a prophet; he probably knew hundreds of prophecies. It was probably why he wouldn't marry, why he thought he'd die young. Maybe he thought our dream was real, that he would die in that circle.

Grief was fickle. One minute I was thinking about what I would have done differently, like yanking Lera off him in the powder room. The next, I was thinking of last night and how I wished I could drag myself to my mother's room and tell her what happened with Brass and Ash. I wanted her advice. For her to tell me I was being foolish or forbid me from ever seeing any of those men again. I had no one to talk to about those things. Then I was crying.

Indigo turned on her roll, and her tanned face streaked with tears as well. She slid her hand into mine and we fell asleep long after our tears dried.

CHAPTER
FIVE

The others seemed dumbfounded about Slate's admission and Steel and Jett looked unnerved that Slate had told us about him being a prophet.

We reached the red canyons, and I could almost smell the water that I knew was deep in the gorge just past the Wemic village. We reached the Wemic around noon.

Rikke sprouted from a gap in the canyon almost immediately. Rikke's eyes were lime green with a vertical pupil, it pulled his inky black hair back into a ponytail. He was bare chested and dressed like the other Wemic would be in a loincloth on and a beaded belt. His short black fur covered his powerful body. They painted him in red swirls that signified that he was a warrior.

"Steel! No business this time," a cat like smile curled Rikke's lips. The dark furred panther man put his forehead to Steel's. He greeted us warmly, "More guests?"

Steel gave a poster boy smile, "You remember Jett? My nephew, and my other niece, Indigo." I guessed Indigo was his niece of sorts since she was my adopted sister.

Rikke's smile wavered sensing Steel's emotion, but he held it, "Welcome! It has been a while, Jett."

Jett nodded, "It has. Good to see you again, Rikke." Jett lowered the scarf around his head protecting his close cropped dark blonde head.

"Come, let us enter the village."

Rikke, Steel, and Tawny led the way. Jett fell back with Slate as we walked through the red dirt canyons and between the little clay adobes the Wemic lived in.

Grief was a torturous monster, it jumped up just when you think you're doing well again. BAM! You're back to square one, reverting into the sobbing slobbering mess you were. But, then you're fine again, no wait, you're crying.

Something inside broke the scab over my very raw wound of my mother's death when I saw the lion man and his practiced human smile. There had only been one completely uncomplicated time since coming to Tidings, and that was with the Wemic. Keen had helped me find happiness that night.

When he saw us from the village edge, he started out with a smile. It wouldn't be appropriate to run into his fur covered arms and start crying, but I did anyway.

My body rocked his as we. He tucked me to him, "Always so sad. Scarlett..."

He lifted a clawed finger to my chin raising my teary turquoise eyes. He had gold fur covering his body that grew lighter under his chin and down his chest and stomach. Red paint swirled around his arms and shoulders. He had golden eyes and long golden hair pulled back with feather fetishes. His muzzle was white with a black nose. I hoped I wasn't a hideous crier; I'd been doing so much of it publicly in recent days. He gave my forehead a bump and placed a small kiss on my lips before looking over my head to our group.

"Good to see you, Slate," he said in English before returning to his purring native language.

I didn't need to be a linguist to know they were talking about me. I breathed deep and pushed back.

He smiled down at me. "We will get you speaking again," he breathed. I nodded, "Introduce me."

Steel helped, "This is Indigo, my niece and you know Jett."

Keen nodded, and he brought his forehead to Indigo's startling her.

He did it to the group, Slate whispered something in hushed tones, but it made Keen smile.

"Come," Keen and Rikke walked ahead with Steel and Tawny.

"He's strangely attractive," Indigo quietly confided.

It made me laugh inappropriately. They looked back at me. Indigo blushed, and I nodded in an answer.

Gypsum was next to me listening, he was nodding, "They're very...exotic."

I wondered if he knew he had said it out loud. I brought an arm around his and leaned up to kiss his cheek. Gyps looked down at me and gave a small smile. His dimples still gave him a boyish quality I hoped he'd never lose.

We reached the village heart. The different cats in the Wemic tribe fascinated Indigo. One Wemic, whom I found very attractive, was a tall snow leopard man who had long white hair tied back with bits of leather strings and feathers. His eyes were a stormy grey.

We passed the trio of cheetah brothers, the one in front gave a flash of teeth. It looked like a sneer if he had been human. Nirrin was as friendly as ever.

We headed into the chief's clay home. Keen went in first, holding his hands out and gave me a wink. We were to wait a moment before entering. Rikke followed in after him. Reski exited with his quiet other brother Nekee and Tikee, the fuzzy faced lynx. Red paint covered his cheekbones down to his jaws and on his forehead into his hairline.

Tikee was jolly. The lynx man had ears long and high on his head reddish brown and spotted fur sticking straight out. He was also the burliest — tall, and wide. Nekee was the lion men's middle brother, someone had dipped his hair in red and plaited it. Red paint covered his jaw down to his collarbones. He was silent and greeted us all with nods.

Reski rested his head to each of ours as did Nekee and Tikee. Reski's golden mane of hair blows as the feather fetishes catch in the wind. "Be welcome in your time of mourning," he said in his rumbling voice.

"Come, eat with us," Tikee said and led us into the chief's home.

We sat on cushions lined along the walls; a small clay hardened table rested in the center of the room. A beautiful tigress came into the adobe and sat down next to her husband the chief Reski her long plaited black hair held in beads. The younger tigress entered behind her, beautiful with golden eyes, it was Tika. The tigress that had come into Slate's guest building on our last visit when we had almost kissed.

"My wife Nata and her sister Tika," Reski gestured to the two stunning tigresses who were near identical in their coloring, but Nata had the bearing of a queen.

Nata and Tika smiled and greeted us, Tika's eyes resting on Slate. I dropped my eyes.

We ate our lunch quietly. Steel had been there for a few days not too long ago to tell them what I had found out about the Merfolk. Reski had been sending out hunting parties to skirt the nearest coasts to see if any new ones had appeared. They feared the Jorogumo had brought it further in land, but portable portals were unheard of.

Keen moved to sit beside Indigo and me. "I would say I am sorry, but it is not our way. Tonight, we mourn, tomorrow we celebrate," he told us.

I didn't know what to say, Indigo told him, "Thank you." He gave her a beautiful cat smile, and she blushed. He had that effect.

He smiled. "You came back. That is good. You brought another beautiful girl, that is better," he gave Indigo his best cat smile. I wondered if blushing was contagious. "I will have to get used to that," he said, noting her blush.

We finished our lunches and put our packs in the adobes. Steel and Tawny in one, Slate, Jett, and Gyps, in the second. Indigo and myself in the third. The cheetah twins that had crushes on Gyps came by and escorted us into a large adobe. We changed into our loincloth clothes and sat patiently while the women painted us.

We all wore black.

There was no giggling this time, no talking as the cat women gently painted their swirls across our skin. They put their heads to ours before leaving. We all stood painted in our black swirls and gathered outside around the fire.

Wemic chanted as they threw things into the fire causing the smoke to change colors. A few Wemic held instruments and played sorrowful music I felt down to my soul. We fasted that night as we watched the puffs of red, blue, and orange smoke rise into the air. When it was over,

Tawny took Steel by the hand and led him to their clay hut. Steel looked sadder than he had in the previous days as if the truth of his sister's death had finally caught up with him.

No one could outrun death.

I wanted to leave my brother and adopted sister and go off own my own, but I didn't think that would be right. Jett moved to sit by Slate and Gypsum as the Wemic passed out their jugs of fiery alcohol.

Rikke came to sit by Indigo, handing her a jug. She smiled at him. I rose and searched Indigo's eyes for permission.

Rikke's lime green eyes glittered, "I will take care of her." He smiled. She nodded looking comfortable with the black panther cat.

I made my way to Keen; he stood to meet me. I said nothing; I grabbed his clawed hand and headed deeper into the canyon. He knew where we were going right away and took the lead unspeaking. We came out on top of the canyon, and he led me to the stone spot where we could lean against it and stare up at the stars.

He threw down a blanket I hadn't seen him grab and pulled me to him as he sat. I rested my head against his chest as I looked up into the sky. I wondered if my mom was peaceful and if she could see us.

"Your sadness runs deep," Keen said, "I am glad you chose me to share it with."

I sighed.

He smiled down at me, "I do not mind. You are always welcome here, Scarlett." Keen gave my cheek a lick, and I nestled into him.

I didn't remember falling asleep.

I woke up entangled with Keen, a sound suspiciously like a purr coming from his chest. It was incredibly soothing. I placed my ear on his chest and it stopped.

He smiled at me sleepily, "I meant to carry you to the hut."

I sat up straightening my loincloth skirt; he had kept me warm in such little clothing. He pushed himself into a sitting position.

"We should get back to the village. Maybe no one will notice we spent the night together," he said with a cheery grin.

I scoffed, and he laughed too, his rasping cat laugh, "When you leave your suitor for me, we will give them something to talk about."

He stood and held down his clawed hands to help me up. I grabbed the blanket as he pulled me to him.

We entered the village, and Keen walked me to the visitor's hut. I kissed him at the threshold and hurried inside.

Indigo slept by herself on the stuffed mattress bed in the far corner. I slipped out of my loin cloth and into a pair of shorts and a tank I had brought and crawled into bed.

I couldn't fall to sleep. I thought about everything that had happened in the last month. I thought about the one thing no one seemed willing to talk about — my mother was murdered. There had been no struggle, she either knew the attacker or it had happened so quickly she didn't have time to react.

I wasn't ready to cross that bridge, so I pushed it temporarily out of my mind. I got up and change back into my clothes. Someone had placed a fresh loincloth skirt and top in the doorway.

The top reminded me of something I'd seen in a music video with a snake charmer. I felt a little exposed, but it seemed ridiculous since I had been wearing scraps of fabric all day yesterday. I hoped Indigo would wear it too.

She stirred, "Oh my. Do you think you could heal me? Their drinks are so strong."

I walked to her bed and healed her hangover.

"That is so much better. I think I made a spectacle of myself," she said, pulling a stuffed pillow over her face.

I laughed.

She smiled her face blushing, "I totally made out with that black panther Wemic." She pulled her blankets over her head.

I laughed again, and the blankets shifted like she was shaking her head underneath them I crawled under the blankets, she scooted to make room for me. We could have done this as little girls. The thought made my throat constrict.

I made a gesture that said tell me about it. I wanted to know; I'd be lying if I said I'd never thought about things with Keen.

"His tongue was rough, like you'd expect," she blushed a bright tomato face red, "He was very good at it." She bit her lip, "Is that weird?"

I shook my head and didn't mention that Slate was fooling around with Tika.

As if on cue she added, "I saw Slate with Tika. She's exquisite. What do you think of Rikke?"

My stomach had done a flip. I stamped down on the unwanted emotions and gave her a big thumbs up.

She made a grimace, "Gods, it is weird. His fur is like silk, I barely noticed it last night." I giggled.

The blanket tent collapsed on us as a certain handsome brother of ours joined the fun. Our heads peeked out of the blanket. Jett looked better, he had a cocky smile on his face and was laying squeezed between us, his booted feet dangling off the bed.

"If you two are done. I'm ready to eat breakfast, I forgot how strong that stuff in their jugs are. Slate had to drag me back into bed. I passed out in front of the fire," he laughed in disbelief.

"You should really be in your loincloth," Indigo told him, and I stepped out of the blanket to show him I was following tradition.

He sucked his teeth. "I don't think that's appropriate to wear in public. I hope that scrap holds those bad boys down," he said gesturing to my top or lack thereof.

A throat cleared in the door. Our laughing tapered off.

A hint of a smile played on Steel's lips, "Breakfast is being prepared."

Jett slid off the bed and helped me up. I straightened my outfit, and he quirked an eyebrow and shook his head. Indigo needed to change and meet us out there.

Slate and Gypsum sat outside in their loincloths shirtless eating breakfast together. The twin cheetahs must have felt like they gave

Gypsum his day off from their advances and were slowly inching towards him. He monitored them as he used his fingers to feed himself.

Keen saw me coming and smiled. I smiled back. He really knew how to make a girl feel good. Rikke was lingering near him not touching his breakfast yet. Steel and Tawny sat with the chief, Nekee, and Tikee. Tikee let out a bellowing laugh at whatever jokes he'd told.

Keen nipped my ear when I sat down next to him. Jett sat between me and Slate with his food. Indigo came out shortly after wearing her loincloth outfit.

Rikke gave a small smile when she came out and patted the spot next to him, she blushed as she sat down with her food.

"Rikke likes your sister," Keen leaned in and whispered into my ear. His whiskers tickled, and I shrank back and giggled.

"What's on today's agenda?" Jett asked him.

"Today we celebrate. Would you want to join a hunting party until then? The festivities will not start until later," Keen told me.

"How about a swim? I could use a dip," Jett said around me.

Keen smiled, "Much better idea."

Slate was stony faced, but Gypsum was nodding along with me. I didn't dare mention that the cheetah twins had heard.

After breakfast Tawny, Indigo, and I grabbed our darkest pairs of underwear and rolled them into our makeshift towels.

We followed Rikke and Keen deeper into the canyons. The seven of us and the four Wemic came, the twin cheetahs would not be left behind. We followed the stream into a ravine and eventually a lake of water. Wemic with nets stood on one side of the water and gave us a wave when we approached the water. Some parts of the water were darker than others, the lake was deep in spots.

"There isn't anything that bites in there, is there?" Tawny asked, eyeing the water's darker spots.

Rikke and Keen laughed, which did nothing to placate me. "We bite harder," Keen snapped his sharp teeth at me.

You forgot how much animal is in them until you saw those sharp canines. Rikke and Keen untied their weighted belts and cloths and dove right into the water. I got more than an eyeful; I got two eyefuls.

Indigo and Tawny blushed. Jett's eyes glittered with playful mischief.

He let out a long exhale, "I guess I'll be keeping these on."

He snapped the waistband of his blue boxer briefs and dove into the water. I unrolled my towel and pulled on my black underwear under my skirt. Indigo followed suit. Gypsum was running into the water with green boxer briefs, twin cheetahs on his heels in their tops in something that looked like underwear, but a hole was where their tails came through. Indigo shrugged and pulled off her cloth to reveal dark red underwear. She turned a similar shade as Rikke gave a cat call, giving new meaning to the term. Steel carried Tawny into the water and dropping her as soon as it was deep enough making her squeal.

I was thankful I had an affinity for boy shorts. Slate stood in his black underwear and watched me carefully. I kept eye contact as I undid my skirt ties letting it fall. His eyes reflected silver.

"Slate, you are not playing fair! You would keep her to yourself!" Keen yelled with his own brand of honesty.

Slate wasn't one to blush, he broke contact and look out at Kee, "Thanks for that, my friend."

I ran ahead of him and dove into the water. It gradually deepened like lakes back home. I wanted to swim to the deepest part and let myself sink. Instead, I popped up at Gypsum's feet.

He yelled, startled, and splashed me which started a splashing fight. I was dunked repeatedly by blurry sources.

When the waters settled, Indigo floated towards me, "It's kind of perfect here." I shrugged and floated on my bubble raft I'd called.

"I miss the girls," Jett said with a half-smile, "They needed time away from me." He turned introspective, "Be careful with Cordillera, Scar. She does what's best for her first and foremost and some of those patrons of hers are dangerous." I nodded and he felt like he did his brotherly duty.

Slate and Keen were talking both were smiling, so it was a good sign. I could count on one hand how many people Slate liked outside of our family. Keen was one of those. I let my bubble raft dissolve and floated to the bottom. When I couldn't hold my breath anymore, I called a bubble of air around my mouth so I could breathe. I opened my eyes and had to stifle a giggle, or I'd lose my bubble, I forgot the Wemic had jumped in the water commando.

I swam deeper into the lake and saw the fish that lived in the cooler depths. A tug on my foot startled me and I almost lost my bubble again, my hair floated in front of my face in golden waves. Slate had tugged my ankle with his own bubble and gestured to the surface. My lips quirked, and I swam further into the lake.

I stopped once fish had surrounded us on all sides. Schools of them in all different sizes lived in the deep lake. They diverted from us. Slate had swum up to my side. I cheated using a little air to push me faster, but he was right along with me. He grabbed me around my waist, his hair floating around his head weightlessly and I thought he would kiss me. The thought caused my bubble to burst. His lips curled and he let me go so I could get to the surface I popped up far from the group.

"You did not come to the adobe last night," Slate said, bobbing up next to me.

I shrugged. He had no claim to me; he didn't get to say where I slept or with whom.

"Did you mate with Keen?" Slate asked as he bobbed in the water tossing back his head like a lion shaking its mane, whipping his black waves away.

I leveled my eyes at him. Slate wasn't like me. I wouldn't sleep with the first man who came along just because I wasn't spending the night with him anymore. That he asked annoyed me.

"First, you have Brass's scent all over you, then it is Keen's," he was sounding jealous again, and talking nonsense about scents.

I rolled my eyes and floated away, but he grabbed my ankle pulling me back without dunking my head, "You are still wearing my ring, Torch. No one has asked about it, but they will soon. Are you thinking on my offer?"

My cheeks heated as he held me against his chest. It was such a familiar spot, but I had banned myself from it. I pushed softly against him. I had forgotten about the ring; he was reading too much into it.

I twisted the ring and then looked back up to him running my teeth along my lip. He said he didn't want it back, but perhaps he'd changed his mind. I held up my hand to him and he closed my fingers around it and kissed the ring on my finger before I could snatch it back.

"I made a mistake," Slate floated closer so our legs were nearly kicking at one another's, "I should have waited."

A mistake my fanny pack. His bed wasn't even cold before he sought Lera out. I gave a solid shake of my head and ducked under the water.

I swam until I could reach the floor again.

"Did you see the fish with the big teeth?" Keen said, jokingly.

"We should head back," Rikke told us, "By the time we get back the celebration will begin."

Keen nodded, and we swam back to the shore. The guys turned around so Tawny, Indigo, and I could dry our tops and hair, and tie back on our skirts. Jett pulled his shorts off happy as you please — look at your own peril — and pulled his pants over his bare skin. The rest tied on the cloths as soon as they had gotten out; the Wemic cupped themselves. I had a feeling that was modest for them.

It took an hour to head back to the village heart. They'd painted the other Wemic and were elbow deep in meal preparations. Keen said goodbye and gave me a lick before heading into the chief's adobe.

Steel gave a small smile, "We should go get painted. You can choose whatever you like. Scarlett, you can choose white if you wish."

I frowned and shook my head. Steel was likely as distracted as the rest of us and hadn't noticed Ash's absence.

I gestured to the blue when the lioness with chestnut hair she asked what color I wanted. She grinned at me as she began.

"I better go with white, or my wives will kill me," Jett said, suddenly in better spirits.

They had painted Indigo. "What does blue mean?" she asked me.

Jett smirked. "Single," he spared her the in-season rhetoric.

Tawny and Steel were being painted white as well. Slate came in after me and sat down next to Jett and Gypsum painted in blue. The twins had shoved off some poor lioness girl to do Gypsum's blue paint themselves. They took their sweet time.

It was late afternoon when we finished eating. The usual blue painted girls fawned over Slate. While they sandwiched Gypsum between two giggly cheetah twins. Jett had moved to sit with Indigo and me, near Rikke and Keen.

"Best to stay away from temptation," he said.

Keen and Rikke spoke with Jett mostly discussing fighting with their claws, and him with his long seaxes. Men and they're toys. I thought.

Jett leaned over and whispered to me, "Looks like you've got some competition."

He gestured with his head wearing a lecherous grin I thought he might have had patented. Tika was at Slate's side talking animatedly to him, a few other females hovered around him in case there was something he might need. Tika was in blue.

Keen caught Jett's head nod, "Tika? She is a desirable mate. Beautiful, her sister is my brother's wife."

I took a deep breath, and Jett chuckled.

"Are you jealous?" Keen asked, it sucked, he was so sincere. Jett choked on his jug of fiery liquid. Keen smiled, "Chang'aa. Scarlett?"

He passed me a clay jug of chang'aa, and I decided I would get good and drunk on our last night with the Wemic.

The musicians played, and Gypsum was quickly dragged out into the group of dancing Wemic. He didn't appear to be fighting them as ardently and Tawny shook her head as they sandwiched him between the cheetah twins.

Jett was of a like mind and getting good and drunk of chang'aa as I was. A drunk Jett was a funny Jett. It wouldn't be funny when someone had to carry him back to his bed later.

I sighed feeling a pang of misery rise in me.

"No need to explain. Your family is my family."

Keen reached down with a clawed hand and kissed my lips when he caught me looking at Jett. His whiskers tickled my face as I leaned into his kiss. I giggled. I didn't know how Indigo made out with Rikke.

Night had fallen, Jett was sleeping, and Gypsum was a hot dancing mess. I was having fun. Rikke and Keen were talking between us, when Rikke asked something from Indigo. She smiled and nodded enthusiastically. I gave her the universal sign for you're all good, with my thumbs up. She smiled back and gave me a thumbs up behind Rikke's back.

I shook my head and smiled. "He is going to show her the stars," Keen told me.

That's not all he's going to show her, I thought.

"Let us go dance," he said getting to his feet.

He grabbed his clawed hands and pulled him into the mass of swaying, sweaty, bouncing bodies. Steel and Tawny were dancing. Keen was behind me swaying with me in the firelight. The crowd's warmth made me feel warm in unexpected ways. They carried me on their vibe of happiness and lust. I closed my eyes and went with it.

They lost me in the music. Nothing but the thought to keep moving, swaying, rolling my body. I saw Gypsum get pulled away with the cheetah twins, and not towards our adobe. Next, I saw Steel and Tawny leave. Indigo hadn't come back yet; I didn't know if I would see her again that night.

Keen led me back to the jugs of chang'aa and we laughed the night away as I listened to him tease his fellow Wemic.

Swimming. Yes, swimming sounded good. I was in my racerback and shorts with my suede boots as I found my way to the gorge. I stripped off my clothes and ran out into the water. The silver moonlight reflected on the still waters except for my ripples. I floated on the top sloshing water over my body.

I tilted my chin up and howled. My voice resounded off the walls, and I listened until it tapered away. I howled louder and louder until I'd stopped swimming and screamed up at the moon. My cries were cathartic.

Why hadn't I done this before? I unleashed my inner animal and roared at the full moon.

I laughed loud and full of self-discovery. My pain had ebbed. I threw back my head and gave my best roar from my stomach. Gods, did it feel good.

I wanted to dance; I wanted to fight, to laugh and love. To love. I wanted to make love. Yes, that was it and I wanted to laugh and howl as I did it. I'd never been that girl to throw caution to the wind. When I lost control, bad things happened — every time.

A low staccato purr made me whirl around and sink down to my chin in the water. Nirrin, the cheetah hybrid tracker was watching me. His golden cat eyes reflecting the moonlight as he tugged on his loincloth.

"You are ready for a taste of something wild, Guardian." Nirrin purred. His black hair was plaited into a mohawk that fell to his neck.

I shook my head, not Nirrin. There was only one hybrid I wanted.

Roaring broke the silence, and an enormous dark creature broke from the crevice that led to the village. Nirrin hissed and crouched as the beast stalked around him.

It was dark and had long pointed ears with three sets of horns protruding from its head. One set like tusks curved around to its jaw, a set curled slightly from behind its ears that were short, and the third set curled like a ram. Its short snout was pulled back in a snarl revealing teeth much more frightening than Nirrin's. The beast man had black hair that hung from its head held back by its series of horns and it stood a foot taller than Nirrin's six feet and its shoulders were twice as broad. The beast rippled with sleek bunched muscles ready to attack as it prowled around Nirrin.

What hunted the hunters? This beast. Top of the food chain.

When he clobbered on my last visit, it ended in a tongue bath. I wanted one now. It was deadly, and I had to fight against my primordial instincts to flee from the savage beast in front of me, but my gut told me it wouldn't hurt me. Not intentionally.

It started relieving himself and Nirrin growled before trotting off into the crevice. The beast man swung its reflective gaze to me looking furious, but I kept walking.

"Go back to the village," he rasped and uttered a length of curses as I walked until the water level slipped past my hips to reveal my bare skin.

The beast wore a loincloth this time, but it did little to hide how rapidly it was recognizing my expression. I wanted it. I wanted to know what it felt like to lose myself completely, I could with the beast. It watched me as the water trickled over my skin prickled chest and down my lean thighs.

I stalked around him and found my gravelly voice for the first time in almost two weeks. "You are mine," I told it firmly, and it stiffened making me smile.

I ran my fingers along his hard chest covered in dark silky fur and around his back. "Say it," I commanded, and he laughed a low rasping laugh.

"I am yours. And you?" he asked.

I stood in front of it and untied the strings that held its loincloth. "I am yours. I give you everything freely," he rose between his legs as I told him. "Say it," I commanded again, and it laughed.

"You are mine," he said in stilted words.

I blinked, and he was on me. My hands hit the sand as I fell on my hands and knees. He bit down on my neck forcing my head down before planting a searing kiss to the nape of my neck. His wide coarse tongue trailed down my spine with painstakingly slowness and up over the curve of my backside until I whimpered with want.

He murmured something in Wemic. The beast was running its fingers through my murky depths and there was a lot more where that came from.

"*It is I, you women — I make my way,*
I am stern, acrid, large, undissuadable — but I love you,
I do not hurt you any more than is necessary for you,
I pour the stuff to start sons and daughters fit for These States — I press with slow rude muscle,
I brace myself effectually — I listen to no entreaties,
I dare not withdraw till I deposit what has so long accumulated within me.
Through you, I drain the pent-up rivers of myself,

In you I wrap a thousand onward years,
On you I graft the grafts of the best-beloved of me and America,
The drops I distil upon you shall grow fierce and athletic girls, new artists, musicians, and singers,
The babes I beget upon you are to beget babes in their turn,
I shall demand perfect men and women out of my love-spendings, I shall expect them to interpenetrate with others, as I and you interpenetrate now,
I shall count on the fruits of the gushing showers of them, as I count on the fruits of the gushing showers I give now,
I shall look for loving crops from the birth, life, death, immortality, I plant so lovingly now."

Walt Whitman?

"I cannot."

He breathed harshly into my hair behind me before shifting away. I turned around instantly and grabbed onto his powerful legs before he could go anywhere. His eyes narrowed as I prowled up him kissing the insides of his legs as I went, the soft fur formed seamlessly to the mold of his muscles as if it wasn't fur at all but dark skin. He watched me warily as he sat back until I reached the tops of his thighs and wrapped my hand around him.

He gripped my wrists so tightly my fingers uncurled reflexively. "Not like this," he rasped out.

I drunkenly whimpered for him, and he pulled me up over his body, so my elbows rested to either side of his horned head.

"You are mine. My mate. I will claim you one day soon," the beast rasped against my skin, as I murmured in response.

"Yours. Mine. My mate."

The sun warmed my face, and I opened my eyes slowly to get my bearings. I was in the Wemic village, in the Guardian guest adobe. I mentally checked my body and aside from a mind numbing headache there was the need to puke everywhere.

It had all been a dream. I found myself horribly disappointed. The only time in my life I had let go and done something spontaneous and reckless — and none of it was real.

The big hand that rested on my back flexed, and I tilted my head back. It could only be one person; he must have had his fun with Tika and climbed into bed with me. He looked heavenly in the sunlight. The hard planes of his face not as tense as they normally were, and his full lips pressed lightly together as if waiting for a kiss.

A soft kiss perhaps?

My mind had vacated the premises and tremors from last night's extremely steamy, very realistic dream was still coursing through my veins. I closed my eyes and breathed in his scent, it'd only been a few days, but I had grown used to it on my skin. Maybe I was obsessed with scents.

He was naked; I realized belatedly, which didn't surprise me since we were with the Wemic. What was disconcerting was that I was naked too. I didn't sleep naked, and how did I end up laying on top of him? By the Mother, how many hours had we been in this naked embrace!

My cheek pressed against the hard ridges of countless bronze muscles and big corded arms were wrapped around me. It appalled me to find that I had hooked my arms around his shoulders as if I'd been returning his embrace. My bare breasts smashed against his stomach as if I'd climbed onto him with his arms outstretched and simply passed out. He held me there with his legs stretched powerfully to either side of my hips.

If this was real, then it looked like it wasn't Slate who had climbed into my bed, but I who climbed into his. Could I have invented the beast man, and it was Slate who I had the pledged my love to down by the gorge?

That thought was most unwelcome. I was losing it. I knit my brows as I pressed my forehead to Slate's hard stomach and sucked in a deep breath. It was a heady scent.

I inhaled deeply lowering my nose to brush the crease between his pecs.

"Lower, Torch," Slate purred with an impossibly deep husky voice as his arms tightened around me flexing his hips so what was growing hard under my stomach pushed into my skin.

I yelped and tried to push off, but it was futile. I'd sooner ease Atlas of his burden than I would pry myself from Slate's fierce grip.

"Let me go," I ground out with red cheeks.

"Says the woman laying nude atop me, kissing my chest," Slate chuckled huskily.

I wouldn't look at him. Not that I could he was holding me so tightly to his body, but if I could, I knew he'd have a lazy, full lipped smile, and dreamy gray eyes. No. I *couldn't* look at him. I was still feeling a strange effect from my provocative dream, and it made Slate's usual charge and tug to me more intense than usual.

Did he have to chuckle so deeply I could feel it low in my belly? Gods! That wasn't all I could feel. He flexed his hips again and my insides coiled hot and delicious.

"I was drunk. Very drunk. Why did you climb into my bed?" I accused, murmuring against his chest.

He laughed all the harder making his muscles in his stomach flex. My skin prickled; my nipples tightened to hard little pearls against his middle. "Hilarious, Torch. It was you who climbed on top of me. Naked, if you do not remember. You were very..."

"Drunk," I said pointedly and wondered if something had happened between the two of us and quickly dismissed it. I doubted one could do something with Slate Sumar and forget it. "And don't make up some nonsense about things we did, because we both know that it wouldn't be true," I snapped.

He chuckled again, but it was low and unfurled in my belly working its way under my skin to curl my toes, "Do you need me to jog your memory, perhaps? I am all too happy to, Torch."

His grip loosened as he slid his hands lower down my back and I shot up furrowing my brow. "Baloney!" I shouted defensively.

Tawny and I hadn't come up with a word for bull poop, but baloney suited me fine. His eyes shot down to my bared skin and where I sat between his legs, and everything in between. I snapped my eyes shut and my hands flew to my chest. Slate's own hands whipped out and caught my wrists effortlessly and pulled me by my wrists dragging my breasts over the length of his hard muscles, so my face was even with his. My mouth went dry with what I saw in his flashing silver eyes. How did any woman stand a chance against him?

"Hey, is Scarlett, in here? She didn't come back to the adobe last night?" Jett asked, stepping into the hut.

A moment ago, I would have done anything to wriggle free of Slate and the world of temptation his very presence on the planet presented, but when I heard my brother's voice, I tried to make myself as small as possible. My hands being stuck as they were in Slate's outstretched arm, I buried my face in the crook of his neck and had pulled my legs up to the sides of him trying to flatten my body to the shape of his and failing utterly. Slate started laughing, roaring with laughter really, making things...move perilously close to, um, other things causing me to yelp and try to wriggle up his body further since the bastard hadn't let go of my wrists.

"Whoops. Sorry," Jett said until I yelped, "Scar?"

I groaned and kneed Slate as hard as I could in the ribs so he'd, A) Stop his incessant laughter, and B) Let go of my blasted wrists. Slate let out a grunt and I yanked my wrists free and fell out of the bed pulling the sheet with me while trying to maneuver off Slate's body. I fell between the wall and the bed on the hard clay floor with a grunt.

Jett loudly cursed a word that rhymed with duck no doubt after getting about five eyefuls of Slate. Handfuls? *A lot* more than he'd bargained for.

"It's not what it looks like," I said, wrapping the sheet around my chest and struggled to my feet after bouncing off the edge of the bed once. My face was purple with embarrassment.

"Are you sure? It looked like you were having sex with Slate or straddling him with the intention of," Jett said, crossing his arms disapprovingly, but not budging an inch.

I looked to Slate for reinforcement, but his expression was a blend of irritation and amusement. He strategically placed a pillow on his otherwise fully nude body. Gods, did he really think we were going to — I refused to finish that thought. An inner voice snidely reminded me I was naked clinging to his hard body like a spider monkey moments before, so who could blame the man for that assumption.

I could only imagine how flushed, and rumpled I looked to my brother, the picture of a woman who'd just had a tryst with a man. I ran my fingers through my hair to present a better image of myself.

"You haven't spoken for over a week and your first sentence to me is, *it's not what it looks like?*" he shook his dark blonde head.

I shrugged chewing on my bottom lip. "It's true. It wasn't. Just a series of compromising events," I offered and moved past my brother to my pack against the wall, "I was pretty drunk last night, but I think I would remember... Slate."

I dug through my pack and wrestled on a pair of white underwear and a matching bra before pulling on snug taupe pants and a long white sleeve linen.

"I am going to take that as a compliment," Slate said in a growl.

"I suppose it was," I said distractedly as I finished getting ready.

"Would you like me to recount details, Torch?" Slate rumbled with a devilish grin.

Jett groaned, "Not while I'm in the room, thank you. How are you feeling otherwise, baby sis?"

I gave him a lopsided grin after I finished my bright tomato faced blush. "I've been better, but I'm okay. How are you?" I asked, tucking my locks behind my ear.

"Been better. I would have left you alone except it's two hours past breakfast and I didn't know you would be in here with him," Jett told him so it sounded like *that piece of sugarfoot.*

I smiled warmly up at my brother and kissed his cheek on my tiptoes. He embraced me, his arm like a steel bar across my back before letting me back down on my feet.

"Did that really happen, or was it some sort of heat stroke and I'm laying out in the desert right now half dead?" Jett murmured against my hair.

Slate scoffed again, "If you had been laying half dead in the desert, I would have confirmed the juice was worth the squeeze."

I drew back from Jett. "Everything is as back to normal as it's going to get," I said, talking over Slate.

Jett let me down and walked back to the doorway eyeing us warily before he left us alone. I sagged to the bed and fell back. Slate rose and walked to his pack displaying one of his finest attributes. It didn't have the same effect on me when he wasn't being arrogantly confident.

Light scratches covered his shoulders and forearms. There was no way I would have done that. I no longer felt confident about anything.

I crossed to him placing my hand gently on the small of his back and he turned around looking down his nose at me and I remembered how imposing he was when we first met. He hadn't lost his predatory gaze, or his ability to make me freeze, but I'd grown used to him and knew how tender he could be.

I ran my fingers tips along the scratches and watched as his skin prickled in response to my touch. "Did I do that?" I asked in a whisper afraid of his answer.

"Forget it, Torch. Pay it no mind," he said coolly, and I lifted my gaze as I healed him.

He displayed no emotion for me. I bent down to pick up my pack and slung it over my shoulder before heading towards the door.

"Your virtue is intact, Scarlett. We did not lay together," Slate murmured with his back to me.

I looked at the profile of his face, normally so arrogant I itched to slap it, but now it was blank.

Sleeping with Slate wouldn't be an event I'd forget.

"I WILL NOT LIE; you smell like Slate, and it is a strange mix on you. You're not the only one to find their way into unpredictable arms last night. Indigo stumbled in drunker than a skunk and I healed her this morning from several questionable scratches. I think her and Rikke did the deed, and don't get me started on our boy Gyps. Did you know he's been hooking up with those cheetah twins?" Jett chuckled, and I cringed as we ate breakfast around what was the bonfire last night.

"I was hoping he'd found a nice girl back home so he wouldn't suck into their web," I told him.

"No such luck, and I don't think he minds getting sucked," Jett waggled his eyebrows and I swatted his middle.

"EW! You're the grossest brother ever. Other brothers would have walked right back out if they'd seen their sister in such a compromising position, but you didn't so much as shuffle a foot!"

"I was in shock! I couldn't tell if it was ending or starting, or in the middle. I think I've done a good job of not mentioning that ring on your finger, and all the nights you've spent in his bed. Gods know, I have no room to judge. Do you care about him?" Jett asked as we huddled close together eating so the others wouldn't overhear.

"Of course I care about him. He didn't even try when he was taking care of me, he never so much as tried to kiss me until the last night. Then I knew I couldn't stay there anymore; it was getting too complicated."

"Oh, honey. It's more than complicated. Ash has been sending flowers every day that I have been throwing out. He has been trying to see you, but since you usually laid around in Slate's bed all day or went out with Slate until dinner, we didn't think it was a good idea to bring it up. Not that you would have spoken up about it, anyway. Slate told me you ended things and judging by your lack of a certain ring, I knew it was the truth. Complicated is a drastic understatement," Jett said as we headed out into the bright sunlight.

They gathered the others around the ashes of last night's bonfire and looked at me curiously when I sat. Slate sat beside Steel, legs outstretched and eating breakfast with his fingers.

Tawny beamed at me, "Scar, you look good. You're glowing or something."

Indigo turned to me and seemed to sport a similar glow, I arched an eyebrow at her and she blushed as Rikke demanded her attention once again. Jett had been right about those two.

My glow was inexplicable, simply wrestling around this morning with Slate shouldn't have given me a glow. It had to be my too realistic dream. Then again, I could still feel everywhere Slate's skin had touched mine when he dragged me naked across his chest, it wasn't like in the shower when I'd been sobbing, and he held me. This was completely different; I wasn't feeling as emotionally vulnerable. I still was, I knew, but he had helped heal me. He had helped me with nothing in it for himself. Didn't he? It wasn't another one of his conditionings like his training me to fight so I'd get used to his touch, was it?

Slowly, but surely, he had inserted himself until I wasn't fighting him with every breath. I welcomed his advances as often as I pushed him away. No, that wasn't true. I almost never pushed him away anymore. I went seeking him out now. Gods. He had conditioned me to him. Even now sitting a few people away I felt cool where his body heat should, er, would have been by my side.

"I had a juicy dream last night." I said sitting cross-legged beside her yanking myself out of my disturbing thoughts to talk about something other than Slate.

Keen had started towards me once I'd exited the adobe and sat gracefully beside me. He leaned over and I met his lips with a chaste kiss and ate from the plate Tawny passed me. Keen cocked his head.

"I did not mention it before because last time you told me it was not polite, but you are in season. Your scent has altered, unless you wished a cub or two," he said taking a piece of meat off my plate.

"She would've if I hadn't stopped her," Jett mumbled.

My eyes widened a bit, "Keen, have you ever seen a dark, *um*, hybrid with horns. Tall, really tall."

Keen smiled. "Has such a hybrid visited you?" he asked nonchalantly, and I narrowed my eyes at him.

"Once or twice. Why? Do you know what he is?" I shrugged.

He laughed and flashed me another feline smile. "I do. I am not surprised he found you. Was he well mannered?" Keen asked, and I blushed.

I nodded not wanting to answer that odd question. Depended on your definition of manners. Our hands were all over one another, but he had given me release before I gave him his.

"So... random question. Totally random. What happens, if say, a human and a hybrid conceive? Would it be even more of a hybrid, more human?" I asked and Keen chuckled, but I'd drawn the attention of those around me and the ever-alert Slate.

"Coming around to the idea of being my mate?" Keen teased, "It would either be human, or a hybrid, there is no in between. I cannot think of such a case, but it is common knowledge. Have you skipped mating and gone right to having my cubs, Scarlett?" Keen prodded and I laughed with a blush.

"Ah, you caught me," I joked.

Indigo leaned over to Tawny once everyone went back to their conversations.

"Do you have that special tea?"

Tawny nodded enthusiastically and pulled out a canister. Indigo nearly sighed in relief. She took a few scoops out a tea tin and heated water in a mug keeping her head ducked as to not meet the gaze of all the Judge McJudgersons.

"I'm not even going to ask," Jett murmured.

We camped in the red hills. Steel, Jett, Gypsum, and Slate checked for any rogues, and we set up camp. Indigo was making food with Tawny as I set out our rolls. Slate was back to being emboldened, every time our eyes met his smirks were lascivious. I cursed myself for being stupid and hormonal.

The men came back and gathered around the small fire eating the meal Tawny and Indigo prepared. Once everyone finished, we'd packed everything away for an early departure. I laid back on my roll hoping to get asleep right away, apparently even dreaming about coital-esque acts was exhausting.

"I feel you hovering," I said hoarsely without moving my arm from where it flung over my face.

"The Shadow Breakers have a mark that bonds us all together. You are the only person who feels me without the mark, Torch," Slate said as he sat down next to me.

"Tell me more about the bond with your lover. I am dying to hear about how close the two of you are," I said sarcastically, and he unfurled a roll next to mine.

"It must be activated. The one you feel for me is constant. There is a way to increase it, if you wished," He coaxed, and I rolled over to face him.

"Why would I want a closer bond to you?" I asked without adding my usual snap to it and pulled my arm down.

"You would feel what I feel when it activated, and I would feel what you felt when yours was," he rumbled as his as scanned mine.

To finally get in Slate's head? Unfettered access.

"Why?"

I felt like it was a trap, or I was some goal he was trying a new strategy on to achieve. "I have been spelling it out for you. Why are you so damn stubborn?" I raised my brows at him. "I want you. It is that simple. In my bed, by my side, and everywhere in between," he said, and I swallowed hard.

I scanned my mind for words I knew I had learned; they had letters in them and made sense most of the time — okay — sometimes.

"So, we're attracted to one another. You'd be hard pressed to find a girl not attracted to you. That's another problem. You've been with Lera for the better half of a decade, where do I fit into that scenario? If you think I would share, you're sorely mistaken. Lera's just one of your many lovers. Try to be practical," I urged, but I could tell in his eyes all he heard was that I wouldn't share him.

I sighed when he cupped my face. "Why did you ask about the hybrid again? Did I not tell you to stay away from it?" he breathed. "You should run in fear of him. The things he would do to you," he exhaled and I thought I heard a little tremor to it.

Tender Slate got me every fiddlesticking time. He softened those silver eyes trimmed in lush black lashes and I felt myself melt.

"It was just a dream. I don't think it was real."

"What did you dream?" he asked, arching an eyebrow.

I tried to shift my face away, but he held it. He gave me a lecherous grin that revealed brilliant straight teeth and I averted my eyes.

"So, it was one of those dreams. I must admit, I am disappointed it was not with me. What does the beast have that I do not?" he chided.

His hand slid through my hair, and I gave him a lopsided grin, "I am not talking to you about that dream."

"Humor me, Torch. Tell me now, and I will not pester you about it again."

I chewed the inside of my cheek as I thought about it. "I told you the time I met him, sort of. Even though he hurt me, I think it was an accident, like, he doesn't know his own strength." I tried not to blush thinking of the clawed hand that had slid against the apex of my thighs. "I know he doesn't judge me. How could he? He's part animal himself."

"You turn into an animal and an elemental?" He teased, and I rolled my eyes with a smile.

"You know what I mean. I can be myself, or how I want to be. Say what I want. Now it sounds weird telling you since it was a dream, but there's something about him..." I bit my lip and looked into Slate's eyes. "What?" I asked, trying not to sound defensive.

"You like him. You do not even know him, yet I can see in your eyes that you care about him," Slate rolled onto his back and I shifted uncomfortably on my roll.

I couldn't separate my feelings from them like some people could. Even though it was a dream, I had experienced pleasure with the beast man. I cared; hoping I'd see it again. It was weird and twisted; I knew all that, but I couldn't help it. If you squinted, it kind of looked like I missed it, er, him. I was certifiable.

"He is barghest," Slate murmured, and I popped up on my elbow to look down at him.

"You knew? What's his name? What's a barghest? Have you spoken to him before?"

Slate shut his eyes tight. "He is not forthcoming about his name; I have spoken to him in a sense. A barghest is a nearly extinct type of canine creature. Vicious and solitary," his tone was modulated, and I scooted up to his chest.

"You don't like him?" I asked.

He arched a dark brow as he opened his eye, "I was not aware that you cared about my opinion, Torch."

"Do you really think you are going to die young? Is that why you are the way you are?" I asked, and I registered the shock on his face, "I'm not blind."

"I will die young. There is no think about it. It is a prophecy, not some palm reader's prediction. I live how I please, Rabbit. Never forget it," Slate turned his back to me for the second time in a week and I didn't think it was possible to feel so cold in the desert.

"WAKE UP!" Slate roared.

I sprung up and away from the dying fire. Shadows cast gruesome masks over an already fearsome scene. Spider hybrids had surrounded us. Slate had rolled to my right. Indigo was crouched to my other side. I sprung my wrist blades. There wasn't a chance to look, but I could hear Steel and Tawny fighting behind me. I let my fire blaze creating a shield that stretched to Jett who was fighting with his two long seax against a Jorogumo. I turned to find Gypsum; he had a long seax out, his short seax deflected pinchers.

Indigo's arrows whistled into the flames targeting their eyes. Jorogumo behind the ones I had burned pushed the carcasses closer to get to us and pushed the flames. I let them go and called to air to catapult myself behind the first one to charge me springing my wrist blades. I landed behind it and slit its humanoid throat. Coming on my rear was another, I threw a knife from my belt into the center of its head.

Jorogumo were everywhere. The sun was dawning; the sky was bleeding red. I retreated to the camp and ducked and cut legs off a Jorogumo before stabbing it through the chest. Gypsum defended Indigo so she could send out arrow after arrow into the waves that came at us slicing and dicing the ones that came close.

Jett's two blades chopped through one spider faced creature after another like a hot knife through butter, he was lightening quick his blades flashing in the dying embers. Slate was darkness personified. Spider creatures died before they knew what had them. They were clumsy running right for us, we only had to sit back and wait, block, and thrust. I knew I had to help Steel and Tawny, I could hear Tawny's cry of frustration as she shot a nonstop flow of piercing arrows, but the Jorogumo never stopped coming. Steel's pronged spear wedged in the torso at his feet, and he was calling blades of air to slice through the endless line of attackers.

I was thankful for flexibility training and conditioning; I ducked under a swing of a spider's legs and brought my blade up, stabbing it through its stomach as I used air to bring me between Steel and Tawny.

"Torch. Get back here!" Slate bellowed when he saw me land by Tawny and Steel, leaving his side.

I ignored his cry as I blasted fire behind the ones Tawny and Steel fought giving them a chance to breathe. I could hear lightening crackle down around us striking the Jorogumo with precision. Slate.

We were losing. The thought came unbidden. There were too many of them. I heard Indigo cry out, which meant one had gotten past Gypsum. I raged. My skin burned, I felt myself light a fire from within and with a burst; I shifted. I was fire.

A red blazing torch with a white-hot core. I would not lose another loved one.

Heedless of the consequences and desperate to save my family, I charged unarmed into the melee and watched the Jorogumo try to fight me at first, but everywhere they touched scorched their flesh, leaving blisters and their skin sloughed off their limbs. Shrieks of burning Jorogumo followed my path of destruction. I fed on it like my flames eating up the oxygen.

I wondered how hot I could get. I stoked my internal flames until my skin burned white and the surrounding air blurred. The Jorogumo around me fled, and I dabbed at them first to test myself, and then ran once I realized I could burn *through* them. I used air to propel myself forward and pumped my arms as hard as I could as I aimed for the black and grey blurs of bodies of the Jorogumo.

The world was wind. I stole its atmosphere.

In moments, I could hardly stand. Jorogumo came for Jett's back and I blew it apart with a blast of air, my external flames unable to kindle. I dropped to my knees on the red clay covered in charred gore and nothing else. I struggled to breathe and blinked slowly as I tried to search out the survivors. I staggered kneeling and landed on my elbow.

"You have a death wish, Torch," Slate cursed before I fainted.

"There is nothing wrong with her. She is resting, it took a lot out of her. I have seen nothing like it," Steel's tone was astonished.

The putrid smell of burning Jorogumo assaulted my nostrils making me feel like gagging. Steel's voice was coming from further away and I tried to sit up. A big hand rested on my chest pinning me to the clay dirt.

"Let me up. The ground is digging into my back and it smells terrible," I said and opened my eyes to find a scowling Slate hovering above me.

"You do not have any clothes on. I suggest you stay put until we can search for something in the packs that were not fried to a crisp while you turned the entire area into an inferno."

Yikes. He was incensed and doing a poor job of reining it in. I looked down at my body which was laid out in the shade of one of the rolling hills and my head swam from the infinitesimal movement.

I nodded. I put nothing past Slate with what he thought was good for me. He ran a hand through his black wavy hair that fell loose around his bronze face.

"You smell terrible. Singed Jorogumo guts covers every inch of you," Slate said with a grimace and handed me my pack.

"Don't try to sweet talk me now that I'm naked. I'm going to rinse off before I put the clothes on, thanks," I said sarcastically, and Slate helped me to my feet.

My lips quirked as Slate held me around my waist to keep me from falling over while the others turned away. I was so filthy it wouldn't have mattered if they saw me.

"I will call. You will scrub," Slate said, blocking the others from me with his own body. I nodded and ran my hands over myself as Slate poured water down over me.

I needed to get blood and guts and charred remains off me and I couldn't call a lick to do it myself. Slate standing over me while a showered was frustrating but necessary to get the job done.

"Maybe you could do it over your shoulder or something instead of looking at me like that," I grumbled.

"Perhaps, but I will not," he said, not caring that I scowled at him.

I pulled on my spare outfit Brass recommended and I made a mental note to thank him. My body was having a hard time adjusting to the new powers I'd developed; it took too much out of me.

"Your sheath did not burn off, neither did your necklaces. They are enchanted by leshys like the sheath," he noted.

I looked up to him. "Leshy enchanted sheath? Slate," I exhaled heavily, "No wonder it cost a fortune."

Leshys enchanted items were rare, even I knew that. There was only one person I could think of that Hopper could get the items from, Styg. I hated the idea of Shadow Breakers making deals with that black market scumbag.

Slate gave me a rueful smile, "Your ring is enchanted too."

I looked down and saw that he was right. My Yggdrasil necklace I'd received upon entering Valla University was enchanted and hung against my chest. Interesting. I rubbed at the emerald ring trying to get the grossness off and felt Slate watching me. My fingers found the fetishes tied to my hair, and I was glad that I still had hair.

"I love the ring. If I had to pick one out for myself, it'd look just like this," I told him honestly, but he walked towards the group ignoring my comment.

I tried not to pout as I joined them. Their heads lifted as I approached, and I saw that Indigo's eyelids were heavy as if she'd had a lot of healing.

"What happened? Are you okay, Indi?" I asked, kneeling by her and was keenly aware that I wasn't okay either as I fell sideways onto my hip.

Slate grumbled from beside me.

Jett dryly pursed his full lips from where he squatted next to Indigo, "It would appear that you knew you could become a human torch; Indigo here is finding out that she can turn into a puddle."

Indigo blinked slowly at me with a sheepish smile. It drained her dry. If we were attacked now, we'd both be useless. Worse — the others would risk themselves trying to protect us.

"We need to get going. If there's more Jorogumo we're sitting ducks. Indi and I are liabilities," I got to my feet shakily and Steel grabbed me under my elbow when my ankle bent.

"Right. Why didn't I think of that? Oh yes, I did. Steel, Slate, and I are going to look for more Jorogumo. We might find the nest or portal they used if the Merfolk were right. We'll destroy it then Steel will have to go back to the Wemic and warn them. That was a lot over four Jorogumo this time. Tawny and Gypsum should be enough to defend you if there's a couple still lurking about."

Jett was in a foul mood. Tawny and Gypsum had experienced their first time killing another life, no matter that the Jorogumo had been trying to kill us. I could see the shock of it glaze their features. You did what you had to do; I knew I was the exception and not the rule. Everything that had life had a mother and a father, and I wasn't heartless. Someone might grieve the loss of these lives, but I also knew it wasn't me, and I wouldn't let them kill me.

"How are you guys?" I asked as the three men left us.

I had decided that sitting was preferable to standing. Standing, I needed someone to steady me. Tawny's wide hazel eyes swung to mine.

"We're all right. One of them grabbed Gypsum's sword arm, and he dropped his seax, but Indigo turned into...water and with your heat — it boiled," Tawny said with a hard swallow.

I winced, "Sorry. I thought things weren't going so well. I've only just found out I could — shift. One day, I was angry and poof. Just like that. I had told no one because there's been so much going on. Indi, are you okay?"

Indigo had her head lowered to her pulled up knees, I noticed grudgingly that her clothes seemed just fine. They had probably only gotten wet when she shifted not incinerated like mine.

Indigo's head nodded, "I'm so tired."

I scooted to Indigo's side and put my hand on her back, so she shifted to put her head in my lap curling alongside me. She was asleep within seconds.

Gypsum's long black hair was loose falling past his shoulders threaded with copper beads. It coated the sleeve of his arm in dried blood, and I sucked in a long air. Tawny looked good all things considered — dazed, but good.

We'd have to tell Alder what happened. There was no way he could avoid it being the ambassador to the Jorogumo. I wondered if I went to Ostara with him and I used my empath abilities if we'd as easily find the traitors as we did with the Merfolk. It was worth a shot even if the idea of going to the Jorogumo lands made me shiver.

I stroked Indigo's corn silk hair and lowered my head. I'd close my eyes for a moment, as I tucked my arm beneath my head.

"That doesn't look comfortable," Steel was standing near Tawny when I opened my eyes.

"Grab Scarlett, I'll carry Indigo," Jett murmured, and I was lifted.

Taking Indigo off my lap while removing me should have been more difficult, but we were both weak and limp like wet noodles. Jett and Slate lifted us in their muscled arms effortlessly and I pressed my cheek against Slate's hard chest.

They stopped for lunch once I stirred. Indigo was still out, and Jett carefully sat with her slim body leaning against his chest. Tawny made him a sandwich, and he ate over her sleeping form.

"Did you guys find the nest?" I asked, trying to ignore the fact that Slate had placed me between his legs to use his chest like a lawn chair.

Jett shook his head with his mouth full of bread and dried meat. "A portal, we destroyed it. Steel went ahead to the Wemic with Gypsum —"

"Which is sugarfoot because I could very well guard his back as well as any man," Tawny huffed.

A small smile played on my lips. I didn't like the dazed Tawny, spitfire Tawny was much better, even if it irked her.

Jett rolled his eyes, "Steel knows that. He wants you safe and Gypsum can fight in closer quarters. Your archery is good — great, but you're no good if Steel can't leave your side to make sure no one can stab you while you're nocking an arrow."

Tawny frowned at her sandwich. I knew how she felt.

"Give the man some peace of mind. That is why Jett and I are escorting the lot of you instead of Gypsum. Steel wants to make sure his wife and nieces get back safe. Your brother is a man. Let him act like it," Slate's chest nearly vibrated behind me with his deep voice.

Tawny's cheeks flushed. We babied Gypsum, we both knew it. For him to flourish in Tidings, we were going to have to back off. It was easier said than done.

"You called more than I would've thought possible, and I am probably one of the most powerful Guardians ever," Jett told me, he didn't sound like he was bragging. "Those Jorogumo surrounded us before they attacked. You've got to be more careful with that elemental business, baby sis. Your heat was eating the oxygen right out of the air, you could have suffocated us all. Luckily, Indigo is our own personal water supply," Jett said looking down at our still sleeping adopted sister, she could sleep anywhere.

I didn't mean to put anyone in jeopardy. It was a quiet, sullen lunch and ate in silence.

Walking proved futile. Slate scooped me up when I stumbled for the third time. I told him I could walk if he'd lend an elbow, but he said it'd only slow us down.

Our usual six-hour hike turned into eight. Tawny pouted the entire way back while they carried Indi and me like babies. Slate's gentle motion as we walked lulled me to sleep with the bright Thrimilci sun warming my face.

Being carried and crying all the time seemed to be my new favorite pastime.

When I awoke, it was early evening, and Indigo was walking on her own. We had reached the shimmering white roads of Thrimilci's town heart.

I patted Slate's hard chest feeling the belt of knives underneath the thin fabric. He swung his grey dubious eyes my way while arching a dark masculine brow.

"I have half a mind to take you straight to my bed, Torch," Slate purred making me blush furiously.

"You have half a mind if you think I'd go," I said pointedly and crossed my arms, "Put me down. I can't argue properly with you while you carry me."

"Keep your panties on. Wait, you are not wearing any. Are you?" Slate's full lips curled before he grabbed the nape of my neck.

Slate crushed his lips to mine while dropping my legs, and I flailed for a hold. He held me tightly to his chest at the small of my back with his other hand buried in my hair. His tongue slid into my mouth. Warmth flooded my system to pool in the lowest regions of my belly where it twisted and coiled making certain muscles pull and tug in anticipation.

Was I kissing him back? Oh, fiddlesticks! We'd stopped walking!

I pushed away hard not thinking of how I was inches above the ground and our lips broke with a loud inhale of air, but it caught my lower lip between his teeth, and I fell on my backside with a grunt. I touched my lip gingerly with the pads of my fingers gaping at Slate.

"By the Mother, save that crap for the bedroom. You're making a scene," Jett whispered harshly, and I looked around.

The shop owners were opening, and several had stood in their windows to watch what was happening.

"He bit me!" I protested and scrambled to my feet when Slate tried to help me up.

I sought refuge next to Indigo and eyed him warily as I licked at my bloody lip.

"You bit me first, Rabbit."

He pointed to a spot on his lip that appeared to be bleeding, but it could have been my blood. I turned around ignoring his allegation, I would remember biting someone hard enough to draw blood.

Tawny mouthed, *WOW*, and I rolled my eyes.

CHAPTER SIX

We retold the fight with the Jorogumo to Alder and the others and since Pearl and Sparrow were on the council of nine, an emergency meeting was called into session, and we had all gone to Valla U to tell the story. They had decided unanimously that the part about Indigo and I being elementals be left out. We agreed wholeheartedly, and Hawk, ever the dashing intellect asked us questions we couldn't possibly have answers to, which was any question really. We did not know how it happened, why it happened, or how it worked. Dominant emotions were a trigger, but that was all.

The entire family was going to the hearing. We left from the portal room in the Sumar palace to enter at the portal room in Valla University. It was a long room with a wall of solid arched intricately carved wood doors with sconces between each one fastened to the yellowed stone that the entire university comprised. Two huge tapestries hung at either end of the room, one of Mother Earth and the other was the Yggdrasil of the university's sigil.

We walked the enormous castle halls to its highest floor and to the double doors of the hearing room used by the council. A granite tiled path that led to the dais which sat the horseshoe shaped desk divided two sections of pews before with nine seats behind it.

I walked with Indigo and the others to the front pew and sat waiting for the rest of the council to arrive. Slate had reverted to keeping his distance, and he sat on the far side of the pew next to Hawk and Alder. Amethyst and Cerise were at the other end with Jett in the middle, and Tawny sat on my other side. Sparrow and Pearl were members of the council, they took their seats in the Sumar and Dagr spots.

Pearl wore her royal blue sleeveless robe that brushed the floor trimmed in gold and an emblazoned gold sun on the back. Hawk was the patriarch of the Sumar family and should have been the one sitting up there, but he preferred to stick to teaching American History at the University. Sparrow was the last Dagr since Tawny had taken her birth father's name. Sparrow's robe was sky blue with yellow trim in the same crushed velvet fabric of Pearl's with a solar cross on the back, a cross inside a circle.

Orion Vetr sat in the Vetr seat in a scarlet robe trimmed in white as pure as the freshly fallen snow from his homeland with an auseklis embroidered on its back, resembling four Ms with elongated legs that connected with one another like a compass. His hair matched the white trim of his robe, his bright blue hooded eyes had lost most of their bitterness since Tawny had welcomed him into her life with open arms. He hadn't aged as well as the other Guardians.

The ebony skinned man sat at the curve of the horseshoe with a black robe trimmed in both silver and gold and emblazoned with the three interlocking triangles on the black. Reed Tio, our great uncle, sat on his left with a coppery brown pompadour and trimmed mustache on his olive-skinned face. His dark narrow eyes had smile lines in their corners. His Tio robe was gold with silver metallic trim, the starburst sigil shimmered on the back.

The room filled with Guardians eager to hear the events that transpired on our trip. We were becoming known for our perilous excursions.

My grandfather strode down the center aisle, his emerald robe dragging behind him with gold trim and gold tree of life on its back with his arm looped through my grandmother's. She was reed thin with porcelain skin and dark hair pulled up in a bun like a ballerina. Wide brown eyes peered up beneath winged brows, her orange robe with purple trim hung loose around her slim shoulders a triceps on her back. Ruby Geol was the antithesis of her husband. Cygnus was a strapping older man with white-winged dirty blonde hair. Powder blue eyes peered from his stern tan face. Our father looked a great deal like him, but with the hard angles of his mother's face.

The last two council members arrived with an entourage. Cassiopeia Natt was rumored to have moved back into the Natt palace in Elivagar, leaving her husband in the Vetr palace. Her blonde hair was curled under brushing the shoulders of her navy robe trimmed in black, a star inside a circle was barely visible on the dark fabric. Her cool blue eyes were set straight ahead as she walked in with my stepmother.

One of the two Natt daughters of Orion and Cassiopeia, Delta, the statuesque blonde had a little wiggle to her walk as her cool blue eyes blazed in her fair beautiful face when she caught sight of our father sitting with Hawk. Delta was all legs and curves with a pouty mouth our half-brother had inherited. Sage strode at her side, tall and wiry, almost too pretty to be a man with blonde hair that was always combed perfectly like a gentleman's. Ash was with him. Those lightest green eyes met mine, and he flashed me his most charming grin. I let my lips quirk a little in acknowledgement and could almost feel the breeze when Tawny whipped her head around to glower at me.

I had found what Jett had really done with the flowers Ash had sent for the last two weeks. They were in the bedroom next to mine and it filled the room with a riot of colors and scents and with them were the most beautiful cards I'd ever read.

Willow Natt had her arm looped through her husband's, her creamy skin just as fair as her younger sister's with the same curves on a shorter stature. Willow had a mass of black chin length curls and violet eyes that she had passed to her son Sterling. He wasn't at the hearing, but his evil twin sisters were, Novaculite and Quartzite. Where one was blonde, the other was brunette, they were both short and Quartz was far curvier. Nova had more attitude with wide hazel eyes eerily like Tawny's.

Their father was Peak Haust, the patriarch of the Haust family in Mabon. He had a unique color eyes so light and bright green against his deep olive skin. Black waves were threaded with silver that looked handsome on the tall, powerful man and he smiled with full lips at others in the crowd. The only thing that wasn't perfect on his face was his nose that rounded a bit at the tip, but I thought it added character to an all too handsome face.

The energy in the room was buzzing with the power radiating from the Guardians contained into a small space. The hearing room filled, everyone wanted to know what we found on the trip. All the greater families were there, including my uncle Jackal and my father's uncle Canis.

Canis was barrel chested with a shock of spiky white hair; his blue eyes were hooded in his round face. There were a hundred different people I didn't recognize aside from a section of red heads announcing the Tio/Rot brood.

I'd taken extra care of my appearance; I pinned my hair up with a cascade of golden curls that brushed my back, and I wore my favorite blush chiffon flowing dress with a sweetheart neckline. I dusted my skin with a shimmering bronzer, and felt like my old self.

Reed called the room to order, and they began by calling Slate up to the high-backed black chair that sat before the curved dais. He sauntered to the chair with every eye in the room on him, including my own. He was glorious. I was suddenly jealous of all those eyes drinking him in as I was.

Which was immediately followed by me kicking myself in the head. Not in the literal sense but it was a close call.

Slate sat in the chair facing the council members and a hush fell over the crowd. Reed and the others had him describe what happened from the point where he woke until we split ways with Steel and Gypsum which included a very embarrassing retelling of how Indigo and I were carried like infants out of the desert while Tawny walked out on her own two feet.

They didn't bother questioning Indigo or me since we spent a great deal of time napping, but Jett and Tawny corroborated Slate's retelling. The Guardians were in an uproar about the portal gate that was destroyed, though the council had hoped it hadn't been destroyed so they could discover where it led but understood why they had. They sent another contingent out to the red hills and Alder was being sent with a separate contingent to the Jorogumo. Alder gave a curt nod to that, a mere jerk of his head with obvious frustration.

The hearing adjourned, and we hung back to wait for Pearl and Sparrow while they discussed what happened.

"Scarlett. Do you have a moment?" Ash leaned forward on the pew behind me, a gorgeous smile on his sensual lips and his celadon eyes glinted full of charm.

I turned and offered a muted smile. I didn't think I had to a right to be upset in the first place; it was the circumstances of which I'd found them that had hurt and everything after it. His eyes fell to my hand before I could respond.

"I did not realize you had any other suitors. He is a lucky man," Ash said coolly, and the smile fell from his handsome caramel face.

I caught his hand on the back of my pew. "I don't. No one else has asked for my hand. We can talk, if you wish," I told him not wanting to be the first one to get to my feet.

He turned back with a smile that made my cheeks tingle. His dark brows lifted a little in delight.

"Have I told you how beautiful you look yet?" Ash's eyes glittered and I fought the idiotic urge to titter.

"Not too bad yourself," Jett said with a wink angling in the pew.

I shot to my feet and scowled at Jett. "Thank you, Ash and thank you for all the lovely flowers. They positively fill the room with beauty," I said still scowling at Jett.

"As do you," Ash purred.

I came around the pew and he offered me his arm as he led me from the room. We walked a little way down from the door together when Ash stopped and turned me around to face him.

"Scarlett, my actions were deeply regrettable. It was not the time nor the place," he picked up my hand, "Crimson and I have history and I fell into old habits when I should have been by your side. I shamefully felt rejected and made poor choices. It should have been me at your side. I should have been the one to comfort you."

He had his moments. Being vulnerable didn't come easy to him like someone else I knew.

"You are not promised to another?" Ash said, glancing down at the ring again.

"No. It was a gift. He wants something different from what I want," I confessed and twisted at the emerald ring.

Ash closed his hands over mine, "What do you want? Marriage? Children? I want to give you both. I want to keep you safe and be your family. Be my wife, Scarlett Tio. I do not want any other."

He clasped my hands together as he stepped closer and searched my eyes. I looked up at him, the gorgeous man who had just proposed to me telling me everything I'd ever wanted to hear. It was much better than his first proposal, which was after an intense make-out session in his room followed by a ring.

My heart thundered in my ears as I scanned his face. Safety. Family. Marriage. Children. I'd never had so many heart strings pulled at once. My mom said to find love, but she said she married Lark before he knew she could fall in love with him. I could fall in love with Ash too if I'd let myself.

He slowly lowered his mouth, tilting it so he could fit it to mine. Ash's lips pressed to mine softly. An eternity had gone by since I'd broken things off. I was a different person with different needs. I needed to feel safe and to feel settled — stability. Ash wasn't one to make promises freely and not keep them.

Ash pressed against me deepening the kiss. His hand cupped my face, while his other slid around my waist.

"Something about you has changed — matured. Be mine, Scarlett." Ash pressed his forehead to mine peppering my lips with kisses as if we weren't in our university hallway.

"I feel different." I breathed, and he took my hand between us and took off the emerald ring switching it to another finger and slid on the amethyst tear dropped engagement he'd given me in a gold setting with three marquis cut diamonds.

"Sleep on it. I will come calling tomorrow, and you can give me your answer. Hawk has already given his consent, now all I need is yours. I have much more than anyone else can offer you," Ash whispered huskily, and I nodded. "Scarlett, I am happy to wait until we are wed to prove myself to you if it puts your fears to rest."

It did. He seemed to sense it.

Ash smiled slow and seductive and kissed me again, cupping my face with both of his hands. I placed my hands on his wrists as I nervously giggled; he was getting carried away.

"Kissing and smiling? I believe the lovebirds have reconciled." Jett said sarcastically from the doorway of the hearing room.

My family had exited the hearing room with the other greater families who were now pouring out into the hall around us. Ash turned and wiped my gloss off his lips with a thumb before sliding his arm around my waist.

"A bump in the road was all, but we are back on the right track," Ash flashed a cocky smile at Jett and then turned to kiss my forehead. I couldn't resist when he was being genuine.

Alder stepped to the forefront and eyed my hand. "I understand you have already arranged a marriage contract with Hawk. I will review it tonight," he said in a cool guttural tone.

Ash didn't falter, "Of course. I asked for her hand some months ago, I am a patient man. She has agreed to give me her answer on the morrow. I will be over for dinner to discuss any issue you may have. Until then," Ash turned back to me and gave me a lingering kiss on my cheek before meeting with his parents to leave.

I stood alone facing my family and some seriously disapproving looks. "What?" I asked defensively and shrugged.

Slate pushed through the throng, and I thought maybe he'd finally lost it, but he walked right past me as if I didn't exist. Indigo and Tawny met me and linked their arms through mine before leading the way back to the portal door.

We gathered in the informal dining room for lunch. It's high domed ceiling started out dark blue at the walls and faded to white at the peak of the dome with white birds painted in the segments between curved white beams trimmed in gold. The walls were predominantly white but with smaller subtler mosaic patterns in teals and blues.

In the center of the room was a rectangular table that sat sixteen made of a light-colored wood with delicately carved and painted in golds and silvers that was made by the trolls. The chairs were the same type of wood and upholstered in heavy gold and silver embroidery on white fabric. Lanterns hung from the walls in copper, blues, and gold in with intricately shaped metalwork framing the glass.

I sat in my seat eating lunch, looking at the blue morning glory vine Pearl grew on our first day there. I was doing nothing with my bachelor's in English. *Sure*, my mom had told me after we arrived all my loans were paid off, but I had pushed myself at neck break speed to get my bachelor's degree and I was a knife fighter. My life had thrown me a curve ball I hadn't seen coming.

"I had planned on saving this excursion until your birthday but seeing as tonight is likely your last truly single night of your young life, we should go out." Jett said jutting out his jaw arrogantly.

"Out where?" I asked skeptically, eyeing my brother.

"Out to the U.S." he smiled brighter seeing my reaction, "You can dress in jeans or something and we'll go to a movie, maybe dinner after. Steel will be back by tonight. We'll wait for him and Gypsum before we go. What do you say?"

"Um, let me think? YES! Oh, Jett it's the perfect birthday present. Thank you," my nose tingled as I grew weepy. It couldn't be helped.

"It's just a movie, baby sis," Jett said hoarsely, and I giggled as I wiped my tears.

"Ugh, I'm so sick of crying," I laughed again.

"Scarlett, where did you get that ring?" Sparrow had grown still and looked at my hand I'd used to wipe my cheek.

I looked at my rings, there were only two on it. "Which one?" I asked stupidly, of course she knew which one was from Ash.

"It was my mother's," Slate rumbled without looking up and my mouth dropped open.

I shut it, then opened it again. What possessed him to give me his mother's ring! My family's eyes swung from me, to Slate, and back again. I was thunderstruck.

Had the ring meant more than I thought it did? He said he wanted me; he wanted me to stay in his room, but he said nothing of marriage or kids. On the contrary, he said he didn't or couldn't have either.

Sparrow was waiting for another response. "Impossible," she said as she pushed back from the table and crossed behind Alder and Indigo to see the ring for herself.

She grabbed my hand high above my head, so I winced, and she inhaled sharply as she shook her head. Pearl and Hawk rose to their feet.

"Please, excuse us. Alder, Slate, would you both join us upstairs for a private discussion?" Pearl said, turning her emerald eyes on Slate, he nodded once and pushed to his feet.

"Should I come, too?" I asked in confusion.

"No," Slate's single word caused me to sink.

Alder was watching him closely as he crossed the room then followed him out. I did not know what was going on and I didn't think I was the only one.

"Did Slate propose to you?"

Tawny jumped all over me the second they turned the corner into the hall.

"By the Mother, Tawny. Couldn't you have waited until they were out of earshot?" I scolded, and she waved dismissively before giving me a look. "Does Slate seem like the married with kids type?" I countered.

"I know for a fact he would never propose to any woman no matter how delusional he was now. What did he ask you?" Jett asked, leaning back in his chair and crossing his corded arms across his chest.

I shifted in my carved cream upholstered seat. "It's none of your business." I mumbled, unable to meet their eyes. "I tried to give the ring back, but he said it's mine now."

"Scarlett Tio, tell us now," Tawny slapped a thin hand on the tabletop and Cherry jumped, "Sorry."

I rolled my eyes. "He wanted me to — I don't know, move into his room. He said he'd only be with me or something," I chewed on my lip self-consciously with my eyes on my plate.

I looked through my lashes at them and watched as Jett dry washed his face, "Tell me honestly, no judgement. Did you sleep together?"

I leveled my eyes at my brother. "It's none of your business," I said without inflection.

"Your secrets are safe with us. I am your sister-in-law as much as Ash's cousin and it's not like Ash doesn't have his own skeletons," Amethyst said, smiling a broad reassuring smile at me.

"Thanks, but *if* I had, that'd be mine and Ash's business — or Slate's if I had," I conceded.

"That's a no," Jett sighed in relief. "Then there's a chance he'll get over this...this whatever it is. Did you do something else with him besides what I saw?" he asked almost scientifically, and I blushed to my toes.

Tawny knew because Steel had told her about the journey from the Merfolk, but otherwise I'd not told a soul. The only other person who knew was Solder, the shop owner from the Armored Armoire. Indigo blushed next to me knowing I hadn't snapped a reply for a reason, that and I couldn't stop fidgeting in my chair.

"In an effort to soothe his wounded ego, I'll tell you so you can talk sense into him. He said if I stayed in his bed, that he would consider that ascent. I left it, offer denied. What happened in the adobe was — hormones and he keeps sneaking into my bed at night — picking the lock. Maybe have this talk with him," I snidely offered.

Jett cocked an eyebrow at me waiting for a reply, "You are the only one out of the two who might listen. You'd have to be blind to not notice how badly he wants you. I don't know if it'll get better or worse now that you're off the market. When you started dating Ash, he went on a bender of fighting, drinking, and —"

"I got it!" I snapped, "He'll have to get over it because I've already decided. I'm going to marry Ash either this spring or next summer. I did something... physical with Slate, but those Merfolk drugged me. It doesn't count."

Jett slapped the table. "Steel knew they gave you rousen! Why weren't we told?" Jett was shouting.

"Um, I don't know, babe. Probably because they knew you'd react this way. She's fine, Slate was with them, and he knows how to take care of someone on rousen." Cherry placated Jett, and the red left his tan cheeks.

"Non're said it was a half dose. He wanted Steel to leave me there, Sear're found out what really happened because I was being...weird." I told them and smiled weakly at Indigo who returned my smile.

"The prince of the Merfolk drugged you!" Jett rubbed his face like he was trying to wipe the slate clean. "You can never go back there. Non're will not let you walk away from him again. Freya's burly boar!" Jett cursed.

"Jett!" Amethyst sounded scandalized, but Indigo giggled covering her pink lips with a hand.

"Sear're saved you. I doubt the king wanted you to leave either. Dion're has not had a human woman in some time, or if he has, she was not from a greater family or engaged to the Prime's nephew who might be Prime himself one day. Gods, he certainly has had no one as pure blooded as you Scarlett. You might as well have painted a target on your —"

"I get the picture," I told him in a stilted tone.

The subject appeared to be closed and I couldn't have been more thankful. My love life or lack thereof was not what I wanted to discuss ever.

Slate appeared in the doorway and the silence was deafening. Neglecting to tell me the ring was his mother's seemed like an awfully big deal to slip his mind.

"Pearl wants you three to meet her in her room," Slate rumbled, returning to his chair.

I hesitated and searched for words. He'd repeatedly told me it was mine now, but I hadn't known the significance.

Indigo looked at me, and we looked at Jett who shrugged.

Sometimes you can see things coming. Other times, you're so self-involved or consumed in your own bubble that things drop on you like an anvil crushing everything you thought you knew.

We meandered our way through the sprawling palace until we found Pearl's room in one turret of the palace. I'd only been there once, so we relied on Jett to steer me. We reached her exquisitely carved double doors with a blazing sun the center piece, half of which was on each door. Jett swung the doors out and revealed Pearl's room.

Our bedrooms were big, but Pearl's room was sprawling. Her massive white bed sat under a recessed arch that was backlit. Ivory silk fabric draped on either side of the massive bed. She had an alcove that held a flight of stairs which led to the top of one of the many domed turrets of the palace. She gestured to an oversized cream chair that felt like cushy gel when I sank into it. I doubted a comfier chair existed.

Indigo stood in the entrance in a cream flowing dress like the chiffon flowing fabrics most woman wore in Thrimilci. Her hair was parted to the side and fell to her waist, her tanned skin looked darker in the cream dress and made her light blue eyes pop. When she smiled the beauty mark on her right cheek lifted prettily, but then everything Indigo did was done with a measure of grace that made you want to hate her, but it would be impossible. She was one of the sweetest people you could ever meet. She was the first person I met outside of Ash. I had immediately liked and so asked her to be our fourth roommate at Valla U with Cherry, Tawny, and me.

I scooted over and patted the spot next to me. Indigo was in Ash's crowd. I'd hung out with her every lunch period and outside of my classes in our room. She had even been a bridesmaid in Tawny's wedding, and she would be in mine as well.

Jett stiffened when he saw Alder sitting next to Pearl on the cream chaise as he sat on the edge in the twin to the chair I was in. Alder's light blue eyes followed his every step.

Pearl wore a dusky blue dress that flattered her voluptuous figure and smiled when we sat. Alder sat rigidly next to Pearl. He wore a deep blue short-sleeved jerkin with silver clasps that buckled in up to its short collar. Not conducive to Thrimilci's hot weather, it was what people wore in Ostara where he was from. His tan pants were snugly fit like everywhere else and tucked into deep brown leather boots that were polished to a shine. He wore a silver buckle of the tree of life in bloom, the sigil of the Var, on his belt.

Jett stared straight ahead; the two men could not have looked more alike.

Alder could've passed for early thirties. Guardians lived twice as long as humans. They matured younger, and their aging slowed at around twenty. The unfortunate side effect of that was that the women could only birth until about age twenty-six, so when most people were living their college years, Guardians were busy having as many kids as possible, and it still wasn't enough.

We were a dying breed. Guardians married humans from outside of Tidings, but it didn't seem to help. The Guardians were attacked almost twenty years ago and the university that trained them was closed in the aftermath. It reopened nearly four years ago, and people were in a rush to be proven tried and true Guardians.

You could always leave Tidings and live like a myopic. A few provosts had before taking their place at the university.

A tribe from Elivagar called the Crathode had a band of rogues who went by the name Red Kings. They were crab/human hybrids or Crathode, and they attacked an induction ceremony that welcomed all the new tyros to Valla University for Guardian Mastery that all the citizens could attend, and it ended in a massacre. They killed hundreds of unarmed Guardians despite their abilities to call. Suspicion had run rampant, and it cut the five islands off from one another except for Valla's town portal. Portal doors were locked tight, and marriages were few and far between resulting in even fewer children. It went on for years until Moon Straumr's only daughter was old enough to attend Valla U. Amethyst Geol was the apple of Moon's eye and Jett's wife.

Tidings was in the beginning stages of repair.

Indigo smiled and her slim figure sat down next to me. Pearl smiled at the three of us and patted Alder's hand that rested on his powerful thigh. Alder swallowed visibly before starting and I shot Jett a look that he returned. What we they all so nervous about?

"Over twenty years ago, Wren and I had a son. I was there when he was born — along with Lark. We stopped seeing one another when Delta announced her pregnancy with Sage," Alder said in his deep guttural voice.

Sage. My half-brother and Ash's best friend, who happened to despise me for no reason. My half-brother was raised with Indigo after my father adopted her.

I saw Jett go even stiffer. In the eyes of Jett, our father had abandoned our mother and us. It was a father's duty to watch over his children and he had let Jett stay with our grandmother while they took me to Chicago with our mother, Hawk, Sparrow, and Tawny. There was no bigger failure in Jett's eyes.

Alder didn't so much as bat a lash as he continued, "On the night of the massacre was the next time I saw Wren; it was once she had married Lark. I saw her sitting at the Sumar table from where I sat at the Var's, and she held a baby girl in her arms. I thought she was his. Wren and I met outside the tent later carrying the baby girl. She handed the girl to me and told me she had given birth again — that they were mine. That was when the Crathode attacked."

I watched Alder swallow hard. Horrors of the past replayed in his mind's eye.

"I went back in and did what I could to find Wren when she ran, but the area that the greater families sat in were crawling with Crathode. Delta had Sage in her arms as she emerged from the tent bloodied. I knew Lark loved your mother and would not let harm befall her. I took the baby girl, Sage, and Delta into the university and went back out, but I couldn't find Wren or my other son."

Alder looked at Jett whose face had gone red. Neither of us had heard the story before and I noticed Indigo was crying. I wrapped an arm around her as I knit my brows at my father. Indigo leaned against me as she cried.

Alder watched us intently as he continued, "At the last masquerade, I saw Wren again. I thought she had died nineteen years beforehand. I had never received word from her of any sort. Then she explained that on that night how she and Hawk had gone to Chicago taking with her our other daughter and that was why she had returned, so her children could reunite and attend Valla U together. All those years while I thought she and my son were dead having no knowledge of another daughter. While Wren had to hope I had saved our other daughter. You see, Wren gave birth to twin girls the day before Samhain."

Jett was looking at Indigo and me. I sat there a moment trying to absorb the information. My mother had two daughters. I was a twin. I replayed all the times my mother interacted with Indigo, how weird she had been hugging her all the time and paying special attention to her whenever she got the chance. Pieces of my life fell into place in a puzzle much larger than I had ever known.

Indigo cried all the harder against me and I looked at Pearl's emerald cat eyes, to Alder's hard blue, then to my brother's wide, disbelieving turquoise eyes. I opened my mouth and then shut it.

"Darling, Indigo is your older twin sister, though Indigo is only older by a few minutes," Pearl told me after a protracted gaping silence.

I blinked slowly and wondered why Indigo, my sister, was crying. She had known. That much was clear.

I rubbed her back again and Jett handed me a black kerchief to give to her. I needed something to do. Whenever I tried to grasp what they were telling me, it slid through my fingers like sand.

Pearl picked up where Alder left off, "On the night of Tawny and Steel's wedding, Indigo was told who her birth mother was, and she wanted to meet her. She was to go up to the room and was to meet with Wren so they could have time together before we told the rest of you during harvest break. That was why Indigo was in the room that night. She did not know it was Wren."

Pearl finished, and I watched as emotions passed through her eyes. She could control their projection, but not keep the emotion off her olive face.

"I thought you tried to kill yourself when you jumped off the balcony. I'm so sorry, Scarlett. If I hadn't been meeting her, she would never have been up there," Indigo sobbed.

Her shoulders shook violently as she gave up all pretense and clung to me.

It was the biggest *ah-ha* moment of my life. I couldn't figure out why Indigo had been crying so much, and why she'd been so strange lately, like she didn't know how to act around me anymore.

"Indi, that's crazy. Whoever pushed her would have found a way to... accomplish their task. I would not kill myself. I had to get down there," I squeezed my eyes shut and reopened them.

My muscles wouldn't do what they were supposed to, and I felt like my face was twitching. I had a sister. *Our* mother had passed away. I was a twin. Jett was encircling us in his arms, and his eyes gleamed with tears unshed. I didn't think he would let them fall in front of our father, but he would always take care of his sisters.

"Now I have two of you to worry about," Jett said in a strangled tone and Indi laughed as she sobbed, "I did not know."

Indi had raised her head and blown her nose; I studied her face. She looked like our father. She had all his coloring, but she had the thin frame of his mother Ruby Geol. I'd only met the woman a handful of times. While she didn't look like our mother, she had the warm quality our mother had that drew you in and made her impossible to dislike.

Jett, Indigo, and I sat like that for a while until I glanced over Jett's head to see our father sitting stoically by himself. Pearl had left the room on tiptoes, so we hadn't even noticed she was gone. This was the hard part. The first step. Tidings men were so prickly about how men should act, I knew it was deeply ingrained in my father. Jett had skirted it being an affectionate guy, but it wasn't so easy for Alder.

I pulled away from my siblings and stood to cross to the chaise where my father sat. I sat down next to him. He was an imposing figure. My mother had been as tall as Tawny, and dwarfed by the man who was a foot and a half taller than her. Luckily, I had spent a great deal of time with giant men lately, so I didn't hesitate to throw my arms around him and kiss the hard plane of his cheek, holding tight until he relaxed under the weight of my innate love for my father.

It took Indigo joining us for him to take a deep breath and return our hugs. Jett sat down next to me but made no move to embrace our father. That relationship would take a great deal of time to repair before it would blossom.

There was something so deeply sorrowful about my father that it must have taken years to cultivate and had only recently been visible from the outside. The four of us sat together in Pearl's room as Indigo worked as a mediator between my father and I. Jett, while present and listening, didn't partake in the conversation. I mostly asked questions about my mother, his side of how they met, a story I'd heard vaguely for the first time recently.

I couldn't help how much I cried, but at the end of our time in Pearl's room, Alder felt comfortable enough to draw me close to him offering me a shoulder to cry on. I couldn't imagine how hard it must have been for him.

"Why did you both move here?" I asked, finally getting my crying under control.

"Delta realized that Indi was my biological daughter, and I did not want her taking it out on Indi. I was not sure if she would, but Sage might have. He has cause to be angry with me. I have disappointed my sons it would appear, but I did what I thought was best," Alder said, casting a side glance at Jett who stared at the floor.

Yes. It was going to be quite a while.

"Does that mean you're getting a divorce?" I asked, confused.

Alder pressed his full sculpted lips together, "Guardians do not get divorced. We separated. She is free to see whom she wishes, but not to remarry."

We lost time in Pearl's room, and I supposed it was dinnertime. Pearl asked that I stayed behind so we could speak, and I gave Jett a shrug as he left, taking Indigo's arm and looping it through his. Alder walked behind them like a living, breathing statue.

I walked back into the room with Pearl and noticed a painting I hadn't before. A silver-haired man with dark eyes that looked very much like Hawk with a goatee stood before what I recognized as the balcony over the waterfall.

"Flint," Pearl said standing next to me, "Your grandfather. He was a great man. He is the reason I am still here today. The night of the massacre, he saved us by sacrificing himself. Some families were not as lucky. The Haust's lost their entire family, only Peak survived with his wife and kids. Moon lost his wife; he has never been the same," she sighed deeply, lost in her memories, "There is something I need to give to you, darling. I almost gave it to your mother, alas her path went in a different direction."

She rose gracefully to the painting of Flint, and I sat in the sofa chair. She flipped the painting towards her and behind it, opened a safe. She took a small rectangular box from it and closed the safe. Returning the handsome silver-haired man's portrait to its previous position.

She sat back down on the chaise looking burdened, her eyes sorrowful, "I expect you have had ample time to get to know something of our Slate, yes?"

I didn't like where it was going, but I nodded anyway.

"Our Slate is a very special young man. He has taken on a substantial burden," she paused a moment seemingly to collect herself, "It is a rare gift like our empath abilities. He had a prophecy — it is coming true." She smiled warmly and patted my hand. I had a feeling it was about me.

"It does not bode well for Slate. Prophecies are tricky things; they do not always mean what you think they do. I hope that is the case with this one. In any case..." Pearl waved her hands through the air to erase the subject.

She opened the box, and in it sat a round stone pendant. It was the size of a dime with a long silver chain. She crossed to me and pulled the chain down over my head. It dangled off the shape of my chest, so I tucked it in, so it nestled within.

"I'm sure you have heard my parents were brother and sister?" I nodded. She didn't look surprised, "She had something like amnesia, they said. Those types of diseases rarely afflict our kind. She lived with them for fifteen years. Then they told her she had to go back. She eventually found her way home and married my father. She had this pendant with her. Before she passed on, she gave it to me and told me I would know what to do with it, to pass it down to my daughter, and her to hers."

"And now you're giving it to me? That can't be right," I said disbelieving.

Pearl smiled, "You are destined for great things, perhaps difficult, but great."

When I got to my rooms, Indigo, Cherry, and Amethyst were digging through my boxes of clothes I hadn't bothered unpacking from Chicago but didn't have the heart to toss out. Tawny had brought even more clothing and boots on my chaise lounge.

Cherry squealed and stepped out of the closet, "This isn't my color, but you will look so hot in this. OH! With these!"

I looked at the clothes she tossed me and laughed as I noticed she'd also thrown me underwear. "No one is going to see these you realize," I told her.

"Maybe you'll get lucky. It is your last night single is you plan on signing your marriage contract tomorrow. A brief fling hurts no one," Cherry's cobalt eyes glittered at me, and Amethyst bumped her hip.

I shook my head and stepped into the pink and white lace thong she'd picked and fastened the matching push-up bra around me. She'd picked an olive-green long sleeve cashmere mini dress and a pair of tan sheath boots. I pulled it over my head and down over my hips before sitting on the couch and tugging on my boots. Since I spent a small fortune on the cashmere dress, I'd been too afraid to wear it in case I spilled something on it. It was short, but long enough to keep things interesting.

I stood up and ran my fingers through my waves of hair and held out my arms. "You've dressed your doll; how do you like it?" I asked, pulling at the low scoop neck.

"I'd do you," Cherry said, and Tawny laughed when she saw my reaction. Tawny and I said that to each other, but we usually prefaced it with if I was a man, Cherry needed no such preface.

We headed down to the portal door, it's blue starry lights reflecting off the mirrored flooring.

Tawny couldn't keep her hands off Steel in his dark blue knit cardigan and blue and white plaid shirt, hunter green corduroy jeans hung off his hips. His smile beamed when he saw how much Tawny liked it. I couldn't believe it myself. Jett must have kept a stock of modern clothes; he loved all things American. He wore grey camouflage chino pants and a black military style shirt with the sleeves rolled up. His smug smile let me know everything I needed to know about who had styled the guys.

Gypsum was in his usual slouchy black hat and red plaid shirt under a grey hoodie with jeans. It felt good to see him in his old clothes, although he must have bought new ones because he was so much taller and broader than he was a year ago.

Slate in distressed denim.

I wondered if a nicer fanny pack had ever been squeezed into a pair of jeans. He wore a black fitted shirt that formed to his hard muscles beneath and a leather jacket with motorcycle boots to top off the ensemble. Freya's burly boar. The man was every woman's fantasy come true, and that was with his clothes on. His black hair hung loose in waves to his shoulder blades, it toppled over his right side, and I noticed he didn't have any beads or fetishes in it, and he ran a hand casually through his long locks and flashed me an arrogant grin.

Dear Gods, how long had I been standing there staring?

"You are very welcome," Jett whispered into my ear, and I blushed.

Sometimes it was like he was as confused by Slate as I was.

I couldn't stop pulling at the hem of the dress and then up at the low scoop neck. "Stop fidgeting, Torch," Slate rumbled, looking much too satisfied with himself.

I scowled at him as I crossed my arms to keep them from moving and his eyes flashed silver at my chest. I was positively pouring out of the dress, so I dropped my arms.

"Looks like you're my date for tonight." Indigo linked her arm through Gyps's, he gave her a dimpled smile.

"I guess I could do worse," he said, and Indigo gave him a light punch on his shoulder as he chuckled.

I made small talk with Indigo as a bright light let us know something or someone was coming through the portal. Right on time, Hawk pulled in a big silver SUV. Jett was going to drive, and Slate sat shot gun.

Hawk gave me a hug before I'd piled in. "Congratulations, Scarlett. Your mother would be proud of you," I'd almost completely forgotten about the Mjolnir.

"Thanks." I said trying not to get choked up.

"I wanted to have a minute to discuss this friendship with Cordillera Blomi," he said edging closer with his head down to meet my eyes, "You're an adult and I can't tell you who you are friends with, just—be wary. I know what she's involved in. She betrayed my mother's trust, she is ruthless."

"Consider me warned. I stay as far from that woman as I can," I smiled at him and he returned it.

"I worry," he confessed, and I waved goodbye.

Jett reversed out the portal door. It was already nighttime in Bristol, RI. It was one of two portals in the US, the other was on the west coast.

I could hardly sit still; I was so excited to be back. The last year had been a bad dream, and I finally woke up.

Jett drove down the dark roads till we reached the town of Seekonk. It sounded like the sound a donkey would make. He pulled into a theater, and I had to look at the faces I was with to bring me back to reality. I was bouncing in my seat; I wanted to get out and smell pollution, jump on the asphalt, eat artificial butter.

Slate walked alongside me into the theater to my surprise. Indigo and Gyps were acting silly skipping with their arms linked. I was so happy to be back, but it had a weight I hadn't expected. My mom's death became incredibly real there. I kept feeling the cry creep up my throat as I held my breath to fight it back down.

The guys let us pick the movie. In the small theater, there weren't many choices, so we went with a comedy. I needed to laugh at something nonsensical.

Slate had never been to a movie, I tried not to enjoy myself too much because I one point, I'd been new to all things Tidings. It was a date. I was on a date with Slate, and it was confusing my emotions in the extreme. I glared at a gaggle of girls giggling and staring at him while we got popcorn. Had they never seen a man be- fore?

Yes, that was what one looked like. Not yours. Back off.

The girl behind the counter batted her lashes at Slate and I thought I could hear my teeth grind.

I shoved him aside with a hip. "Two waters and a large popcorn," I ground out, and she nodded absently as she sauntered away never taking her eyes off Slate.

He arched an amused eyebrow down at me and I turned around crossing my arms. Did these women not see me standing there?

Jett sat in the back with the girls, Steel and Tawny sat behind us and Indigo and Gyps a few seats over to give us some space once we got into the theater. I took a deep breath and counted when a pair of girls spotted Slate and the empty seats next to him. They walked over, happy as you please, and sat down beside him giggling. I looked up at Tawny who had probably been glaring at them from the moment they walked into the theater obviously on a mission to meet men, and then arched a brow at me.

No, ma'am.

"Switch seats with me," I whispered to Slate, and he did an annoying brow arch looking too amused.

"What for, Torch?" he asked with a lip curl, and I could feel the heat rise in my cheeks.

I narrowed my eyes. I would never admit to what I did next, but I called. A tiny, itty-bitty spark, that started the girl's purse on fire nearest Slate. She jumped, spilling her pop all over herself and the seat dousing the flame out as well.

Whoops. She cursed and her and her friend shucked off. I sat back with a hint of a contented smile and ate my popcorn.

"What was that?" Slate asked.

"Spontaneous combustion. I hear it's going around," I told him, facing the screen.

When the movie was over, we hung back and let the crowd pass so we could leave with the rest of the group. When the first girl brushed by Slate rubbing her chest on his arm, I blinked unable to react.

I knew what Slate looked like. I had eyes. He wasn't built like the average man, none of them were. The Mother picked guardians for their strength and beauty when the first Leshys gave them their ability to call the elements. She did a darn good job.

Regardless, the floozies needed to keep their eyes, hands, and other appendages to themselves. When I saw a second one coming, spotting my escort, I stuck out a foot so after she rubbed her ample bosom over his forearm needing to squeeze past even though there was three feet of room ahead of him; she face-planted on the sticky theater floor. I chuckled to myself and when I turned back around, Slate was giving me an unreadable look.

Jett's cheeks flushed as we left the theater, and I was determined not to know. Steel and Tawny are holding hands gazing adoringly at one another after them. Gyps and Indigo are continuing their silliness and Slate and I were still not really talking or touching, but we'd been together, and I didn't know what to do with the foreign emotions I was feeling.

"Sugar lips?"

I froze, my heart rising to my throat.

Only one person on the planet called me sugar lips. He'd taken me out of our senior prom and into the limo on our one and only date. What was he doing in Massachusetts?

I turn around and came face to face with Chris. I hadn't seen him since the night before we moved to Tidings, and he had tried to fumble his way into my panties. We had been good friends once, now my cheeks stung at the sight of him. We had done things on our prom night that had left me feeling less than stellar.

He was taller than he was a year ago and broader, college football had done him good. As his baby blues looked me over, he ran a tan hand through his chestnut hair. He dressed like a frat boy with his white polo collar popped and a shirt that matched his eyes underneath. He'd known me as a gangly teenager, and I had been so flattered when the captain of the football team had asked me out.

"Chris," I said trying not to use any inflection.

I heard Tawny gasp behind me.

"Wow, sugar lips. Have you been working out? You look...wow. You always looked good, but now..."

"Thanks. Still playing football, I see. You look good, too," I said and hated that it was true.

He flashed me a dreamy smile that used to make my heartbeat faster and slower at the same time. "What are you doing on the east coast? You live here now? I transferred colleges, first string now," he said with pride.

"Yeah, on the coast now. That's cool. It must psych the coaches," I told him and I found I was happy for him.

He rubbed his full lips together and looked nervous, "I tried to call you, but it always goes straight to voicemail. You moved, I found out. I wanted to apologize for... last time. Maybe I could make it up to you. Take you out to dinner?"

I felt a flurry of butterflies in my stomach. Chris was from a lifetime ago; I was getting engaged. I felt an arm sling around my shoulders and watched as Chris's eyes narrowed. Dear Gods, Slate!

"So, this is your boyfriend?" Jett gestured with a thumb to Chris, and I cringed. Chris's dreamy eyes glittered, and his permanent smirk broadened to reveal a megawatt grin that had made girls throw themselves in his path. I would know.

"My brother. Jett. This is Chris. He was my prom date."

Chris offered his hand, "I didn't know you had a brother. You two look like twins."

Jett waggled his eyebrows. "He's pretty, baby sis. You sure have a type, don't you?"

What was that supposed to mean?

"Goodbye, Jett." I said shoving him off only to be replaced by Tawny.

Chris's cheeks reddened. "Oh hey, Tawny. What's up. I was just talking to our girl here. Um, sorry you know, for calling you a cock block last time we chilled. I was wasted. When I drink, I know I am a dick. I was just asking sugar lips if she'd let me make it up to her. Take her out since we're both on the east coast now. You out here too?" he asked, looking edgy.

What Tawny lacked in height she made up for with mouth, "Her name is Scarlett. You had your chance —"

"Hey man, I'm Steel," Steel interrupted his little spitfire wife and offered his hand to Chris who was being bombarded by my relatives, while his friends hit on girls working behind the concession stand.

"What's up?" Chris said, shaking his hand.

"We should be going. It was good to see you again, Chris," I told him trying to get out of there before something happened, like Slate reappearing.

"*Aren't* you going to introduce me?"

I sucked in a lungful of air. Did he have to be so quiet? Such a big man should be loud when he moved.

"Slate, Chris. Chris, Slate," I said in a stilted tone hoping Slate would get the message.

The tension in the air was palpable as the popcorn. He waited for me to mention him, and I'd failed. Chris was instantly on guard. Chris was used to being the biggest guy around, and here was Slate, bigger and much badder. I almost laughed when I saw Chris stand a little straighter, lift his chin a little higher. It had to be a volatile testosterone combination that caused reactions like that.

"Slate, huh? That's different. How do you know sugar lips?" Chris asked with an obvious inference to how he had known me.

Slate's lips curled, but it wasn't a friendly smile and I realized Chris's life might be in danger, I improvised, "Slate is my very overprotective boyfriend. I should have mentioned him earlier. I'm sorry, babe. Chris hasn't seen me in a while."

I pulled on the leather jacket Slate wore and gave him a quick peck on the lips. Steel choked as he walked away, dragging Tawny with him. Slate wanted to deepen the kiss, but I didn't let him. That had to be enough of a show for him to quell his blood lust. Slate gripped me tightly to his side and Chris's eyes followed Slate's hand to my waist.

I was mentally pleading for Chris not to say something that would trigger Slate; he was unpredictable when he was like this, and after the time we'd spent in his room, he kind of acted like I belonged to him.

"Lucky guy."

He could have left it there and it would have been fine, but I'd forgotten how Chris had gotten into more than his fair share of scuffles back in high school.

Chris shrugged his shoulders. "I have the same cell number. You already know it. Call me if you change your mind," he said with a smirk.

"She won't," Slate retorted in more of a growl than with words.

I wondered if Jett was nearby to help if this got ugly.

Chris's smile quirked up in the corner. "Did she tell you about me? We've got a thing, sugar lips and I," he said low so the others wouldn't hear, "We'll always have that together."

My cheeks stung, and my breath caught. "That is a real sugarfoot thing for you to say to him."

Chris smiled his dreamy smile, "You still use those cute names instead of cuss? I've always liked how sweet you are."

"Let's go," I said, turning to Slate.

I saw Slate's face and panicked. The others were already outside the glass doors. I pulled Slate's face down to mine and kissed him deeply letting his arms wrap around me tight. I understood what he needed. Me. He needed me to validate something primal in him that had claimed me as his territory and another man had invaded.

When we broke apart several breathless moments later, everyone was outside. Indigo and Gypsum who had been playing in the arcade must have passed us on their way out the doors. Chris was gone through and so were his frat friends.

I looked up at Slate and searched his eyes for the ferocious beast I'd almost seen unleashed. It was still there but caged again.

"Sorry about that. Chris gets all alpha around guys he doesn't know."

"You forgot about me," he accused.

"I didn't forget, I was temporarily distracted. You could have spoken up at any point. I said I was sorry," I crossed my arms. "I kissed you in front of my fiancée's cousin. Can I please have credit where credit is due?"

Calling Slate babe had almost made me laugh out loud if I'd hadn't been so terrified that he might rip Chris's arms off and beat him with them. The kiss had been nice though, too nice. We'd never kissed in public, and I'd enjoyed it far too much.

Slate moved so our faces were level. "You have given that boy your pleasure," he ground out between clenched teeth, and I set my jaw.

He seemed at a loss; I wasn't about to set him straight.

"You've been inside countless women. Pot, meet kettle," I whispered harshly, not wishing to make a spectacle, and pushed past him to join the others.

He stopped me before the doors and yanked me back to him. His chest was heaving with barely controlled rage, "I must have you. Now. Right now."

I searched his face. Was he serious? "Slate, everyone is waiting outside," his brows knit as he scanned my gaze for a compromise and found none. "Come on. Let's finish our date," I said taking his hand, but he pulled away.

"Give me a moment, Torch," Slate growled as he stalked down a hall.

I turned and went outside with the others. "Slate is taking a bathroom break. He'll be right out," I said, not looking at anyone.

"You have terrible taste in men," Jett said grumpily, and Amethyst nudged him.

"Of all the theaters in all the world, he had to walk into this one," Tawny shook her head.

"Old boyfriend?" Indigo asked obliviously.

"Something like that." I muttered.

When Slate finally came out, he wasn't speaking to me. He wouldn't even walk near me. I sat between Gypsum and Indigo at the steak house. Everyone else had gotten over the incident. Jett was in a great mood and insisted on ordering for everyone from a very flirty waitress that Amethyst looked ready to throttle. They did not hit on Slate; his face went all hard and intimidating when he was angry. He was a force to be reckoned with.

Jett laughed when Amethyst placed her hand possessively in his lap when the waitress refilled his glass for the third time in ten minutes and winked.

"Married and I still got it."

Steel had his arm around Tawny's chair as she gazed at him adoringly. Jett and the girls were just as bad as they fed food to each other. What saved the night was Gypsum and Indigo mocking them. My stomach hurt from suppressing my laughter. Slate had even smiled, but not at me of course. I couldn't put my finger on why it bothered me so much. I should have been thankful for it, finally he was leaving me alone.

Jett paid the bill with his store of American currency, and I tried not to be cross that he'd spent so much time on the east coast and had never looked me up. He drove and let the radio blare. I sat in the back again with Gypsum and stared at the back of Slate's head until I huffed and looked out the window checking out the few people who had already decorated for Halloween.

Jett pulled into Colt State park, and I knew our time in the U.S. was almost over. I felt the tears prick at my eyes. I tried to hide it but did a crappy job. Tawny and Gyps understood. Gyps pulled me to him. I wasn't sure when it happened, but he could easily throw his arm over my shoulder as I leaned into him.

"Don't sweat it Scar, we'll come back again. Maybe we should come back more often. It felt good to be back, didn't it?" he whispered.

I nodded, "I miss my mom."

Gypsum's eyes teared up, and he nodded and held me closer. We pulled through the portal door and parked. I wanted to get out of the car fast so I could go cry in private.

I gave Gypsum a squeeze and hopped out quick. "Thanks for dinner and the movie," I told Jett as I hurried out through the door.

I heard someone trotting after me; I knew who it was.

"Come."

"You think I'm some shivering little rabbit chock full of provocative daydreams about you and me. Frustrated and waiting for you to cure me of my ails, but you're wrong. I'm going to tell you once. I'm a grown woman and tomorrow I'll start planning a wedding to a man who wants to give me the world. What do you offer that would make me follow you up to your rooms?" I asked, squaring my shoulders.

Slate's eyes flashed, "Do I push you further than you will go? Force you? I was inviting you back to my bed tonight. What you decide from there is up to you, Torch. I have made my stance clear."

The image of him and Cordillera in her office made my stomach roil. It had hurt. I had slept in his arms and thought... I was wrong. He did exactly what I was afraid he would do. Thankfully, I hadn't given myself to him beforehand.

"I'll be sleeping alone from now on. Thanks anyway."

"You mean, when you are not with the Straumr boy," Slate growled before stalking off.

I exhaled with a shudder listening to his boots echo down the hall. The problem was — I wanted to go to that bedroom.

"Scarlett?" Steel asked, as I walked back into the portal room.

"I just need some air," I said distractedly.

Their voices faded as the white light of the portal door engulfed me.

I didn't go out in search of a destination. So, when I found myself standing in front of the wooden bedroom door of Brass's bedroom, I jumped when Brass opened it before I could knock.

He stood clad in only a low-slung pair of navy plaid linen pants. His dark honey muscles, dusted with silky dark hair over his chest, tapered down to a happy trail that had that mind numbing corded 'V' that disappeared under his waistband. Sleep disheveled his thick dark hair, so he ran a hand over through it.

"Hey, Scarlett. Is everything all right?" Brass asked in a sleep thick voice.

I'd lost my ability to think much less speak, but I remembered why I had wound up there. He finally took in what I was wearing, and his brow creased.

"Scarlett?" he asked again in his smooth deep voice sounding less sleepy.

"Can I come in?" I squeaked out.

"Yeah. Sorry. I am out of sorts," he said opening his door wide to reveal the bedroom I'd been in a few days ago.

Instead of sitting on his couch, I moved past it and walked to the bed. His sheets were tossed back, the bed still warm. I didn't know what I would've done if he had been with someone.

He stood by the armrest of his grey couch baffled why I was in the skimpy dress sitting in his bed in the middle of the night. I ran my teeth over my lower lip looking at him through my lashes.

"Scarlett..." his tone had changed.

He was going to talk me out of something.

"I'm going to say yes to Ash tomorrow. He's asked me to marry him again, and he loves me...in his way," he interrupted, and I held up my hand begging him to let me finish, "I'm a romantic, but I'm also a realist. I don't think I can go my entire life with one man, never knowing what it was like with another."

"I —"

"Please, I'm almost through," he nodded leaning on the armrest as if his head was spinning. "I care about you and if I'm not completely mistaken, we're friends. Very good friends. I thought I had been with a man before, but... I was drunk for the first time in my life and remember incorrectly. You only get one shot at your first time. I trust you," I licked my lips and looked down at my hands, "you won't hurt me and that we can be friends after. I was hoping you would say yes and, um, be my first."

My cheeks felt as if they'd caught fire as I briefly flickered my eyes to him. He looked dumbfounded.

A gust of air puffed from his lungs as his lips parted. "You should be in love with the first man you are with, Scarlett. If you are not in love with Ash, that is the problem, not your maidenhead," his face reddened with mine as he said the last word.

I got to my feet. I couldn't take his rejection.

"There's more to marriage than love. Sorry to have woken you," I muttered, crossing his room rounding the opposite side of the couch from where he stood.

Brass moved from the couch and was at me in a blink, "What about Slate?"

I looked up at him, searching those sleepy amber eyes, "You think I could trust Slate with my heart?"

"I think I do not want to be your last option."

"You're not. I've never asked anyone before," I swallowed, feeling weak and tingly.

Brass gave me a dry look. "Because you do not ask, Scarlett. It should not be a negotiation. It should overcome you with passion. This is what I mean about marrying Ash."

I dropped my eyes. Unless it was a fight, I never lost myself in passion. I was too afraid I'd end up like my mother, pregnant and alone. I didn't know as much about her situation as I thought I did.

"You're right," I said, feeling shaky.

I rushed past Brass and into the hall. What I needed to do was catch my breath, but I was feeling completely mortified and the first thing I needed was to get out of Shadow Breaker headquarters.

My booted heels stumbled down steps as I tried not to succumb to self-piteous tears. The rumpus room was all but abandoned as I blew through the usually bustling playroom. As the secret door painstakingly opened with the grinding of stone against stone, I balled my fists before bursting from the expanding crack.

I groaned shaking my fists at the sky. Lightening crashed, and I spouted a Wemic curse Slate had taught me. Because *of course* it would be raining. I'd been outside HQ exactly two seconds and my dress dripped down my legs.

So Brass was safe. I liked safe. I wanted safe. What was wrong with safe?

He wasn't just safe. He was gorgeous, sweet, reserved for a Guardian, and sexy as hell.

It was Slate. They were friends and Slate had staked his claim in me. I'd be lying if I said I didn't want Slate, but he wasn't good for me. He wasn't good for anyone.

"Scarlett. By the Mother, did you not hear me calling your name?"

Brass turned me around by my shoulder. I'd only taken a few steps over the glistening cobblestones from the door. I hadn't heard him, but the sound of my heart was making it difficult to hear anything.

"I have passion!" Over the rain, I shouted at him, "I'm brimming with passion!"

Brass knit his brow giving me a rueful look, "Come in out of the rain. We will have a beer and talk about it."

I was indignant. I could incite desire. I'd shown him passion.

I closed the distance between us and brought my hands to his jaw rising on my tiptoes to kiss those soft plump lips inhaling his cinnamon scent that seemed intensified not muted by the rain. I found his lips molding to mine as I ran my fingers through his thick hair.

Then Brass started kissing me back.

My body trembled with titillation. I was a cliché. Maybe it was adrenaline, I did not know. I had an odd mix of excitement and nervousness coursing through me I couldn't tell heads from tails of. My mission to make love to a sweet, caring man who wouldn't rip my heart out was underway and —I was drowning in pleasure.

Maybe he wasn't so safe.

A fluttering in my chest began. If I had a heart attack while attempting to seduce Brass, I would just *die*. His muscles flexed beneath my fingers as I ran my hands down his back. He took my face in his hands. His tongue met mine, and the world blurred.

His hands slid down my face and skimmed my chest as if he wasn't sure if I meant what I said and was trying to test the waters. I was ready to plunge in. It was the longest I'd kissed him aside from the day I used my manipulations on him. Now he wanted to, and it was better.

His kisses were always heated and passionate, but it was the first time I had wanted more. I was pushing for more. I never pushed.

As I blinked at the rain in my eyes, I followed kisses down his throat. My hands wandered lower to his pajama pants; he had nothing underneath them.

"The most urgent lips are often not in a hurry two kisses later," he said throatily.

I was just as intent as I had been in his bedroom. I ran my thumbs along his ridges of sculpted muscle as I kissed down his chest swirling my tongue against his skin. He grabbed my shoulders and brought me back up. Brass searched my face as rivers of cool rain ran over us.

"I have to ask —" he shouted over the rain.

"Do I have to spell it out for you? S-E-X. I want it. With you," I said in a raised voice, wiping rain from my eyes.

His chest heaved and he looked up to the dark sky that wasn't allowing any light in the dark dead end. I could barely see him, but I had a mental map of where all the essential parts were. I took a bold step forward and curled my fingers in the waistband of his pants.

"You are using me," he said, looking down at me.

"Trying to," I said, giving him a sheepish smile.

"Gods forgive me," Brass murmured to himself, and his posture seemed to change.

Brass wound his arms around me and kissed me so thoroughly, my toes curled in my boots. His tongue slid along my throat as I panted.

"This is where we first met," he said roughly, tugging my earlobe between his teeth.

Was it?

I couldn't remember my name with his hands caressing my skin as they were, much less useless details like where I was. He chuckled and ran his palms over my hips. His fingers bunched up the fabric of my dress as he walked me backwards until I ran into the brick wall.

I moaned out loud when Brass's hand curled around my thigh and braced it over his hip. He pulled my arm high above my head and laced his strong fingers through mine the grit of the brick digging into my knuckles. My legs wanted to wrap around him, but he held me firmly busying my mouth with his, my other hand around his neck tangling in his hair. His hand slipped between my legs and my silly strip of fabric that passed for underwear pushed aside.

My eyes shot open. I was really doing it.

I tried to reach for him. His eyelashes stuck to one another with droplets running to his trim beard as he kissed me, strands of his hair matted over his forehead from the rain. I melted. I was *actively* melting.

Yes. It felt right. It felt good. Great. It was — Oh Gods, it hurt!

I wanted to shout for him to stop — or to hurry. I didn't know which, but it felt like my body wasn't made to accept things in such a way.

"By the Mother," Brass gritted, "Try to relax, love..."

Words were lost on me. I could feel him rubbing between my legs. The delicious friction and slipping was causing a tightening in my belly. Then he had tried to move into me, and a sharp pinch had made me go rigid.

The pain grew sharper, and I clenched my jaw holding him tight and burying my face in the crook of his neck. His heavy breaths moaned in my ear as the pinch ebbed and I felt him sliding into me. My muscles loosened.

That wasn't so bad.

Brass moaned, and my loins pulsed. I assumed they were loins since it was an unidentifiable body part fluttering away inside of me. It was like nothing I had ever felt before. The feeling of fullness and pleasure beginning to intertwine. He held me effortlessly pinned against the brick, my skin slick from the rain, and from the passion. Frigga's sweet grass, the passion — the loss of control. It frightened me and I was enraptured.

My head leaned back against the wall as he kissed along my throat. Not so bad had suddenly turned into positively marvelous. A rope inside me twisted tighter and tighter with every glorious thrust of his hips.

When we were girls, Tawny and I sat on the swings and she would take my legs, spinning me as the chains bunched and pulled. Until the chains were so entangled, she could no longer twist me. I knew I was going to get dizzy, that I could get hurt, but that in the few seconds I was spinning wildly out of control — I was free.

Brass was like that; the feeling was just too fantastic to suffer without it. All I could do was hold on and pray it never stopped.

He moaned pressing his lips to the sensitive inside of my neck, "Curse the Gods."

I took his curses as a compliment.

He eased his hold on my thigh and I braced my weight on his shoulders to lock my ankles around his waist. Suddenly, the rope that had slowly been twisting could twist no more, and I was spinning out of control. I came undone, moaning like an animal as waves of pleasure washed over me like the rain and every hair on my body seemed to stand on end at once.

"Scarlett," Brass said roughly as he thrust, his stubbled beard chafed my face and neck, but I barely felt it as I went limp in his arms.

Slowly, he set my feet down. My face slid from the crook of his neck to his chest as we both panted. Brass pulled his sopping wet pants over himself and adjusted my dress for me before taking my chin in his hand and tilting it up so he could get a better look at me.

"I am taking you inside. I am going to bathe you, dry you, and make love to you. You are going to spend the night, and, in the morning, I would like you to have breakfast with me. Here or elsewhere, it does not matter, but not under any circumstances will you run off after I fall asleep. Is that understood?"

Brass's amber eyes flitted between mine. His lips swollen from my fevered kisses and love bites on his neck where I had gotten carried away. The deed was *finally* done.

"You don't have to invite me in. I know you were reluctant to help me —" I said, yelling over the crackle of lightning.

"Help you?" the lightning drowned Brass's guffaw out, and I frowned.

I did not want to be laughed at after that.

I was getting ready to stalk away when he swept my legs out from under me and carried me over to the entrance. I even let myself rest my head against his chest justifying the needless affection by telling myself it was all still a part of the lovemaking.

One night wouldn't hurt any.

Brass was a man of his word. No one was in the shared bathroom at the end of his hall, and he locked the door after us. He filled the tub with lavender scented bubbles and had me wait so he could remove my clothes himself.

If he noticed the way I trembled, he was kind enough not to mention it. I caught my first glimpse of Brass fully aroused and magnificently nude and balked. No wonder it had been so painful.

His lips quirked as he ducked his head — always reading my mind.

He meticulously washed my skin as he sat in the tub having pulled me into his lap, so I straddled his hips. I shook the entire time until he rinsed my skin and nuzzled my chest. Brass ran his nose along the swell of my breast stopping to kiss every square inch before glancing up at me and wrapping his lips around my pearled peak.

I gasped, and it seemed to exhilarate him. He guided my hips with his capable hands as I took him into me again.

By the time he carried me into bed, I was deliciously exhausted. Brass pulled a white cotton shirt over my head before giving up on trying to dry my hair and curled into his four-post bed behind me.

I was asleep before his arm finished winding its way around my middle.

"Tea. Special tea. I hope you do not mind I took it upon myself to get some for you."

A steaming jade teacup sat on a saucer over Brass's knee. He was wearing another pair of forest green pajama pants and no shirt though he'd had to go down to the kitchens for the cup and the tea. I sat up groggily and gave him an embarrassed smile as I took the tea.

"Thank you. It was good thinking; I don't have any of this tea," I told him sipping from the glass.

He watched me drink, and I set the cup down on the saucer as I finished. I felt like something profound should've been said or maybe I should thank him. Maybe a pat on the back and a handshake, I didn't know the protocol.

The man was a mind reader and dear sweet Mother how he put that skill to use.

Brass took the saucer and cup from my hand and used his calling to float it over to the coffee table. "How are you feeling?" he asked with a smile so warm and inviting I nearly swooned.

"Good. Better than I expected. Not too sore," I said, blushing down to my chest.

Brass had told me he would heal me, but I couldn't use calling on the places that would ail me.

He shifted on the bed and raised his hand, then thought better of it and let it drop back to his thigh, "I have never been a woman's first, Scarlett. You should know that. I feel responsible for you somehow, it is a strange feeling I am not sure what to do with now."

"Oh, *um*, nothing. I'm good, really," I said awkwardly, wondering if he was asking me to leave.

He shifted his hand from his thigh to mine. "Feel free to say no," he said looking down at my thighs that peeked out from under his blankets, "breakfast is not for some time."

I involuntarily squirmed. Brass wanted me. In our strange relationship, he didn't know how to go about asking for it and he wasn't comfortable diving right in. I bit my lip. I shouldn't. Ash and I were going to get engaged today. Technically, I supposed all our lovemaking was after midnight, so it was the same day.

Brass was reading my mind again. He didn't wait for a response before taking the hem of my shirt and pulling it up over my head. My skin prickled as my hair fell and his eyes raked over me.

"You are breathtaking, Scarlett Tio," he said in a smooth whisper. "I am sorry I did not make love to you for your first time," he said pushing his pants over his hips to reveal what I feared and revered, "but I intend on making it up to you now."

I was speechless.

Brass pulled me down the bed, so my head fell against the pillows as he prowled between my legs. I was shivering as I watched his corded arms flex with each movement.

"Why do you tremble? Relax, love," Brass brushed his lips lightly against mine like the beat of a butterfly's wing. "I will never hurt you. I swear it. You can trust me," he promised.

I melted for the umpteenth beneath him.

Since it was Sunday, Quick and Shale were sitting with the ever-perky Ama. I waved a hand in a very unmercenary like way and saw Shale's shoulders shake with suppressed laughter. I'd dressed all in black like they did for the day.

"Good morning," I said, smiling my best smile at the four gathered at the table as I sat.

Brass and I had spent too much time in bed and decided it would be better if we came down separately since I was adamant about no one else knowing. He seemed disappointed when he gave me the spare clothes I kept in the prep room's cubby.

"There have been better mornings, but it is certainly looking up now," Shale said in a raspy tone with a smile.

"You are speaking again," Ama said with a little clap.

"What brings you in, Scarlett?" Quick said with his usual charm.

"Ash is coming over later, and I wanted to get some training in," I said dismissively.

Brass's amber eyes watched me intently, "A minor distraction would do me some good. We will go run the Crash Course."

"Are you sure? We really don't have to."

He shook his head, and a lock of dark brown hair grazed his cheek, his ebony beads clicked against the bronze. I had braided them in myself that morning.

"I am sure. Besides, there are only a few hours left of your single life. You might as well make use of that time," Brass said and Quick looked at him through narrow eyes.

Brass's eyes looked at me knowingly, and I gave a shy smile, "I'm going to accept Ash's proposal when he comes over tonight. Don't worry, I won't let it affect our training."

Shale's smirk fell and Quick gave a small sneer.

"How was the movie?" Quick asked.

Slate was there, one guess where he was now.

"It was a good movie. I ran into an old boyfriend of sorts, which sucked, but otherwise it was good," I said without blushing again.

Ama leaned forward on her elbows finally speaking. "Ooh! An old boyfriend, what happened?" she smiled brightly, wanting a little girl talk.

I shrugged and sipped my drink, "What you'd expect a guy like him to say when he thinks you've moved on. Which I have, just not in the way he thought. Long story short, he pissed Slate and my brother off."

Ama cocked her head of bouncy blonde curls, "The ex thought you were with Slate. Why?"

"Um, it's a long story. I think it was a testosterone thing," I rambled, rolling the glass between my hands.

Brass chuckled, "You told him that Slate was your boyfriend."

I cringed, "It was the only thing I could think of that would assure Slate I wouldn't make the same mistake with the ex again. It backfired."

"Did you really call him babe? I would have paid to see that. Though from your memories he seemed not to mind at all," Brass knit his brows with a smile, and I could almost feel him rifling through my thoughts, "In fact, I think he liked it. He is not the only possessive one, is he?"

Shale was laughing, and Ama was hiding a smile. Quick looked like someone just told him a purple unicorn riding a hot pink dragon had flown through the rumpus room and he'd missed it. Utter confusion colored his handsome face.

"No. What are you doing to him? Why was he in a rage this morning? I thought he was going to bite my head off," Quick shot me a look.

"He's always angry," I tried desperately to control where my eyes roamed to the point of drying them out, so I had to blink rapidly to moisten them.

"We should get you a mark, a bond like we all have. You are almost one of us now. Well, if Lera does not find out that Slate enjoys being your boyfriend," Ama said perkily, not bothering to lower her voice.

"We're nothing — family. I'm going to be married within the year. He's all hers."

Quick shook his head, "You should have quit while you were ahead —"

I shot to my feet before he could reveal whatever he thought was a lie. "Are we going to train or not?" I said too loud and sat back down when a few heads turned my way, "What I mean is, I'm done. Ready to go train."

As if on cue, Slate emerged from Cordillera's office and seemed to find me the second he stepped through the door. It felt like someone had poured ice down my shirt.

I was a rabbit.

"Enough story time, let us go train. Any other takers?" Brass said, straightening up from his seat.

"I am in," Ama said, getting to her feet.

"We will be here. If we see Lera heading downstairs, we will send you warning. Try not to give anything away in your face. Lera does not like Slate's other women hanging around," Quick teased.

My face contorted in disgust. "I'm not one of his women," I glared at Quick, and his lips curled.

"Truth."

No small amount of satisfaction wound through me. Slate hadn't slept with any of the other Shadow Breakers, that was interesting. I nearly jumped when Brass slid his arm around my hips. My love life was more active than it had ever been, all at once and disastrous.

Brass noticed my little jump and shot me a smile so full of warmth I nearly simpered. He bent his head down to my ear, so his lips grazed it as he spoke.

"Have you ever heard the adage, all is fair in love and war?"

I nodded.

"Guardians adhere to that sentiment," he whispered in that smooth deep voice of his.

Three insanely good-looking men had kissed me in one week and I had let each one. I let out a breath as I saw Brass's eyelids slide lower over his amber eyes. If he was reading my mind and knew I was thinking about our night together I was going to kick his fanny pack. He laughed rich and warm, and I knew he was.

Brass stopped at the entryway to the stairs and Ama kept going, Brass tilted my chin up with a finger.

"I am going to marry Ash. Tonight, I am telling him," I said, watching as hair fell from behind his ear.

His lips parted in a sad smile, "I know. That is why I must steal as many kisses as possible before you leave."

I laughed, but he pressed his lips to mine raising me onto my tiptoes with the arm that tightened around my waist, his other hand slid from my chin into my hair. It only lasted a few seconds, and he didn't deepen it. Brass's kisses were felt inside, he poured emotion into them that was impossible not to feel. The man did nothing halfway.

When we parted, his eyes flitted to the corner, and I turned my head. Past Quick and Shale's incredulous faces were Slate and Lera. Lera's dark eyes shifted to look at Slate, and his was a thunderhead. I gulped as Brass leaned down to my ear making me blush since he was still holding me up on my tiptoes.

"You needed to be kissed," he whispered and set me back down on my heels before guiding me by my waist. Ama was waiting on looking at us amusedly as she leaned on the wrought-iron balustrade.

"I read auras. Do you want me to tell you what I see in yours?" Ama said with a small smile.

"Um, maybe some other time," I said very aware of Brass's warm hand at my hip.

I thought now I understood his reason for kissing in public — Cordillera. She thought I was after her pet, Brass sought to put her mind at ease. Since I hardly put up a fight, Brass did that in the simplest way possible. Just a small kiss here and there. I smiled a little at its simplicity. I felt Brass's amusement, and I looked up at him as we headed to the prep room.

"You're rifling through my thoughts again."

Brass's amber eyes swung down to me, "It is very easy to do when you touch me."

I hadn't even realized I'd wrapped my arm around his hips, and I bit down on my lip to stop the smile, "Thanks."

"My pleasure, really, I thoroughly enjoy kissing you. It will disappoint me when you return engaged," Brass said.

I would not read too much into that, but my insides pulsed traitorously.

Brass rubbed his hands together. Lips pulling back into a genuine smile, "Show her the ropes."

Ama gave a devilish grin and trotted down to the end of the Crash Course. I turned back to Brass who urged me to follow. I gave him a smile as I raced after her.

Ama started explaining, "We do not expect you to cross it the first time. Do as well as you can, no calling involved. I will go first so you can mimic my movements, Brass will walk along with us to instruct and coach. Understand?"

I was brimming with excitement. I looked down the expanse of obstacles and couldn't wait to start. We stood in the combat ring, Ama turned around to give me a last reassuring smile with her little pouty mouth before she was a whirl of blonde curls and black clad limbs. She ran, duck, and rolled as she jumped from ledge to ledge narrowly escaping the wicked blades that swung, sliced, and diced in an attempt to mince her.

They looked much sharper than the ones in our Gauntlet at the University. I was suddenly happy for my snug clothing. A loose piece could get cut through easily and throw me off balance. Excitement, nerves, and anticipation consumed me. I'd watched Ama do it closely. She was nearly through the bladed portion of the Crash Course. I took a deep breath and exhaled slowly. I got this.

I started at a run. I counted every nanosecond between the swish of the blades. Shing Shing, the sound of the knives slicing sang all around me. I was a blur. My emotions melted away, and I just was. I was speed; I was the wind. Nothing could touch me. I ducked, jumped, rolled, and at some point, I flipped. My mind was perfectly clear as I exited the blade portion.

I ran and launched myself at a tree. My upper body wasn't very powerful, but I was flexible. I could reach holds and dig in better than most. I scaled the first tree without a problem. Ama was kicking off the treetops in midair, jumping from one treetop to the next. I'd never done that.

"Do not look down," Brass shouted.

"Why would you say that?" I shouted back at him; it was met with his warm laugh, "Now I want to look down!"

I rolled my eyes at myself and tucked my feet against the treetop's limbs before aiming for the next tree top and pushed off. My entire body was sore from my escapades with Brass the night before. I did not know sex would use so many muscles, or perhaps that was only sex with Brass.

I was flying. My shoulder hit the tree and stared to slip. I groaned and tightened my grip into the thick bark. It took a second to collect myself as it shoved its way under my nails. I wondered if I'd bruised my collarbone. I shimmied back up to the top of my current tree and tucked my feet again and shoved off. This time, I didn't aim to catch myself on the tree, but to stay in motion and propel to the next one. That was what Ama had done.

I flew, my foot connected with the bark of the tree, and I pushed off aiming for the next tree in succession. I managed to do this until the second to last tree when my foot slid against the bark. My thighs squeezed around the side of the tree until I was upside down. My head hit with a *thunk*, and I saw stars.

It slowed my descent, and I ground to a stop. I could feel the bark embedded into my back as my vision cleared. I hung upside down, my legs squeezing the tree just breathing waiting for the pain to dull.

"Are you quitting already?" Brass shouted at me.

I was pretty sure I had splinters in my fanny pack. A slew of curses came to mind before I could stop myself from thinking them.

Brass laughed, "Get up then and finish so you can make good on those promises. And stop thinking about sex, it is distracting you!"

I grit my teeth as I flushed. He did *not* just say that!

I didn't want soreness to set in so I wrapped my arms around the tree as best I could and slowly eased the tension from my thighs. My arms alone held me above my head, which were below my body. As I brought my legs down, I used my weight between my arms and head. I felt like an acrobat; I thanked Slate for every ridiculously hard trial he ever put me through. During my slow flip, I thought my shoulders were going to dislocate, but that was right before my legs made contact with the tree trunk and I squeezed with my legs again.

I shimmied back up the tree, I aimed, and sprung to the last tree. I clung to it and crawled down and managed a smooth landing from about ten feet off the ground with a bit of called air.

Ama was already across the earthquake portion, so I had no clue how to begin, but it was self-explanatory. Don't fall in a crack, don't get hit by a falling boulder. There was no rhyme or reason to the boulders falling. Every inch of me was sore from my treetop parkour. It'd made me feel weak and *boy oh boy* someone was going to have to take these splinters out of my backside.

I didn't even bother to touch my fanny pack. It was achingly sore and probably badly scraped. I hoped my pants would hold up.

"Now is as good a time as any!" Brass shouted.

I gritted my teeth and started forward. The ground shook under me. It was a lot harder than it looked. It threw me onto my already smarting backside and had to roll from a falling boulder and back onto my rear. I cursed. I could stand being stabbed but put a few wood slivers in my skin and I turn into a baby.

After a few more falls, and a boulder nearly throwing me into the lava pit. I had made it through. My toes gripped the soles of my boots as I fought to balance myself over the edge of the lava. Damn that boulder.

All I had to do is balance on the floating rocks and keep away from the lava geysers. Easy Peasy.

The first jump was the hardest. How does one knowing jump into a pit of lava? I lunged. The floating rocks were much more unstable than they looked. It bobbed as soon as I landed on it and tilted from side to side.

"Is it stupid to ask if this is real lava?" I shouted to no one in particular.

"Do not fall in and you will never find out," Brass yelled.

... *You don't fall in* ...

Brass laughed. Stupid mind reading abilities.

I jumped over and over. It was achingly slow. Sweat poured off me. I was looking forward to the whirlpool in front of me. Halfway through, a geyser erupted and caught my arm. I should have had a solid sheet of blisters along the side of my right arm, but it was flawless.

I stood before the whirlpool trying to get a feel for how it worked and trying to catch my breath. What I wanted to do was drink all the water swirling around, the lava having left my throat drier than the Wemic desert.

I slipped on the wet surface as I jumped and grabbed for the first raft. My chin hit it and my teeth clacked. I dug my fingers in between the pieces of wood and pulled myself up as quickly as possible grunting with every painful movement. I swirled closer and closer to the center of the whirlpool. Waves crashed against me. Ama landed safely on the other side, and I noticed she and Brass were standing there watching me.

I gritted my teeth and pushed myself up into a crouched position. They started cheering for me. I felt my adrenaline surge. I was coming back around the circle. Two more rafts would line up close enough for me to jump across. It was now or never. There was one last spurt of energy. I put my muscular legs to good use. I jumped, took a step, jumped, and then pushed off with both feet off last raft as it sailed past the dock where Brass and Ama shouted for me.

I knew I would not make it a second too late. Sugarfoot. My hands hit the dock, but so did my head. The world around me grew foggy as my head sunk under water. I blacked out as I saw hands thrust into the water above me.

All my worries were over because I was dead. Hopefully, no one mourned. I could see my mother again. Nope. Someone was crushing my chest. I felt air forced into my lungs and someone was crushing my chest.

Out of my way, I've got to puke!

My eyes slid open, and Brass's mouth was over mine and not romantically. Oh Gods, I was going to puke in his mouth! He jerked back and rolled me over. I coughed up everything *ever*. I thought the whirlpool might be empty because I drank it all. Brass was dripping water over me, but he was smiling.

"She is fine," he told them helping me to sit up.

Ama was kneeling next to me and handed me a towel, "You cracked your head on the dock."

I gave her a dry look wiping my mouth with the back of my hand, and Ama blushed.

Brass helped me to my feet, and I winced. I looked over my shoulder and lifted my shirt tentatively. Oh yeah, I was going to need some healing. My back was doubling as a pincushion for slivers.

"Let us go take care of that," Brass said to me.

I gave him a lopsided smile, "Thanks," I noticed movement in the glass enclosed stands. Cordillera stood watching us and turned to leave.

"She came in once you started," Brass told me.

I only nodded. I was sore all over, and I couldn't heal without removing the splinters. Ama and Brass grabbed an arm to either side of me and helped me limp into the prep room.

They set a padded table up for injuries, there were five in a row. Ama helped me take off my shirt. My arms ached in places I wasn't even sure had ever been used. I unbuttoned my pants, and she helped my pull off my boots. I laid down on my stomach in relief and Ama threw a towel over my backside.

I folded my arms under my head. I really wanted to fall asleep, but the aching prevented it. She pulled my towel down a little further and tucked it under my hips; Wood embedded in my skin all the way to the top of my backside. I guessed I should've been happy it wasn't on the lower half; I imagined that would hurt even worse. As it was, the thick bark had scraped off strips of my skin, so it looked like I had a severe road rash.

"Ready!" Ama called, "I will see you upstairs. You deserve a drink after tonight. You did well."

I snorted, "You're kidding right? I dove right into the dock headfirst."

"It took me three months after I joined the Shadow Breakers to finish the Crash Course. You were amazing," Ama told me, patting my arm.

"You did extremely well, you would have completed it if not for that last raft," Brass came into sight, freshly showered with still damp hair.

"Drinks are on me when you are done." Ama said as she skipped away.

Brass came to my side; his voice was soothing, "Relax, you are in expert hands." I heard him smile.

I turned my face towards him to see what he was doing.

"Getting a feel for what I need to do," he explained.

He held his hands up so I could see he was going to place them on my skin. I appreciated the warning. His warm hands rested on my back. Slowly, I felt the tiny splinters pull from my skin.

"I have seen anyone do that on the trees," he said, smiling.

I watched him as he worked at my side. His hands never left my skin.

"What, turn into a porcupine?"

He chuckled, "What you did after. Most people would have tried to curl back up and grab the tree, but you let gravity do the work."

I snorted, "I did a little work."

He turned to meet my eyes and smiled. I tried not to squirm under his hands and kept my mind blank. Must not think about being naked under his hands. He continued to smile as he worked. I couldn't help watching. A lock of his wet hair fell from behind his ear and grazed his chin as he removed splinters from my backside. After last night, I was feeling humiliated and clumsy.

I thought back to when I came to and nearly puked all over him. "Did you dive in after me?" I asked.

He nodded, "It was like watching you fall in slow motion. I dove in right after you. It was foolish, I should have called and used air to pull you back up, or water to push you to the surface. We could have both been sucked down."

Yikes. I hadn't thought of that, "Thanks anyway."

"You say that as if I had a choice," he arched a dark eyebrow at me.

"You do, everyone does," I told him.

He pulled a full bottom lip into his mouth before releasing it, "It was instinct."

"Couldn't you have pumped my stomach with air or something?"

Jett's side glance when I gave him C.P.R. came to mind when he'd nearly drowned.

"I could have, but where is the fun in that?" he asked, teasing me for my thoughts.

I narrowed my eyes at him, and he chuckled.

"That is all of them. Maybe next time try not to become a tree yourself," he joked, "I will heal you now."

Warmth spread through me and the scrapes on my back faded away to nothing, not to mention the aches from the morning's bed play. I felt warm and fuzzy.

"If you want to shower, I can rub you down afterwards. I will wait here," he said, standing back.

I turned my face away as I blushed. I prayed he wasn't reading my mind and swallowed, "Okay, I didn't bring any other clothes."

He unfolded the towel at my hips and pulled it over my back. I grabbed a corner of it and sat up wrapping it around my front tightly. Was he blushing?

"I will get you some clothes and meet you back here."

He walked away briskly, and I groaned internally. My promise to Ash could not possibly come any sooner to abolish my new indecent line of thinking.

After a long and thorough scrub down, I wrapped my towel around me and called to dry my hair as I walked back to where Brass had healed me. He had changed the blood dotted sheets and was sitting on the table waiting. I paused. His tall form sat slightly hunched as he organized bottles on a tray. Even doing something so simple, I could see the muscles move in his arms. His hair had dried. It had a little wave to it. That rogue lock was sliding against his cheek bone above his stubbled jaw.

He was rubbing his lips together, "Are you ready?"

I started, "Um, yeah. Sorry."

He shook his head, and I climbed back onto his table. He gave the towel a tug and pulled it from my front and lowered it, so it covered my backside loosely.

"I've never had a massage before. Do I just leave my hands on the table?" I asked, feeling ridiculous.

"Yes, that is good," he said as he pulled my hair over my shoulder.

His fingers glided over my skin like silk, and it felt like an intimate gesture. I swallowed hard as my skin prickled. My body had a mind of its own. I felt the need to validate it.

"Is it customary to get a massage after training?"

Please say yes and ease some of this guilt, I thought.

He rubbed oils on his hands from the bottles on the trays, "Not always. I only offered because it was your first day of training, we usually get a massage and get sloppy drunk."

I hoped I hadn't insulted him. My overthinking was getting the best of me.

Brass put his hands lightly on my shoulders and worked his magic. It would be awkward if I started moaning. My lips had parted, and I pinched them back together. My eyes slid closed of their own volition. He rubbed my shoulders, my neck, down my arms, my hand and down my back.

"I can't believe I've never had a massage before. This feels amazing," my voice came out low and throaty.

His hands stilled for a moment before picking back up its motion. I flushed; I hoped my back didn't turn red as well. His hands slid down to my feet, and I fought the urge to pull them away.

I could hear the smile in his voice, "If it tickles let me know, I will stop."

I bit my lip, had it been my imagination, but his voice sounded guttural.

"Don't stop."

Oh. My own words sent a roll of pleasure through me.

He cleared his throat and continued. He rubbed my instep and along my ankles, and the pads of my feet. Sprinkling a little more oil on his hands, he started rubbing my toes. He pinched the pads, one toe at a time and rolled them in his fingers.

He worked his way up to my legs, pushing the towel up to expose the tops of my thighs. He pushed the towel between my legs, a small offering at modesty. His hands slid up to the top of my thighs kneading their way down.

"All set, Scarlett," Brass said and lifted the towel up and tucked it under my chest and turned around.

I sat up grasping it before hopping off the massage table. "Thanks," I said, clearing my throat, "If that was weird... I'm sorry."

"Hmm..." he tapped a finger to his lips. "A beautiful woman enjoyed my skilled hands. I am deeply offended," he said sarcastically, and I smirked reluctantly at him.

"It wouldn't kill you to keep your thoughts to yourself," I said, pulling my towel tighter.

Brass's amber eyes scanned my body, and I tried not to shift under his scrutiny. "Clothes are by your cubby. Lera has an uncanny knack for sizes, I am sure everything will fit you. Dry your boots first. That is... unless you would like some company?"

Freya's burly boar!

The man knew every single time I was thinking about him. I was doubting my flawless plan until his hands gently removed mine from the towel and he pulled it open to expose my oiled skin. His hands glided smoothly up my taut stomach and over my breasts with a moan.

No, still a good plan. A great plan. My best plan.

Brass smiled as he kissed me and lifted my backside back onto the table. "I have always wanted to do this," he said plucking one of the oils off the tray and handed it to me before he removed his shirt.

Oh yes. Best plan ever.

"What if someone comes in?" I breathed, watching him unbuckle his belt.

"It is lunch, they will be eating. You will have to be quiet to not attract attention," he said, his usual warm smile heated until it smoldered.

As his eyes closed, I rubbed the lotion into my hands and ran my hands over his shoulders. I was oiling Brass's muscled torso. I felt like I needed to be slapped so I snapped back to reality. He moaned aloud uncaring if anyone walked in as he pushed his pants down over his hips.

"I want to kiss you here," he whispered in that seductive tone of his and my eyes widened.

"Just a kiss," I whispered.

His smile was back, and I bit my lip, looking away, "You can ask me to stop anytime."

I nodded as he pulled my hips to the edge of the massage table and pressed his gleaming body flush to mine as he cupped my face and showed me exactly what kind of kiss he wanted to plant between my thighs. An embarrassing moan rolled into his mouth from mine and the ropes were back, twisting tight until they frayed, and I nearly blacked out. His lips had made their hypnotic route over my chest and down my stomach.

My heart raced as he moved over my thighs. My hands went to his hair, it was too much for my delicate frame of mind.

"Brass, wait... wait," I whispered frantically as he seared his first kiss at the apex of my thighs.

He straightened, and I wanted to crawl under a rock. Brass was undeterred. Fiddlesticking mind reader.

He lifted me down from the table and kissed along my shoulder as I turned, pulling my hair aside. "Only what you are comfortable with, love," he whispered in my ear.

My eyes slid shut. His sculpted lips must have secreted some sort of drug.

His hand slid around me to where he'd just kissed and he wound his fingers, coiling that rope, pulling it tight as he ran his palm over my back. "Your body is perfection," Brass purred rounding over my rump and giving it a good squeeze.

I arched my back for him and was rewarded with his moan as he slowly pushed into me. His hips pinned mine to his hand between the table as he moved. His other hand ran up my stomach to catch my swaying breasts.

Cinnamon and morning dew would never again smell the same for me. His body slipped and slid against mine until my rope frayed making me come undone.

So much for being quiet.

CHAPTER SEVEN

We drank little, and Slate didn't join us though I saw him cross the rumpus room and head to the opposite staircase, the ones that led up to the higher floors and the bedrooms.

When it came time for me to meet Ash, things finally got awkward between Brass and I when he asked me if I still planned to go through with it. Five orgasms in twelve hours — I wasn't planning on much but getting sleep. If Brass was disappointed by me wanting to keep our lustful day a secret from the Shadow Breakers, he was arctic when I told him nothing had changed.

When I went home, and Ash was already waiting. We were engaged. It was official. They sent messengers out to all the greater families the moment I signed the marriage contract after dinner. Ash was ecstatic, and he had never looked more handsome. He vowed his fidelity as soon as we were alone, and I gave mine. An official engagement party was already in the works and Dahlia wanted me to plan immediately so we could do it after the Wild Hunt during Yuletide.

Tawny caught up to me in the hall after dinner, and I was glad for it, "Do you have some of that tea?"

She looked skeptically at me with her wide hazel eye, "Yeah, do you need it now?"

I nodded, and we walked the mosaic filled halls to the family wing of the palace. Ash had gone ahead to my room to wait. When we got to her room, she handed me a box filled with little tea bags. I laughed, there had to be fifty little bags.

"Tawny, I need one, not all these."

She smiled knowingly at me, "I know you don't want kids before you finish at the university so it's better if you are proactive rather than waiting to see if your fiancée will knock you up with a happy accident."

My heart tightened in my chest, "Thanks Tawny."

"Do...you want to talk about it?" she queried hesitantly as she tossed her long dark waves over her shoulder.

I sat down on her and Steel's new couch that had arrived after the wedding. They had redecorated the entire wing of rooms before my mother's death. The walls were a dark teal with matching throw pillows on the plush grey couches. The bedroom was behind another door entirely, which was exclusive to the family or couple's rooms.

"I rather not," I confessed, "But I will say it was one of the best nights of my life." I glanced down at the tea packets.

"It's good you've gotten it out of your system before you said yes," she sighed and offered me a wide mouthed smile, "At least that itch was scratched."

I buried my face in my hands and shook my head, "Not Slate, Tawny." She made a choked noise, and I looked at her.

She was laughing, "I think it's safe to guess who else would be a viable subject."

"My love life isn't a science experiment." I grumbled, and she arched a brow at me making me groan.

    I had little experience with hand holding, but Ash guided me with ease from the yellowed stoned portal room of Valla U and downstairs to the hall's classes.

    They made the entire castle of the same yellowed stone, tapestries depicting the greater families' sigils and previous Prime's hung on the walls. Our very first class was Dahlia Natt's and when Ash told her the good news and of our intentions to plan an engagement party for Yuletide, her normally pinched face smiled.

    Dahlia was the headmistress for the first-year girls and the History provost. Through the heavy wood doors on the second floor, was her classroom. There were tiers of stone steps with mismatched cushions resting side by side. They were seats and from behind them we could pull up an inverted 'L' shaped wooden desk the tier in front of us.

    The room was lit by artfully crafted pewter sconces, all the classes had rounded stadium seating that faced the provost's desk and often, a laptop and screen behind the desk to project the computer's screen onto. Old world met new modern in the state-of-the-art battle grounds, or the room specifically built to house any technology you might wish to use. Valla U was the only place in Tidings with internet access.

    Quick was in our class and sat on Tawny's other side, much to Ash's irritation, but it would take more than a few dirty looks to chase Quick off. Sage sat opposite me on Ash's other side, the five of us sat together in every class. All the others were in the Ask course with the same schedule on opposite days. Crimson Rot entered the class after we sat, and her red puffy eyes bespoke her thoughts on our engagement. A big part of me sympathized, she was in love with Ash, and he had chosen someone else. I'd have to remember to send her a note, she was my great uncle's granddaughter after all.

    News of our engagement and our true patronage were all anyone spoke of which put me smack dab in the spotlight which I loathed.

Classes ended with the *dong* of what sounded like church bells, and we moved through the crowded halls.

Since I'd spent all day with Ash, I sat with Jett, the girls, Tawny, Quick, and Slate for lunch. The dining hall was much longer than it was wide with long tables and benches along its marbled floors. The walls were the same yellowed old stone, carved pillars lined the rooms while sculptured people lined the edges of the ceiling looking down at us. Chandeliers were on each side of the hall, two by two all the way down. The most amazing part was the ceiling. Between artful rafters were circular stained-glass mosaics depicting the phases of the moon.

At the head of the hall, the provosts sat at tables before an unlit fireplace, with long narrow windows to either side. Our Headmistress and Headmaster were sitting at a table directly in front our rows. They wore black robes with a thick gold trim, sleeveless with the university sigil on back in silver. Only the headmistresses and masters wore black robes with gold trim. Moon's had both, his sigil designed with both silver and gold. We sat towards the middle of the hall, the left side was for first years, to the right were second years.

I slumped down on the bench next to Quick who raised his eyebrow at me, "Lover's quarrel?"

I scoffed. Ash and I had had a heated discussion when we talked about what had happened, or hadn't, while we were on the outs. I wasn't a liar, so telling Ash that I had been spending time with Slate and had a teeny tiny fling went over horribly. The first time he delved, he'd know I had been with a man.

"We're not lovers. He's my fiancée, and yes," I rubbed my temples until Quick placed a hand on my back and called.

"Truth. At least you will stop making out with my brother at headquarters," Quick mumbled loud enough for everyone to hear.

I forced a laugh, but his name sent a thrill spiraling through me.

"Brass is a grown man. If he doesn't like it, he wouldn't do it," I shrugged, feigning nonchalance.

"Truth," Quick cursed.

Jett shook his head, "Tidings is bad for your virtue, baby sis."

I gave him a lopsided smile. "For once, we agree."

Tawny laughed at Jett's expression. "So, what were you two arguing about?" she asked, piling a savory slice of chicken onto her plate.

"*Um*, activities while we were on a break."

I wanted to slink away. I should've hidden my emotions better.

I was a firm believer that honesty was the best policy but telling Ash I'd had a fling hadn't come as a shock. That made me feel awful. Ash didn't ask the details probably because we had done little without calling and I would not volunteer information; I hadn't asked about Jonquil or Crimson. The problem was, he thought the fling had been with Slate.

I could hardly believe I had done it myself. Images of us rain soaked and bared in the dead end, the slow way he had washed me in the bubble bath, how we were together in the bed which could only be called making love, played over and over in my head. Then there was the slipping and sliding in the prep room.

Jett chortled, "Why am I not surprised? I figured he wouldn't want him in the wedding. Nothing stays secret for long in Tidings."

Insane laughter bubbled up as I filled my plate, "If you're referring to whom I think you are, there was no affair. It's my wedding too, I can have whom I want in it."

"How did I come up?" Slate asked with a mocking smile.

I sighed, "He asked about our time apart. I wanted a clean slate so to speak, so I told him I had spent time with you."

They met my statement with silence until Amethyst spoke, "I think it's admirable that you told him about bedding Slate."

I choked on my bite until Quick, laughing, smacked my back. My eyes were watering when I lifted my head to them.

"I did not sleep with Slate."

I said nothing else as I stuffed my face so I couldn't speak any more even if questioned.

"Who did the illustrious future wife of the next Prime take onto her bed or his bed?" Quick teased.

If Quick knew I had slept with Brass, he'd freak out. They all would. Tawny hadn't said Brass's name out loud, and I had wondered if she thought it was someone like Solder.

"None of anyone's business," I snapped.

"There is only one man she trusts enough to go to," Slate growled and punched the table so hard our cups fell over.

"Oh. Oh no. You... No. No. No. He would not," Quick protested in disbelief.

"For her? He would," Slate growled before stalking off.

Quick cursed and chased after him. Jett was the only one staring at me. Cherry, Amethyst, and Tawny gave me sympathetic looks, but I felt as if I'd betrayed Slate and food had lost its appeal.

Quick met us in our Arithmetic class taught by Magnolia Rot, a curvy red head whose daughter was the miserable Crimson. He wasn't speaking to me. I understood. I wouldn't speak to him either if he'd slept with my sister even if it was unconfirmed.

It was a relief to leave Arithmetic and be away from the sad glances Magnolia kept shooting at Crimson. I finally understood what Slate had meant about Ash breaking hearts. Crimson was heartbroken, and it was torture sitting next to Ash as if we were rubbing in our happiness.

What I didn't expect was when I went to leave the class, I dropped my book and waved everyone ahead of me. I thought it was just Magnolia and me in the room until I felt the anguish.

"Watch your back. Not everyone is happy about your upcoming marriage," hissed Crimson as she passed me.

My head shot up in alarm as she passed me. Girls who fought over men were idiots in my book, but I wasn't fighting over Ash. I'd already won.

Her threat proved baseless. Not that I was complaining, but all I did was go to classes with Ash and then stay the night at his palace after staying late planning the engagement party in two months. I told myself I wasn't avoiding headquarters. That I would feel the same way about seeing Brass as I had before. He had nothing to do with me not training.

It was the end of the week and we had finally nailed down the date of our engagement party and planned the details. I could describe the theme in one word, purple. One of the Straumr colors was purple, so they incorporated it in everything. I didn't mind so much since purple was one of my favorite colors, but I would have liked a bit more say in the matter. Dahlia was a planning drill sergeant and on more than one occasion Sparrow looked like she was ready to throttle the woman.

Each day composed of six classes, on our first day we had Hawk's American History class but had exchanged it for a second battle class usually taught by Fox Straumr.

The battle grounds were twice the size of the ones at the Sumar palace. You expected Russell Crowe to walk out at any moment and ask if we were entertained. A track spanned the tiered stone seating with an enormous globe of domed stained glass that capped the room. There was a section for weights and archery like at home. A combat ring of artificial grey turf padding accommodated four simultaneous pairs of fighters. There were no welcoming flowers like at the palace, only weapons, weights, and they lined it in gravel. They sometimes rolled out an obstacle course we called the Gauntlet and made us run it over and over while swinging hammers tried to pulverize us. There was always a lot of healing at the end of class.

I stayed back to chat with Fox waving Tawny on ahead and watched as the tyros from the second and first years filed into the prep rooms. I needed to blow off some steam and Fox was always good for some harmless flirting/training.

Fox embraced me when the others left. "Can I welcome you to the family already? I knew Ash would win you over, the boy never gives up on anything he really wants, and he really wants you."

I gave the youngest Straumr's brother a smirk. "Thanks, yeah, he's persistent," I joked.

I'd been so busy with the party planning; I had hardly spoken to my family. After Slate stormed out of the dining hall I'd sat with Indigo and Ash the rest of the week. I knew things would be awkward between Slate and I, but not him becoming a card-carrying member of the We Hate Scarlett Tio fan club. I seemed to gather a stalwart following. That might have been what Crimson had been talking about. There were several girls who'd been giving me the stink eye since Ash and I became engaged. Ash was the most eligible bachelor and I'd taken him off the market. They hated me.

Fox practiced a real knife fight with me, and I didn't mind grappling with the twinkly eyed trainer. I'd drawn Fox's blood surprising us both. He'd called it quits and healed me before I left the battle grounds.

"Good to know your betrothal has not made you soft," he said with a flirty wink.

I peeled off my gear and hit the showers. I was late for dinner but feeling good. Tonight, I'd see Brass and get extra training. I'd stay to have a late, strictly platonic dinner and hope I didn't run into Slate and Lera doing anything that would make me want to dump acid into my eyes.

A shower started somewhere on my left. It wasn't unusual since it was a shower room. Then I heard more showers turn on. Showers were turning on all along the walls. I finished rinsing my face in time to see the fist flying towards my nose. I went sprawling along the tiles to hit the wall.

I didn't have the luxury of recovering gracefully, Jonquil stood with her gang of haters. They were in their gear and I was as naked as the day the Mother made me. I thought Jonquil would jump all over me once I was down, but she was going to savor it. Her nearly white, blonde hair was combed to the side, the sides shaved. Her big cobalt eyes watched me with malice. Red lips pulled back over her mouth with too many teeth in a sneer.

"I have been waiting a long time for this," she said before she lashed out again.

She wasn't using weapons, and she wasn't calling. Her friends weren't jumping in, I vainly hoped they were only there for reinforcement.

Being naked and wet worked to my advantage. When she tried to grab me, I slipped through her fingers. I kicked her under her breasts with my bare foot, knocking her back, but she kept coming.

She swung high, keeping me low, then tried to stomp on me with her boots. I rolled out of the way and swept her feet out from under her. I jumped on top of her and punched her in the face, my wet hair slapping against my face and obstructing my sight. Her wenches dragged me off the tile floor with my knees after I got in three good hits. There were four of them and one of me.

I wanted to call, but I was afraid to hurt them badly and get expelled. The secret would be out if I went elemental. I was relying on my hand-to-hand combat skills and four against one naked, sopping wet girl were bad odds.

Jonquil rose to her feet wiping her face. One girl walked out and healed her, Jonquil washed her face in the stream of shower water. I took the chance to fight the girls holding me why Jonquil and the other girl were distracted. They were going to kick my fanny pack otherwise.

My wet body went limp and with no clothes to hold on to, I slipped through their hands. I jammed my open palm into one girl's nose breaking it instantly and punched the other girl in the throat. I used my body's momentum to slam her face first into the shower wall. So much for not hurting them badly.

I was trying to knock them out, but Jonquil and the girl who healed her came at me as one. I was hoping if I could incapacitate Jonquil, the other girl would give up, go home lick her wounds.

I threw the dice. Jonquil was quick, she got in a few rib shots before I knocked her back, her head slamming on the shower floor. The other girl hesitated, and I thought my gamble had paid off until Jonquil screamed at her.

"Get that bitch!"

I blocked her fists flying at me but tripped over the girl I'd slammed face first into the wall. My feet slipped, and the girl jumped on me. My head cracked on the drain, and I tasted blood. Nausea swelled in my throat and my vision swam, the girl sat on my chest and wailed on me. Pain exploded in my face. There wasn't a singular point where it began, it was my entire head that pulsed with sharp pain. Somehow, I wriggled free. Being nude and wet was becoming my only advantage. There was blood in my eyes, and I could hardly see.

I should have felt them, I thought angrily. My stupid need to be alone in the shower with no one else's thoughts or feelings caused me to mute it. The four girls were back on their feet but looking worse for wear. I wondered if I looked any better than they did.

"Hold her down," Jonquil ordered.

The four girls charged me. Even though I hated running from them, I had to run. I came at them like I was going to attack, but I ducked low and rolled between the girls in the middle, their fingernails clawing at my back as I slipped through making me wince. I was on my feet and running down the showers when I felt arms around my waist and slammed face first into the shower floor. They had caught up quickly with their booted feet versus my bare ones. Perhaps nudity had its downfalls.

Someone rolled me over. I couldn't see through all the blood in my eyes and when I tried to open them, pain lanced through my throbbing head. I was pretty sure every bone in my face had broken.

At least one girl was kicking me in the stomach. Jonquil, I thought ruefully, and I coughed up blood with my vomit. That was when the searing pain started. I tried to scream; I gave up trying to fight off my elemental power and wanted to shift. Someone grabbed my head and slammed it into the floor.

My world went dark.

There was no rescuer, no one saved me. I woke up cold, wet, and alone. I couldn't see, though I remembered everything. One of those haters had broken my ribs when they kicked me and my right arm. My breathing was shallow, and I hurt from head to toe. I had never hurt so much in my life. Not when the baulk gutted me, because I was in shock, not when my throat was slit, not when Jonquil had stabbed my chest, or when the Jorogumo attacked me. I'd always healed almost immediately. Now, I was in agony. Every breath was a thousand knives. I wondered if they had punctured a lung.

They knew I'd survive. They could've made sure I'd died if they wanted to. It was sadistic. I crawled on my good hand and knees blindly out of the showers. They had turned them all off, so the prep room chilled my bare skin. I was afraid to touch my face and find out what they'd done to it. Oh Gods, my teeth!

I remembered the searing pain, and I was sure it had been a knife on my flesh. I hoped they didn't Hannibal Lector me and chopped off pieces of my face. There'd be no healing from that. The pain came from my stomach. I wanted to give up, lie down on the floor, and try to sleep. It was the blood loss and shock talking, but I didn't care.

I crawled out of the showers and tried to find my way out of the bathroom. It didn't matter if someone saw me naked; I had bigger problems. My crawling was achingly slow, but I couldn't move any faster with the pain blazing through my body. I didn't shift into an elemental; I didn't use calling, only defended myself. That had to count for something with the council. I was worried if they found out they'd expel me.

I was so afraid of getting kicked out and never becoming a Guardian and failing my mother; it had gotten me beaten into unconsciousness. I didn't even know how long it had lasted. Five minutes? Ten? Was I even out for very long?

The gentle rise and fall of my chest was too much for me to continue. I had to keep going; I didn't think I was dying, but you wouldn't catch me waiting around to find out. With the pads of my fingers clinging to the tiles, I groped ahead on my good hand and knees again but slipped in my blood. My body crashed back into the floor. I cried out.

I hoped Jonquil and her gang weren't still in there laughing at my cries. I laid my head on the cool floor and tried to breathe. It was all I could focus on. After another minute, I started again. Move my hand, shift my knees, move my hand, shift my knees. It became my mantra when my body protested, not wanting to give another inch.

I could save myself. I could do it.

I made it to the door. It was a swinging door; I didn't know if I had the energy to shove it open. I climbed to my knees and threw my body forward. Someone would find me in the hall, that'd be okay.

I was wedged half in, half out of the door. It felt like someone was stabbing my insides anew. I pulled myself out through the doors by my fingers. When I cleared it and it closed, I coughed up blood. I laughed, at least it was supposed to be a laugh and more blood frothed around my mouth.

Crap, I might've been dying.

My jaw was mush, and I couldn't speak. I started yelling as best I could, I would've given a zombie a run for its money with the noises that came from me. I was giving up. It was time to accept it. I laid face down on the floor, the stupid door nook still hid half of my body, but anyone walking down the hall would notice my top half laying on the floor.

I heard footsteps. I felt worry. As loud as I could, I groaned — this was it. Either this person would find me, or I'd lie there slowly bleeding to death. The footsteps picked up into a run.

CHAPTER EIGHT
JETT

Jett

It'd only been ten minutes, possibly less.

They followed Slate's lead as he barreled through Valla U even faster than Quick.

Jett stopped next to Slate and fell to his knees, his hands held palm up. His eyes darted all over Scarlet's body. He didn't know what to heal first. Blood covered her from head to toe in blood, not a stitch of clothing over her body. She laid on her stomach and if she had not opened her turquoise eyes, Jett wouldn't have even known it was her, her face was so badly broken. Fear twisted in Jett's chest; he couldn't lose Scarlett after losing Wren. Neither could Indigo. Jett feared Scarlett's twin was having a much harder time than she was letting on.

Slate moved beside Jett and stiffened. His jaw clenched, and he looked as in- credulous as Jett felt. Scarlett's matted head moved as Slate came into view of her eyes and he flinched. Secretly, Jett was happy Slate had had the same reaction he'd had to how mutilated her face was, but those eyes were unmistakable.

Jett shook his head at Slate whose eyes were changing. Slate had to keep his cool until they could help Scarlett. Brass sucked in a deep breath as his eyes settled on Scarlett. The three men looked helpless, afraid to move her, afraid to touch her and see the extent of the injuries. Maybe it wasn't real, and this was some horrible prank. She groaned and Jett winced.

Quick slid into Jett like he was stealing second base and she groaned again, Brass smiled, and Jett took it as a good sign. She obviously had enough going on in her head to hate having four men standing over her naked. It was a worse sign that she couldn't voice her complaints.

"We cannot move her until we heal her first, I do not think she can take it," Brass murmured as his hand fell against her cheek.

Slate nodded, "Do it."

Jett glanced at Slate. He knew after their mother's funeral that things were changing between Slate and Scarlett until he'd gone and messed it up. Something had changed in Scarlett, like she thought life was too short for regrets, and had had her cake and eat it too. Now she was engaged to the future Prime and had spent the night with Brass. Even if it was unconfirmed.

Not that Scarlett was being destructive, on the contrary, she had taken extra battle training from the Shadow Breakers and had appeared to make a clean break from Slate. It was Slate whose pernicious brooding was leading him into fights for the last five nights. That was only the half of it. There was palpable tension between Brass and Slate. The two men were like brothers. Judging by the fond way Brass was looking at Scarlett, that was all the confirmation Jett needed to know why they weren't spending all their time together as they usually did.

Scarlett would be trouble for Brass. He had to know how badly Slate wanted Scarlett. He'd never shown so much interest in a woman.

Quick's dark eyes were painfully sad as he reached for Scarlett. Jett watched as Quick and Brass put their hands to her shoulders as they called. Her body shook as she took a deep shuddering breath. Jett's square jaw clenched in rage at his sister's pain and couldn't wait any longer. He gently rolled her into his arms, cradling her body trying to offer her as much cover as possible with his own. Freya's burly boar, did whoever did this not care that she was painfully modest? They could have tossed a towel over her after they beat her, seemed the least they could do.

"Get me something to put over her," Jett said and swallowed at the detachment in his own voice. He felt as cold on the inside as he sounded.

Quick headed into the prep room at a run and promptly fell slipping in the bloody trail she'd left dragging her body through the room. He cursed and got back up and ran more carefully. Slate and Jett brought her back into the prep room behind him and Brass locked the doors.

They healed her enough to be conscious, but not enough to talk. Jett tried not to look down at her where she was gazing up at him with enormous almond eyes the same color as his own in that broken face. It swelled her full lips beyond recognition, those high cheekbones bruised and impossibly shattered. Her celestial nose was smashed and the beginning of two black eyes were forming around the only part of her that was recognizable. Jett felt a wave of fear again and drowned it in the urgency to get her better.

Rage and fear would serve no purpose.

Quick came back with his hands full of towels and Slate laid them out in a makeshift bed over the cream marble floor. Jett laid her down and took the towels from Quick laying one over her breasts and over her hips, but low on her hips because they would need to see as they healed her. Jett sat back down on his heels and brought his eyes up to the other men. Slate was kneeling across from Jett, Quick leaned over her head, and Brass was at her feet. It felt morbid to Jett and his blood heated with rage.

"We can't fuck this up," Jett told them in all seriousness.

He couldn't say out loud that if her face wasn't fixed, as well as her internal injuries, that he was liable to kill everyone in the building in a rage if Slate didn't do it first. He met silver eyes brimming with primitive fury, amber eyes filled with genuine concern and care, and last, deep chocolate strained with self-recrimination. Quick was supposed to be guarding her, but she had been sleeping at the Straumr palace all week, he couldn't have known she'd change her mind.

Scarlett's swollen fingers moved at Slate's side and Jett looked away at the flicker of emotions that crossed the man's face as he brushed

Scarlett's knuckles. The four of them placed their hands on her bare skin and Jett closed his eyes as he delved, knitting her together. Her broken arm righted itself. The swelling around her eyes faded. She blinked her turquoise eyes at them. Quick let go and disappeared and Jett watched as her lips returned to a normal fullness that most found alluring, but she despised, and her nose and cheeks returned to their original forms. He sighed as she did.

"Please don't close your eyes, Scarlett. I need to see those big beauties looking at me with thinly veiled indignation," Jett said tenderly when her bright eyes moved under her long lashes.

She opened them again and looked directly into his. She tried to wet her lips with her tongue and her cheeks twitched. Blood.

"I'd hold off on that until Quick gets back," Jett said, forcing a smile.

Slate's hands rested on her hip. He closed his eyes in concentration. Brass still had his hands on her feet and looked very far away as he gazed down at her. Yes, Jett could understand why there was tension. Brass had deep feelings for Scarlett. Jett cursed his luck. Why had Slate brought Brass if he didn't like him around Scarlett? Brass was stable and didn't have a reputation for sleeping with married women, Slate was neither stable nor was his reputation exemplary. She would never go for a guy like that, that's why they let Quick around her. Quick may have every other woman hypnotized by his smile, but it was powerless against Scarlett.

Slate released a long-held breath sighed. "They healed it so it could never fade."

Jett's eyes focused on the skin under Slate's hand, it had to be a woman who attacked her.

Scarlett's throat started working and Jett put his hands on her face, cupping to either side of it and closed his eyes. He was determined that every pore on her body would be back to its previous perfection. Quick was back with three wet towels and a small glass bowl of water.

"Open," Quick said, lifting the bowl to her mouth.

She parted her lips, and he let a little trickle in. She worked her throat again and her lips quirked. Relief flooded through Jett and was suddenly very defensive about his sister's state of undress in front of the other three men and tried not to glower at them.

"More," Scarlett rasped. She sounded like she'd risen from the grave.

Quick flashed that smile of his, "I would have paid to hear you say that any other day."

Jett scowled and noticed they mimicked his expression on the other two men's faces when Scarlett's lips parted into a beautiful heart-stopping smile and Jett could feel the tension break like ocean waves on a headland. Slate's hand moved again brushing hers. Jett knew he was craving her attention, and not enjoying sharing so much as her smile.

Jett took a wet towel and wiped at her face, and Slate followed suit to wipe her chest above the towel. Brass called glancing up at Slate before cleansing her legs. Jett did his best not shake his head at the careful distance Brass gave Slate, Slate had just as much right to Scarlett as Brass did. None. She was Ash's. Jett could just see Quick where he had disappeared with the other wet towel.

"I can move now. You don't have to baby me," she told them gently.

"You'll let us baby you if we want to," Jett said, irritated. He hadn't meant for it to come out so brusque, but there were many dynamics at work, and it was making Jett edgy.

"Would it be vain to ask if my face is okay?"sShe asked afraid to touch it.

Slate smiled in a way that made Jett's eyes widen. "Better than okay," his hand stroked down her cheek, and Jett closed his eyes and counted to ten.

Scarlett's hands went to her face, then her throat, and she sighed when she felt her necklaces. Her hands slid down over the strategically placed towels and Jett sucked on his teeth as her hand neared the scar.

"Can I sit up?" she asked, rubbing the tips of her fingers over the white slightly puckered skin.

"Wait, a little longer," Slate said.

"You're showing serious restraint in not asking me questions," Scarlett smirked, a little of her humor coming out.

His lips curled, "I am."

"Is that because you plan on milking Brass for everything he sees in my mind?"

Brass chuckled, "Yes, they will."

Jett cursed internally at the daggers Slate shot Brass for engaging her. It was gone in a blink, but Jett had caught it. Brass was cautious, but not willing to back down completely.

"I was going to come to headquarters tonight. I stayed late to spar with Fox," she took a deep breath searching Brass's eyes. "Not that I'm complaining, but couldn't you guys have brought Ama or Shale with you? Does every man in my life have to see me naked?" Scarlett teased.

Slate's jaw clenched as Jett turned his head to Brass narrowing his eyes. Slate was balancing on a knife's edge. Brass's eyes flickered down to her.

Slate had shut his eyes and appeared to be trying to tame his anger.

"Naked?" Jett glared at the two Regn brothers.

"I need to take a shower. Jonquil and three of her friends jumped me during my last one. I should have known better. They waited till everyone left for dinner and I was showering. They didn't call at all, and they didn't use their weapons. I thought at first, they might just let Jonquil and me fight, but once I had the upper hand, they moved in."

Scarlett interrupted Jett's questioning and temporarily distracted Slate's wrath. Jonquil — Jett should have known. She'd been on and off with Ash for years, of course she'd be irate that Ash had chosen Scarlett over her. There were more than a few nasty rumors going around about Scarlett that Jett knew weren't true and had been doing damage control against so she wouldn't hear them and break her heart. Guardian politics would be the death of her; she felt too much, burned too brightly, and Jett would die before he let one of those jaded greater families dim his sister.

"I didn't want to show them I was an elemental. I didn't call because I didn't want the council to have an excuse to expel me or instigate the girls start all calling at me. They would have killed me if they wanted me dead," she continued.

"They used a weapon, Scarlett," Jett said softly pressing his full lips together.

"I don't think so. I don't remember that," she protested, but Jett could see the denial in her eyes.

Slate pressed his lips together and helped her into a sitting position, he shifted the towels around her chest to keep her covered. He lifted the corner of the towel at Scarlett's waist and displayed the bumpy skin she'd felt there. Someone had carved KHORAZ into the skin. She touched it again with her fingertips; it was rough but white.

Slate had worked too hard to heal it. She squeezed her eyes shut and Jett wanted to raze the earth for the pain in her face. His innocent sister branded for life, he fought the urge to tear into the portal room and track down Jonquil and murder her.

"They healed you so it would remain," Brass explained.

"What does it mean?" she asked them and looked from face to face.

Jett couldn't bring himself to tell her, so he looked to Brass.

"One who desires, literally. They are Guardians who covet the tribes or have transactions for certain services. There are others who have become addicted to a person through rousen," Brass informed her in a smooth delicate tone.

Jett's heart twisted as her lip wobbled. She ducked her head and Jett fell forward wrapping his arms around her not caring if there were at least two other men who would prefer to be the ones to comfort her; she was his sister. He resisted stroking her blood matted hair, it would only upset her.

"No one will see it, baby sis. Only your husband, and if he has something to say about it, then I'll have something to say to him," Jett promised.

"Shadow Breakers have tattoos so they can find us, they must be activated with calling, but it has proven helpful. You could incorporate it into a tattoo of your choosing. I could take you if you like and get that covered up," Brass offered, and she broke away from Jett with streaks of tears on her cheeks.

"Yeah?" she wiped her face with the back of her hand.

Brass smiled warmly at her, his amber eyes glittering, "It would be my pleasure, Scarlett. There is no laser surgery for it, it is permanent. It would have to be cut out from your skin to remove."

She ran her fingers over my lumpy skin, "Anything would be better than this. Could you take me in the morning? I don't want anyone else finding out. I'm grateful they didn't do it on my forehead. They got revenge after Ash proposed." Jett looked across to Slate who clenched his jaw, not looking at Brass.

"You want to do nothing?" Slate asked incredulously.

"I didn't say that. I said, I didn't want anyone else knowing. They'll get theirs, but I'll have to wait for the right moment. Revenge is a dish best served cold," her tone was ice cold when she turned to face Slate and he looked taken aback.

Slate watched her, searching her expression, "Fine. I am going to bring you home. I will help you shower because you will be weak, and then in the morning I will take you to get the tattoo."

Quick walked up with several bloody towels in his arms, "I do not know how you dragged yourself all the way through here and out the door. There was blood everywhere."

"You cleaned it yourself?" she asked, raising her slightly arched eyebrows a shade darker than her caramel hair.

"Of course," he beamed a dazzling smile at her, and Jett noticed both he and Brass smiled when it had no effect on her.

"How is it that the four of you were together and knew where I was? I have been spending the night with Ash, so it's not like my absence would be cause for alarm," she looked at each one of them looking for answers.

Several ideas ran through Jett's mind, but the truth wouldn't work. He never thought he'd have to lie to her, but it was for her own good. Jett looked at the other three men, the resigned look on Brass's face, the surprised one on Quick, and the expressionless one on Slate. Jett cursed himself once more.

"Slate brought them over. You weren't going to Ash's, and we saw you sparring with Fox. We realized you were missing; we came here first by luck," Jett said quickly, and she looked at the other men for confirmation.

She wanted to believe the lie; Jett could see it in her face. Deep down she knew there was a reason she had shied away from Slate for so long, why there were so many holes in their story, and a few others they'd told her.

"Get the tattoo, Torch," Slate rumbled.

"Okay. What do I need to do for the Shadow Breaker mark?"

She kept deferring to Brass and Jett could almost feel Slate's frustration. Brass held much of her regard. He wondered how much of that regard Brass had experienced since she blushed when she looked at him even in her condition.

"You use Shadow Breaker blood, and we insert a tracker rune into your tattoo to blend in. Mine is under my hairline, so is Slate's, Quick integrated his into his body art," Brass explained.

"Would you mind?" I asked and Jett's head swung to Slate who had dropped his silver eyes and balled his fists so his knuckles turned white.

"As long as Slate promises not to kill me," Brass teased not lifting his amber eyes from Scarlett's.

"He promises," she said dismissively without looking at Slate.

"Not for the mark," he ground out, and Jett wiped a hand over his face reminding himself he needed to shave.

Scarlett was playing a dangerous game that she did not know she was even playing. She didn't see the looks the two men were giving one another, and she did not know how differently Slate acted with her. How could she? Slate's discipline went out the window with his rules for her, and it wasn't a good thing. He had those rules for a reason. Gods, she must have some inkling of how Slate thought of her.

"You are trouble. I do not want you hanging out with my brother anymore. I thought I would be the one hooking up with dangerous women. Not Brass. Brass is the sensible one. You, are trouble," Quick pointed a long finger at Scarlett and for once Jett agreed.

Brass shrugged, "It has been a long time since I have gotten into trouble." He flashed her a warm smile and rose to his feet.

"Not that long," Scarlett's usual tone dropped an octave.

Brass's eyes glittered as he bit back whatever he wanted to say in front of the other men, "I will see you in the morning. Good night, Scarlett."

She craned her head back holding the towel over her chest and flashed Brass a smile that gave Jett a headache. Didn't she know she couldn't flash that thing at just anyone? Slate's teeth set on edge from the simple parting of her lips. She had the female equivalent of Quick's smile that incited desire and the need to please her no matter the cost, all with a twist of her lips.

Couldn't Jett have had a couple of hermit sisters? Life would be so much easier if Scarlett and Indigo had been plain, maybe a little frumpy.

Quick grabbed Brass's arm with a scowl and dragged the other man from the prep room, their work was done.

Jett started incinerating the towels Quick used to clean the prep room, disposing of the evidence and Slate helped her to her feet. She couldn't stand on her own, and it was apparent that Slate was the only thing holding her upright. Jett took the towels that had been under her and burned them as Slate walked Scarlett over to her cubby.

The prep room smelled of the polished wood that made up the beautiful walnut cubbies not a hint of the blood that had trailed behind her. The benches were chocolate brown padded leather that ran the length of each aisle. Jett saw Slate carefully get her into a seated position on the padded bench with the towel wrapped tightly around her and pulled out her clothes for her. Jett moved away not wanting to see what happened next. There was no way she had the strength to dress herself. It counted in Slate's favor that he cared about Scarlett in a way Jett did not know he was capable of.

Jett finished cleaning up after the mess before coming down the aisle happy to find her dressed if swaying slightly as she sat next to Slate. Jett stroked her head unable to stop himself and frowned at the dried blood in her hair.

"Gods, Scar. You look like Carrie White. Let's get you home," he said in a voice that was almost as deep as their father's.

Slate didn't wait for her reply before he scooped her feet out from under her and Jett gave him a glare good enough for both. Jett rested his hand on Scarlett's head and called her to sleep.

Slate arched a brow at Jett, the two men could meet eye to eye, being taller than most the men in Tidings. Jett jutted out his jaw arrogantly as he wanted to do before looking at Slate coolly as he held Scarlett cradled in his arms.

"She needs the rest, and I don't want her to hear this," Jett started.

"Hear what?" Slate rumbled with flashing silver eyes.

"She's going to find out about that mark, then what? I covered today because she's not ready to hear it, or maybe I should say you're not ready for her to get irreparably pissed at you. Just what are you going to do when she fucks her husband, as wives do?" Jett hammered his point home with as much visualization he could punch into it.

It had the desired effect when he saw Slate's arms tighten around her and a muscle in his hard jaw leapt, "She will not marry him; she will not sleep with him before then. Help me complete the bond, Jett."

Jett nearly staggered. It was as much a plea as he'd ever heard from Slate. Slate begged nothing from no one. Jett sucked in a deep breath.

"She slept with Brass, Slate. Why him and not Ash?" Jett knew there was more than met the eye with those two.

Slate couldn't resist looking down at her, and Jett fought the urge to slap sense into Slate, "Only she knows that, but I can feel what she feels when we are alone. She cares even if she pretends otherwise when others are around."

Jett shook his head and leaned against the door of the walnut cubby, "I also see the way her and Brass look at one another. Does your plan take him into account? Say she doesn't marry Ash. Why would she choose you, who can't offer her a future, when there's Brass who can, and they have a connection?"

Slate's demeanor changed, and Jett knew he'd hit a nerve. He uncrossed his arms and rested his hand on Slate's shoulder.

"Life is too short. Your life in particular. You are my brother; I don't want to see you lose it because Scarlett chooses someone else. Because you will," Jett dry washed his face; he wasn't even making a dent.

"I do not expect you to understand, but all will reveal itself —"

Jett held up a hand, "Spare me your prophet talk. I'll help you complete the bond, even though she'll hate me when she finds out. You'd better take great care she doesn't. Couldn't you have gotten attached to Amber or Lynx, or one of the countless other women willing to have you in their lives?" He rubbed his close-cropped hair roughly feeling the soft tiny spikes run across his palm.

Slate's lips curled, and Jet knew he'd only heard one part of his diatribe. "Thank you, brother. I swear I will take care of her tonight," Slate said, and Jett crossed his arms.

"Who said I was letting you take my baby sister to your rooms? You'd better not try to seduce her, satyromaniac," Jett raised his brows waiting for a response.

Slate chuckled darkly, and Jett narrowed his eyes, "I would do nothing the lady would disagree too. Honestly, what do you take me for?"

"I'd worry less about me, and more about how she'll react once she wakes up in your bed."

She pursed full pink lips in a petulant little pout, and her lashes fanned across her high cheekbones. Jett's eyes flickered to Slate, and he almost rolled his eyes. Did he know no restraint?

"Leave the vial on the coffee table and I'll take it once I drop off some clothes in your room. We'll have to get Brass in on it too, I'll run the vial over to him tonight so he can give it to Dhole. By the Mother, what a damn mess." Jett said.

CHAPTER NINE

Warm water spilled over my head, and I moaned in my sleep. I couldn't stay awake; my eyes wouldn't stay open.

"Scarlett." I felt Slate stroke my face.

I wanted to sleep. More water spilled over my head as hands worked their way through it, and I murmured words even I didn't understand. I was laying back against something warm and a hard band was around my waist holding me in place.

Hands in my hair again and I felt myself drifting off at the relaxing feel of someone massaging my scalp until warm water poured over my head once more.

"What?" I mumbled in a voice deeper than my usual gravelly tone.

"Getting the blood out of your hair," Slate rumbled close to my ear.

"Can't... stay awake," I told him trying to pry my eyes open.

"I will take care of you," he told me, his voice like a wound about me in a cocoon of strength and safety.

I was warm and fuzzy all over. I was vaguely aware of where I was as I leaned my head back against that something soft and felt more warm water slosh over my skin. Dimly, I moved my hands, and my fingers ran into flesh. I pried my eyes open and saw two powerfully built thighs to either side of me. I squinted at them trying to make sense of what I was seeing before I saw a hand come into view and sluice water over my partially submerged chest.

My hands rested on the thighs with silky blue-black hair too fine to be Brass's and I stared in disbelief at the feel of them. They were real. It wasn't a dream. Healing and fighting had sucked the energy right out of me. I had more healing than usual, and I was sapped and delirious. I tilted my head back to see what I was leaning against, and my head dipped sideways.

Slate's arm lifted catching me as my head slid down his chest. I opened my mouth and closed it as he looked down at me with an unreadable expression. I blinked several times to no avail. His eyes were silver and full of lust. It had to be a dream.

"*This is thy hour O Soul, thy free flight into the wordless. Away from books, away from art, the day erased, the lesson done. Thee fully forth emerging, silent, gazing, pondering the themes thou lovest best. Night, sleep, death, and the stars.*"

I closed my eyes, and I swore he kissed me before sleep rolled me under.

Wiping a hand over my face, I opened my eyes. Fiddlesticks, it had been a terrible night. My stomach rumbling had woken me up, I was starving. My heart lurched when I realized where I was. I hadn't needed to open my eyes to smell the earthy scent of Slate mingled with the spicy clove scent.

His arms were wrapped around me like a straitjacket. I pressed my face to his hard chest, and I instinctually knew we were both naked. Gods, even when I'd bathed him after the bauk attack, I'd dressed him! He could have done that much.

My body felt worn out, and I didn't know if I would have to fight with Slate for him to let me leave. We were in his bedroom, so Jett knew we were there or at least in the palace. I closed my eyes. Slate had bathed me in his enormous bathtub. He had been in it with me, and I seriously doubted he wore a swimsuit while he did it. When I had bathed him, I'd had free reign to clean every inch of his skin and I doubted Slate had shown any restraint.

Sighing, I relaxed my muscles and let my head fall against his hard chest. It wasn't the only thing that was hard either; he was poking me in the stomach, but I refused to wiggle any more than necessary and risk waking him and having a conversation about how totally inappropriate it was.

My eyes were heavy as I tried to summon the energy to leave.

Slate's hands roamed freely over my skin until I awoke. I was groggy, but not in any pain. A thick feeling had settled over my mind like I stuffed it with cotton balls making it difficult to process things, like where I was, what happened, and the fact I was holding Slate, not Ash, when I awoke.

I'd fallen back to sleep!

He had pushed my hair over my shoulder, so it spilled over his ribs and was running his fingers down my back as I came to.

"What are you doing?" I murmured, working my mouth before calling water into it and swallowing.

"Caring for you, Torch," he said, and I shifted my head, so my head rested on his chest on the ridge of his pecs.

I pulled my hands under my chin as I looked up at him. Slate when he first woke up was quite the sight. Bronze and sexily sleepy with tousled waves that molded over his shoulders and onto his chest with dreamy grey eyes. Like a big cat lazing about on a jungle tree limb.

"You took a bath with me last night."

It wasn't a question, but he answered anyway, "I did not want you to have to wake up with blood in your hair."

He ran his fingers through my golden locks. "Did you need to climb in with me?" I asked, quirking an eyebrow at him.

His full lips curled lasciviously, "I guess we will never know."

I narrowed my eyes at him. It would be pointless to remind Slate of all the reasons this was inappropriate in the extreme. He wouldn't care.

"Thank you for taking care of me last night, but you should have dressed me, or at least yourself. You know if Ash saw me right now, he'd break things off. You put me in a compromising position. Not that you care, but it's my reputation on the line when things like this happen."

"You are taking it remarkably well. I had expected to have to restrain you when you woke up, Torch."

His hair toppled on his left side; the ivory starburst threaded on a midnight braid resting on his collarbone that matched mine. I smashed my breasts up against him, his hands stroking my bare back, he was straight out of a girly magazine.

Unwanted feelings soared through me just by being in his room, add a naked Slate, a naked self, add the knowledge of wonderful carnal appetites could be, and it equaled world of trouble.

I grabbed his satin sheet and pulled it around me as I got off him. Not looking back to see everything I'd revealed. Adrenaline was shooting through me; it must have exhausted me to have fallen back to sleep.

My nerves were jittery, I couldn't be in this tiny room with him. He shouldn't be allowed in such confined spaces with all that mass, taking up all the space and air. I could hardly breathe with him filling his giant lungs, stealing my oxygen.

"Stay the day, Torch," he said following me into the sitting room where clothes were sitting on the coffee table.

A heather grey fitted t-shirt that said LOVE on it and a pair of pink sweats awaited me. Slate's hands slid around my waist; his bare body pressed against the satin sheet around my hips. Slate's stubbled jaw rubbed against my cheek as he made a contented noise deep in his throat. I clenched my jaw as pleasure shot down to my toes.

"Did you not like sleeping in my bed?" he purred in my ear, and I flashed back to those nights he held me while I grieved.

"It was... nice." Very nice. "If I thought we could just lay together, maybe I would stay," I wasn't strong enough to turn around and face him, so I waited for him to drop his arms from my waist.

"I saw you the following morning with Brass. Were you the least bit guilty for having left me to be with him?"

His voice had taken on a cool edge, and his arms had tightened around me. He was angry. Maybe even jealous. I would have been too in his position. Last night was the first time I'd seen Brass since we'd made love and I couldn't keep a reign over my wild emotions.

"Brass only kissed me because he tried to call off the dogs. Your lover hates me and thinks I'm after you. He does it so I can keep training with the Shadow Breakers," I snapped.

He spun me around and pulled me hard against his body. Slate's eyes were hard, his full lips pinched.

"Brass kisses you because he wants you, same as me. Do not make him out to be more noble than he is. Explain to me how taking your maidenhood helps me. Confess. It was Brass."

I blinked up at him and worked my mouth, "What bothers you more? That I had sex for the first time, and it wasn't with you or that when I did, it may have been with the only man you feel threatened by?"

For a moment, I thought Slate darkened, but I blinked, and it was gone. "Scamper off then, Rabbit. I hope you got your use out of me," Slate's arms dropped from me, and he walked back to his bedroom, his powerfully sculpted back and everything below it strode from the room.

I hugged myself accidentally dropping his sheet to the floor. That had not gone as I'd hoped.

Brass was waiting for me in the portal room of the Sumar palace. It bathed him in blue light, his lips parted in a warm smile when he saw me freeze in the doorway.

"Surprised to see me, Scarlett?" Brass's smooth deep voice perked up my mood.

"Yes, but I'm happy you're here. I thought I was going to have to hunt you down at headquarters, but door-to-door service is much better."

He rubbed his plump defined lips together and looked away, "Not having a delightful morning, I see."

I bet he did.

"Can we please get out of here? If I think anymore, I'm going to rock myself in a dark corner."

Brass held out his arm, and I walked under it holding my breath so I wouldn't wind up melting against him with his intoxicating cinnamon scent. He draped it over my shoulder offering me comfort as we exited through the bright white light of the portal and into Valla's town heart.

I ignored the fact he was rubbing his lips together again and let him lead me away.

"Hungry?" he asked as we traversed the cobbled roads.

... *Yes* ...

"I know a place that makes pizza."

I stopped in my tracks. "You're only telling me this now?" Brass's full lips spread into a smile.

He led me into a dimly lit bistro, complete with red checkered tablecloths. I sat in the wrought iron seat happily and looked at the menu.

"Deep dish?" I exclaimed gleefully.

Brass smiled, "They have every type of food here if you know where to look."

"Brass, I could kiss you right now," I beamed.

He started rubbing his lips together. If the pizza was good enough, no matter that it was for breakfast, I would kiss him. The thought of melting into him made me wriggle in my seat.

We split a small deep-dish pizza loaded with sausage and mushroom while I listened to him talk about his brothers and the Shadow Breakers. He'd known Slate and the others for a decade. They tutored together in fighting, then Lera got her red talons into Slate. I kept my opinions to myself since I felt Brass holding back as he told me about it.

"Do you have a girlfriend?" I asked boldly, as I ungracefully ate sloppy pizza.

Brass leveled his amber eyes at me, "Would I go around kissing beautiful women if I were seeing someone?"

I blushed. Kissing was all we were discussing. Did he just call me beautiful?

"I suppose not. Why are you single then?"

Brass laughed richly making his eyes crinkle. "It tends not to work out when the women you date think about other men, even if they do not mean to, it bruises the ego," he gave a rueful grin.

"Do I...?"

"When we are alone, you only think of me," the corners of his mouth quirked.

"Most of the time inappropriately, and I thank you for not mentioning it," I toasted him with my ice water hoping it would bring down my rapidly heating temperature.

He leaned forward on corded dark honey forearms. "I really do not mind. I am only glad you cannot read mine," he said silkily, and I bit the inside of my cheek to keep a ridiculous smile from blooming on my face. "Do not worry, Scarlett. I am not trying to seduce you...again."

"Good, because it's not working," I smiled playfully as I looked at him through my lashes.

A little flirting hurt no one, I told myself. He knew I was engaged and what we shared was a personal favor he'd done me. I thought he had enjoyed himself, or else he kept wanting another go around hoping he'd only imagined how horrible it was the time before.

Yet, there he was flirting, and I felt like I had a friend. A real friend. I real gorgeous friend who knew me in ways no one ever had. I told him about Chicago and my life before Tidings, how I was so focused on finishing school that I never had a boyfriend, never did the things other kids my age had done. Brass was only four years older than I was, and at twenty-four he seemed so much more mature.

By the time we left, he stuffed me with pizza and information. Brass was even chivalrous enough to pay for our dinner and I couldn't help but smile more and more.

"I had an idea for your tattoo, if you want it," he said.

"I do. Lay it on me," we walked with his arm around my shoulders, and it was most comfortable I'd been with a man who wasn't related to me.

"An inguz rune, it means new beginnings. They would incorporate the tracker into it. Scarlett, are you sure you want to use my blood?" Brass asked.

"I always imagined if I got a tattoo, it would be for life. I prefer that it's your blood instead of someone else's."

No need to say who, I would bet Slate had used Cordillera's. My face heated at the thought.

We entered a darker portion of Valla I'd never been before, and I kept checking my weapons Brass was kind enough to bring back for me from my cubby at Valla U.

"You're not planning on murdering me, are you?" I asked facetiously.

"Do not give me a reason to," he rumbled in a perfect imitation of Slate.

A bubble of laughter escaped me, "Good to know I'm not the only one he speaks that way to."

"He was threatening well before you came along," he chided.

He walked over to a metal door that looked like it hadn't opened in years. No way that was the place. Brass knocked on the door and a slide shifted to reveal a slot. It slid closed, and I heard locks tumble and the door swung open.

A bald man with a brown goatee that hung to his chest opened the door wide. "Brass. No Quick today?" the man asked in a gruff voice.

Brass smiled and pulled me inside after him, "No, not for Quick. Dhole, this is Scarlett. The tattoo is for her."

He pushed me forward for Dhole's inspection. Dhole was a burly barrel-chested man in his late twenties. Twenty hard years for a Guardian. He regarded me with equally hard dark blue eyes, and something nagged at me.

Whatever he saw seemed to satisfy him, "Come on back and tell me what you want."

He led us down a narrow hall with a high stone ceiling to a larger carpeted room. It was wall to wall designs with hanging catalogs, there were four little cubicles behind a stone counter. Two of them had men leaning over people getting tattoos. The third person raised their head, but lost interest once they saw Brass. I guessed Dhole was the one who exclusively designed Quick's tattoos.

Dhole sat at a modern black chair that looked softly padded and rolled easily across the floor. He gestured to the reclined seat in the center of his cubicle.

"Show me what I am working with," Dhole said gruffly.

He breathed loudly out through his nose; I realized what I thought was facial hair along his neck was an intricately scrolling tattoo that continued down under his collar.

I laid back on the chair and undid my pants so he could clearly see my hips.

"I'm looking to get this covered up," I told him.

KHORAZ in crooked, sloppy scrawled scarred letters marred my otherwise flawless tan skin.

"Ex-boyfriend?" Dhole asked, breathing heavily through his nose after inspecting the skin, "That is a lot of scarring, I could cover it up easily enough." He sat back.

"She wants a tracking mark in it as well, within the tattoo so it is not obvious," Brass added. His eyes were glued to my hip, his full mouth turned down in a grim- ace.

Dhole nodded. "You are a Shadow Breaker?" he asked.

I shook my head, "No, training with them."

"What were you thinking? Have an idea or do you want to check the walls?" Dhole asked, gesturing.

Brass had rolled up his sleeve, and Dhole was pulling out a syringe and some other items.

"I know what I want. It's a rune. Inguz," I told him.

Dhole yelled out to the other guy not working on a client, "Grab me a rune book, would you?"

The guy nodded and dug around under the counter and brought over a book for me to look through. I found what I was looking for. "This one."

Dhole nodded. "Good choice, inguz. Life finds a way, or where there is a will there is a way, if you prefer. New beginnings. How do you want it done?" he asked.

I pointed to his neck, "I really like that. Like a twisted Celtic knot. No color, keep it black, please."

Dhole arched an eyebrow at me and turned to Brass bringing the syringe to his arm. Brass didn't even flinch as Dhole took a little of his blood and healed him without looking. Dhole took out some black ink and pushed the syringe of blood into it. He mixed it up and put it aside.

... This seems very unsanitary...

Brass chuckled, "Guardians do not get fluid transmitted diseases."

Dhole laughed, "Your brother would be in big trouble if we did."

I smirked. Quick was such a womanizer, I wondered if Jett was before he met the girls. The two seemed so similar, kind of like Solder.

Not Brass though.

Dhole was incinerating the hairs on my hip; I was glad my fire power didn't absorb the thin stream of light. "You know Solder?" Brass asked.

"Yeah, you mean you hadn't gleaned that from me yet?" I smiled at him knowingly. He looked guilty instead of amused and my smile fell, "What's up, Brass?"

"I am going to start," Dhole interrupted, "This here instrument." He held up his tattoo gun. "It is Leshy enchanted so your tattoo will not come off. Ever. You sure you want this?" he asked obligatorily.

He'd probably asked this every single time before he started.

I ran my fingers over KHORAZ and looked to his dark blue eyes and nodded. I'd always know it was there, but I didn't want to look at it. Dhole had already drawn my tattoo design and transferred the image to my skin. I fought the urge to ask if it would hurt.

I bet he got that a lot.

"Why not grab a chair, Brass?" Dhole asked him. When Brass disappeared around the corner, Dhole looked to me, "The Breakers will find you anywhere with this, if you die, they will know. If you do not, they will know. You say the word and I will switch this with plain old black ink."

"I thought you liked the Shadow Breakers?" I asked him, astonished.

"I like good people. Brass is good people, so is his brother, but not all Shadow Breakers are good people, you hear?" Dhole said gruffly.

His speech unnerved me, but I was resolute, "I want it."

He nodded once and set to work.

My stomach twisted at his words. I thought back to what Quick said about them being mercenaries. I couldn't imagine Brass killing anyone, or even Ama. Quick was an interrogator, that meant his hands got dirty more than a few times.

But Shale? Or Slate? Could I see them killing someone? Yes, I could if they thought they deserved it. My skin prickled.

"Have we met before?" I asked Dhole.

Something kept nagging at me about his voice as if I'd heard it before, but I knew I'd never met him.

"No."

Brass came back with a chair and Dhole had already started. Brass was rubbing his lips together, and I reached out and pulled his chin down. He smiled ruefully at me.

"Dhole, I have one more thing I need you to do," Brass started.

Two hours later, I gave Dhole a nice fat tip for a job well done. The best part was that it already healed. It healed as soon as Dhole had finished. One 'X' on top of another in black Celtic ropes rode my hip, it wasn't huge, but it wasn't small either. He had gone lower with it so it would hide part of it under my bikini, and it was just wide enough to cover the KHORAZ, you could hardly see the white scar beneath it. I loved it. The Celtic ropes so detailed they looked three dimensional on my skin.

When Brass had Dhole add the second part of the tracking mark to my lip, I furrowed my brow. It was the rune of cosmic union, the EH. I didn't ask; I assumed it had something to do with the fact that it was permanent. I couldn't believe how fast Dhole had done the intricate design on my lip; a vertical line intersected by a second line that tilted to the left. When I pulled down my lower lip I could see it, but otherwise I never would have known it was there.

Brass leaned forward to explain how the tracking tattoo worked. We had to try it out.

"When you need to be found, you call darkness here."

He pointed to the center of the bottom 'X'. I looked closer to the detail on my hip and noticed a small runic compass.

"I've never called darkness before," I confessed.

"It is the same way you call anything else," Brass told me.

I focused. *Black, night, dark, darkness...*

A wispy pitch-black stream poured from my finger and into where my finger rested over the center of the bottom 'X'.

Brass smiled, "I feel you. That is good, it worked." He placed his thumb over my 'X' center and called. I didn't feel any different, but if Brass insisted.

"It will work for you too. Everyone will wonder what is going on. I will explain when I get back to headquarters. Watch."

Brass reached his muscled arm behind his head and called. I felt an explicable pull to him. Not like I did to Slate, not a draw of electricity, but of need. I needed to find him.

"Wow. That's strong."

He shrugged, "It is while you are alive. If you should die, the signal will go away," he said solemnly.

We said our goodbyes to Dhole who seemed happy with his work. I told him I might come back again, and he said I'd be welcomed if I did.

Then Brass became my favorite person. I sat with him in a small, crammed ice cream parlor. Apparently, it was the place to be.

"You might be my new best friend," I told him licking my chocolate, chocolate chip cone.

What I would've done last week for one of these...

Brass laughed. Watching him eat strawberry ice cream from a cone that looked minuscule in his big hand was delight enough. I had had a great day, and I was glad it covered the scar. For once, I felt like a normal girl. I should have saved our date for my birthday.

Brass walked me back to the portal gate in Valla under the moonlight. We had spent the whole day together. We turned to face one another. Suddenly, I felt very awkward.

"How did you like our date?" he teased.

I couldn't get a read on his emotions, probably because all of mine were cattywampus, "It was lovely. Thank you for everything, Brass."

I looked up at him through my lashes. Why was it suddenly so uncomfortable?

He seemed to feel it too, "It was my pleasure. Your new body art suits you."

"Whenever I look at it, I'll think of you. You know, because your blood is literally decorating my skin."

He chuckled, "You are nervous."

I couldn't tell if he was nervous or if my awkwardness was contagious, Brass didn't strike me as the nervous type. When we had been together, it was he who was constantly comforting me. Soothing and warm and so incredibly inviting. It was a date. We'd strolled attached at the hip with his arm around me all day. He bought me dinner and ice cream and made me laugh.

He was utterly amazing.

I giggled with a slightly hysterical edge; this was more of a date than Ash had ever taken me on. Any man, now that I thought about it.

"At the end of a date people usually kiss goodbye."

I nodded, focused on his hair falling free from his ear and his bronze beads caught the moonlight. I wanted to run my hands through it, to give him that goodnight kiss. One tiny little kiss couldn't hurt anything. It could be brotherly, fatherly...

I gave him a small knowing smile, "I'd settle for a hug."

He smiled, and I tucked the lock of his hair that had fallen across his cheek. He stepped up close and wrapped his arms around me. I turned my face, so my cheek pressed against his and wrapped my arms around his trim waist. He smelled like cinnamon and spring rain. His stubbly chin grazed the top of my head as he kissed it.

"Today was effortless. We'll have to do it again soon."

I opened my eyes; I hadn't even realized I'd closed them. Holding him like this made me think of the massage tables. I wanted to ask him how he felt about it all. If he felt... anything. I wanted him to take me back to headquarters back to his bed and for him to kiss me how I hadn't let him before.

"Do not thank me yet," Brass muttered something that sounded like a curse.

He let me go slowly, and we both took a step away from one another. My empath abilities picked up astonishment and lust with a variety of other emotions. I could identify the person it was coming from and the thrum of electric charge from the other.

Slate had a blonde under each arm, and his full lips were curled on his bronze face. The blondes each had a hand on his stomach as they walked with him giggling in too tight myopic dresses for the cool fall weather. Quick had his own blonde who was nearly as tall as he was in super high heels.

Brass's arm brushed mine as he moved closer, and I could feel the reassurance he was passing through his emotions. Only someone who understood what it was like in others' minds could know how to comfort another one of us with our talents.

My stomach twisted. "Hey guys. Out for dinner? Brass was walking me home," I offered them my best smile, but I wasn't fooling Brass for a second.

"I do not know about dinner, but we did plan on eating, Rabbit," the front of Slate's hair was pulled back in a leather throng to reveal his wicked grin that made my heart feel like someone was squeezing it in their big, calloused hands.

"How did the tattoo go?" Quick asked in an unusually considerate tone.

"Very well. Both of them," Brass said, and something passed between the brothers.

I smiled at Quick thankful for the distraction. Once the youngest Regn brother tricked me into seeing his tattoos, so I know I had something to show him too.

"Want to see?" I asked with my best smile. He laughed, knowing what I insinuated.

"I have something to show you too," the tall blonde purred as she turned Quick's face to hers with a seductive smile making the other blondes giggle.

"We will see you later, have fun," Brass shifted his body towards me.

"Or you could come have fun with us," one blonde under Slate's arm said.

Brass flashed her a smile, "Maybe some other time."

My heart was pounding in my ears, and my whole body was burning.

Brass's hand brushed mine, and I pivoted towards him. "Come," he said under his breath.

A thin hand reached up, and it happened in slow motion. "That is a bad idea," Brass said smoothly without taking his amber eyes off me.

"You did not tell us you had such cute friends," the blonde said as the hand moved to rest on Brass's belt.

I saw red. My pinky twisted as I whipped around, and my blade was at the blonde's throat. Instinctually, I side stepped moving in front of Brass.

"If you want that hand, I suggest you keep it to yourself," I said in a detached tone.

Blood beaded where my blade rested. Her eyes were wide, but her friend recovered faster.

"You crazy bitch! What is wrong with your eyes?" she gasped.

I knew my eyes would be two hot coals where my turquoise should be. I moved my blade away and Brass wound his arm around my waist preparing to pick me up physically if need be.

"We should go," Brass said.

I squeezed my eyes shut and shook my head to clear it. "Keep your dogs on a shorter leash," I snapped, and Brass pulled me roughly towards the portal.

I cast a last glance over at my shoulder before we walked through the free-standing stone gate with sculptured tree branches twisting up it, a sculpture of a woman, hands extended forming into branches crested the top. Slate's silver eyes glinted in the moonlight as he bared his teeth that made him look more animal than man. My breath caught. I thought I saw his teeth sharpen just before the bright light of the portal enveloped me.

"Are you alright?"

Brass gripped my shoulders as he leveled his eyes at me. I nodded trembling, and he pulled me against his chest.

"You should not shift in front of people. It makes you vulnerable, takes too much out of you. People cannot find out about you, not yet" Brass said, and I drew back.

"I lost my cool," I said numbly.

Brass slung his arm around my shoulders and led me from the portal room and into the mosaic lined halls of the Sumar palace.

"It was incredibly sexy. No woman has ever shown so much protectiveness over me," Brass gave my shoulders a squeeze as we climbed the stairs.

I laughed uneasily and gave him a lopsided smile "Sexy isn't what comes to mind. Crazy. Crazy is a good word. I don't know what came over me," I sighed feeling worn out.

Brass opened my bedroom door, and I didn't question how he knew which one was mine. He probably knew from when Slate had him watching over me. He shut the door behind us, and I fell onto the chaise lounge. I needed to practice shifting, so it didn't drain me so badly. Brass was right, it made me vulnerable.

Brass walked into the hall and came back a moment later. He pulled my boots off and sat back on the royal blue sofa chair; he sank back so his boots thumped on the carpet.

"You don't have to babysit me," I said as he rested the back of his head on the couch, his dark hair fell away from his face.

"I am hungry. Are you hungry?" he said without looking.

"I could eat," I told him carefully, turning onto my side.

"You should practice. I am here to make sure if you burn anything down, we can promptly put out the fire," he lifted his head, "Besides, I think Slate will wait for me back at headquarters to have me skinned alive." Brass's amber eyes held mirth as he gave me a grin.

"Slate acts like I'm his favorite toy that no one else can play with. He won't have you skinned, he knows I like you and let you get close to me... for guarding purposes. Practicing sounds like a good idea."

Why did admitting that I liked him feel like a deeper confession? I was attracted to Brass. I could acknowledge that. He was everything any woman could ask for in a man. He should've been married by now. How some clever woman hadn't made a husband out of him was beyond me.

"All true, but you are no toy. I do not think you would let any man play with you, Scarlett."

Brass got to his feet when a knock sounded at the door. I had let him play with me. It had been fantastic.

He came back with two plates of Italian pot roast with roasted carrots and potatoes that were still steaming when he set it down on the octagonal coffee table. My mouth watered instantly, and he walked back to the door. He set a carafe of red wine and two goblets down on the table next to our plates.

"You thought of everything," I scooted to the edge of the lounge and picked up the fork.

"I am buttering you up so you will let me sleep on your couch," Brass said, laughing.

"No need to rough it on the couch," I told him after swallowing a bite of the pot roast.

We ate, and I shifted. I practiced for a few hours until I got ready for bed. A shirtless Brass got ready after me and had laid down on his back in my gigantic bed. He was hesitant at first, but I told him it seemed silly to sleep on the couch or a cot since we had shared a bed many times. Recently we shared much more.

I put on my least sexy pajamas, grey sweats, and an oversized shirt from my college with NEIU across the chest. I dropped my eyes when he pushed his pants off over his hips before climbing into the bed.

"Do you need any more pillows?" I asked hesitantly in the archway.

He folded his arms under his pillow giving a display of the dark honey muscles of his biceps. "All set, Scarlett. Thanks," He said then focused those amber eyes on me making me pause.

"What is it?" I asked.

"I am sorry."

"For what?" I asked piling my golden hair in a sloppy bun on my head and his mouth pulled to the side as I climbed into bed.

"You will know. I like your hair like that," he said cryptically.

"Like this?" I laughed, pointing to the mess on my head in my attempt to look sloppy and unattractive.

"Yes, you have a graceful neck."

My hands flitted to my throat, and I gave him a funny look, "I think that's the first time anyone's ever complimented my neck before."

"That is likely because there is so much of you worthy of compliments."

He raised his eyebrows to look up at me from where he laid. I thought of all the parts of me he complimented that night.

I pointed at him trying my best not to blush, "Goodnight, Brass."

I drew my blankets up.

I knew what had been going through my mind when I lost it on those blondes, and it shook me to my core. I had been territorial. Possessive even. Brass was sort of right when he said I was being protective. I loathed the idea of another woman touching him. He'd been my escort, and it was the same feeling I'd gotten when the girls at the movie theater kept hitting on Slate.

What's mine was mine.

Seeing Slate with those women he was going to shack up with had driven me right over the edge, but it wasn't the first time I'd seen him with women. Then one of them had hit on Brass as if I wasn't even there. Slate fine, it was his choice, but not Brass. Brass was my escort, and I'd be darned if a woman would make a pass at any man I was with unchallenged.

Brass slid in bed and cautiously snaked his arm around my middle. He must have read in my mind I'd let him. He was right. I lifted my elbow, so his palm rested on my stomach.

"Goodnight. Sleep tight, love," he whispered in a seductive whisper.

I shook my head ruefully. It was an invitation. I'd be damned if I didn't want to turn in his arms and start something that wouldn't finish for hours later.

It was the best day of my life. Which was saying a lot considering all I'd gone through recently. Falling asleep in a man's arms who cared for me was the perfect ending to the perfect day.

After my day with Brass, he joined us for breakfast which the whole family was present for. He had won Pearl over in a matter of seconds and revealed she had been great friends with his grandparents. Aside from Slate's cold shoulder and Jett's side glances, everyone enjoyed his company. He was charismatic like Ash, but he had his own charm that radiated genuine warmth and those smiles that may have been the sole source of global warming.

The morning after hadn't crossed my mind when I let him spend the night in my bed. My father's brows had quirked ever so slightly, but it was enough to make my cheeks tingle with an embarrassed flush. Thank goodness for Steel who had greeted him with a broad smile and a laugh before inviting him to sit beside him. The two were good friends and hadn't seen one another since the wedding. It distracted everyone from the fact that he'd come down to breakfast with me.

Only Jett and Slate knew I'd spent the night before in Slate's arms and now I was coming to breakfast with Brass. I'd gotten engaged last week!

"What happened to you last Friday night? It scared me witless!" Tawny scolded as we walked down the halls on Monday.

"Long story. But here I am," I gave her smile.

Quick snorted, the bastard.

"You're dishing, if I have to get the details from Quick, I won't be happy,"hHer hazel eyes were happy despite her attempts at threatening me.

Quick leaned past me from where he walked on my other side. "That sounds intriguing. Scarlett, you should probably let me handle this," he joked.

Another day of relentless flirting courtesy of Quick and Tawny. Fantastic. I turned my empath abilities way down. It was going to be a long day.

Slate passed in my line of sight at the end of the hall. He was kind of hard to miss towering and dark in the suddenly cramped yellow stoned castle. My heart flip-flopped, and our eyes met over the score of tyros making bile rise in my throat.

"Are you feeling alright?" Tawny asked. "You want to go freshen up?" she offered, and I looked away from those silver soul stealing orbs.

I nodded, and Quick followed us standing outside the girls' bathroom.

"Spill," Tawny said.

My stomach wanted to upchuck, but I laughed. I went into more detail about the night I discovered I was an elemental, about the fight with Jonquil, the morning after with Slate and the following day with Brass. I felt like I brimmed with secrets. When the invisible monkey left my back, all my secrets would be GONE.

"I left you in there for those girls! Scar, I'm so sorry," Tawny sobbed. I comforted her.

"It's not your fault, like I told Quick. If it wasn't then, it would have been another day. They were waiting for an opportunity," I hugged her as she blew her nose.

"What are we going to do with those wenches? Whatever it is, I'm in."

Her hazel eyes were fierce. It's what I loved most about Tawny, as hot tempered as she was exactly proportionate to how much love she gave. She had my back no matter what.

I shook my head, "I have no idea, but they won't get away with it."

"Can I see it?" she asked.

I lifted my skirt to reveal the inguz rune on my hip. She cursed aloud.

"It's awesome, but we're gonna get them," sinister intentions filled her eyes.

"No kidding. Let's get out of here. We're going to be late for Energies and Wights."

Quick was still waiting, if somewhat impatiently, for us by the door. "By the Mother, did you fall in?" he asked, "Maybe you do not mind extra work, but I would like to head home tonight."

The bell tolled, and they ushered us like cattle to our next class. Tribal Affairs, taught by another of my red-headed cousins. Butterfly Rot was the youngest of the Tio/Rot brood and was married to Quick's eldest brother. When the petite redhead saw Quick come through the door, her face lit up.

"Silver, I have not seen you at home lately," Butterfly gave Quick a big kiss on the cheek, he had to bend down for the tiny redhead since he stood at least a foot taller than her.

"Busy, busy. How is my nephew? Not spoiling him too much, I trust?" Quick dazzled her with his smile.

She smiled back, her brown eyes shone with the love of a big sister, "Copper gets bigger every day. He misses his uncles. Brass at least *tries* to come see us."

"I will be by soon, I promise." He gave her a last smile, and we moved up to our seats.

When we settled in, I turned to him in mock surprise, "I don't think I've ever seen you talk to a girl without hitting on her."

Other than my mom, but I kept that thought to myself.

He laughed, "Saying inappropriate things to my oldest brother's wife would be a new low for me. You did not think I could repress my animal urges?"

His lids lowered as he growled the last part, very animal indeed. I gave him a shove, and he smiled brighter; Ash frowned as he took the seat next to me following Quick with his celadon eyes. Ash wasn't sure what to make of the newest addition to our friends.

Tribal Relations went quickly, as did Arithmetic with provost

Magnolia Rot. Crimson's eyes slid right over me. The game we were playing was ignore all the bad things that have happened to Scarlett.

I won every time, at least until we reached lunch.

I really thought I was okay with what had happened the night in the showers but seeing Jonquil with her friends sitting at the table made me want to scream. When I walked down the aisle her eyes met mine, I wanted to kill her. I'd never actually wanted to kill someone. I didn't think I'd go through with it, but I wanted to try. My hands curled into fists, and I couldn't stop myself.

We filled the dining hall with people talking and laughing, eating their lunches on the long tables and benches. The smell of fresh baked bread and garlic hung in the air. I marched along the marbled floor, oblivious to the clatter of utensils on plates and constant chattering of tyros.

She saw me coming, her wide eyes glittered. Quick was whispering feverishly and Tawny was trying hopelessly to hold me back. My hand whipped out as I smashed Jonquil's plate to the floor. The entire room turned to me, and she leapt to her feet.

"Need another ass kicking? I can oblige," she said smugly.

"You did a sugarfoot job. As you can see, I'm still standing," we were inches away from one another. You could have heard a pin drop.

She laughed with a smirk, "Now he will know what you are every time you take you disrobe."

I laughed in her face, "Is that what this was about? Are you jealous that he wants to marry me and not you? Why would he want you when you to give it up without him having to promise anything?"

It was cruel, but I was in a cruel mood.

Her eyes flashed with anger, "I am going to kill you."

"You could try. What's stopping you now?" I egged her on.

Ash stepped between us and pushed us apart with his body which only made us both angrier. I hated fighting over a man and that's what him standing there made it look like.

There are two types of anger in my experience, hot fiery anger, and cool, calculated anger. I was cool now; I wasn't making any friends, but she had pushed me to my limit.

Slate was in my peripheral and I was off my feet. I thought at first

Jonquil had called, but no. Slate had just given permission to Quick to toss me over his shoulder like a sack of potatoes.

I was furious; I felt my eyes get hot, and I had to close them or everyone in the lunchroom would see my fire. The last thing I saw was Ash turning his back to me and place his hands on Jonquil's shoulders. As it was, Quick was going to feel my fire as soon as we passed from everyone's eyesight.

There were several empty classrooms in Valla U, there weren't as many Guardians as there used to be. Quick opened the door to a room and tossed me onto my feet none too gracefully. He retreated immediately closing the door behind him. I cursed and opened the door.

Slate swung it, so it almost hit me in the face. I backed up and his storming eyes met mine.

"What happened to revenge is a dish best served cold?" he asked, prowling forward, looming over me like an oppressive storm cloud.

I refused to back up. The back of my head was almost touching my shoulders as I looked up at him.

"I can't! She deserves it. I want to strangle her!" I let out a scream of frustration turning aside and clenching my fists. I wanted to punch things, "You told Quick to do that. I saw you. Why? I was handling it just fine."

He narrowed his eyes. "The council would have you thrown out in a second if you had laid a finger on Jonquil in front of the entire university. Not even your precious husband could save you then," Slate said mockingly, the muscles in his chest and shoulders bunching.

I lost control, my eyes went red, but I didn't care. I lashed out at him, and he deftly blocked my punch.

"You get sloppy when you are angry. The Shadow Breakers will train that out of you," he prowled around me.

I came back at him, punching and kicking in a blur. I wasn't thinking only reacting. My movements guided by instinct. He hadn't hit me once, but I had landed more than a few blows. I landed a punch across his jaw and took a step back as I saw blood bead to drip from the wound.

I felt guilty. Slate was only trying to protect me; it wasn't his fault I'd lost it front of every single person in the lunchroom. He had probably saved me from certain expulsion.

Slate licked his bleeding lip and gave me a salacious blood-tinged grin. Sensations flooded me and I doubled over gasping. Rage and love, both blind, assailed me so fiercely it took my breath away.

Gods — the lust. A bone deep lust that never ebbed.

"I can feel you," I gasped between stilted words.

His emotions were suffocating, no wonder he constantly kept them walled, and why could I abruptly feel them?

Holding my stomach, I raised my head to read his expression.

Oh.

He slammed into me, knocking the air from my lungs further discombobulating my already confused emotions. He pinned me against the wall as he reached down and pulled my leg up, pushing my dress around my hips. He crushed his mouth against mine and I tasted his blood.

"Sugarfoot!" I gasped, turning my head roughly away from him. "Slate!"

I couldn't tell where what he felt ended, and my own emotions began. My heart was beating like a bass drum in my ears, and it aroused me beyond reason. The internal battle I waged wasn't even mine to fight!

He panted against my mouth as he freed himself from his pants and my hands found his stilling them. It was escalating quickly, and I couldn't even see straight.

"Slate!" I cried again, trying to get his attention, and he growled before shoving away roughly from the wall.

His back was to me as his bunched shoulders rose and fell rapidly and I was afraid to move or even speak. I squatted against the wall panting. It was the most out of control he'd been with me. By the Mother, he'd tried to have sex with me in a classroom with my fiancée in the building!

I licked my lips, and his blood tinged them with its coppery taste, and he stiffened. Slate's hands moved to his pants, and he turned around once he tucked away, but nothing but a tent could hide that bulge. I kept my eyes firmly on his and shook my head.

"I don't understand," I said, and his lips curled.

He stalked over to where I stood and grabbed a fistful of my hair, so my hands flew to his hands to keep him from pulling too tight and he pressed his lips to mine while I was on my tiptoes. It was a chaste kiss despite the hair pulling and when it was over; he drew back and wiped a thumb across his bleeding lip and brushed it against my lower lip. His hand loosened in my hair, and I didn't feel him anymore.

"Get out of here, Rabbit," Slate growled, looking down his nose at me.

I pursed my lips and his eyes flitted down to them and then lower to my hands to settle on the ring he gave me I wore on my right ring finger.

"I'm not a rabbit," I protested, "Explain to me what happened."

He chuckled darkly, "What was going to happen if you were not scampering off? You know exactly what I was going to do and how much you would have relished it."

He couldn't intimidate me into backing off. My cheeks stung anyway.

"I felt you like never before." I told him waiting for an explanation.

Slate scanned my bewildered expression and narrowed his eyes, "Show me your marks."

"No way. You've seen enough of my body to last a life — AH!"

Slate grabbed my chin in his big hand and pulled down my lip and sucked in a deep breath. I felt like I had little baby fists as I punched at his brick chest not making a dent in such an awkward position. He released my face, and I rubbed my jaw. Slate arched a straight black brow at me, and I glared at him. His eyes flitted to where my tattoo was and back up to my face.

"You're a cache hole," I muttered as I pulled up my black caftan uniform exposing my leg and my blue floral lace panties with pink blooms.

I had to pull the dress to my hip to show him the inguz and moved my belt higher up my waist while he squatted on his heels on the floor in front of me. My cheeks heated when he ran his thumb over my hip bone where the tattoo was subsequently running his pad over the lace.

His eyes lifted to mine without moving his hand, "New beginnings?"

"Brass picked it out, and I thought it suited me to a 'T' since it's been a new beginning since I moved here," I said, breaking eye contact.

"Brass," Slate breathed, and his finger slid under the lace from underneath almost distractedly and I looked back down at him.

"Are you quite finished?" I asked, rankled that he was so casual when playing with a woman's underwear — specifically mine.

His grey eyes focused, and he looked at his finger beneath the lace and pulled it out, so it snapped back against my skin before he rose to his full six and a half feet making me feel dwarfed.

"Just because you are bigger than me and stronger, doesn't mean you should do whatever you want to me," I huffed, straightening my dress.

"Trust me, Rabbit. If I was doing everything, I wanted to you those little lace panties would be in my pocket as a token of a well-spent lunch hour."

I thought my eye twitched. "Go find one of your cock jockeys to sate your carnal needs. There's a whole other world out there for couples who share themselves with each other exclusively. A deeper kind of feeling your empty trysts with vapid hidey-holes don't even scrape the surface of," I was nearly shouting up at him.

Slate slammed the wall to either side of me, but I glared up at him defiantly and didn't even shy away when he brought his nose so it brushed against mine.

"Do you share yourself with Brass exclusively? Does your betrothed know how you parted your thighs for the middle son of a lesser family? That he still shares your bed?"

I'd never kneed a man in the groin before. There'd been cause, but I couldn't bring myself to do it. I had no such qualms now as I slammed the door behind me leaving Slate holding himself between his legs as I stormed down the hall. Gods, I thought my kneecap was going to crack he had been so hard.

Only two months until the Wild Hunt. We were being drilled on common calls, tribal attributes, and battle, battle, battle. My life was the battle grounds. I felt good about my calling, Ash was helping a great deal in that department. He insisted we practice religiously at the Straumr palace every night after dinner at Valla U.

The day before we Provost Ford Tio made good on his promise to take us to visit Mabon and the community of fairies and trolls there, we had a full day of classes.

Ash pulled me to him entangling his hand in the hair at the nape of my neck nuzzling it.

"Good morning," his lips pressed to my neck.

It made me smile. Ash was always at his best with everyone around.

"Good morning. Sleep well?"

"I did. Ready for another scintillating history lesson?" he always mocked his mom's lessons.

We sat Tawny, me, Ash, then Sage sat in a row every single class. Half the tiered seats were full, no one took sick days because you could heal almost anything with your calling as long as it wasn't on yourself. Provost Dahlia Natt was sitting behind her desk readying her slides, her gaze had gone back to her computer after we passed. My future mother-in-law went back and forth on whether she liked me. Which was fine by me, because although I respected her as my provost, she wasn't the friendliest person.

"Today we cover the most tragic love story in our history. This pertains to most as you since we are nearly all descendants of Wind Dagr and Storm Natt," she clicked a slide.

The stained-glass mosaic of our shared room ceiling lit the screen, the male figure made up of night embracing the female figure made of light.

"There has been much speculation about their relationship, but what we know is they were man and wife. Before we kept detailed records," she puffed up at that, "they say the pair were deeply in love and led the Guardians together. They achieved a perfect balance for many years. Storm Natt became obsessed with science and calling. He claimed to have devised a way to keep nature in balance forever with one of his projects. This created a divide between Wind Dagr and Storm Natt."

She changed the slide. It was a drawing of a circle divided into eight segments, runes along the circle's edge, "There is no record of what this project did, but Wind Dagr believed it would give Natt ultimate power. Even though she loved Natt, she came against him believing such power was not meant for Guardians. A war raged between the Guardians — the only one. Dagr confronted Natt after his side fell."

Another slide. A painting depicting a dark man holding a woman who was in his arms bleeding out onto the circle of eight segments. The dark man's face was pained, but the woman's face peaceful.

"Dagr went to him and sacrificed herself to stop Natt. Storm destroyed the project, but the energy we know as The Mother was heartbroken. She came to Natt revealing her displeasure. Mother took away the elemental powers of the Guardians and separated the lands hoping with more space and less power, they would never war again. The Natt line has only been women since. We created the council, named Guardians to separate tribes, and have worked together as a people much better than those in our history. It was the only time a Guardian saw the energy, Mother Nature. The project is believed to have sunk into the ocean when the land divided and has never been found, although many have gone searching for it. Some have never returned."

I had to hand it to her, Dahlia knew her subject. I had wondered why Guardians couldn't transform into elementals anymore; it was such a sad story. The look on Storm's face when Wind was dying, at least in the painting, was of utter and complete ruin.

"What happened to Storm after the Mother left him?" I asked unable to hide my curiosity.

Dahlia smirked; she always noted how little I knew of our history. Which was all of it.

"He killed himself."

"They had two daughters, Dagr and Natt. They each took a name. Not a male Dagr or Natt since," Sage added like someone asked.

I wondered, but I was glad I hadn't spoken up.

"Correct, Sage." Dahlia gave a simpering smile.

Tawny rolled her eyes. Class was over, and we headed out the door.

"Your mom doesn't like me," I'd told Ash this before. He only ever laughed.

He did again, "Only my opinion matters, do not worry about hers."

He grabbed me by the nape of my neck and kissed me softly and I leaned into it. I wrapped an arm around his hips; it was a rare P.D.A. I allowed myself to give him.

The Embala course headed to Energies and Wights with Wisteria Rot. Tawny and she got along well. Tawny had been a frequent visitor of hers since she was the herbalist, i.e., no babies before graduation.

Butterfly Rot's class was the one I'd been waiting for. The tribes were difficult to deal with and the giants were the most reclusive and independent of them all. The happy little red head welcomed us in.

"Risar and Jotnar, the giants. Risar live on Mabon. They are considered friendly — for giants."

Butterfly clicked a slide; it was a man and woman around eight feet tall with rust-colored skin. Otherwise, they looked like overgrown humans, just wider set. She clicked the slides again.

"Jotnar live on Elivagar. They keep to themselves, have not been involved with matters outside of their community in centuries."

It showed a similar man and woman on the slide, but with a grey/blue skin painted in white which reminded me of the Wemic. Their expressions looked more threatening than the Risar. Butterfly went into detail about their customs, they knew unfortunately little about the Jotnar.

They were head and shoulders taller than Slate and twice as broad which seemed like an impossibility.

I could go my whole life without meeting the giants and not feel as though I'd missed out.

CHAPTER
TEN

Ford was bringing Provost Butterfly for good measure. Cherry's dad was meeting us in Mabon. Viper Enox was ambassador to the Centaurs, Mabon's only ambassador.

We lined up in the portal room at Valla. Over a hundred tyros and two provosts. This was going to be interesting. Indigo, stood with Tawny and me waiting for our turn to head through the intricately carved doors.

"It's supposed to be a party tonight," Indigo said excitedly. Her long blonde hair was loose around her face. "Troll ale is really strong, should be a good time," she beamed.

Indigo, always happy. I was glad it was only first years going otherwise Sterling's sisters, Nova and Quartz, would join us. They were vile, and I felt like I hadn't seen her in ages and wanted to get in some sister time. Jett and Cherry stood less than five feet behind me with Slate and Quick bathed in the incandescent light from the sconces that shone from between the multiple portal doorways.

Ash snuck up behind me nuzzling his face to my neck and my hand rested over his on my waist. "Vanilla and spiced apples. Your scent lingers in my bed, you have frequented so often as of late," he whispered in my ear, and I turned my head to kiss his soft lips.

"Last year, Quartz threw up the next morning through the portal. It came back and hit her in the face," Sage laughed.

Tawny rolled her eyes; she may have disliked him more than I did.

Ash held me from behind, it was such a normal hold, I'd seen kids do it at my high school. It didn't feel like it fit in here. We were wearing our training gear, everyone in black. They had informed us; we were staying one night and coming back in the morning. Everyone was looking forward to it, they had very strict no partying rules at Valla U, but this wouldn't be at the university. You could feel the buzz of the crowd.

"Party favors," Sage opened his hand, magic mushrooms and little purple vials.

I'd seen the little shriveled brown pieces enough times to recognize it. I'd yet to try it. Ash popped three pieces into his mouth. Sage offered them up to us. We rejected them. I blanched when he held up the vial. Rousen. The Merfolk aphrodisiac. I'd never take it again, and I'd only had it the once because I did not know what it was. Sage had been doing his best to ignore Indigo and I since our father claimed us, but in front of Ash he tolerated us as one would the cries of an infant in a restaurant. You may not like it, but there was nothing you could do about it. He went down to Jonquil and her wretched friends, they happily accepted.

Big surprise there.

Ash ate them; he hardly ever partook in anything that would make him lose the slightest bit of control. We were up. I grabbed my roll and headed through the door with my group.

I smelled autumn the moment we crossed over. I missed fall. Golden, crimson, and copper leaves hung on the trees. I knew they grew that way; it made me homesick for Chicago. The portal gate hung between two trees, carved on the massive doors were scenes of fairies, centaurs, and what must have been trolls. It was a cheerful scene, everyone gallivanting about. Two giants stood within the trees; you could just make out their forms in the carving.

Viper and Butterfly stood with the groups of students who had previously come through, "Welcome to the town center of Mabon. We have a hike ahead of us so do not wander off."

Viper Enox was a no-nonsense type of man; he spoke quickly and clipped his words. It was strange to think this was the same man who raised Cherry. She ran up to her dad and gave him a big hug, Jett, in tow shook his hand. Jett towered over most people, Slate and our father being the exceptions. Viper was only a few inches shorter. Viper had warmed up to Jett mostly while Jett still looked a little nervous around him. It was kind of endearing.

Our group joined the people gathered around Viper and Butterfly. Ford came through last. We grabbed our packs and headed through town to go to the fairies' and troll's village. Mabon reminded me of pictures I had seen of Ireland and Scotland. Mossy hills and a lot of ancient stone buildings. It looked the oldest of all the islands except for Valla.

I could see the Haust castle from there. It looked Medieval. I half expected a knight in shining armor to come riding out of it. It had an actual moat around it complete with drawbridge. Mossy stone bridges were everywhere, we crossed the first one just outside of the town. Unfortunately, we trooped the opposite way of the castle. I was hoping to get a better look.

Cherry, Jett, Quick, and Slate walked along with Viper at the head of the snaking group of tyros. The ground wasn't particularly hard to cross with the bridges to help, so we made excellent time. It still took about four hours to get to the village.

I wasn't sure what to expect, everything I knew about fairies and trolls that was accurate I'd learned over the last ten months at Valla U. Otherwise it was from cartoons. Fairies were usually tiny pointy eared humans with wings, trolls were usually some kind of evil in cartoons. They were neither.

Viper led us into a clearing in the middle of the forest. Tall trees to either side with small bridges that crossed through the treetops. The fairies flitted from tree to tree, some hung over bridges to watch us approach talking excitedly and pointing. Fairies were only about a foot high and looked like a part of a tree had come to life and started speaking. They were bits of nature shaped like people with wings, their eyes were green and blue glowing slits in their tiny twig and grass faces. They were fascinating. The trolls weren't much bigger; they came up to our waists at varying heights. Wide tanned faces with skinny limbs and round bellies, the trolls smiled big wide smiles on their wrinkly faces.

When I had first met Ash, we talked about fairies after Tawny joked about maybe being one. I felt good about us at the moment. I laced my fingers through his. He looked down at me and smiled. Sage was looking at the troll scowling. I did not know how he and Indigo were raised in the same household.

Indigo was smiling and shaking hands with the trolls as fairies weaved their way through the crowd. Her powder blue eyes were bright as she spoke with a fairy who danced in the air around her head. Even the quiet Sterling was chatting.

"We will make camp in the clearing here. Appreciate our hosts. They say the Centaur will visit at nightfall. This is indeed a rare occasion."

The tyros murmured, the Centaurs had their own community and didn't frequently travel outside of it. They had never come to the village while the Valla students visited.

We found a suitable spot under a fairy tree home. Indigo had spoken with the fairies who lived there, and it elated them to have us stay under their tree. I turned up my empath powers I had been keeping off lately and could tell they were positively giddy. Tawny camped with Jett, Cherry, Quick, and Slate. I couldn't blame her; Sage wasn't her favorite person and she and Quick got along well.

Jackal had been right about how bad my language skills were. I could barely understand the fairies and I couldn't speak a lick. Trolls were easier, some of them spoke English and talked to the tyros. The trolls had homes made right into the little hills, I could see small carved doors every dozen feet built right into the grass.

Too big to fit inside, we poked heads in to see their little hand carved furniture. It was their primary source of income, furniture making. I could see why, the details their little hands could make were so intricate. I thought they must've made our dining table in Thrimilci.

"It was," I heard a small voice that was high and croaky at the same time, "Down here."

A little wrinkly faced troll with a puff of white cottony hair sticky straight up stared up at me. He or she wore a shirt and shorts made of moss and leaves with grass blades in a crown around its head.

"What was?" I asked, resisting the urge to lean over it.

"Made here. I remember."

"I don't understand."

"The table you were thinking of," It said as if I was dense.

"You can read minds?" I asked skeptically.

No one was listening to our interaction; it didn't seem concerned.

"No. I pick up images. I saw it in your head. It was not on purpose," It poked the dirt with a long bare toe.

"Sorry, I didn't know you could do that," I said surprised. I'd have to watch what I thought about.

The troll shook its head comically, its little tuft of hair shaking, "Not all of us, I am special. My name is Baboo." It held out its little hand with long fingers.

I shook it, "Pleasure to meet you. I'm Scarlett. Thank you for inviting us to your village."

It gave a high snicker, "You come every year. Very exciting."

"You speak very well," I noted.

It seemed to swell up at that, "I do. I do the dealings with the Guardians. Lots of experience."

It ran off then suddenly distracted. I watched in run into a nearby knoll. I wondered if I would see the little troll again and if I did, would I recognize it from the other trolls.

As night fell, I noticed little blue glowing mushrooms that sprouted from the fairies' trees. It gave the clearing an ambient glow. The clearing wasn't big, trees lined the length of it, all homes of the fairies, where there wasn't a tree, there was a knoll where trolls lived. They had little dirt paths that crossed through it and a little platform in the center. A few trolls were bringing out platters of food I had been smelling for hours. A band of trolls climbed on top of the platform and started playing tiny instruments. It was a folk music. I imagined there being a traditional jig to the strum of the string instruments and the tooting of the wind.

I sat between Ash, and Indigo eating our meals off tree bark plates with our fingers. Fairies spun in the air doing their own version of dancing, twirling glowing mushrooms. Trolls passed out flagons of ale as we ate, everyone in good spirits. Even Sage wasn't making snide remarks which was a first. I was afraid to ask what we were eating, but since it tasted good enough, I ignored the strange textures and kept filling my stomach.

Trolls came out and danced to the folk tunes they played. They're skinny bodies jerking this way and that. None of the students danced, probably afraid to step on one of our hosts, I know I was.

"How are things at home?" I asked Indigo as we clapped along to the music.

Alder was looking forward to our trip this weekend, and I was looking forward to some family time with the father I barely knew. My schedule revolved around Ash and training lately and I felt like I'd been neglecting my newfound family. I never asked in front of the others, gossip was the number one currency in Valla. Especially in a university full of powerful young adults.

She gave a halfhearted smile, "Good. I haven't spoken to Delta since... and Sage won't make eye contact with me, but it could be worse."

"I'm sorry, Indigo," I tried to give her a comforting smile.

"How about you? Things okay?" she gestured with her eyes to Ash.

"I don't know. The wedding is going ahead. June, it's happening fast," I sighed.

She put her hand on my lap, "We should talk. Really talk soon. I must tell you something."

I knit my eyebrows. She mouthed, *later*.

"How's your love life?" I'd never seen her with any guys except family, either adopted or through marriage. Even in the blue light, her face turned red, "You didn't tell me you met someone! Does he go to Valla U?"

"Later, okay? Not in front of everyone," she whispered.

I nodded smiling conspiratorially. I had been trying to find someone for her all year.

The little white-haired troll came running up to us. I laughed, it was all knees and elbows.

"Hello again, Baboo!" I shouted to it.

"Come, I would show you our swirling springs!" It said in its simultaneously high croaky voice.

"Okay, okay! Indigo, come with," I grabbed her hand and pulled her with. I waved to Ash to let him know I'd be back.

Baboo brought us through blue lit trees and rolling hillocks which were undoubtedly troll homes. We reached a stream a few minutes into our walk pooling from a small waterfall.

"Oh Baboo, it's beautiful," Indigo told them.

"Go swim, it is always cool."

It dipped its toes in as if to prove how ideal it was. Baboo was smiling and nodding up at us.

Indigo looked delighted and promptly pulled off her pants. I shrugged and took off my shirt, boots, and pants. I felt bare without my knives though, so I strapped my seax to my thigh. Indigo jumped in.

"Oh, it is warm!" Indigo said.

She was lit from below; small green and blue glowing plants lit the bottom of the stream. Baboo made jungle call before plunging into the watery depths. It was hardly a waterfall I realized, more like a few steps the water poured over. The water swirled in circles rapidly all around. I stepped into the water. I wasn't worried about being wet, I could call heat to dry my clothing.

The warm water swirled around us, it looked like a giant had pressed its thumb print into the water, leaving its permanent mark. Baboo squirted water out through its mouth and kicked happily on its back through the water. Indigo swam towards the waterfall. I let myself sink to the bottom and opened my eyes to get a better look at the glowing plants. The entire village was magical. I never imagined I could experience anything like it before, and there I was. I knew now why Guardians kept it a secret, I couldn't imagine what the rest of the world would do if they knew places like this existed.

I called an air bubble around my mouth allowing me to breathe underwater. Steel had taught me to do it in our pool at the Thrimilci palace after my run in with the vodyanoy in the River Mani. I had never tried it outside before. It took me a minute to even my breaths. The hardest part was maintaining the call, if I stopped for even a moment the bubble would disappear.

Something was disturbing the water above me and saw ripples through the swirls, so I came to the surface.

"Oh!"

Drinking water from the stream was a male Centaur, and he was glorious. Indigo was up to her nose and red faced in the water. Long waves of blonde hair fell to his waist, which then became a horse. He had stunning sapphire eyes and tanned skinned that seemed to make them glow.

"Lewt!" Baboo waved its hand, "Taking some student Guardians for a dip. Will you join us?"

Lewt, the blonde centaur with the body of a palomino horse smiled as he straightened.

"Sorry we are late Baboo; we ran into an issue. All is well now. Come out, we will join your feast," he smiled again.

"Hi, I'm Scarlett. This is Indigo," I gestured to Indigo hiding behind a boulder in the stream.

I laughed, it was funny!

The horse body kneeled and reached out a hand. I looked at it, exactly like a man's hand. I looked back to Lewt's blue eyes and held out my hand. As he stood back up, I flew out of the stream.

"OH! Thanks," I said as I caught my balance.

I dried my clothes as I pulled on my shirt, pants, and boots. There were more Centaurs behind Lewt watching us. I heard Indigo let out a yelp, and I knew Lewt must have helped her out of the water as well. She put her clothes on in a blink and dried them afterwards. The Centaur were smirking at us. I felt like an idiot.

"We stopped for some refreshments, my clan and I," Lewt gestured to the three other Centaur behind him, "others went on ahead. This is Goep, Hute, and Fert."

Fert was a female Centaur. She was all woman down to her waist. A strip of fabric that hung around her neck made my Wemic garb look downright modest. Her long brown hair also fell to her waist.

"Do you know what would dry your hair, so it smells like the wind?" Lewt asked.

"What?" I asked the glorious pony boy.

"A ride on my back. What say you? Want to feel the wind?"

Something told me they didn't let people sit on their backs often and he was enticing. I looked at Indigo; she was mouthing no repeatedly. I couldn't help but laugh.

"Okay." I heard Indigo groan behind me.

Baboo scrambled out of the water gleefully, "Do you mind?" They held their arms out waiting for me to dry their mossy clothes.

"Um, okay," I called warm air.

"Much obliged," Baboo said as they scampered up the female Centaurs body.

She was smiling like Baboo had tickled her.

Lewt held down an arm to me, I grabbed it hesitantly, and he swung me up so fast I almost fell off the other side.

"Squeeze gently with your legs and wrap your arms around my waist," he told me. I could hear the smile in his voice.

His cohorts chuckled. One with waist long dark curls scooped Indigo up with a squeal. She was blushing behind him. He was enjoying it very much. They took off at a run, I almost fell off before I threw myself at Lewt's back holding on for dear life. Horseback riding was not something we did frequently in Chicago. His powerful hands clasped over mine that were locked in a death grip.

We were back before we knew it. Everyone was already chatting with random Centaurs, so our arrival went unnoticed mostly until Indigo started laughing.

"That was fantastic, Hute!" she had done a one-eighty while on Hute's stallion back.

"If you and your friend are up for a ride later, I think Lewt and I could accommodate."

The dark-haired Centaur gave her a smile that would've melted the coldest hearts. She giggled like a schoolgirl.

"I think we'd like that. Right, Scar?"

I smiled, "I would."

Lewt smiled, but noticed Viper and Ford, he waved farewell and trotted over them careful of the dancing trolls and fairies. His Centaurs followed; we'd lost track of Baboo again. I thought disappearing was a part of its personality.

Tyros were watching us as we came in on the backs of the Centaurs, one in particular. Slate. He sat in the shadows with Quick their eyes glittering in the firelight. Indigo and I went to our rolls under the fairy tree.

Ash was drinking out of a wooden mug and was being uncharacteristic, so was Sage. He was hanging on me. He handed me a mug sloshing with what smelled like troll ale. Indigo said it was strong, plus he had eaten those magic mushrooms. I hoped he hadn't drunk the rousen.

I sipped my mug and watched the trolls and fairies' dance. Ash kept kissing my neck and murmuring all the things he wanted to do to me making my eyes widen. He had definitely taken the rousen. I glanced down at my mug and wondered if he would have slipped it into my drink. I dumped it out beside my roll and got up to go refill it. Tawny met me at the barrel.

"Ash seems extra snuggly tonight," she said watching me with her wide eyes.

"I think he took some rousen. He's on me like white on rice. I think I'm going to have to take him out of here before he tries to get frisky in front of everyone," I said in a low tone as I refilled my mug.

"Do you *want* to do something?" Tawny asked as she took her turn with the barrel.

Good question, I only shrugged.

"One day, but not while he's a rousen. It takes the sweet part out of it. There's some crazy part of me-"

"That's in love with Slate?" she offered, and I leveled my gaze at her.

"Not what I was going to say. I was going to say, there's some crazy part of me that wants all the romance of my first time with Ash. Flowers, candlelight, maybe some sweet tunes. Not rutting in the dirt like an animal. Besides, being in love with Slate wouldn't be crazy. It'd be stupid. Terribly, terribly stupid," I stood next to Tawny as we watched the dancers. "How are you and Steel?" I asked, making small talk.

"Madly in love and blissfully happy," she said dreamily, and I knew she was rubbing it in, "In love with Brass then?"

I sighed, "Brass. I shouldn't have — he's one of Slate's closest friends. Seeing as he only has two, Brass is off limits if they're going to remain friends. I don't want to come between them." A boy and girl locked their arms and twirled together in the center of the dancers as I sipped my ale, "I'll get there. Ash is as charming as he is gorgeous."

Tawny snorted into her mug, "On a scale of one to volcano, how bad would Ash blow his top if you came to hang out with us for a bit?"

"What he doesn't know won't hurt him," I said, waggling my brows.

We walked into the shadows and I double checked on Ash to make sure he was preoccupied, which he was, laughing and entertaining a few members of his fan club with Sage, Indigo and Sterling sat with them in their little circle.

I was good to go.

Tawny and I snuck stealthily around the back until we reached where Cherry, Jett, Slate, and Quick sat, "Look who I found drowning her sorrows. She looked like a lost puppy, so I brought her home. I hope you guys don't mind," Tawny teased, and I plopped down squishing between Jett and Quick, if the two big men couldn't hide me, then nothing would.

"You guys move those broad shoulders in front of me. My husband doesn't know I'm here," I joked and rewarded with laughs from all but Jett and Slate.

"If I had a silver crescent every time woman uttered those words to me," Quick said, and a laugh bubbled up from my belly.

"Ugh, thank you, Quick. I needed that."

"If I had a —" he started.

"Yes, we get the idea," Jett snapped. "I didn't realize you two were married already. Apparently, he doesn't know that either."

I looked to Ash; he was whispering into Crimson's ear, and she was blushing prettily while he smiled.

"Harmless flirting. We are not married yet," I muttered and Quick grabbed my hand and made to leave.

"In that case, let us go find out how fiery you are," he teased, and I pulled him back down laughing.

"I would never. How's that for your truth detecting?" I asked smugly as I sipped from my mug.

Jett looked at Quick then with an arrogant smirk, "Oh, you wound me, Miss Scarlett."

"Untrue," I murmured, and Jett laughed.

"We missed you, Scar. I feel like the team's back together again," Cherry said, reaching over and giving my thigh a squeeze.

"I didn't realize Quick was part of the team. When did this happen?" I asked, nudging Quick.

Something about Quick made me like him despite his bawdy comments.

"I will take that as a compliment. You know you have noticed me, from your first night here, and the Ausa Vatni. You would know I often sit with these lunatics at lunch except you have been absent as of late. The husband cracking the whip?" Quick asked.

I sniffed, "No, things are great. We're busy, planning the engagement party, training for the Wild Hunt —"

"Reacquainting yourselves," Cherry chirped in with a waggle of her thin raven brows.

Tawny scoffed, and Quick turned back to me. His dark eyes glittered when he dazzled me with a smile.

"Uh-oh. Lover boy has discovered you're missing," Jett nodded towards the circle of Ash's fans.

Sure enough, Ash looked to where I had been sitting earlier and his light green eyes scanned the camp. I ducked my head behind the two big men.

"Tell me. Is it normal for a fiancée to hide from another?" Quick asked.

"Sage gave him rousen. I just need to dodge him for a little while," I whispered huskily since my body was at such an awkward angle.

Slate leaned back so his eyes met mine, "He took rousen tonight, and you are going to sleep next to him?"

"Sleep being the operative word," I said as I peeked over Quick's shoulder.

Those were the first sentences Slate, and I had exchanged since I kneed him in the groin. Ash was on his feet; he'd come straight to us.

"Party time's over, folks. Thanks for the laughs Quick. You're not bad for a pervert," I told him sitting up.

"And you are tolerable for the patron goddess of temptation and tease," Quick said with a seated bow.

"All I heard was goddess," I stood and dusted off my fanny back and Ash found me immediately and I scowled internally. I was not a tease. How could Quick think that?

"Hey, just saying hi to Jett and the girls," I told him and noticed his dilated pupils.

That must have been what mine looked like the day I'd drank the rousen.

"Lie," Quick muttered, but I didn't think Ash heard him.

"I missed you. Come, my love. I have something I want to show you," Ash said, sliding his caramel hand into mine.

"Truth. I bet I know what he wants to show her. OW!" Quick said, laughing.

I wondered who hit him since they sandwiched him between Slate and Jett.

"Come on," Ash said with that charming smile of his.

We were palm to palm as he led me into the woods. Ash spun me around against the bark of a tree and as I gaped at him, he ducked down to crush his mouth over mine. He wrapped his hand in my hair and pressed his lips to mine and eagerly deepened his kiss. This was it. He wanted me, right then and there. He pulled my head back and his lips trailed down my neck and down to my clavicle.

A million things passed through my mind.

"Slower," I whispered, and I saw something pass through his eyes, but I must have imagined it because it was gone in an instant.

Stop... slow... pause...

"Relax, my love. You are so tense," Ash peppered my neck with kisses as his hands ran over my back.

Maybe it was because we weren't married. With Brass, I knew exactly what it was. A friendship closer than friends. With Ash, it was more. He said we could wait for marriage — he was changing the rules. I was mentally prepared for kissing and maybe a little light fondling, but nothing more.

"Ash," I whispered against his mouth.

"Scarlett?" he breathed.

"When we —I want it to be romantic," I told him nervously, and he drew back with a curious look.

It drew together his brows as his light eyes scanned my expression. I hated that I could feel how disappointed he was in me.

"We have the rest of our lives for romance. This is but one night of a thousand," he said, not giving up.

"I'm not comfortable outdoors — naked," I said, biting my lower lip.

Ash drew back, visibly irritated with my constant reluctance, "I begin to doubt you will ever be ready for me. Perhaps on our wedding night you will have an excuse then as well."

I dropped my eyes as Ash stormed off into the woods towards the stream. I leaned against the tree blinking at shameful tears.

I stumbled away sniffling as I debated whether to follow Ash and make up with him. There would be only one outcome if I chased him down and again, I wasn't ready. Not with Ash. That little voice in my head who'd nagged me for years about being careful was mute my night with Brass. With Ash, it tapped me on the shoulder and whispered in my ear. *Wait*, it said, and I couldn't force myself to convince it otherwise.

A roar sounded through the night, and I stiffened. I knew that roar.

I turned around when the barghest hybrid collided with me taking me down to the lush grass at my feet. My head didn't hit nearly as hard as I'd braced for.

The barghest roared inches from my face making me close my eyes and turn my head away even though that only made my ears ring from how loud he was.

"You want him?" he rasped, pressing his short canine snout against my cheek.

Dark in the moonlight with long pointed ears and three sets of horns curling from its head, its short snout pulled back in a snarl revealing teeth as long as my fingers. The barghest man rippled with sleek bunched muscles ready to attack as it pinned me to the earth.

"Ash? No. I swear it," I said honestly, and it opened its maw over my throat and pierced my skin ever so slightly.

Gritting my teeth, I tried to speak again with minimal movement of my throat.

"I mean, I'm not ready! Nothing happened."

"You say you are mine. You went to another and mated with him and promised yourself to yet another," it lifted its teeth from my skin enough to speak as its lips grazed against the tendons in my throat.

My head swam, and it wasn't only from the troll ale. If this beast was speaking the truth, and I wasn't hallucinating again, then what happened in the Wemic lands had really happened. That wasn't possible.

"But I..."

I had nothing to say. No defense.

He took his mouth from my throat completely and his wide course tongue slid against my skin licking the beads of blood I knew were there.

"You are mine," he rasped, "for the rest of my days."

My lips parted as I turned back towards the barghest, he was shirtless, but had pants on for once. It was the most dressed I'd ever seen him. I tentatively brought my hand up and slid my hand between its tusk to cup its face and he closed his eyes to lean into my hand. He made a contented noise deep in his chest that made my loins pulse.

"Does that mean I promised myself to you first, so you have some sort of dibs?" I asked and smiled when I heard rasping laughter come from its throat.

"Did we mate?" he asked, opening his eyes and gazing down at me.

My eyelids were heavy as I peered up at him and his array of horns, and sleek dark fur. I wasn't even sure what color it was; I'd only seen him in the middle of the night, but I thought it was a charcoal gray.

"Why didn't you take me in the gorge?"

"You were in season," he rasped, and I remembered Keen had said the same thing.

I hooked my hands in his tusks and his eyes watched me as I tugged his face close to mine. "And now?" I asked boldly.

He made a noise it his throat that was primitively animalistic, and my toes curled in my boots. My fingers slid along the muscles of his shoulders covered in sleek silk fur. He raised his hips enough so I could move my legs to either side of him and I moaned when he pushed hard against me.

"I want to kiss you... like we did that night," I breathed trying to maneuver around his tusks.

The hybrid stiffened and raised his snout to the air. "Another time, mate," he rasped and pulled me up with him.

The barghest towered over me a foot and a half higher than my meager five foot six. Frigga's sweet grass, he wanted me. His clawed dark hand gripped the nape of my neck with no concern for being gentle carefully making sure his tusks did not impale my face, he pressed his lips to mine. His wide coarse tongue slipping into my mouth and forcing my jaw wide, so I had no choice, but to let him. He claimed my mouth as he would my body.

Bushes rustled wildly, and the barghest broke away as a palomino broke through and cantered over to where I stood. It was Lewt. I looked where the barghest man had just been and found myself alone. My pants unbuttoned. I blushed and quickly walked over to Lewt, surprised my feet would bear my weight.

He smiled as I approached, pushing his long blonde hair out of his face. "Scarlett, ready for that ride?" he smiled.

He offered his arm. I reached for it and he swung me onto his back but this time I was ready, and I gripped his waist closely.

"Let us go for a real ride," he said. I could hear his smile.

He galloped out of the clearing. I looked back at the camp and only saw one face watch me go. Slate.

Lewt felt like power between my legs. His blonde hair blowing behind him as he galloped along the stream. His bare chest was completely smooth, I would know since I'd been holding it the better half of an hour.

"Mind if we trot for a while?" he asked.

"Of course. Do you want me to get off?" I swung my leg around him, but he put a firm hand down on my thigh.

"You are not getting off me that easily," I heard his smile.

I smiled with him. "How far do you live from here?" I asked, offering some conversation.

"Two days walk for a Guardian. You really want to talk about that?"

I smiled, "I was curious. What kind of issue did you run into?"

"Ah, yes you are curious. No matter," Lewt said, smiling.

"I ran into Jorogumo this summer. That was an issue," I offered. I had a feeling it was tribal related.

He kept up his strolling pace, "Yes, we had heard about that. I did not know you were the Guardian girl that was attacked."

"I'm not a Guardian yet."

"You will be, and then you will not be so willing to take a ride from a Centaur, or swim with the trolls."

"Why do you say that? Why would it change me?" I asked somewhat offended.

"That is how it happens. Tribes are problems to be dealt with," he said plainly.

I shook my head, "I wish I could look at you while we speak. I have made friends with every tribe I have met, not Jorogumo, but surely there must be some friendly ones."

He grabbed one of my arms from around his waist and pulled me around to land in his arms — so he cradled me.

He smiled down at me, "Now I can see your face."

I gave a crooked grin, "Carried like a damsel in distress wasn't what I had in mind."

"I like it, I will carry you until I run again," Arguing with men, any type of men, in Tidings was hopeless. He continued, "There were Minotaur on the coast." He sneered.

I knew Minotaur lived in Elivagar; I also knew they weren't supposed to island hop without permission, "What happened?"

"We attacked; they were just arriving."

I didn't need to ask what happened. I could tell the Centaur had killed them all. Then something dawned on me, "Did you see how they got there?"

He was looking down at me; he was very handsome, "I saw a portal door near them. They deactivated it before we could investigate. I fear some of the Merfolk brought the doorway to Mabon, and that is how the Minotaur arrived."

My silly insignificant problems seemed quite small now.

"I thought the ability to make portals was gone. This is a *huge* problem."

"You may think so, we have no proof."

"You saw it."

Lewt laughed, it was not a pleasant laugh, "Tribes are lesser, they will doubt my word."

"You're wrong. Some will believe. I believe right now," I said defiantly.

He smiled down at me, "You are special, Guardian," he said it intimately, it made me aware of the fact I was being cradled in his arms. "Ready for another run?" Lewt asked, tossing back his mane of blonde hair.

"Am I!" I said excitedly.

Riding on the back of Lewt was surreal. I felt as fast as the wind. I was sure my backside would pay for it later, but I could get healing. He swung me around to his back and sped off into the forest.

Crisp autumn air whipped my hair around and I just breathed. Sometimes, it just felt good to breathe. The scent of the wind reminded me of Slate, but I pushed the thought away. I hated the idea of having to tell my family that another portal was on Mabon instead of Thrimilci this time and that the Jorogumo weren't the only tribe with rogues.

"Refreshment break?" Lewt asked as he slowed to a canter, "Yes, please." I wasn't the one running, and I was parched.

I heard the babbling of the swirling stream before we came to it. Lewt walked. As soon as he slowed, I heard it.

"Stop!" I whispered harshly.

He smirked, "You wish to watch?"

I didn't answer; I slid off Lewt's back, which looked a lot easier to do in movies than for someone who had only ridden a horse once. A little further and I'd confirmed what I thought I saw.

The moonlight reflected off the stream, but even without it, the green and blue luminescent plants made their faces glow. He was behind her, bare breasts in his hands, moving up to her throat. He nuzzled her hair. Ash and Crimson. She was panting with each thrust. After I caught them together the night my mother died, I thought they were over for good.

I had to admit; I hadn't expected it. Jonquil —yes — but I didn't think Ash would risk anyone finding out. *Me* finding out. I wondered how many of his fan club members he had been with. I should have stormed to the stream and made a scene, let him know I caught him. Scream and shout, do *something*. I was too hurt. After I came clean and we made up — we were good. Not sex, but I came as close as I dared while I shared his bed every single night. It wasn't enough. What I had to give was never enough.

I turned around and headed back to Lewt as I angrily rubbed tears away.

His eyebrows furrowed, "What is wrong?"

"Nothing. Thanks for hanging out with me Lewt and giving me the ride of my life. You blow horses out of the water, I have never been on one before," I said trying to put on a smile, but didn't have the energy. I could have slept right there.

"I am faster than a horse," he scoffed, "You know them?" He asked.

"I do. I think I'll walk back, thanks. Until we meet again. Lewt, I'm going to have to tell the council about what you saw. Is it okay if I tell them I heard it from you?"

He looked at me seriously, "It is. Be careful Guardian. You are quite special and liaisons with barghests never end well." He reached down and kissed my hand before turning and trotting off.

I turned away from the stream and stumbled my way back to camp. Lewt had seen the barghest, had probably chased him off. I could tell them I was sick and had to go home, but it was a lie, and they would just heal me anyway. I sat down on a random log and ran my fingers through my hair.

I picked myself back up and walked to the village. Almost everyone was sleeping. A few people had indulged in the troll ale and were singing off tune songs I'd never heard. The provosts had a tent set up, two low ones on either side of camp. I saw Jett with his arms around Cherry passed out, Tawny curled up behind them. Indigo and Sterling were sleeping back-to-back. I didn't see Sage; he was probably in the stream with a girl or maybe a boy. My half-brother hadn't a clear orientation.

I exhaled a large breath of air. I wondered again if I could get out of the rest of the trip. This was the last place I wanted to be. I didn't see Slate or Quick; I didn't want to know where they were.

Were these grounds for breaking off the wedding? I knew they had affairs and spouses weren't happy about it, but they stayed together. That much was clear, but what about beforehand?

I sighed again and sat down on my roll. It was next to Ash's vacant spot. I wondered if this was karma for Slate kissing me. No. I didn't think Ash would have cheated if I'd given myself to him, but I didn't want to.

Indigo stirred in her sleep, her back flat against Sterling's. I wondered if they all cheated.

"Poor Guardian," Baboo said, "Terrible thing to make you so sad." Baboo was standing in a small bridge between two trees.

"I'm not sad. I'm nothing," I told them.

"Come Guardian, I will take you home," Baboo landed gracefully on their feet.

"It's a four-hour walk back to town; the provosts would be upset," Baboo laughed, "Not your home, my home."

"Baboo, I won't fit," I told them, trying not to get annoyed.

"You will. Come. Come," Baboo took off.

I sighed rolling up my things, pulled on my pack and followed Baboo to Gods knew where. We didn't go far until Baboo stopped at a large knoll, larger than most of the others, but still way too small for me to fit under.

"Baboo, I can't fit in there."

"You will see," they hummed merrily and opened the small door.

The door was maybe two feet wide by three and a half feet tall, but there were stairs as soon as you opened the door that opened to a five-foot-high ceiling. I could fit, it was snug. It was a long house too, well long for someone who came up to my waist.

Baboo smiled up at me, "See."

"I see, you were right. Thank you for inviting me to your home," I really was grateful.

Baboo gave a troll blush, at least that's what I thought it was, "Yes, yes. Do not be so sad."

"You're right again, Baboo."

"You can sleep here," Baboo pushed their little wooden table and chairs into the wall so I could lie down my roll.

"Baboo, thank you. You know what's funny. Funny strange not funny ha ha, the tribes have all been nicer to me than many of the Guardians."

Baboo nodded, "Not all Guardians are very nice."

"I'm sorry if a Guardian was ever mean to you, Baboo."

I couldn't believe a Guardian would be mean to the spunky little troll, the thought made me even angrier. Baboo shrugged. Nothing would keep Baboo down for long.

My dream had always left me with a sour taste in my mouth, but since the woman had taken my mother's face, it was profoundly worse. I'd slept in fits. I woke up a few times not knowing where I was. The events from the day before hitting me like a ton of bricks. I did not know what to do.

"Good morning!" Baboo said cheerfully. I didn't think Baboo operated under anything except cheerful. "I made eggs!" they held up a frying pan.

I smiled, "Smells delicious. Do you know if the tyros broke camp yet?"

"No, no, still early. They are only stirring. A Centaur stole a couple's clothing last night while they bathed in the stream," Baboo smiled.

I'd have to thank Lewt for that the next time I saw him, "So, I guess the entire camp knows?" I didn't much like that, it made me feel idiotic.

Baboo shook its head, tuft of white shaking, "Only a few. The naked man got into a fight, that is why people found out."

"A fight?"

Who would have fought with Ash? Did him and Sage get into an argument?

Baboo was scanning images in my mind; I could feel it, "That is the one, the tall, dark one."

"Slate?" I asked in disbelief.

"Yes, Slate. They tried to sneak into camp and Slate tripped them. They fell on the sleeping tyros and woke the provosts. It was quite humorous," Baboo held its mossy pot belly as it shook with mirth.

I was happy Ash hadn't snuck into camp, happy as you please, but it felt like Slate did it just so I would find out and that hurt. Slate, Jett, Quick, Tawny, and Indigo, all of them, thinking I was an idiot, really hurt. I didn't want to go back out- side. I wondered what the leave of absence policy was at Valla U.

"Eat," Baboo shoved a plate into my hands, and by plate I meant a tree bark plate, "Time."

"What's that?"

"Time heals all wounds. I have heard it said."

"Yes, but what if you are almost out of time?"

"I do not know. You have a long time, Scarlett."

Baboo never used my name, most of the tribe members I'd met didn't, except for Keen. I smiled when I thought of Keen. Maybe I would run away and join the Wemic. Once again, I rued that if I was Wemic, I'd marry Keen in a heartbeat... then again, there was my barghest.

Mine.

"Baboo, I want to ask you something. It is an indelicate question. Bear in mind my ignorance..."

"I am a girl," Baboo laughed.

I laughed too, my face turning red. It felt good to laugh.

After breakfast, I readied my pack and freshened up. Baboo came with me. My anxiety mounted as we approached the village center. I felt like puking. I was in some sort of weird denial and yet I accepted it, kept hoping something would prevent me from meeting up with them all.

No such luck. Some people started murmuring as I walked into the clearing. I saw Crimson. I let my eyes glaze over and walked straight to Tawny, praying the burning in my cheeks wasn't as noticeable as it felt. More than a few sets of eyes followed me as I went through the crowd.

"Hey! I've been looking everywhere for you. Where did you go last night? We must talk, like now," Tawny's face was blotchy, and her heart faced pinched like she had a terrible headache. I healed her. "What was that for?" she asked.

"Only one of us should be upset. I already know. I don't want to talk about it."

Jett and Cherry came up behind her, "Scarlett, are you okay?" Cherry asked.

"I'll kill him," Jett said darkly. I was afraid he meant it.

"Look. I don't want to talk about it. I don't know what I'm going to do yet," My creepy monotone voice freaked even me out.

Slate leaned against a tree with Quick. I wanted to yell at him; to thank him. I didn't know what I wanted, that was clear, so I just stayed away. Ash stood talking with Sterling and Sage, Indigo off to the side. She saw me and walked hurriedly over to me. Ash followed her with his eyes until they rested on me. I broke contact first but kept it long enough, so he knew I knew. He narrowed his eyes, as if he had cornered the market on anger.

"Scarlett, I'm so sorry," Indigo gulped.

She was tearing, so I healed her too. She stopped crying and dried her face.

"What are you going to do?"

"I need some time to think," I sounded a lot more even keeled than I felt.

"Well, I'm on your side."

Indigo planted her feet firmly next to me as if she had just drawn an invisible line between camp Scarlett and camp Ash.

Ford and Butterfly were wrapping up their tents with air. It reminded me of the night Thrimilci held its feast. Tent poles and fabric flew into neat piles, it was like a dance. Ford didn't look like he had a good night, probably because he saw his naked niece with a man that was supposed to be getting married in eight months.

Butterfly looked a little better, "Okay, break camp and file in. We head back to the portal in ten." She shouted to the group.

I could sense Ash coming up behind me, anger and frustration oozed from him. I didn't want to have an altercation there, that might not be a point. Taking him back was the furthest thing from my mind.

I heard galloping before I saw them.

Lewt, Hute, and Goep trotted into the clearing. Lewt smiled down at me, blue eyes shining, blonde hair falling over his tanned shoulder as he leaned down for my hand, "Thought you would need a ride."

I shot a quick glance to Ford whose lips were in a firm line but nodded. "Can I bring two friends?" I asked breathlessly.

This was about as close to a fairy tale as I was going to get. My white knight was golden and had merged with his steed.

His smile widened, "Hute missed your blonde friend, and if you have one for Goep, I'm sure he would be happy." I grabbed Lewt's arm, and he swung me around.

I waved Indigo and Tawny up. Indigo was beaming and Hute couldn't get her up fast enough. Tawny paled, but she still let Goep with his flowing brown mane and Clydesdale body pull her up. He laughed as she clung to him. I can only assume Lewt shot Ash a dirty look as we galloped off. I felt a dangerous wave of anger crash into me from Ash.

Lewt galloped at the head of the trio, Hute and Goep at his sides.

A half hour in and Tawny's smile was ear to ear.

"This is awesome!" she yelled.

The Centaurs laughed. I wished I could take away their fatigue, when they ran, it was like really being free.

We slowed to a walk when we grew close. "You stole their clothes last night," I said to Lewt leaning into him so the others wouldn't hear.

He turned giving me a big grin, "Perhaps."

"Thank you," I said low so only he would hear.

"Who is he?" he asked.

"*Was* he? My betrothed."

"Was?"

"I don't know," I said, confessing to a near perfect stranger.

"Sometimes it is good to say things out loud," he said as if reading my mind.

He couldn't, I was sure.

We arrived at the portal with time to spare. I swung down from Lewt and reached up for a hug; he scooped me up, so my feet dangled and placed me gently back on the ground.

"I really can't thank you enough," I told Lewt, I thought I would cry again like I did with Keen.

He gave a big golden boy smile, "We took three beautiful women out for a ride. I think I should thank you."

Indigo was possibly in love with her pony boy who was whispering into her ear as she stood on the ground blushing. Tawny was windswept and red-cheeked and looked dazzled.

I laughed, "Thanks again."

We watched the three Centaurs gallop away.

It was before noon; the Centaurs made great time. We weren't supposed to be back until tomorrow.

We were still giggling from our ride with the Centaur. The three of us took our giggle fit to my room. We took turns showering and Tawny ran to grab a dress from her room but came back to get ready. Indigo changed into a blue dress that matched her eyes, and I slipped into an olive green strapless.

I felt like I was on a high after the run with the Centaurs. Indigo and Tawny were just as giddy. We came down to lunch, and it was nearly empty with only Steel, Sparrow, Gypsum, and Pearl. Steel jumped out of his seat and Tawny planted a kiss on his lips. Apples of red bloomed on his cheeks.

"What's gotten into you?" he asked, still bashful in front of Sparrow.

"We just ran with the Centaurs!" she gushed.

It was exhilarating.

Without preamble, I spoke swallowing my last bite, "Minotaurs were on Mabon. A Centaur friend of mine saw them and attacked. He said they came out of a portal onto the coast, most likely by a Merfolk traitor. The Minotaur came out of it once it was on land. The portal was deactivated or broken by the time the Centaur's attack was over."

I didn't know what effect this would have on everyone. Steel had his jaw clenched. Sparrow's mouth had popped open while Pearl sat silently in contemplation.

"A widespread invasion. The other islands are at risk," Steel said dumbstruck.

"Your friend will have to tell the council. He knows that?" Pearl asked, pursing her lips.

"I told him. Viper will help, I think," Steel's face didn't look too hopeful, "You will help him? I don't want him thrown under the bus for defending his lands from an invading tribe."

I got away with killing Jorogumo that disappeared, but rules were different for tribes. I frowned.

"Yes, we'll help. I must go back to the Merfolk," Steel threw down his napkin.

"Not right now, surely?" Tawny said, voice rising.

Steel sat back down in his seat. "No, I guess we should tell the council first," he wiped a hand over his face, "This has been a nightmare. First Thrimilci, now Mabon. Why?"

"Nowhere is safe," Sparrow pointed out.

The mood at the table grew solemn, I regretted killing the mood. I didn't want to make it worse for everyone by telling them my marriage possibilities were falling apart, so I kept it to myself.

Jett came in with his usual saunter, "Ready to go see some really big spiders?" He gave a smug smile. I shivered.

Jett, Cherry, Quick, and Slate had booked it back to the portal and came straight home, arriving during the night. It helped when your provosts were your mother's cousins and wife was the Prime's daughter.

Alder came in with Indigo, a green cloak with a white linen shirt tucked into brown boots. Two long seaxes rested on his hips. I wondered if Jett knew that. There was an awkward tension between the two like a cinderblock wall with only a few cracks and chips to let in a sliver of chance of a relationship between the two.

"It will take all day to get there, and a day to come back. If you would like to change your mind, now is the time," Alder told Jett and me.

"No, I want to do this," I told him. Jett shook his head; he wasn't leaving either.

"We are ready," Indigo told Alder.

She didn't look very excited about visiting the Jorogumo. Her hair was in a ponytail, and she wore a beige cloak with matching pants and a loose taupe top, her bow and quiver rested over her back. We walked through the portal door to Ostara.

The smell of the flowers blooming in perpetual spring greeted us and I inhaled deeply. My father's homeland was breathtaking. Ostara had the only portal door that wasn't in the town center.

We headed down the road and into town, Alder leading, Indigo and I walking side by side and Jett taking up the back. We wound past the intricate wood carved homes and the riot of vivid flowers in every available patch of land. The women wore pastel caftan dresses like the black ones we wore at Valla U. The dresses almost swept along the road made of crushed glittering white stones. It crunched beneath our feet with each step.

The townsfolk smiled and waved to Alder, he occasionally stopped and spoke with them. At one point he started introducing us, he told them we were his son and daughters. If I was shocked, then Jett was stupefied. We babbled a bit, nodding like bobble heads and then gave each other side glances as we started walking again. I didn't know what Alder was getting at, but since I could see the castle his wife, son, and parents were in I thought maybe he had lost it. Either that or he was hoping his wife would hear that he was there with his other children and send her flying monkeys after us. I liked neither scenario.

The pastel homes appeared fewer and further between, we came to a narrower white crushed road that led underneath arches of hanging purple and white flowers. The colors alternated, Guardians had a hand in creating their beauty, it didn't diminish it any way. In fact, I wondered how one got a career in cultivating. That would be a pleasant pastime while popping out children, if I ever had time to.

"What do you plan to do after Valla U?" I asked Jett.

He raised his brows, surprised where my thinking had taken me.

He blew out a hard breath, "I'll probably feel the council out for an ambassador position."

I nodded. I had thought the same thing for myself at one point, it would require a lot of traveling so it would be impossible if I stayed with Ash.

"I'd like to leave Tidings and come back to teach," Indigo said, and I smiled. She would be a wonderful teacher.

Alder cleared his throat. It was an awkward noise that cut into our conversation. "I have been meaning to speak with you, Jett," I saw Jett's face go smooth; his step slowed for a split second. They didn't have conversations, "I plan to claim you and your sisters as my own officially before the start of the new year."

Jett's brow knit. I scoffed in disbelief, "That's in two months."

Alder nodded, "It would mean a great deal to me, if you would take my name, Jett. You are my first-born son, my heir. The heir to the Var castle and ruling family of Ostara."

Jett stopped. He looked angry. I bit my lip. Alder noticed we weren't behind him. Alder stood stock still, he looked like a king. The sun shone bright in his light blonde hair; his deep-set blue eyes locked on Jett. Alder was the biggest man I'd seen in Tidings; he was even more intimidating when he set his gaze on you like he was doing to Jett.

"I need nothing from you," Jett said softly.

"Jett," I said. I tried to grab his hand, but he pulled away.

"I've done well in the twenty years before you. That need not change."

Jett swallowed hard. This confrontation was a long time coming.

Indigo knew it too; she stood back fading unnoticed into the background.

Alder knew it was coming as well. He strode back to Jett, entered his personal space bubble, and met his eyes. I thought I was having an anxiety attack. I didn't want them to fight. Jett was younger and probably faster, but Alder was stronger and more experienced, it would not be good.

"Are you finished?" Alder asked in his guttural voice.

Jett's hands clenched into fist. Alder's gaze was unwavering, I wasn't even sure if he saw Jett's fists, "You abandoned our mother. I was raised by my grandmother. My sisters torn apart, you get one, mom gets one while you sat in your castle with your new family. You want to come into our lives now and *what*? Be a father? Show me how to be a man?" Jett laughed; it was a nasty, harsh sound.

Alder took it all, he inhaled Jett's pain and anger and exhaled patience and love, "I love your mother still. If I would have disobeyed them, it would be akin to risking her life. We married when they told me I would have to marry Delta. You are legitimate. Her wedding to Lark was in the Guardian way, but we went to the States with Hawk as our witness. I could never have left her. I kept my distance so she could have our son and so you would be safe from the repercussions of our decisions. Staying away from Wren was impossible. Delta never knew about Wren and me. I regret not giving it all up and going with your mother when you were born. I left my wife after Wren returned and have only been there when Indigo and Sage were home. I have only been with your mother since her return."

Jett's eyes brimmed with unshed tears, but his jaw was still set. I was weeping freely. Alder broke eye contact with Jett as I raised my arms to be held by my father. He held me tight and stroked my hair. I peeked out to Jett who had blinked rapidly, but his face was doing some weird twitching like he was fighting several facial tics at once. I raised my arm to him, and he stared at it. Alder lifted and arm towards Jett, but Jett didn't move.

Indigo appeared out of nowhere and gave him a nudge. Jett stumbled into us, he was too proud to come on his own, but Indigo gave him just the right motivation. I was doing most of the hugging and all the crying and Indigo came in to join us, but I finally felt like we were a family. I only wished my mom could've been there to see it.

We started walking again after I got it together.

Jett laughing at me broke the ice. "What about Sage?" Jett finally asked.

Alder was walking in front of Jett and me again, "I love Sage, he is not the right person to run things in Ostara. A father knows this about his son. He is destined for other things."

It sounded like Alder had thought it through and had not decided lightly. I could not have agreed more.

We had gone off the path and passed by the arches now and had entered a thickly treed area like a jungle, a narrow path passed through the heavy vegetation. It was cooler than Thrimilci, but it maintained its spring like weather with more humidity.

"Won't he be upset?" I asked.

I didn't tell my dad about Sage's not so subtle bullying of me or the fact that he loathed me.

Indigo frowned as she whispered to me, "Sage will be crushed."

Alder nodded, "He will. Quite a few people will be in fact, but I am heir, and I will name my own." He looked back to Jett and gave a small smile.

Jett was in a bit of shock. He hadn't thought he would be the head of his own greater family before, so Alder had dropped a bomb on him, "When you finish at Valla U, we could spend more time in Ostara to groom you for the years to come. You could be an ambassador here until you are ready, you have the disposition to be a great ambassador."

Jett wasn't used to compliments from someone who wasn't Amethyst or Cerise. "Amethyst will be happy," he muttered.

He had told me Amethyst wanted to run a house bigger than the Geol family's, which was currently uninhabited. It would be a dream come true.

Alder smiled. I thought it might have been the first time he'd smiled since my mother died.

The day had drastically improved. We journeyed through the jungle and listened to all the noises of the surrounding creatures. Loud insects calling to one another sounded from all angles. It grew dark, with the trees we couldn't see the moonlight. The path led us to a few darkened stone cottages. Alder opened the door of one of them and hit an energy plate, the cottage burst with light. It was very quaint, but comfortable. Much more rustic than the country cottages of Valla.

"There are two bedrooms upstairs, we can use another cottage if you like. I will stay on the couch," Alder told us.

"I can room with Scarlett," Indigo smiled at me.

"I will take the other room," Jett brought his pack upstairs, and we followed.

The beds were smaller than the ones at Sumar palace, but it wouldn't be a problem with Indigo and I. Jett came into our room as we set our packs down.

"No," I said without waiting for his question.

Jett laughed. His hands folded behind his close-cropped blonde hair.

"I didn't even ask yet."

"No, you will not fit on the bed with us. Even if you did, you have serious boundary issues for a brother," I told him with a small smile.

Jett's full lips turned into a pout as he rolled onto his stomach, "Indigo doesn't mind if I sleep with you guys. Do you, little sis?"

Indigo's mouth curled as she gave Jett an indulgent smile, "You try to hold us while we sleep Jett, it is unbrotherly. I would know, I grew up with our half-brother."

Alder had set up a small dinner. He had a pantry full of dried food stores and seeds in containers so moisture wouldn't seep in, so we ate like kings for the night.

Alder tried to fill us in on what to expect, but all I heard was giant spider people were going to talk to us. I was by far worst at Jorogumo in my language class. Wait till I saw Jackal again, he'd give me an earful.

"Jackal is going to be so ashamed of me," I told my dad.

Alder smiled as his brows knit, "Why is that?"

"I am miserable at languages; he teases me constantly in class."

"I had not realized you two knew each other so well," he said.

I smiled, I liked Jackal, "Well, Crag is a Straumr, and Ash is his cousin... we hang out in the same circles I guess."

My hands had suddenly become very interesting.

Alder grunted, "Father did not like when Jackal took the teaching position, worse than when he brought Crag home. Canis liked it even less."

The humor had gone out of Alder. Indigo was watching him though as if waiting for more, I didn't think it had to do with Jackal.

"They wanted him to be an ambassador?" I asked.

Alder gave a familiar half smile, "They wanted him to do what they wanted. Only I was ever that foolish. I admire Jackal for doing what he wanted. He is much happier his way."

"Scarlett, wake up."

I opened my eyes and Jett's confused face was inches away from mine. Marks from the pillow pinked his cheek and his eyes were still groggy.

"You were yelling for Slate; I hope you don't do that when he stays the night."

I blushed and rubbed my eyes. Jett turned sideways to fit on the bed with me and Indigo who could sleep through anything.

"That was creepy. Were you murdering him? I wouldn't blame you."

I looked at him ruefully. "No, I was not murdering him," I told Jett about my dream even though Tawny had already described it, "Do they make replicas of the pieces? I have this." I pulled my stone pendant up from my favorite racerback and held it up.

He nodded as he ran his thumb over the stone, "Perfectly logical explanation."

"I don't know if he was dying, he was just lying there," I said defensively.

I knew instinctually though that he was dead or dying in my dream.

I shifted, so I was on my side looking at my brother with my hands pressed together under my pillow, "How are you doing? He dropped some doozies today, huh?"

"Doozies. Good word. Apt. I'm all right. If he doesn't expect me to call him dad or something, we'll be fine. What about you?" he asked.

"Other than my brother thinks it's okay to climb into my bed in his skimpy underwear? I dunno. It's weird. I was drawn to Indigo, like a kindred spirit, you know? I can't imagine how hard it must have been for all of them. I didn't know how sad mom was until we came here, Alder has that same sadness, but worse."

Jett nodded, his close cropped dark blonde hair rubbing against the pillow, "You can't marry Ash. You're not the wife he needs. He needs someone too timid to care what he does, or a ball buster who can give as good as she gets. That's not you. You need an equal partner who you can give to who will give alike, see the difference? You're not a taker."

"I took from Slate after mom died," I said pointedly, and Jett shook his head.

"No. You gave as well. Don't deny it. Ash cheated on you," Jett said as his turquoise eyes glittered. His strong jaw shifting as he pressed his full lips into a hard line, "You deserve better than that. I know the girls think he's quite the catch, but you've got options, Scar."

It was much too deep a conversation for a middle of the night talk, "Jett, I care about Ash. It sucked beyond belief to catch him with Crimson, but I can't think of anyone who would take better care of me, of my future children. I'd be secure with Ash."

That was what it always boiled down to for me.

Security. Stability. Reliability.

Ash was predictable, and I could count on knowing what he'd do next. I knew he'd cheat that night because I didn't submit to him, and I could deal with that because I saw it coming. Things weren't always that predictable with other people and there was nothing I hated worse than having the rug pulled out from under me.

"If you say so, baby sis. You know, when you are finally ready pump the brakes on this freight train, it just might be too late," Jett said, knitting his brows at me.

"I'm reasonably sure that you can't pump a freight train's brakes," I teased, but I got the message.

It was light in the room, and we needed to interrogate the Jorogumo fast so we could get out before dark. Alder said no one ever stayed the night with the Jorogumo.

I woke up to Jett's enormous body clinging to me like a spider monkey, "Jett, by the Mother, how do your wives stand you? I can't breathe!"

He woke up groggily and noticed he had tossed a powerful thigh over my hips, his arm slung over my chest to grip my shoulders. He had to weigh well over two hundred pounds, easily twice my weight. A lazy smile grew, and he stretched languidly as he drew his limbs back to himself.

Indigo had woken up at my exclamation and shook her head at Jett, "Your poor wives."

"Must be despairing without me," he said as he hopped up and hopped from foot to foot waking himself up.

I shook my head at my big brother.

After breakfast, we walked for about an hour before the jungle spread further out and came to what looked like giant tree trunks with door size holes in them. They reminded me of post-apocalyptic apartment buildings.

Jorogumo hustled about quickly, their movements made me want to run or draw my knives, it was a toss-up. Most of them didn't pay us any attention as they went about their daily business. I was struggling with the bit of panic I felt at seeing them. I wished Slate was with me for about a second.

A dark grey spider with a fat sack for a back the size of hippo wattled up on its eight legs and started speaking to Alder with it's too human head and face. Pinchers extended from the sides of its jaw. Alder didn't so much as flinch. It turned to us and flashed us its teeth. It took every ounce of strength I had in me not to scream.

I thought it was smiling.

Jett had a hand on my back, to comfort me or to keep me from running I wasn't sure. Indigo moved up beside Alder as they spoke to the spider with the fatback. Indigo was an Ostara native; you could tell by her relaxed posture.

They each looked so different from one another. Some were like the one they were talking to, with big sacks on their backs, others had fewer spider legs and human torsos. Then there were the ones that looked eerily like humans. Human legs before there spider ones with the body of a human, but with several eyes and pinchers. The last was the one I had a close encounter with my first fight ever. That wasn't the only difference, they were also different colors. I'd only seen dark colored Jorogumo, but now I thought they had rubbed mud on their more vivid shades to blend.

The Jorogumo was leading us away, Alder waved us on to follow. Jett kept a hand on my back, I knew now it was so I wouldn't bolt. The Jorogumo were everywhere, and they moved just like their smaller brethren. I had a serious case of the shivers; I couldn't stop imagining them crawling up my spine.

The grey sacked one brought us into the hole that ground level in a giant tree stump. Jett had to do a little extra pushing to get me through the dark entranceway. It was dimly lit, what I noticed right away was the enormous web and the Jorogumo that was obviously a female crouching in the center.

She had three sets of eyes in her ridged face, long black pinchers protruded from her jaw. She had black legs with lime green slashes, her torso was all woman with just a tinge of green. Rows of human like breasts hung from her overly long torso which was completely without nipples.

She climbed down from her web, black human lips curling back into a smile that turned my insides to liquid. That's when I noticed the web cocoons along the walls. Animal bodies hung ready for devouring still alive.

"Ambassador Alder, how unexpected," she stood on her eight legs; spider torso low so she could look him in the eye.

"Empress She'ik, we have news. The Merfolk traitors have been exiled. We have a new way of finding those who wish to remain undiscovered," Alder told after a nod of his head.

"How mysterious. Do tell," she didn't rattle in her throat like the ones who attacked had, her voice sounded like a woman's only raspier.

"These are my children Jett, Indigo, and Scarlett," We inclined our heads; I was grateful they weren't the handshaking type. "My daughter can read emotions. She rooted out the betrayers in Thrimilci," Alder told her.

I had my empath abilities cranked. I knew right away the empress wasn't involved, her mood ran between amused and disgusted. Amused we were there and disgusted with the betrayers.

"What would you have me do? Parade my people through here so your daughter may find them out?" She'ik studied me intensely.

I couldn't wait to leave. A cocoon just mooed.

"Whatever is most convenient for you Empress, I know you wish this matter closed as much as we do," Alder said, inclining his head again.

She tapped a human finger to her cheek, "I do. However, I have already succeeded. If you had not come, I would have sent someone for you. I had Drik'er followed. He met with some Anguillan and returned. My spy returned and relayed what had happened. There was a confrontation. I am sure you noticed all the commotion." She lifted her human arms.

Good to know they rarely swarmed about.

"Do you know where he went? Did he take many with him?" Alder's eyes were ablaze. He knew whomever this Drik'er was.

She'ik gave another ghastly smile, "Only about five hundred, traitors all. I do not know where they went. We must protect the nest."

I shuddered; it did not go unnoticed. She'ik's six eyes rested on me, "You should run along. I believe your council will want to find them before they use their portal again and find themselves inside a university."

It wasn't a threat, she just enjoyed being evil. It was her nature.

Alder nodded, "I think you are correct. We must leave immediately. Is there anything else I should know She'ik?"

She used her spidery legs and climbed back into the center of her web, "Yes. I am very sorry they have done this, Alder. I hope the Guardians fry them to a crisp."

Yikes. There was no way She'ik would accept them back. That much was clear. I felt her want for revenge. Drik'er had offended her on a personal level.

The sack back grey Jorogumo led us back to the path and chattered with Alder. Alder smiled at it making my eyes bulge. We headed back the way we came through the jungle.

"I should have known. Drik'er was She'ik's consort, but he resented he could not be emperor. I never thought he would try to overthrow her; her people love her. He is a fool. Now we have five hundred rogues Jorogumo loose in Ostara. The council will be in an uproar. The town is in danger. We cannot rest tonight; we must go straight back. Jett, if you could warn the council, I will tell my father – and the people in the castle," Alder's blonde brow pulled down as he thought.

Jett nodded; he looked even more alarmed than Alder. I was sure he was thinking about the Wemic and how close the original portal was to their lands. Steel could be out there. I was thinking it, too.

Alder's pace on the way to the Jorogumo was a cakewalk compared to what we were doing on the return. I wasn't used to walking through jungles and I seemed to trip on every snarled root. If I didn't know any better, I'd say they curled up as we attempted to walk over them. Jett walked behind Indigo and me with his hand under our arms to keep me from breaking anything. It was dark by the time we reached the flowering arches. Alder pushed on.

The Var castle glowed in the darkness, all the spheres along the two bridges reflected moonlight. We crossed through the sleepy town and headed for the portal.

"Who is the ambassador for the Anguillan? They should be alerted too. Obviously, they're involved as well," I asked, huffing.

My stamina was embarrassing, but at least Indigo looked just as winded. Anguillan were eel human hybrids. Why couldn't there have been something like bunny hybrids or chipmunk hybrids. Eels and spiders? Shiver.

"My uncle, Canis," Alder said as he reached the portal gate, "I will go back into town and let people know, then I will head to the castle. I do not think I will be back tonight. Thank you, Jett."

I hugged my dad. Alder sensed Jett was not prepared for hugs and gave his shoulder a squeeze.

"Take care of your sisters," he told him before he headed for the bridge. Jett let him go leaving words unsaid. I hated that.

It was in the middle of the night, but an emergency council would be called. Jett went to Pearl's room as I headed to Sparrow's.

I knocked gently on the door, not wanting to wake Hawk up, but needing Sparrow to know what was going on. Hawk answered the door anyway.

He saw it was me and his dark, intelligent eyes grew alarmed, "Scarlett, is everything okay?" Hawk's silver hair was in disarray as he tied his navy robe.

"I have to speak with Sparrow, something's happened."

I was dead on my feet, the anxiety of having been around the Jorogumo had worn on me. Not to mention all things concerning Ash and the long walk. I just wanted to talk to her so I could go to bed.

Hawk nodded and let me through the door. Sparrow must have heard it was me. She threw her long dark hair over the back of her burgundy robe, cinching it tight.

"Scarlett, what's happened?"

I told her what She'ik told us and where Alder had gone. She cursed and headed into her closet to get ready.

"I'm sorry to wake you," I said, sinking into a sitting chair.

Hawk dismissed it with a wave, "She needs to know these things. They'll try to send troops tonight would be my guess, at least around the town for protection. The Var's will be the real problem. They won't look too kindly on having a force there."

"But it's for their own protection," I said in confusion.

"Some greater families value their privacy over their safety, especially if they believe someone is trying to seize power away from them," Hawk whispered.

"People can do that to greater families?" I asked. The prospect sounded frightening.

"It has happened. They install a more manageable family member instead of a strong patriarch or matriarch," Hawk nodded knowingly.

Sparrow was ready in a hurry, but I never saw her leave since I fell asleep halfway through Hawk's answer.

I awoke sensing the stop of movement but was too tired to open my eyes, "I can take her. I am not sleeping as it is."

Hesitation.

"If you wish."

Someone passed me higher and held tighter. More hesitation.

"You are a good young man. I don't know if you knew this, but your father was my closest friend. I see much of him in you."

Silence, the hands that held me stiffened, "I remember. The prophet talent I inherited from my mother allows me to remember everything."

"If you ever want to know more about them, my door is always open. You take care of her," I felt a hand brush my brow, "She's like a daughter to me. I would like to see her happy. Wren liked you two together."

"I hope she can find happiness as well," the voice was low and monotone.

"Prophecies are rarely black and white. Remember that. Depriving yourself of happiness won't make life any easier. But you don't have to listen to me, I sound like a man much older than myself. You'll do the right thing, I know," I heard a light patting and steps that led away.

The movement started again, and I fell back to sleep.

I awoke in my bed for the first time since Brass spent the night and I had a different man in my bed. Slate. We had said two sentences to one another in a week and I had kneed him in the balls.

Forget for a moment that his midnight waves spilled over his bronze back and over my gold satin sheets with the morning sunlight coming through the stained-glass windows next to my bed to color his skin in reds and blues and that his thick long lashes fanned across his cheeks in a way that almost looked vulnerable. And certainly, forget that his full lips were slightly pursed as he slept nearly making the high cheekbones that made the planes of his face look hard, soft despite the blue-black shadow of a beard that grew overnight. Forget all of it. Especially that little flat spot on the bridge of his straight masculine nose I imagined came from Jett doing something wild and Slate being too proud to have it healed.

His muscled arm was under my head, and he wrapped the other around my waist. His expansive chest was bare exposing those perfect dark pink nipples. — Gods what in the world was I doing.

I looked down at myself and shook my head inwardly, he'd made sure I'd had clothes on. I was wearing the ivory nightie he'd bought for me. It was the only bit of lingerie I'd brought back with me into my room from him. He must have found this piece deliberately amongst all my other pajamas.

I didn't bother looking to see if he had anything on under my bright gold sheets. Slate could surprise me, but I didn't think he would. I shifted back in his arms to face the stained glass and held my breath when Slate's corded forearm tightened around my waist tucking my body to his. If he didn't sleep next to women, he sure had a good feel for how he wanted them to lie with him. His hand snaked up my middle to rest between my breasts.

Funny thing was, he was still asleep. I could hear his even breathing, feel the heavy exhales on the top of my head. I knit my brows. He was awfully comfortable with me. His powerful thigh was between my legs, which I grudgingly found very comfortable, and I fit right along the curve of his body like a spoon. I guessed that was where the phrase came from.

A kiss to the nape of my neck sent a thrill shooting down my spine and I fought against a shiver of delight that made my skin prickle. I failed and the ivory satin over my breasts bespoke just how much.

Another open-mouthed kiss seared behind my ear and the scratch of a stubbled jaw rubbed the side of my throat. I clenched my teeth to stop my lips from parting when the crashing waves of excitement swept over me.

"I have never made love to a woman after slumbering the night," Slate's head lifted to place another kiss at the crook of my neck making his long waves brush the back of my neck. "By the Mother,

Torch. Your scent makes my cock rock hard against my stomach," he purred.

I inhaled sharply; he couldn't leave well enough alone. I shifted in the bed, so my backside was away from my most evident problem and bit down hard on the inside of my cheek when I looked up at the being gazing down at me with silver dreamy eyes and flexed bronze muscles. It had been a bad idea to turn to face him.

"That sounds like a personal problem. You might want to go take care of that. I'm sure there are plenty of willing volunteers outside just about any portal door. Lera is a short fifteen-minute walk away, twenty, if you dress first," I said in a cool modulated tone that didn't betray a hint of what I felt.

Slate's full lips curled in an arrogant smirk, and I narrowed my eyes, "I do not want another. Only you, Torch."

A traitorous gasp escaped me when his head lowered to mine, his hair sliding silkily over my throat and chest as he kissed the corner of my mouth and then smiled with a rare cheek creasing flash of perfect white teeth. He had me and he knew it. I quickly scanned my mind for the moment I'd suddenly stopped fighting him and I was at a loss.

Another kiss along my jaw and the sound of my heart beating was deafening. He had to hear it, if not, then he surely saw the shallow breaths I was taking.

Panic rose within me; I'd always known the right thing to do. It was whatever hurt the people around me the least, and I had been acting selfishly since my mother's death. He had trained me and the time alone with him when I was weak and vulnerable was the extra push, l needed so I would trust him without reproach, mostly.

"Torch?" Slate's straight black brows drew together as he looked down at me, inches away from my face.

He'd felt the change in my mood. I'd been malleable and not completely unwilling until a heartbeat ago. Now I was furious. I felt duped. Training conditioned me to him. How easily I'd forgotten about walking in on him and Lera and the two blondes. Who knew how many women he'd been with since then. Ash had been with — one. I didn't think he'd cheated before that; I was almost certain.

I turned my face away from his. He leaned back on an elbow as he watched me roll off the other side of the bed and walk around the massive canopied four poster and into the sitting room. The urge to yell at him or slap him was making my palms itch and my lips pressed firmly together. I would not engage.

Slate followed me with narrow silver eyes until I left the room. I kept going until I reached my bathroom door before; I spoke needing the security of a lock and a door between us.

"When I come out of this bathroom. I will expect you to be out of my bed, Slate Sumar," I said softly before slamming the bathroom door behind me.

CHAPTER
ELEVEN

It might have been the first time he'd ever listened to one of my requests without a huge fight. It was late afternoon when I left my rooms and went down to the kitchens. The staff wore Grecian styled gowns of royal blue with golden belts and torques. They seemed scandalized I had made my way into the kitchen to get my food, so I took my plate of seafood couscous paella with a saffron infused broth back to the dining room to eat alone.

Messengers arrived at the end of my meal with arms full of flowers and a note from Ash begging me to grant him an audience. I burnt it to ashes and crumbled it between my fingers. He would not win me over with flowers and words that were just as sweet and lasted just as long.

I could have been with Brass the night we'd had our date. It wasn't innocent. Belatedly, reality had sunk in. I'd given an immense piece of myself to Brass, but at least it was safe with him.

Alder, Pearl, and Sparrow were in meetings with the council while Hawk, Steel, and Gypsum had gone into town with Tawny. Knowing

Jett, he'd spent a night away from his wives, so he'd be making up for lost time.

I did not know where Indigo was, but I was forming plans of my own.

Shadow Breakers filled the rumpus room. My body shook with exhilaration and nervousness. I was afraid someone would ask why I was wearing thigh-high boots. I was even more frightened that someone would see the flash of my hot pink push-up bra underneath my black cloak.

If Slate was around, I'd lose my nerve.

Brass, Quick, Ama, and Shale walked in pairs from the Crash Course stairs where they had been training. They looked freshly showered and carefree. Ama and Shale were laughing when Brass's steps slowed as his mind found mine. Quick noticed the change in Brass and he searched the room for the source of Brass's intense gaze.

Oh, Gods. What was I doing?

He was in front of me. Had I been walking towards him?

"Brass, what do you want for lunch?" Quick asked nearly tugging on his sleeve to pull his eyes away from me.

Brass's sultry amber eyes locked on mine and my heart thundered, "I am not hungry."

"Lie," Quick grumbled as he walked towards the bar with the girls to place his order. "Not for food maybe," he muttered under his breath.

Brass didn't speak. He took my hand and hastened to the stairs. I was skipping to keep up with him taking the steps two at a time and giggling like an insane person. We were at his bedroom door before my feet could catch up with where my brain had led me.

He pulled me into the room after him and used air to shut the door as he spun to me and unclasped my cloak letting it fall to the floor. Brass sucked in a deep breath as he took in my ensemble.

"My birthday is in the early spring. There are two months before Yuletide. Midsummer has passed. I am trying to grasp why I deserve such a gift, but I do not care if you are for me," Brass said in a rushed smooth whisper.

"You've already unwrapped your present," I said biting down on my lip, "Do you intend to play with it?" My cheeks heated at how forward I was being, but the look in his eyes was worth it.

Brass's lips quirked just before he pulled me to him, and his cinnamon laced lips parted mine. I wound my arms around his neck as he walked me backwards to his sitting room couch.

"Frigga's sweet grass, Scarlett," he whispered as he dove back to me after shedding his shirt, "You are going to stay, yes?"

"Yes," I murmured against his lips.

"The rest of the day and the night. I will bring up food for dinner."

"Stop talking," I said roughly, trying to push his pants off his legs with my heel.

Brass chuckled and his hips slid between my legs with a moan.

We stacked empty plates and bowls on the coffee table from our dinner. The smear of chocolate on the white bowl the last bit of evidence of our dessert that my supposedly safe Brass Regn had used creatively. He tied my hair on top of my head and danced with me to my favorite Arctic Monkeys' song. My ancient mp3 player was in my cubby, and he'd gotten it with dinner intending to listen to it together.

His brown linen shirt fit down to my thighs as we swayed with our bodies mashed together. I was getting very good at matching his body's rhythms. My hands twisted in his hair above his bare shoulders. His charcoal gray boxer briefs was the only article of clothing he wore. Love bites trailed from his left ear and down his chest to the corded muscles at his hips where I'd stopped. I was bold, but shy about most things even after the multiple times we'd made love. He'd watched me looking amused and asked if I was practicing.

That had made me turn as red as my namesake.

Brass never pushed. He only did as much as I was comfortable with. I felt safe and cherished. He didn't ask why I had come for what had happened with Ash, which he must have learned from Quick. He just enjoyed my company, only speaking after I teased him to inquire about my dinner.

"Happy?"

"I'm always happy with you," I said, gazing into his soft eyes.

He slowly shook his head, "You are dangerous for me, and I do not mean Slate's infatuation."

I nearly snorted. Slate was only infatuated with himself.

"Ash wants you to be his wife. It will insult him you have been with me. My grandfather would say I am killing my future marriage prospects."

When my movements slowed wary of where the conversation was taking us, Brass took my hips and swayed us to the slow beat of the song. "I do not care. You do not have to marry him," Brass lifted my chin up to meet his eyes.

I bit down on my lower lip to prevent the question that popped into it from leaping from my mouth. A lock of dark hair grazed his cheekbone, and I leaned on my tiptoes to press a kiss to his lips.

"We could try," he whispered so quietly it was barely audible, but he'd sent it out there into the world where it took flight and buzzed around my head as insistent as a mosquito so I couldn't ignore it.

How could I marry Ash when any time we were apart I went running to Brass's bedroom? Brass was more than gorgeous. He was my friend, and I'd only ever given myself to him. Willingly diving into the pool of emotions I held for Brass whose bottom looked black and depthless was almost as frightening as submitting to Slate.

"Maybe," I whispered back against his delicious lips, and he lifted me off the floor bringing me to his bed.

His smile so bright I should have looked away or else risk going blind.

He convinced me to spend the night. It was not an uphill battle.

He told me about the illustrious Spinel Regn, his grandfather and how his mother, Robin Geol, died in the Red Kings Massacre. Twin sister to Peak's younger brother, Brass had strong ties to the Haust family. My mother had told me some of their background, but vaguely. He was a first cousin to Sterling and his evil twin sisters and a distant cousin to

Amethyst. The other lesser families disliked the Regn family for it and the greater families preferred to pretend they didn't exist.

His father had become reckless in his grief and perished two years later in a bar brawl in Ostara. Spinel had raised him and his brothers with Cordillera, his father's twin, which explained a lot.

He remembered precious little of his mother, and he never faulted his father. Robin had been the love of his life and they had had Coyote Regn against their parent's wishes long before they were married. Too young, Brass had said. When I did the math, I realized that meant his mother was fifteen or so when Coyote was born for them to have been able to have Quick be almost a decade younger than his brother. I wondered how Pearl could have Steel and Hawk and my mother with their large age gap, but my uncle/brother conspiracy would wait.

Laying between his legs with my ear pressed against his chest, not a stitch of clothing between us, I was having a hard time coming up with reasons I couldn't date Brass. He was perfect. I couldn't find one thing I didn't love about him.

Brass awoke when I did in the early hours of the morning and when I laced my fingers through his; he had moaned aloud knowing my intentions.

Brass watched me straddling his hips as I took him. I leaned, so it pinned his hands at his head. He looked as though he saw through me, saw into me, and was lost in the emotions I provoked in him.

My confidence had taken an elevator ride to the top floor of a skyscraper being with Brass. I was terrified of the fall off that windy roof, but now I was holding on to its spire head thrown back, eyes closed. Daring the world to just try to knock me down. I felt invincible.

It could work. I never felt better than when I was with Brass. He made me better.

Brass nuzzled my chest when I shifted to slow my movements, my body curling against his with my every thrust. So intimate, it felt like more than our bodies intertwined.

"Ah, Brass," I moaned unable to stave off the fall any longer.

I was in the murky depths and sinking to the bottom. All nonsensical emotions poured from me and filled my mouth pushing on the back of my lips to be freed. Brass kissed me deeply buying me time before the deluge of unnecessary words spilled forth and I was vaguely aware of his shuddering.

His calloused palms crossed my back holding me still as we laid together and his kissing tapered away. My mouth was being freed and words bubbled from my lips much huskier than I'd intended them too.

"I'm not using you for your body. Since I show up to your bedroom, I know how it looks. I still must tell Ash," I began as we hid from the outside cocooned in the waves of my hair that outlined his face from where I hovered, "but I feel like —"

My nerves weren't as steady as I would've liked so when his bedroom door crashed open, I screeched like a banshee before Brass rolled me off him. Framed in the splintered doorway was six and a half feet of enraged Slate.

Brass was stepping into a pair of black plaid drawstring pants when Slate entered the room. I hadn't moved from the bed paralyzed by confusion and embarrassment with the gray sheets pulled up over my chest. Behind Slate, Quick, Ama, Shale, and Cordillera hovered looking groggy as if Slate had stormed in before they'd had their coffee.

I was beyond mortified. Brass bore the evidence in the plum-colored trail like a road map of where I'd traveled.

"She makes her own decisions," Brass said softly.

The linen shirt I'd been wearing the night before flew to me probably from Brass and I pulled it over my head and only felt slightly better. My underwear was next which I ducked under the blanket to wriggle into.

I felt betrayal, fear, and sorrow.

Slate didn't speak out loud. Whatever he said transmitted directly from his mind to Brass's. It must not have been much because Slate leapt clear of the couch and tackled into Brass. Ama's shriek joined mine as Quick tried to break them apart and was elbowed in the nose for his troubles.

Barefoot and smelling of cinnamon, fresh fallen spring rain, and sex, Shale and I tried to grab hold of Slate's arm. Cordillera took my wrist and yanked me backwards.

"You caused this. They are closer than brothers. Leave. I will clean up your mess," she said in an irritated tone.

I was only half paying attention. The brawl that was slowly breaking apart using the combined force of Ama, Shale, and Quick's calling to control Slate who seemed to stretch and darken.

Cordillera was shoving me out the door. I felt a droplet splash on my arm as she thrust my cloak and boots at me and realized I was crying.

"Go home, girl," she said in an aggravated tone I didn't understand.

The door shut in my face, and I jerked back staring blankly at it.

"Stop! Stop it!" Ama's shouts were followed by panting from several sources.

"My nose broke, you bastards," Quick spat.

"Here," Shale's muffled voice came through the door, and I thought I'd better put my boots on to leave.

The knuckle dragging barbarian who had staked his claim in me spoiled my perfect night.

"You have no right!" Brass's voice sliced through my hot frustrated tears and brought me to attention.

"She is in love with me! Promised from my first prophecy!" Slate growled in a frightening voice full of rage.

"Do you want her or not? You want her to give you all but promise her nothing. You say she is supposed to be the death of you," Brass retorted breathlessly.

"What do you promise her?" Slate shouted.

"I do not have to make promises. She can have whatever I have to give! She does not need to ask."

"Enough!" Cordillera yelled and both men went silent, "You are family. You do not let a girl come between you!"

That was what I did.

I'd heard all I needed to hear and pulled my cloak over my shoulders, clasping it at my throat before I walked from the living quarters. I pulled the hood of my cloak up and slunk from HQ.

I rushed from the Shadow Breaker headquarters trying very hard not to run until I was in the streets of Valla. Then I broke out into a tear faced bolt uncaring if anyone saw me. No one would recognize the blur that whipped by.

Once I made it through the portal gate and back in my rooms, I began stripping off my clothes and eager to wash away the heady scent of Brass from my skin; I stepped through the wall of water that led to the showers.

The dozens of pulsating shower heads built right into the pearlescent tiles shot water at me from every angle in a constant flow of warm and fuzzy heat that melted my furies away. I'd take an extra-long shower that morning, so I'd be sure the feel of him was gone.

"Scarlett?" Ash called.

I sighed. He was already in my room and would come into the bathroom once he realized that's where I was. I was still engaged, and things had to be addressed. I couldn't run away.

I shrugged on my satin champagne half robe and wrapped my hair in a towel before leaving the bathroom taking a deep fortifying breath and shutting the door behind me.

Ash saw me and drank me in. I hadn't dried myself well, and the robe clung to my curves. He entered my bedroom and closed the door behind him with his most charming smile. I crossed my arms and lifted my chin to look at him.

Ash wore traditional Mabon clothing, a light grey jerkin with silver moon buckles that lined the front to the hollow at his throat. His black pants tucked into black mid-calf supple leather boots. His lightest green eyes glittered when he looked out at me from chestnut brown winged brows.

"Ash, I did not expect to see you anytime soon since you have been spending so much time with Crimson," I said pointedly and took the towel down from my hair to soak up the water.

"I deserve that. Please, may I sit so we can speak?" Ash said, gesturing to the chaise lounge.

I nodded and sat. Better to get it over with.

My wet hair hung over my shoulder and Ash's eyes kept drifting down to the outline of my breast under the dampening fabric, "I took rousen the night we were in Mabon. It was not a well thought out plan, I admit, but I thought I would spend it with you and so did not see the dilemma until it was too late."

He turned to me and took my hands from my lap, "I know I have humiliated us both. I am very sorry, Scarlett. Rousen makes you-"

"I know what rousen does, Ash," I interrupted and his eye twitched.

"Of course," he said diplomatically, "I would never have cheated if I had not been on rousen. I swear it. I will declare it to anyone you wish me to. It does not excuse my actions, but I would like to put it behind us. I want you to be my wife, Scarlett. I should never have thought you would want to make love in the woods our first time together," he gave me the most apologetic smile he could muster, "I promised romance and gave you rousen. I am deeply regretful."

I let out a gusty breath, "Ash, do you think you could ever love me?"

He cocked his head, "Of course, my love. I do love you."

He was telling the truth. I could feel it. He thought he meant it.

I interrupted him, "No. You were right. I'm the one who should be sorry. Please forgive me and we'll go back to the way things were before all of this. Just you and me. I don't need to wait. It just has to be private." My tears fell.

The smartest thing I could do for myself was to marry Ash and put all others out of my mind. My dedication would be rewarded with his. One thing I could feel from him was that he honestly, beyond a doubt, wanted to marry me and make good on all his promises. All I had to do was let him.

Ash's brows shot up, and he wrapped his arms around me pulling me into his lap, "You are forgiven, Scarlett. shall start fresh. All else is the past. I love you, Scarlett Tio." Ash tipped my chin up and placed a kiss on my lips, "Our first time together will be all I promised you. We will go to the Straumr cottage in Valla. Leave the planning to me. It is the least I can do."

I nodded as he held me uncaring that my wet hair dripped on his fancy jerkin, "That sounds amazing. Thank you for being so understanding."

CHAPTER TWELVE
JETT

Jett

Jett didn't know how badly until he had to sit through a painfully awkward breakfast while Scarlett pushed food around her plate between Ash and Indigo. Jett didn't need to be an empath to feel the palpable tension between Slate and Scarlett. The strange part was the tension between Ash and Slate that had been there since the first minute the two men discovered his sister had somehow changed. Instead of Ash being more threatened by Slate he seemed less so, even dismissive.

Jett couldn't believe the change in Ash and Scarlett. They were a real couple, whatever happened after the confrontation with Slate had made Ash give Scarlett the space, she needed to have a little of her own life which she was choosing to spend with Ama and Shale at Shadow Breaker headquarters when she wasn't practicing calling for the Wild Hunt challenge at the end of the year with Ash. Brass was as cut off as Slate.

Scarlett didn't want to talk about her change of heart whenever Jett had tried to broach the subject and he didn't think she was talking about it with anyone else either. Tawny hadn't the slightest clue what Jett was talking about when he'd tried to feel her out for information.

If Slate's plan was to try sleeping with her until she went running for the hills and right into the arms of her future husband, then he succeeded. She wouldn't even look at Slate, if she glanced at him in the halls the angriest little snarl formed with her full lips. Jett had seen Slate's reaction to that expression, and it had not been good. Slate was M.I.A. from their shared room at night, and Slate missing in action was always a bad thing in the past.

Scarlett avoided them all.

Slate didn't know how to activate Scarlett's bond so he would know where she was, and it was driving him crazy. Jett hadn't realized how much he had depended on it himself until it was gone. Luckily, she had reported to HQ whenever Quick hadn't seen her leave the university with Ash. It didn't help that Slate told him Scarlett was using her manipulation talent to push him away like an invisible barrier. He could, but it was extremely hard. She made you think you wanted to do something, so when Slate would walk towards her, suddenly he thought he wanted to turn right, or turn around.

Jett was glad she had never used it with him, though it was sometimes funny to watch Slate freeze in the middle of the hall and look like he wanted to walk into a wall. Scarlett seemed indiscriminate which way he turned as long he did. The worst part of the entire ordeal was that Indigo had told him she'd heard Scarlett crying when Ash hadn't spent the night. Jett hoped it was because of their mother and not over Slate, or he'd have to kill him.

There would be no escaping one another when they went out to celebrate the twin's birthday. It was Indigo and Scarlett's first birthday together and though they celebrated yesterday with the family and their father, Jett had had a get together at a club in Valla. They were going to celebrate turning twenty in style if Jett had anything to say about it.

Amethyst laid back in their bed watching Cherry. She hadn't felt like joining, but Jett thought her mood might've changed.

Jett's eyes fell from Amethyst propped up on the pillows to Cherry on her knees. He inhaled sharply and set his hand in her hair. His head lulled as she hummed.

"I changed my mind."

Jett barked a laugh and flashed Amethyst a smile as she threw back the blankets covering her.

"Cherry or me?"

Amethyst's lips curled, "Both."

Cherry staccato laughter vibrated along him and he clenched his jaw. He curled his fingers in her hair and spilled. Cherry popped up after a moment and kissed his slack lips. She wasted no time in crawling over the bed to Amethyst.

"You are so beautiful," Amethyst ran her fingers through Cherry's hair to cup her face.

"I love you," Cherry braced her weight on her palms over Amethyst and kissed her.

Jett hated himself for checking the time.

"He checked the time," Cherry giggled against Amethyst's lips.

"I'm sorry!" Jett wiped a hand over his face and looked around for his discarded boxer briefs, "They trusted me to plan it. It's a big deal."

"We can finish later," Amethyst promised Cherry and planted another kiss on her lips.

"Or during," Cherry giggled again, and Amethyst smiled.

"I'm sorry."

Cherry plopped down beside Amethyst and pulled the blankets over them both when they needed to get up and get ready.

"Look at his face," Amethyst chuckled.

Cherry did, too, and leaned into their shared wife, "Don't be sorry. You are excited. It *is* a big deal. We are just poking fun."

She opened her arms to him, and he arched a brow.

Amethyst laughed, "He thinks we are tricking him into bed."

"We weren't?"

Jett's lips slowly curled, "I'm trying.

"We love you more for it," Cherry crooked her finger at him, and he couldn't turn her down a second time.

A knock at the door cut his shuffle to the bed. He held up a finger for them to wait before leaving the bedroom.

He could hear them ignore his request and follow him to the sitting room. Jett looked again for something to wear, but he'd forgotten it all in the other room. Amethyst offered him his boxer briefs and lifted her jaw.

Jett kissed her and sighed, "I'm distracted."

"It is warranted. I shall get the door."

Cherry met her at the door wearing a red half robe to Amethyst's long black one.

"Good evening, Amethyst. Cerise," Alder rumbled, "I was hoping to speak with Jett. Indigo said he had an evening planned for her and Scarlett's birthday?"

"He does. Please, come in," Amethyst opened the door and Jett bolted into the bedroom to find his clothes.

"We're going to a nightclub in Valla," Cherry explained, "you should come!"

Alder grunted and Jett smiled as he imagined his face, "That is very kind of you. The girls should have their night out without their father looking over their shoulders. They have Jett to do that."

Cherry burst with a giggle at the surprising joke.

"He does do that," Amethyst agreed, "A moment."

Jett found his clothes for the evening and quickly dressed when Amethyst walked into the room. She gave him a rueful smile. Her relationship with her father was complicated so she understood better than most.

"He too is trying."

Jett gave her a flat look and buttoned his shirt, "It would've counted for more if she was still alive."

Amethyst sighed and wrapped her arms around his waist. She gazed up at him with luminous dark eyes that had captured him in an instant. He rubbed her arms and sighed.

"I'll speak to him."

"You will be glad for it," Amethyst kissed his lips lightly, "Send Cherry in and we will ready."

"I don't deserve you."

"You strive to."

Jett fucking loved her enigmatic ways. It had driven the suitors Moon sent her crazy.

Alder was still standing when Jett entered the sitting room. Cherry popped up from the sofa and kissed his cheek as she passed.

"Be nice," she whispered and sauntered back to Amethyst.

They would finish what they started while he was preoccupied.

"I did not mean to interrupt," Alder began.

"We were just getting ready."

Alder nodded and the awkwardness was a third person in the room.

"It's a myopic dance club I thought Scarlett would like," Jett finally said.

A rare smile hinted over Alder's lips, "That is considerate of you. Indigo would like the change. She is not conventional," he shook his head, "she has gone out of her way to be nonconventional."

"In Tidings," Jett corrected, and Alder nodded.

"In Tidings," Alder repeated and stared at Jett. He stared so long that Jett glanced towards the bedroom door for an outlet, "I wished to thank you for including Indigo. She has always been on her own. Sage would take her places, but she has never made friends easily. I would worry about her. It seems," he paused, "she only needed to know who she really was to find her people."

Jett's throat constricted as emotions swelled, "She was happy to tag along before. We don't really give her that option. She's one of us."

"Precisely," Alder nodded, "I should have found a way to contact Pearl. I should have done a great many things."

"Do it now," Jett said point blank.

Alder searched his eyes, "I will. Please wish the girls a happy birthday for me."

Jett nodded, "I will."

"Goodnight, son," Alder hesitated at the door.

"'Night," Jett stared at the shut door.

He should've called him father.

Arms wrapped around his waist, and he held Cherry's hands at his stomach.

"You're a good man, Jett Var," Cherry murmured into his back, "Give yourself time."

Jett sniffed and patted her hands until they fell, "We have to go."

Amethyst was shimmying into a little black number when they walked into the room. She pushed her hair from her face and Jett waved Cherry away so he could help Amethyst with her zipper.

"My father said he has no issue backing your claim."

Jett sighed, "He says that now, but when Dahlia starts yapping in his ear or Basil's ear because she will. Cassiopeia will never *ever* let her grandson lose his position."

Amethyst turned around and combed her hair with her fingers, "Do you think Moon Straumr listens to his only daughter or his sister-in-law?"

Jett smiled and shook his head, "Forgive me for questioning you."

She smirked and lifted her foot to put on her heels. Jett took her outstretched hand to balance her.

"You are forgiven, my love," her eyes slid back to him, and she subconsciously scanned his outfit, "Ash will not be there tonight."

Jett's brows shot up, "No. Shit. Amethyst."

"She did that on purpose," Cherry chirped as she dressed in the closet.

Amethyst shrugged and walked to her vanity, "I like Scarlett for Ash. I hope they have things worked out now."

Jett gaped at her as she put on earrings, "He's been fucking Crimson, Jonquil, that common cook, and Sienna Aurr! I'd rather Brass date her!"

"Aww... I'm rooting for Slate," Cherry leaned past Amethyst and applied lipstick in the vanity mirror, "he is so into her. It's a nice change for him."

Jett's nose wrinkled and both girls giggled. "Scarlett would be good for Ash," he conceded, "but only if she influenced him."

"She does," Amethyst argued, "you don't see it because you dislike him."

"Hate. I hate him. Because he's a rude, great son asshole, and because he does Scarlett dirty."

Cherry shook her head at him beyond Amethyst.

Amethyst arched a brow at Jett, and he threw up his hands, "She is bedding a lesser son while betrothed to Ash."

"Don't tease him!" Cherry giggled as Jett's face heated.

Brass and Quick were like brothers —favorite cousins — and the thought of Brass, Jett shuddered at the thought.

When he looked up both girls were chuckling at him.

CHAPTER THIRTEEN

After an hour and a half of stretching in a room, we grabbed our clothes and trudged downstairs to the prep room. We all rinsed off. I was in the last frosted wall shower. They might see me when they walked past to their lockers, but only if they looked back, which Shale did. I had realized belatedly that Shale and Ama were a couple, and while Shale was very much into the fairer sex, Ama was an equal opportunity employer.

I hurriedly put on my armor and blades. Patting my Yggdrasil necklace and stone pendant, I checked on both rings and the three fetishes in my hair. I took none of them off.

"It might not be a good idea for me to come with." Brass said softly as he met me in my aisle of the prep room.

"Don't be like that. We're — friends. You can be my platonic date."

For my sanity, I had been avoiding Brass. I wanted to kick myself. I couldn't stop hearing the seductive moan he made when we were together. How his lips had more talent in them than most men had when utilizing every part of their bodies. The way his trimmed beard left its calling card wherever his mouth had roamed.

I wanted to know what he tasted like everywhere I hadn't yet explored. No, not that.

Slate was what it always boiled down to.

"Is there anything I can do to change your mind? You deserve a night off as much as the girls do, maybe especially since having to deal with me," I batted my lashes at him in mock innocence.

That got him to smile.

"I guess I could go," he licked his bottom lip, "Scarlett, forgive me for having to ask an indelicate question."

I cocked my head and watched as he dropped his eyes uncomfortable with his next question.

"May I?" he held up his hand in the traditional manner before using calling or delving into me.

I nodded, and he placed his palm on my stomach. His warmth flooded through me, and my stomach dropped when I realized what he was doing. Every muscle in body pulled taut with tension until he let his hand fall and gave me a smile that looked as forced as my own had been.

"I doubt you drank the tea the other day. I wanted to be sure," he said in a gentle tone.

The lights in the prep room blurred as I grew lightheaded, "No. I... guess something distracted me that day. So...?"

"No," he told me.

"No?" I parroted back to him.

"No, Scarlett. You are not carrying my child."

He led me out through the prep doors and into the arena.

I tried not to stagger as we met up with Shale and Ama. I was tired from not sleeping and feeling wrung out from the hot stretch session not to mention that he just delved into my womb looking for a little Regn baby. It might've been my imagination, but we both seemed disappointed. He had quickly closed his emotions off to me which was a dead giveaway.

Brass and I were friends, good friends.

I'd been such a mess all kinds of thoughts were seeping out of me and making him bring me in even closer, as if he could protect me from my own thoughts. Then there were my rogue sexual thoughts. I didn't have a defense for them. Brass was an attractive man, and I watched him a great deal, unfortunately for both of us, he knew it.

With this new revelation, I should have felt relief, but I didn't. I didn't know what I felt. My own mind was a mystery. What did Brass's mind hold?

Brass was fighting a smile as Shale outlined what we'd do today. Shale was going to bark orders from the sidelines, Ama was going first, and this time Brass would prod me onward from behind. I didn't have a choice, so I only nodded along. They'd been running me ragged at every visit and I relished it. It was a welcome distraction from all things.

Ash and I were better than ever. I was happy when I was with him and since we'd finished planning the engagement party, Dahlia and Pearl had taken over the guest list. Ash was like a different person and this person was charming all the time. I kind of loved it and kind of feared it.

Cordillera was back in her glass box as soon as Ama started. I wondered if she had a video feed in here or alarm that alerted her to our presence in the arena. She had been watching me every time I came into headquarters and making me so mad I could spit. I dismissed her presence and focused on the goal. I wanted to complete the Crash Course so bad I could taste it, unfortunately it tasted like blood.

I had underestimated the stretch session, didn't get enough sleep, and was feeling crappy about my skills.

"You are getting in your own way! Get your head on straight!" Shale yelled at me on my second go around because the first time I had my ankle shattered by a falling boulder about ten steps into the earthquake portion.

I felt Brass wrestle with the instinct to pull me out of harm's way, but it was Shale's job to wrap me around with air and drag me to her so I could be healed. Luckily, you didn't need to remove bone fragments before healing, if they were yours, they had told me grimly.

I ran, duck, and rolled through the Guillotine of blades, I jumped from tree to tree and made it to the earthquake portion. Those jumps were harder on me than any other part of the Crash Course. I wanted to catch my breath before continuing, but Brass was bearing down on me. He swung through those trees like a fiddlesticking monkey — hardly fair.

I sucked it up and began making my way over the cracks that could pull a car under and the boulders that fell the size of a sofa chair. I barely made it across. I had to pull it together. On less sleep, I did more.

I took one last deep breath before jumping onto one of the passing rocks in the lava. I went back and forth on the rock trying to time the other rocks just right. One. Two. Three. GO! I used my launching approach like I did with the trees to get me across the rocks.

I would not give up even though I desperately wanted to. My movements seemed sluggish to me, that second round of tree hopping had spent me. I wondered how many times they normally did it in a day.

I leapt to the nearest raft as it passed around on the current of the whirlpool. I misjudged the speed of the water and only one foot landed on the raft. My weight teetered on one leg before cursing and plunging into the roiling water.

My expression was dour as someone dragged me onto the dock. Ama offered me a small smile as I coughed out a lungful of water. Me not needing to be resuscitated was a minor consolation. I still hadn't made it across the Crash Course. I stood up as soon as Shale released her air.

"We are done for today," Brass told us, "you pushed yourself hard enough. You did not give up, that is important."

I was still surly; I nodded and headed towards the prep room. Ama caught up to me and linked her arm through mine.

"Did you bring anything to wear tonight?" she asked.

I cursed again, "No."

Dinner with the family and unable to push Slate away had made me see red. I didn't want him anywhere near me. I got to celebrate my first twin birthday with Indigo so that was good. Ash had told me I'd be on my own tonight after dinner because he had volunteered to lead the mission into Ostara to find the missing Jorogumo. It was disappointing, but Brass would be there, and he could be my dancing partner. I'd have to reign in my raging hormones for the night.

"You can borrow something of mine," Ama's smile was so bright it was hard not to return it.

"If you're sure you don't mind," I said carefully. "Not at all."

"Pick a color, any color," Ama said in her usual bubbly voice.

"Black," like my mood.

"Humor her, she does not get to play dress up often," Shale said, smirking at Ama.

Ama stuck out her tongue, and Shale raised her eyebrows. Ama giggled. I felt like I was intruding; I cleared my throat.

"Black is not a color. Pick another," Ama urged.

"Green, it's my favorite," I said, trying not to roll my eyes.

Ama clapped her hands giddily, "I thought so! I have something perfect for you. You can keep it too; green does not look very good on me."

She threw me two things, a turquoise green mini bandage halter dress that crossed at the back and a gold pair of heels. It matched my eyes, and I arched an eye suspiciously at Ama with a smile.

"Thanks for the dress and the shoes Ama. I love them. It's a wonder that you had shoes in my size since yours are two sizes smaller than mine," I said, smiling knowingly at her and she beamed brightly as ever.

Not wearing a bra was going to make this an interesting night, the laundress had washed my underwear from yesterday and my armor so at least I had those.

Ama approached me warily, "Can I do your makeup, Scarlett?" She held her hands up from behind her back, in them she had a bunch of cosmetics.

I shrugged, "Sure, why not."

Ama squealed and set to work.

Her face was close to mine as she worked, she smelled like sugar. Her dark eyes were ringed by long fluttery lashes, and her pouty cherub mouth was glossed to pink perfection. Shale came to sit beside her and mouthed thanks. My guess was Ama had few friends if she was so excited to be hanging out with me.

Shale wore black leather pants and a tight red tube top, not a stitch of makeup on. She didn't need it. Her dark intelligent eyes watched Ama work; her thin lips curled in the corners in a constant smile. I wouldn't call her beautiful, but she was striking.

"Done," Ama said. She leaned back and clapped. I gave her a questioning smile, "Go look in the mirror. Tell me if you like it."

The full-length mirror was in the closet. I looked how I had back home; I felt homesick. Chicago home sick. The dress turned out to have a built-in bra and was tighter than all things holy so my breasts would be on display all night even without my necklaces drawing attention to my cleavage. I was sure it was what Shale intended and rolled my eyes.

Ama had done a beautiful job on my make-up; she accentuated my features without making my make up look heavy. I was a gold shimmering angel the way Ama had quickly given me tousled waves and done my makeup. I pulled on my gold shoes and completed the ensemble.

"Ama, you're a miracle worker," I told her when I walked out. She clapped giddily again.

As we waited for Brass, I clasped my mother's cloak around my throat. I'd have to keep my eyes averted to not send out anything that would make him uncomfortable. I could pay him a compliment verbally, that always worked out better.

We ate in the rumpus room as we waited. Brass came down the stairs, and I faced my plate so I wouldn't think anything yet. He sat down and I smelled him, cinnamon and morning dew in the spring.

"You ladies look nice," he said in his usual warm tone.

It made my lips curl; he was so genuine. I looked up to pay him a similar compliment because, of course he would look good. How could he not? He was already smiling when I met his eyes.

"Loud and clear," he said, and I rolled my eyes.

I failed. He looked good. Leather pants tucked into black boots and a deep red shirt that stretched nicely over his pecs.

"Loud and clear," he repeated, smiling deeper.

I went back to chewing my food, feeling like an idiot. I was going to make this impossible.

We met Jett and the girls at the portal gate in Valla's town center. The weather was growing cooler now that it was November, and the moon was full brightly lightly the cobbled roads. Indigo came through with Tawny, Steel, and Gypsum and after a nervous hug, I was ready to be on my way.

"Are we ready?" I asked, trying to shimmy my way into warmth, and Jett shot me a dirty look.

"Quick and Slate are coming, as you well know. They're bringing dates too so be nice." Jett explained and I bristled.

Brass rubbed a hand on my back, and I shrugged him off.

"Ash is leading a scouting mission to help find the Jorogumo in Ostara. He's not coming," I watched as Steel and Jett exchanged a look.

"They thought it would be better if Slate brought a date since you would be with Ash," Brass whispered into my ear.

"Is anyone else coming?" Tawny asked, breaking the ice that had frozen over our little group.

"Diamond," Gypsum said nonchalantly, and I grimaced.

Indigo stared wide eyed at Gyps, "I invited Sterling, Gyps. I'm sorry."

"Great. This is going to be awesome," I said caustically and rolled my eyes, "Anyone else? Jonquil perhaps? Chris?"

"I'm going to take the birthday girl ahead. Ama, Shale, would you like to join us?" Brass asked, grabbing my arm.

"It's POP, do you know the place?" Cherry asked, parting her plump red lips at Brass.

Brass nodded.

"See you there," Ama said perkily and cast a glance at Gypsum that made me purse my lips.

Brass gave me a scolding as we walked towards the Urd gate through the little three-story city. I missed skyscrapers.

"Try to have fun. You are being a party pooper."

I guffawed, "I'm not a party pooper. More like party animal."

Shale guffawed, and I shot her a stink eye, "You need to get laid. I am sure someone could see to your needs, perhaps before we arrive so we can all have fun tonight."

Brass and I caught her not-so-subtle implication and promptly quieted.

"I'll be nice. Promise," I said after a lengthy silence.

Ama wrapped an arm around my waist as she balanced on her super high heels. "We love you either way, but would it not be nice to let loose and have a little fun for once? You are at a dark red and I would like to get you down to a pink," Ama said with a little aura reading humor.

I was being a crab fanny pack. I would be friendlier, have more fun, not glare at everyone with biting comments. When did these three become my friends? It seemed to happen without me noticing. I'd never had friends in school aside from Tawny, I didn't have time for it pushing myself like I had.

"You're all right. I'll stop now. Sorry."

Ama smiled as her curls bounced, "Now that that is settled. Tell me, who was that dark-haired guy with the copper beads? He looks scrumptious."

I groaned as Brass chuckled.

Jett had missed his calling. He should have been a party planner. If I could have picked anywhere to spend the night dancing away, POP was it. Two levels decorated in ambient pink, blue, and white and all the latest American hits.

I was in heaven.

It was cool in the club, none of those hanging fans either, it was upscale. Tufted pink couches revolved around round white tables on the wood floor next to the bar with more couches against the far wall opposite the bar. The ceiling over the bar was lit with the blue and pink back lit lights on the white ceiling and floor.

My mission was to get drunk now, get healed later. I walked right up to the sleek black bar that had white lights lighting around it and the DJ on a platform at the end, a black screen was between the bar and the DJ that showed the sound waves of the songs she was playing. After ordering a bay breeze for myself, I turned around to find a suitable spot to sit.

Brass was speaking to one of the black clad bouncers and waved us over. Jett had gotten us a V.I.P. section up on the couches by the bar against the wall. We sat on the pink leather couches and took off our cloaks. I got excited. I hadn't danced since following Styg at the Iron Maiden and had gotten thrown out.

POP's dance floor was black lined with tiles that graduated from blue to pink with pink and blue laser lights that shone from the vaulted white ceiling.

"You like?" Ama beamed, pulling her ample breasts up in her teeny tiny white dress that looked like mine.

Brass was used to the two girls, and Ama's change barely registered with him.

"I love," I told her unable to hide my smile.

Jett knew me so well; I hoped Indigo liked it as well. It felt so delightfully normal. Even my dress was something you'd wear to a nightclub. I turned around with a mischievous smile.

"How much do you all have to drink until I can force you out onto the dance floor?"

A half hour later, three shots and on my third bay breeze I was feeling like a girl who had just turned twenty and didn't have a care in the world. When Jett came with the others, he was smiling before he had even reached me. I doubled over laughing at Shale's impersonation of Ama's guide to seductive dancing.

The tiny, haughty woman could be funny.

I sat next to a laughing Brass when I spotted them and waved them all over. Brass had his arm around the back of our couch, and I tried not to lean into it inhaling his scent like a creeper. Nothing could spoil my mood. Nothing. I was giving hugs and kisses to everyone. Diamond walked up after Gypsum and gave me a kiss on my cheek. The caramel skinned girl looked gorgeous. Her chestnut hair fell in full waves to her gold mini dress.

"These are my friends. Amber and Garnet."

I greeted them both. The blonde attended Coyote and Butterfly's son's Ausa Vatni, giggly Garnet. I hadn't met Amber before, so I introduced myself.

"Pleased to meet you. Any friend of Diamond's is a friend of mine," my smile beamed across my face.

Amber sized me up. It wasn't the first time a girl had done that, and it wouldn't be the last. She was gorgeous, girls like that view all other girls as their competition.

She had strawberry blonde hair that came down to the middle of her back and big blue almond eyes. She had a full mouth, her upper lip nearly fuller than her lower lip just like mine. I didn't know why I noted it. Her eyes glittered.

"Nice to meet you. Scarlett, right? Diamond has told me so much about you."

Her eyes lingered over my rings. My thumbs rubbed at them.

Amber hung up her cloak, and I noticed her figure for the first time. A perfect hourglass figure, her perky breasts balanced her curved hips. She was walking sensuality. Something nagged at me. It was probably Diamond and Gypsum's emotions screwing up my own. The two were trying to be near one another while Sterling and Indigo engaged in a polite conversation on the pink couch.

Slate was behind Quick when I greeted them, and my smile never wavered. He was head to toe black, with leather pants and a shirt that looked like Brass's. His fetishes were in his hair and a few narrow braids pulled the front back. His silver eyes were searching for mine and I pasted a cheerful look.

"Hi, thanks for coming," I said, beaming a megawatt smile that was sickly sweet until Amber nearly knocked me down rushing to Slate's side.

The pieces fell into place, and I spun around before I saw the two make-out. "Birthday shots! Come on, Indigo. Sterling, please join us. We never get to talk," I looped my arm through Sterling's and walked to the bar with Indigo and Tawny.

Indigo looked amazing in a capped sleeve mini that showed off her slim figure in a color that matched her powder blue eyes. Tawny looked equally beautiful in a maroon tube dress that made her face look even fairer and wide hazel eyes shine. I never paid much attention to Sterling, but his violet-blue eyes were unique. He had a boyish look and playfully styled golden brown hair with prominent brows. His lashes were so long I thought I would feel a breeze when he blinked.

"A round of shots please and another bay breeze," I slapped down two gold daymarks and Sterling and Indigo's eyes widened.

"How much do you plan on drinking? I promised Ash I would take care of you," Sterling said in a raspy sexy voice. It was the longest I'd ever heard him speak.

I laughed tossing my light brown waves and Tawny looked at me like I lost my mind.

Too much? I had to tone it down.

"Just getting the party going, I'm starting a tab," I told the bartender who nodded. I was going to need it.

It turned out that Garnet was Quick's date; the blonde was sitting on his knee, and Amber was Slate's. What a happy little incestuous pool of friends I had. I slammed a shot, then ordered another after grimacing and slammed the next one before picking up my drink.

"Happy birthday to my favorite twin!" I cheered to Indigo, and she smiled prettily as if she had another way, the little beauty mark on her right cheek lifting.

"Happy birthday. I am glad we got to spend it together," she smiled with a quirk of her pink lips.

"Come on. I am just itching to dance." I was bouncing at the bar, and she shook her head.

"I am so not on your level right now. A few more drinks," she smiled nervously at Sterling who was smirking down at her.

"Tawny?"

"I promised Steel I wouldn't ditch him right away. I'll be out there; you know I will."

"Scarlett?"

I turned around to the familiar voice. Haarder was average height and leanly muscled with a trim waist. He wore a sleeveless blue shirt and the typical black pants tucked into black boots; he was also wearing wrist blades. His black hair spiked, and his up tilted eyes crinkled when he beamed at me.

"Haarder? My favorite dance partner!" I turned him to the others, "You guys this is Haarder. I met him at the Iron Maiden." Haarder had been the one to point out Styg who had eventually led me to the Shadow Breaker headquarters.

They greeted one another. "Did I hear something about you wanting to dance?" he asked with another beaming smile.

My eyes widened excitedly, and I almost slapped him when I bounced, "Yes! See you guys out there."

Haarder slipped his arm over my shoulders, and we walked past the others who I gave a little wave and my very best smile to as we walked out onto the dance floor. Haarder was a fabulous dancer, he was the guy at the club you made room for just so you could see what he was going to do next.

When I recognized the mainstream pop tunes, I threw my head back and squealed making Haarder laugh as we started dancing, my hair bouncing as I did.

"If I start drunkenly twerking, you have my permission to slap me!"

Haarder laughed at my proclamation.

Jett had picked an awesome place. This was my type of music for carefree dancing. Haarder was already attracting attention as I swung my hips around to the beats bouncing in my gold heels. I'd almost forgotten how much fun I had with Haarder last time we'd danced.

All the top hits were playing and eventually Tawny and Steel joined us followed by Indigo, Sterling, Diamond, and Gypsum. Shale and Ama came out once Gypsum was on the dance floor and Tawny narrowed her eyes at them making me laugh.

I fanned myself as I strut past the couches flashing Brass, Jett, and the girls a smile. I got another drink and walked back ignoring Quick and Garnet sitting with Slate and Amber. The two couples were all over one another and it made my stomach turn. I sat next to Brass, and he wrapped his arm around my shoulder.

"Are you going to come dance with me? You're the only one without a girl tonight. Maybe there's one out there for you and she's just dying to see how you move," I teased, and Cherry and Amethyst laughed.

Brass smirked down at me with plump defined lips, "I am your date. You are getting a fan club."

"What?" I asked playing with the little red straw in my glass.

"The surrounding men cannot help how short that dress is and how long your legs are. Watch your drink," he said in seriousness, and I rolled my eyes.

"Cherry? Amethyst? Are you guys coming out?" I asked, standing up and tugging on the hem of my dress.

My legs were tan and long, and one of my best features, they looked fantastic in the dress Ama gave me and I was proud of them. I was lifted off my feet and I squealed trying to balance my glass so my drink wouldn't spill.

"How many birthday spanks have you gotten so far?" Solder asked, tossing me over his shoulder.

I laughed breathlessly and smiled like a loon, "Solder, set me down! You're going to make me flash the club."

Either my fanny pack or my breasts were going to spill out of the dress. He set me on my feet, and I pulled at the neckline before I embraced him, "Did Steel tell you to come?"

The stocky armor salesman was my height in my heels. He was one of the few Guardians I'd met with a scar, his eyebrow had a slice through it above his cobalt eyes, but it was his luscious lips that drew the eye.

I had a thing about lips.

"I happened to be here and saw him on the dance floor. He told me it was your birthday. Happy birthday, Scarlett and may I say that you look positively naughty sweat sheen and breathless," he quirked an eyebrow, and I laughed placing a hand on his chest.

"Look whose naughty. Steel will have your tongue," I told him, giving him a sultry smile until I heard Jett clear his throat.

I flashed him my most innocent smile over my shoulder, and his brow drew down. I was going to have to work on my innocent act.

"Do you want to dance?"

I grabbed Solder's hand before he responded. Solder followed me with a sexy smile on his lips and we intertwined our legs as we moved to the song. Haarder was doing dance moves in the middle of a circle that I could never replicate in a million years and Solder had his hands on my hips moving my body with his.

"You're taking this song seriously," I joked as the lyrics directed a man to do what he wanted with her body. Solder's eyes glittered when he turned me around and we moved together.

I wasn't the least bit surprised that Solder was a superb dancer. It somehow translated into the whole fighting, flexibility thing. After a few songs, I led Solder back off the dance floor holding his hand and we got drinks before going to sit on the couches.

We sat together on the couch Tawny had been at and I couldn't stop smiling. Solder slid his hand into my lap when I sat back and it didn't faze me, it wasn't the first time he'd done that. Tidings men were innately possessive.

Brass scooted to the edge of the pink tufted couch and stared at the hand in my lap.

"I did not know you still hung out with Steel," Solder said, and I looked at him wondering who he was speaking to until I saw Brass's jaw flex. "It would be a good idea to stay out of my mind tonight," Solder said laughing.

I could only imagine what was in Solder's head with a club full of hotties.

"Brass is my friend. I invited him," I told Solder. "You two know each other. Oh! That's right, you went to the university together," I smiled crossing my legs, but the tension didn't ease.

"Roommates with Steel and I," Brass said in his silky deep tone, "you are doing it purposely."

I spared a glance over my shoulder when I felt someone stiffen beside me. Quick was watching Brass, and it made my hackles rise. Even Slate was ignoring Amber who had her little hand on his jaw trying to get his attention. What was I missing?

Solder laughed, "You blame me? Have a drink, Brass. You look like you need one."

Brass's amber eyes looked as angry as the day Styg tried to get me killed. I shot to my feet and placed my glass on the round white table. I bent at the waist in front of Brass and placed my finger to his chin lifting his gaze to mine, my lips curled when his eyes hitched on my cleavage. Good to know he appreciated my feminine attributes.

"I want you to dance with me," I said in my most sultry voice.

He rose, and I slid my arm around his waist. I hooked my thumb on his belt and waved back to Solder who was sitting back with pursed lips, "Talk to you later."

I flashed my very best smile and my eyes slid to Quick who was gaping, and I wondered if I gave them a show bending over like I did, or if it was because I deftly handled Brass. Then I saw Slate and almost laughed. Amber was watching me too.

I flashed them both my megawatt, super smile I saved for rare occasions, such as, look at this hot guy I have my arm around and I am having a fantastic time. By the way, I look super awesome in this dress.

Brass didn't know what he was getting into when I dragged him onto the dance floor. Ama and Shale cheered when they saw Brass. Sterling, Diamond, Indigo, and Gyps were nowhere to be found, but Tawny and Steel were still out there get- ting down and dirty. Patrick Swayze had nothing on my moves. Brass couldn't do anything but go with the flow as I slinked my body all around his.

"Are you playing to an audience?" Brass asked as I placed my hands on his hips from behind, his front to my back as my hair spilled over my shoulder swaying with Brass against me.

"I thought you would appreciate rubbing it Solder's face a little. Yeah," I flashed him a conspiratorial smile over my shoulder and met a slow, lazy smile from Brass.

"I think you have more than one audience member. Are you having fun?" he asked and his breath tickled my neck filling my nostrils with cinnamon.

"I am, you? I haven't noticed any other girls checking you out but let me know if you need me to get lost."

"Other?" he asked, chuckling.

I bit my lip. "You wouldn't even know it if you couldn't read my mind," I said defensively and his fingers tightened on my hips.

"I do not mind you looking at me, Scarlett. I am having a good time with you. You are as beautiful as you are dangerous."

I turned around and wrapped my arms around his neck tangling my fingers in his beaded hair, "I really am sorry I was such a crab earlier. It could've been worse, but it's been good. You always make sure I'm taken care of. No one has ever been so attuned to my feelings as you are, you're —"

He placed a finger to my lips. I was getting too deep. All the drinking was making me emotional. We had stopped dancing had it was very noticeable; my hands were in his hair and his arm around my waist, and I blinked up at him. I kissed his finger at my lips and curled them into a smile. His amber eyes peered down at me, and his lips curled too.

"Let us get out of here. Something is going on tonight that you might want to see."

Butterflies beat in my stomach excitedly as my imagination ran wild. Brass took my hand and led me off the dance floor as I waved goodbye to Tawny and Steel who beamed at me. I felt a thrill shoot through me.

Was Brass taking me back to his room? Gods, I hoped so.

CHAPTER
FOURTEEN
JETT

Jett

Jett had sat with the girls drinking while watching Indigo and Scarlett interact with everyone. People usually thought Jett was drunk, but he had a very high tolerance for alcohol. Slate had brought the infatuated little girl who looked just like Scarlett which both girls had noticed. Amber hung on Slate like a cheap suit. Garnet and Quick were mutually all over one another.

The four had met at Copper Regn's Ausa Vatni last year and had had a few interactions here and there. Scarlett had been in prime mode when they'd arrived, a complete one-eighty from when she'd left them. Brass brought out the best in her, of that Jett couldn't deny. The girls didn't feel like dancing, Amethyst was pregnant and pretending to drink which left Jett to glower at the dance floor every time Scarlett took another dance partner.

For someone supposedly inexperienced, she was a damn scandalous dancer. Every man in within eyesight was watching her and where did she get that dress? Shirt, more like. Jett had only seen more of her legs when she'd been naked! She looked amazing; she was radiant, and it infected everyone around her. Indigo had danced for a short time before sneaking off.

There was a lot of that going on tonight.

Jett hadn't known things were so bad with Solder and Brass, but Brass looked ready to punch the pretty boy out. Jett only needed one guess to know what would make a man want to do that, and it was a woman.

Damn it, Scarlett was at it again. She'd left Slate alone, but Solder had been all over her on the dance floor, then she came back here and bent over. For fuck's sake!

Cherry's eyes had even widened when his baby sister had bent at the waist her long legs disappearing into a dress that barely covered her butt then ran her finger along Brass's jaw. Jett had saw Brass's eyes hitch at her chest too, respectable maybe, but he was human. Quick had been staring open-mouthed at that point and Slate's teeth ground so loud Jett could hear them.

Brass's face when he looked up at her though was the kicker. He was putty in her hands; he looked up at her like she was the sun, the moon, and the stars. She was his world. Fuck! Why? Jett shook his head when Scarlett wrapped Brass's hands over her hips as she ground her back into his front.

"They might as well be naked," Cherry purred and slipped her hand into Jett's lap.

He'd clamped a hand over hers stilling it, "Not now. If Slate tries to strangle her, I have to stop him."

"It is only dancing. She looks like she is blowing off some steam. I haven't seen her this happy — I don't know if I ever have. Let her have some fun, Jett," Amethyst told him, and he picked up her hand, placing a kiss to the inside of her wrist.

Maybe she was right, maybe he needed to stop being so overprotective. What were they doing now?

Scarlett had her hands wrapped around Brass's neck and she pressed against his chest, his finger at her lips. They weren't even dancing! Didn't they know they're all siting here? Scarlett puckered her lips to Brass's finger, and they smiled at one another. He knew that look they were sharing. Jett dry washed his face and looked past Amethyst at the other men.

Quick cursed and Slate's silver eyes reflected in the multicolored lights. Thank goodness they kept the club cool otherwise they'd be throwing off some serious heat. Oh good, they were walking over holding hands.

Why didn't they just skip?

They were both smiling like idiots when Brass grabbed their cloaks.

"Good night, everyone. We're out of here. Thank you all so much for coming."

Scarlett's almond eyes were bright and glassy with the booze. She tossed waist length caramel waves over her shoulder, and she fanned her sweat slicked skin. Jett forced a smile. She did look happy; her high cheekbones were prominent every time she smiled which was every few seconds. Especially when she met Brass's eyes.

Her eyes followed Brass everywhere.

"You are leaving together?" Quick asked, incredulous blinking at his brother.

Scarlett rolled her eyes with a drop-dead gorgeous smile, "Yes, Quick. Don't worry. Your brother is a gentleman."

Brass chuckled in a way that made Jett want to curse as he brought over her cloak. "It is not him I am worried about," Quick muttered.

"What's that supposed to mean?" Scarlett pouted or looked like she pouted.

She was probably trying to glare, but her full lips made everything look like a pout, it was Jett's favorite feature about her.

Brass interrupted, "Silver does not know what he is talking about. Come."

Brass's hand slid over her stomach in a way that looked comfortable, he was at home touching her and from the way she didn't flinch away from him like Jett had seen from others; she was comfortable with him. Slate shifted and her eyes never flitted to his. It must have been eating at him all night.

"No offense, Scarlett. Honestly, but you are nothing but trouble for Brass."

Scarlett's mouth popped open as she stared at Quick. Jett sat forward on the pink couch.

"Baloney! I am not trouble. Far from it!" she blinked at Quick. "I'm a good girl," she mumbled as if she wasn't sure if she believed it anymore.

Brass pulled at her, "Come, you have both been drinking."

Jett moved to stand up, and Amethyst placed a hand on his thigh. "She's doing well on her own," she whispered to him, and Jett set his jaw.

"Yes, you were good until you hooked up with these two," Quick pointed a finger over at Slate and Jett sucked in a deep breath.

Brass's face was a thunderhead, and Scarlett's cheeks reddened, "I never hooked up with Slate!"

"Lie," Quick said pointedly and Scarlett's face went purple.

"You fucked her?!" Amber nearly shouted it and Jett saw Slate's head drop.

"I swear, I've only been with you," Scarlett told Brass who nodded, trying to calm her.

Slate was irritated beyond belief with Amber, Jett could see the regret in his eyes all night.

"Amber, do not speak that way," Slate said in a low tone to placate her.

The strawberry blonde wasn't having any of it. She stood up, and it happened in slow motion. Scarlett faced her doppelgänger, and the girl threw her drink in Scarlett's face. She gasped in disbelief and instead of going elemental like Jett thought she would; she cocked her fist back and punched Amber so hard she fell back. Scarlett didn't stop there. Something inside her had snapped. She grabbed the girl by the hair straddling her chest and punched her again as the girl clawed at Scarlett from beneath her.

Brass and Slate each grabbed a girl. Scarlett's chest was spilling out as her dress from Brass's arm pulling her off the girl. Slate had Amber in a similar position and Jett stared stupefied by what just happened.

"Khoraz! Slutty khoraz!"

Redundant for Jett's taste, but Amber had got her point across.

Scarlett's eyes tightened as she flashed her teeth at the girl. "Enjoy fiddlesticking him tonight but know that he'll be thinking about me the entire time. A poor man's Torch," Scarlett spat and heard Quick suck in a breath.

"Holy shit," Cherry said next to him. Jett's sentiments exactly.

Jett probably would have dropped the 'F' bomb, but even when trying to be catty Scarlett had a hard time swearing. Jett stood up to walk between the two girls.

Slate was staring at Scarlett as if it was his first time seeing her. Frigga's sweet grass, Jett felt that way too.

Amber cried out and ripped free of Slate while he was dumbfounded and nearly plowed Jett over when she launched herself at Scarlett making him duck in time to see Amber knock into Scarlett taking Brass down. Jett cursed and was going to pull Amber off Scarlett when he saw Scarlett cock back her fist and punch Amber in the jaw, so her eyes rolled back, her teeth clicked, and she toppled off her.

Brass sat up with Scarlett on top of him and they were both sitting on the floor when Slate moved to pick his date up. Jett's eyes were wide. Thank goodness they were in the back away from prying eyes. Scarlett sat between Brass's legs as Brass gently inspected her face pushing her hair out of the way.

Jett sighed and Quick moved to kneel next to Scarlett, "I am a stupid bastard. I am sorry Scarlett."

Quick helped her to her feet, and she gave him a small wary smile and cursed sugarfoot when her heel gave out.

"I got it," Brass said as she balanced on his shoulder while he took off her heels.

"Thanks," she told him doing that gazing into his eyes thing again.

Jett moved, "Well, I hope you had fun before now."

Scarlett turned to him, and it was like being warmed by the sun when she flashed her smile, "I did, we'll have to come here again. Maybe no dates next time."

She looked past Jett to see Slate laying the girl on the couch.

Jett saw the fire in her eyes, but she quickly extinguished it, "I didn't mean to knock her out."

"Whatever. She deserved it," Jett gave her a big hug and set her back down on her bare feet.

CHAPTER
FIFTEEN

Brass had his arm around my waist as we walked through the club. I hated the feel of all the spilled drinks on the bottoms of my feet, but my mortifying brawl with Slate's lover had broken my heel. Brass said he'd look at it once we got outside.

Someone tapped me on the shoulder, and I turned around. I found it diminished my empath abilities when I drank. I didn't even feel Slate come up behind me, which was startling since I always felt the electricity crackling around him.

"I am sorry about Amber," he rumbled, looking down at me.

Her name on his lips incited me, I could feel my eyes twitch from it. I was determined not to let him ruin my night.

The only person who could have been worse was Lera.

I pasted on the smile I'd worn when facing him all night. "No matter. Enjoy the rest of your night. I'm sorry your date is unconscious," I said sickly sweet, and Brass coughed through a laugh.

Slate's eyes slid past me, and Brass's hand fell from my waist.

"Don't go just because he asked you to. He's not your captain now, you're my date. I asked you to come with me," I said, knitting my brows at Brass. Brass rubbed his lips together, and I spun back to Slate. "I have nothing more to say to you. Goodnight," I spun back around, but Brass didn't move. I lifted my eyes to his. "Don't make me talk to him," I whispered harshly, and Brass gave me a small smile.

"I will wait outside and see what I can do about these heels," Brass said leaning down to give me a peck on the cheek.,

I sighed and turned back around to face Slate and crossed my arms, "Well?"

"I apologize if I frightened you. I fear I chased you back to the Straumr boy because of it," Slate said, looking down his nose at me.

"You did me a favor."

He pursed his lips, "Brass is better than Ash."

I scoffed. "Forget it. I've made my choice. If you can't be my friend, then stay away from me, okay? We are volatile together —"

"Unlike you and Brass?" he asked in a low dangerous tone that sounded mildly hurt.

I narrowed my eyes as our faces turned from blue to pink under the lights, "He cares about me, and I care about him, and he doesn't constantly put me in compromising positions while trying to get into my pants. Like I said, you want to be my friend, you know where to find me."

The heat rose to my cheeks when I turned my back to him. I couldn't be so close to him. I just couldn't. He was too much! He was sucking all the air out of the room, and I desperately needed air.

I felt Slate as he stepped closer, close enough, so his chest touched my back, "I do not want to be your friend. You know what I want."

I whipped around, "You come here with another girl and say these things? You always do that! I'll believe you one day when you are alone, just you for a while. Not having to dip your wick in every single woman who passes before you. Your words mean nothing when you say them the same days you have been inside other women. Don't you know that? Your actions speak volumes. Did you already have sex with her today?" My hand shot up to his mouth, "Dear Gods, don't answer that."

Slate stared down at me with my hand over his mouth saying nothing until I pulled my hand away, "Understood, Scarlett."

Did I just hear that right? Was he agreeing with me? Not groping me or trying to cajole me to go into some seedy stall with him so he could jump my bones?

"Happy birthday, Torch. Have fun with Brass," Slate said, and he reached down pulling me into an embrace.

I went numbly into his arms thinking must have drunk myself into oblivion for Slate to be acting this way. Maybe Amber had knocked me out, and I was dreaming? No, I knocked her out. Call me a khoraz. Ha!

I forgot who held me and melted against him. His scent intoxicated me further as I buried my nose in his wavy mane. Gods, I loved his hair.

"Torch?"

"Hmm?" I moaned dreamily.

Someone bumped into us, and Slate growled at them, but it was just what I needed to bring me back to reality. I let go of him and took a step back knowing my face was red.

"See you at training tomorrow," I muttered and spun away.

I could feel Slate's eyes on my back as I walked away. He hadn't paid me a single compliment that night and I hated that it irked me to no end. I met Brass outside and wrapped my cloak around my shoulders. He'd even fixed my shoe.

The man was perfect.

CHAPTER
SIXTEEN
JETT

Jett

Slate sat down next to Jett after he'd gone after Scarlett. It surprised Jett he didn't have a slap mark marring his face. He was sure Scarlett would have found a reason to slap him for something. Jett thoroughly enjoyed it when Scarlett slapped Slate, Jett thought it must be the only time Slate had someone strike him and he not retaliate.

Jett lifted his amber drink to his lips and drank deeply, the girls had gone to the bathroom and Quick had left with his date to Gods knew where. Everyone had left, coupling off and disappearing. He had to get the girls home so he could do his own coupling. When they were back from the bathroom, he was leaving Slate with his coma patient.

"I am going to wed her," Slate rumbled.

Jett spit his drink out, spraying himself and the ground in front of him. He started coughing when he inhaled immediately after. He turned to Slate who must have done some sort of hallucinogen on his way back from Scarlett.

"Amber?" Jett asked in a wheeze and sipped from his glass to coat his burning throat.

Slate turned to him and gave him a look that said, do not be an idiot. Jett gave him a look back; you can't possibly mean Scarlett because she is already engaged.

"Scarlett," Slate rumbled, and Jett shook his head, maybe he'd heard him wrong.

"Okay. Let's pretend this is possible. Which it isn't. That she agrees to this. Which she won't. Then what? You two are married and you die?"

"Brass will take care of her," Jett blinked at Slate.

He was going to need more booze.

CHAPTER SEVENTEEN

"Look, it's my birthday. Please don't have me murdered," I told Brass as we walked under yet another blacked out lamp post.

"Why is it whenever I take you out, you think I am going to have you killed?"

"I think it's because you take me to some seriously unsavory neighborhoods," I chided as I shot him a smile.

"This is not a fun trip. It is business. Are you up for it? I think you are; you did not call or shift when the girl came at you. I take that as a good sign. If you are not ready, we can wait, but it will be another month before we can go," Brass said cryptically and arched a brow down at me.

"I'm good. I'd be better if I knew where we were going."

"I was not sure until I felt him activate the tracker. I do not know where we are going either," Brass confessed, and I stopped walking.

"You're not doing much to reassure me I won't be dead in the next ten minutes," I said raising my brows at Brass.

Even in the darkest dankest spots of Tidings, the air was still clean and fresh. The fall breeze was irritatingly reminding me of Slate in the most unwelcome way. I didn't understand why he was being so weird when I'd left the club. It had been a strange, unpredictable night. Case in point, I was in a dark dead-end street with Brass when a half hour ago we were dancing in a pink and blue lit night club to Katy Perry.

My life was full of curve balls.

"The Stygians. They hold a tournament of sorts every so often. We have some- one who has infiltrated their ranks, he was to notify us when the tournament began. Only their higher ups know when it will be," Brass explained, and my chest constricted.

Jett had found a slip of paper on a man who had been trying to capture Slate that had STYG written on it. It had been raining and I had asked my uncle Jackal about Styg. It was how I first met Brass. Styg wasn't the culprit which left the Stygians, the rivaling mercenary group in Tidings. Jackal had said it would not be good if the Stygians were after Slate because they never give up on a contract. They kept coming until they completed it. The thought made bile rise in my throat.

It sobered me, "I'm good. I wouldn't turn this down for anything."

Slate and I may be on the worst of terms at the best of times but hurting him was unacceptable. If anyone was going to kill him, it'd be me, and figuratively. Brass was looking down at me with an amused smile playing on his defined lips. His hair fell forward shadowing his face so I couldn't see his eyes, but I knew they'd be glittering.

"Do you mind if I make a few adjustments?" he asked.

"Um, okay?"

A few adjustments meant he was curling my hair again and straightening making my appearance less bar-fight-chic and more I-actually-comb-my-hair. After he asked if I had some 'something for your lips', I rolled my eyes and applied some with a few swipes of my Bliss Stila lip gloss and smacked my lips at him. I wiped under my eyes, just in case, turned around and pulled an Ama adjusting my breasts. Luckily, whatever Amber had been drinking dried clear, so it hadn't stained my dress. Luckily for her.

I twirled sending my cloak swirling behind me and held my palms up, "Do I meet the high standards of Brass Regn?" I teased.

Brass smirked and grabbed my curls in his hand, "You know, I prefer you in my shirts with your hair piled atop your head, but this will do for the Stygians. Act like my arm candy. Women are not highly regarded within the Stygians."

He trailed his dark honey hand through the curls he'd made, and I nodded swallowing.

"I think I can feign interest in you," I hoped I didn't sound as throaty as I did to my own ears.

Brass chuckled and wrapped his arm around my waist turning me back to the dead end. There was a riveted metal door to the left that looked freshly polished, and a hand painted mark was over it. A red sickle that looked freshly painted high on the door blazed even in the moonlight giving me chills and made my hackles rise.

"You are safe with me," Brass said softly as he handed me a half mask then slid one over his face.

Safe. Brass was anything, but safe for me.

It was a plain black leather mask; I looked at mine and saw that it was gold. The Shadow Breakers must have thought I was made of sunshine. They were always casting barely masked looks of amusement whenever I showed up in anything other than black. I couldn't help it if I liked pinks and greens. They suited my coloring well. When I slid the mask over my face and fixed my hair around it, Brass reached past me to open the door.

No. I was definitely getting murdered tonight. Red overhead lights shone down for lethal ambiance; it creeped the sugarfoot out of me. Aside from the door, it didn't look like they'd wasted time cleaning the joint up.

It didn't have a foul smell, but the air was tense. Part way through the stone hall we could hear the cheers from a rowdy crowd. I placed the smell that was putting my teeth on edge. It was fear.

Fear, cruelty, and lust, for blood and bodies. So very much of it and contained in a large room of maybe three hundred bodies sitting around a round combat ring I half expected someone to throw some chickens into, or maybe a bull to chase down a rodeo clown.

They crammed the place with people with lights focused on the large circular ring at the center, but I could smell the booze and the bodies that sat along the stadium seats. The classes of people were obvious. A small roped off area seated a few very well-dressed people, and it seemed to be willy-nilly from there. No rhyme or reason for the mass of bodies who were watching two bare-chested men fight with nothing but their fists.

Brass led me in deeper and I noticed cloaked men that lined the upper most row that looked like they would do more than toss out someone up to no good. I wondered what would warrant the need to be thrown out since they seemed to be lenient as it was.

Brass was trying to shield me with his body from the worst, but I saw topless women serving drinks getting groped by patrons and it made my skin crawl even though the women were smiling. I was genuinely intrigued to hear what the Stygians offered them. Everyone wore masks or they painted their faces granting a sordid anonymity to the whole tournament.

We moved close to the roped off area and sat on the end of a concrete row, or I tried to sit, but Brass pulled me into his lap and unfastened my cloak for me. Suddenly, I felt like I was naked even though I had a dress on and was very much covered. Brass pulled me high on his thigh resting me against him possessively with a hand in my lap and his arm around my back.

Many of the women sat in similar positions aside from the ones in the roped off seats who got to sit on tufted cushions. Brass's hand slid over my back pulling me out of my sulk and my eyes focused on the two men in the circle and I gasped.

Their faces were blurs. It was disconcerting. They had to have features, but my mind couldn't see them.

"Black market distorters. They have rings on that make their faces warp to the human eye. Styg found this place for us after selling them the pieces. Try to pretend you like me, Scarlett," Brass teased.

When I wasn't pulling on my hem, I was sitting ramrod straight with my palms flat on my thighs. I blushed. I was bad at the undercover thing. My arm slid around Brass's shoulder and leaned into him as I crossed my legs, his hand moved to my thigh which coincidentally kept my dress from sliding up any further.

"Our guy is up next," Brass murmured, turning his head, his eyes widened slightly when his nose collided with my cleavage.

"How long has he been, um, under cover?" I tried to whisper since the masked man beside Brass was giving me the side eye.

"He is not suspicious; he is wondering if he can lure you over to him or take me on. Chafer has been under cover since the new year," Brass whispered.

Nearly a year and they were only now making progress?

"There is an initiation process. It takes a long time until they trust you. Chafer does not have a weak stomach; he has gone through their guild at a rapid pace," Brass tightened his jaw, and the crowd jumped to their feet.

One man had blood pouring down his muscled chest, but we couldn't tell exactly where it was coming from. He stumbled backwards and fell onto the gritty red dirt to the cheers of the masses. They quickly exchanged money as the victor held his arms above his head. He roared and his muscles bunched before he ducked his head. A door in the pit's side opened.

We were still standing when Brass moved so swiftly; I did not know what happened. Then he was leading me away. I looked past him and saw the man that was sitting next to us was holding his heart. Dark red blood was bubbling over the man's fingers when Brass turned me around to move me faster.

"It was me or him. I do not take killing lightly, Scarlett," Brass whispered harshly over the crowd.

I'd just witnessed a man's murder in a room full of people and we walked away. No one had even noticed the slumping man yet when we took up a new seat closer to the circular pit. I felt queasy when Brass pulled me back into his lap; he placed his hand on my stomach and called calming the roiling waves.

"I barely saw you move," I whispered numbly, and Brass shifted his head to look up at me.

In the ring, the man who'd lost was being carried out none too gently adding insult to injury. "Do you trust me?" Brass asked, searching my eyes.

"Of course, I do. I'm just in shock or something," I sucked in a fortifying breath, but it didn't help.

One of the masked men looked around the crowd and I felt Brass's thigh stiffen under me, "What's —"

Brass roughly pulled my face to his and slanted his mouth over mine. The crowd was still boisterous, but it faded into the background when Brass's defined lips molded to mine, and I tasted his cinnamon scent mingled with the amber liquid he'd been drinking giving him a rich masculine taste. Our tongues stroked and caressed until I forgot where I was.

My fingers threaded through his hair when his big hand squeezed my thigh. My body arched to his unwittingly. His talented lips. A loud laugh in front of us was like a stone being thrown into the still lake of silence and Brass turned away looking into the pit.

"There he is," Brass nodded towards the pit.

I rubbed my lips together spreading the gloss out and attempted casualty when I disentangled my fingers from his hair forcing myself not to shift on his thigh. My nostrils flared as I tried to even my breaths without panting. Two men were in the pit. They must have entered from the short door in the side.

"What's the plan?" I asked and cleared my throat so it's throaty sound would fade.

Brass shifted me towards his body so I could face the pit better. "We are here to watch his back and get any messages he might want to pass along," he said, facing the pit.

I nodded and tried to take a deep breath without him noticing because my neckline was so close to his face and shuddered out my drawn breath. I cursed myself when Brass spoke.

"Are you okay?" He asked.

...Yes. I'm a terrible actress...

Brass grunted, "You are doing well, Scarlett. Try to relax."

Not the first time he'd told me to relax.

I leaned into him again and watched the match start. There was no preamble, nothing to introduce the fighters. People collected coins from the crowd placing bets and then a bell sounded signifying the start of the match.

The match was brutal and bloody. I now understood why the pit walls were six feet high, the blood sprayed the concrete walls and the crowd cheered making my stomach turn. I didn't want to watch. Beating someone to a pulp wasn't entertaining, it was disgusting and morbid. You couldn't even tell if the guy who lost the last match was alive when they carried him out. At least the faces were distorted so you couldn't see how mutilated their faces were.

"You do not have to watch the match. Try to school your face, keep it devoid of emotion," Brass whispered.

I wanted to roll my eyes. I looked at what the other women were doing, the ones that were dressed, and gave the top of Brass's head a dry smile. Others were fawning over their male counterparts. I could fawn over Brass.

I ran my palm over his chest and shoulders letting my fingertips trace the ridges of muscle beneath. Bringing my mouth to his ear, I nibbled on his earlobe as I looked past his head. People were standing again, and angry faces mixed with the thrill of watching men hurt one another and winning. The sick sound of flesh hitting flesh made me drop my eyes. Brass stood up quickly, catching me before I slipped off his lap. I looked towards the match and one man was down but was rubbing frantically at his blurred face.

"We have to go now," Brass barked and dragged me up the steps.

"What happened?" I asked as he held me in a vise grip to his side.

"Something is wrong. The opponent blew acid into our man's face. They know. It is not safe for you," Brass rushed along the top tier towards the red lit hall.

Brass froze when we came to a wall of black cloaked men then spun around, but another wall was closing in behind us. I didn't have a single weapon on me.

My seax didn't go with the dress, and I was kicking myself for my vanity. Guardians always wore weapons.

"Let the girl go and I will come quietly," Brass said to one that stepped forward.

They all wore half masks, but I wouldn't have been able to recognize them to begin with the way the room was dimly lit, and their cloaks hid so much of their faces in shadow. I saw the wicked smile that spread on the pale man's face.

"I am afraid we cannot do that. See, she killed many of our

associates. You may go, but she stays," his voice was high for men, but impossibly smooth.

I knew Brass had a blade in his hand without seeing it and he shoved me behind him close to the wall so I wouldn't be exposed to the men behind us. Brass cursed.

"They have nix torques. We cannot touch them with calling," Brass said gruffly to me, and my heart leapt.

"Go. Let the others know and you can come back for me," I urged.

I didn't want Brass getting himself killed for me.

"Never," he ground out.

If I ever become a villain, I'm going to give the good guys a fighting chance. I'd shout something like "Attack!" or "Get them!" before I do. I'd at least monologue my evil intentions before throwing one of my knives.

The blade went through the back of my hand and into Brass's back pinning us together. Brass let out a grunt, it was very masculine and would have made the toughest man proud, but having my hand pinned with a blade to a man's back while blood ran over my wrist made me shriek.

Then something cold snapped around my neck and I tried to pull my hand to touch it, but they pinned it to Brass.

I promptly fainted from the pain.

They pulled a black sack from my head, and the overhead light was blinding. I tested my wrists and feet. They secured me to a metal chair, with my arms tied behind me and both ankles tied to a chair leg. Whomever removed my bag was gone and tall since the lamp swung in the dark room.

Brass.

He sat across from me tied the same way as I was with a thick pewter torque around his neck. A nix torque. He was bleeding, what I could see of his face was a mass of bruises and it had swollen. I flexed my right hand a pain shot all the way through my shoulder.

"Brass," I hissed, not knowing if others lurked in the shadows.

He raised his head lazily, and my eyes widened. He must have fought after I passed out, his eye sealed shut. I hadn't seen it in the shadows of his long hair.

"Oh, Brass," I cried, and I struggled against my bonds not caring that I was in excruciating pain.

Brass parted his lips in a bloody smile and my brows creased as I swallowed against the lump in my throat, "That bad?"

I shook my head. "Not at all. You'll always be beautiful," I choked out.

"How fucking romantic. Did anyone else know you were coming tonight?"

I'd missed the man hanging on my right. He was bare chested and if I thought Brass was bad, this man was worse. Much worse. I couldn't make out any facial features besides dark brown eyes below brown winged brows and a matted mess of short brown hair. He was muscular, less so than Quick, like he practiced martial arts, so he wasn't bulky at all, but ripped.

"No. Your tracker was only active for a short while and I was the first one to answer it. Slate and Silver omitted it. I was the one to collect your messages," Brass admitted.

The man, Chafer, hung from chains wrapped around his wrists outstretched over his head that he gripped with blood slick hands. Someone chained his ankles to a bolt in the floor. The acid covered his face with red pocked holes from what had blown into his face during the fight. Seeping ulcers oozed on his cheeks.

"What gave us away?" Chafer asked, spitting on the concrete ground.

We must have been in the lowest part of the building. No way they could have moved us three without being seen.

Brass shook his head and then winced, "No idea."

"I bet it is that bright shiny daymark you brought to this dump. She radiates naivety," Chafer glared at me.

"I'm sorry," I strangled out, aware I was crying, but not sure why.

"It is my fault. Someone more experienced would have been better," Brass lifted his head to me, and his brow furrowed, "I am sorry for getting you into this."

"You? You should have left when you had the chance. They only wanted me," I cried.

"Stop your sniveling!" Chafer hissed and my eyes widened at him, "Think, girl. Bite your lip."

"Excuse me?" I asked in disbelief.

"Bite your fucking lip or no one will know where we are," Chafer spoke to me like I was an idiot, and I narrowed my eyes.

"Do it, Scarlett," Brass said sounding breathless, and I worried there may have been worse damage done to him that was visible. "You must draw blood," he added.

I nodded and bit my lower lip as hard as I could and felt the skin give as the coppery taste of my blood tinged my tongue.

"Now we wait," Chafer said from where he hung a full foot off the floor as if waiting was going to be easy.

A bar slid across a door and a lock clicked before more light blinded me and a series of footsteps resounded off the high-ceilinged room, "Shadow Breakers. I trust you have not had time to activate those trackers. I would hate to flay your skin away to dispose of them."

"No. They were not activated," Brass admitted.

"Very good."

It was a different man. Taller, about Brass's height, but a little narrower at the shoulders. He too wore a cloak and mask so I couldn't see his features, but his brown bearded jaw, that was trimmed and well kept. Evil men should have scraggly beards and crooked teeth, not the million-dollar smile he flashed.

He walked behind me making me try to turn in my chair to see him, but I didn't have to. He rested his tan hands on my shoulders lightly as he spoke. Others, at least six men were behind Brass and next to Chafer.

"We have a proposition for you," the man started.

"No. If it has anything to do with her, the answer is no," Brass ground out.

I could hear the smile in the man's voice, "It does, I am afraid, but we wish to be fair. You had a spy in our guild, and we don't want an all-out war. This is our offer. The girl fights to the death against one of ours, if she survives, you all go free with a message for your Grand Mistress."

The man spat Grand Mistress as if he was saying khoraz. Not a fan of Lera's.

His clean long-fingered hands ran along my shoulders in delicate strokes that made my skin crawl. He slid the straps down over my shoulders and my eyes went wide. There were worse things in my mind than having to fight.

"What happens to them if I lose? Can they go free?" I asked with my heart beating in my throat.

The man behind me ducked his head and inhaled deeply before responding. "No," he said, exhaling gustily and his hands were moving again.

I felt vulnerable strapped to the chair unable to stop the man from exposing me, or worse, but he stopped pushing the top of my dress down at my biceps.

It was to humiliate me, to disable me from thinking clearly, and it was working. My heart was pounding, and I was trying to keep my eyes on Brass's, but he was livid.

"You were going to release him if I came. Why can't you still do that?" I pressed even though I had no room to negotiate.

The cloaked men chuckled as I stiffened, the man behind me slid his hand into my dress and curved his hand to my left breast. "Ah. Your heart beats fiercely, girl. Does it beat for this man? We believed it was the other your heart yearned for," he slid his hand from my dress, but not before trailing his fingers over my peak making me stifle a sob.

Brass struggled futilely, and they chuckled again, "Both. I care about them both. I'll do it, just heal them so they don't have to wait in pain."

"Seems fair enough. What about your hand? How is it feeling?"

"Delve and find out," I snapped, and the man froze with his fingers on my shoulders.

He crossed in front of me and gripped my chin lifting it roughly with his fingers. "I do not think you will need this dress to fight in," he flashed his teeth in a way only an idiot would have taken for a smile.

He leaned down pulling a blade from his boot and pressed the point between my breasts, so the threads gave, and the point slid to my skin. His arms flexed as he gripped my neckline. He tore it down to my belly button. I hung my head, so my hair fell in front of my chest and thanked the Gods my mother never let me cut it short.

Brass had fallen sideways in his chair and was being righted again by some men. They had his face healed. I shifted my head and saw the other man's face. It was still covered in blood, but now I could see his sharp angular features and a wide thin-lipped mouth. His face had a cruel look to it. A wicked grin spread on his lips when he caught me looking, and I shifted my head to better cover myself.

I felt warmth flood through me and the pulsing pain at my hand disappeared. I thought that was a good sign. They did not untie my hands, but another man sawed at the ropes around my ankles. A hand on the nape of my neck yanked me, so I was on my tiptoes as they pulled a bag back over my head. I heard Brass growl at how I was being handled.

They shoved us through what I assumed were stone or concrete halls until I was tossed face first onto the ground. I didn't move afraid of what would happen next and felt the gritty dirt under my fingers. There was the pit. I yanked the bag off my head and found myself brightly lit by an overhead light and a row of men sat all the way around the first row of the pit staring down at me. An idea came to me, I covered my chest. I slid my arms out of my dress and turned it around, so the crossing fabric was over my chest and my back was exposed instead. It was the best I could do, but I felt better already.

Someone chuckled at my actions, and I tried to memorize as many details as I could. They threw a blade into the pit at my feet, and I grabbed it up. Two feet long and three inches wide, it was essentially a big machete, and I'd never used a blade so big to fight. I tried to get comfortable with the blade while I waited for my opponent in my desperation.

They forced Brass and Chafer to stand with cloaked men all around them, their hands tied behind their backs. Brass's jaw clenched so hard his neck strained. Chafer looked like he'd resigned himself to die.

Thanks for the vote of confidence, I thought.

I wished Brass didn't have the nix torque on so he could read my thoughts, or that I didn't for that matter so I could go full elemental on those jerks and fry them all.

I heard the door open behind me and I backed up to the other wall. A black hole gaped, and I saw several of the men lean forward. The wait made me aware of the gravity of the situation. I had probably tipped off a year of undercover work. Chafer had been right, the Stygians had spotted me. Maybe they had suspected Chafer, but I'd confirmed it.

The doorway filled, and adrenaline shot through my system. My body did not want to fight, it wanted to flee. Out first came a hoofed foot followed by a powerful deep brown leg, then it stepped out sideways. Eight feet tall, covered in brown fur and burnt umber skin, its horns curved to its head like a ram with another set of horns that curled up in a 'U' shape. It had come out sideways because its shoulders were so broad. I was facing the devil.

I didn't tear my gaze away from the burning red eyes it locked on me like I was a tasty little morsel; I knew the second I showed any weakness it would kill me. It was a bies. Like the bauk and the vodyanoy, it wasn't supposed to exist, or if they did, they kept to themselves.

The creature's smile was grisly before it came at me in a run. I didn't stand a chance besting it physically, so I dodged, rolled, and jumped and prayed.

I prayed a lot.

I couldn't fail Brass or that jerk Chafer.

I hoped I was wearing it down, because it was wearing me down, but its charge, and swipe moves were predictable. My moves must have been just as predictable because I was mid leap when it swung its head and I felt myself being lifted into the air. It had impaled me on one of its 'U' shaped horns and dropped my only weapon to keep the horn from driving through my back when it lifted its head.

I wasn't the screaming type. I grit my teeth in determination not to let myself die. As much as I didn't care about my own life, there was Brass. I'd live and fight for him.

My blood slicked the horn as I grappled for a hold to keep my weight from killing me. The only thing that kept me from passing out from the pain was the shock that sent an overload of adrenaline through me. I let out a cry of frustration when I couldn't find purchase and the beast shook its head like a dog. I curled up my legs, and I felt my heel sink.

The creature roared in pain and swiped its clawed hands at my legs, and I jerked my legs free. My broken heel had sunk into one of its burning red eyes. I would have laughed if the motion would not have forced more of my blood out through the wound I was clutching at on the top of the beast's head.

I pulled my other foot up and while it tried to shake me loose; I was trying to ram my other heel into its working eye. My brand-new gold birthday heel sunk deep into its eye socket, and it roared in pain. I didn't stop. I jerked my foot all around hoping there was some way I could reach its brain, assuming it had one, and if it did, that it was in its head. You never knew with these things.

It shook violently and fell to its knees. My feet hit the gritty ground hard, and my legs buckled as it toppled onto its side pulling me with it. I breathed for a few seconds and braced my hands on the horn before yanking myself off. I cried out as it disappeared from my body and fell onto my back looking up at the light that hung above me. The bies's body disintegrated into embers that floated away.

A shadow blocked out part of the light and I followed it with my eyes as it landed next to me.

It was Brass. His hand tore the nix torque from my neck and warmth flooded through me as my wounds healed. I sucked a breath and watched numbly as he helped me to my feet. Chafer was there with him, no longer shirtless and he held our cloaks.

The cloaked men lined the top of the pit, and the bearded man looked down at us, "Tell your Grand Mistress next time we will not be so gracious when she attempts to infiltrate us."

I tried to shuffle forward, but Brass held me firmly to him. "What about the contract against the other man? Can I buy it from you? Pay you to give it up? Whatever the price, I'll pay it," I shouted.

The bearded man spread his lips in a million-dollar smile. Million dollars? Done. Pearl could afford it.

"We are simply the weapon, not the wielder," he said cryptically as he turned around, "Be glad we are not extracting a higher price for the deaths you caused, girl."

My mind wasn't working right, and I was angry. He couldn't so easily dismiss me, covered in blood and the stench of the musky dead creature behind me after I had a full day. I wanted straight answers.

"If you want to get out of here in one piece. Keep your mouth shut," Brass whispered harshly at my side.

I snapped my mouth shut with an audible click.

There wasn't a soul left in the building as we tried to find our way out. We finally found a hall they met the red lit hall and back to the metal door with the red sickle. We had our cloaks on and Brass had evened my heels. They were blood covered flats as we walked down the cobbled roads back to Shadow Breaker headquarters with all the wonderfully terrible news.

Before we reached the alley that led to headquarters, I'd stumbled even with Brass holding me, so he scooped me up and carried me the rest of the way unspeaking.

It was in the wee hours of the morning when we walked into the rumpus room. Two Breakers sat at the bar pouring their own drinks in the otherwise empty room. The smell of leather was still there, but not that of the food from dinner earlier. The round wood tables were wiped clean, and the dark carpets called free of all dirt and food.

"I am going to bring her to my room and then we will see Lera," Brass said to Chafer.

Chafer nodded once looking exhausted as I felt, and we all headed to the stairs at the far purple wall that led upstairs.

Brass placed me on his couch and smiled for the first time. "I will be back in a little while. Borrow whatever you wish and make yourself at home. You know where the showers are," he pushed my hair away from my face as he leaned over me, "You did very well tonight."

I squeezed his hand before he left closing the door behind him. I raided his closet immediately and set out a white cotton 'V' neck for when I returned from my shower. Extreme exhaustion would make a hot shower impossible, so I had to hurry.

With no intention of wasting energy drying my hair, I looped it into a bun high on my head and stole a pair of Brass's navy blue boxer briefs hoping it wasn't crossing the line, but I really wanted something on my fanny pack after having flashed a half dozen strange men. I was rolling them up at the waist when the door opened behind me.

Brass's mouth quirked up in a lopsided smile. I returned it shyly, then slid into his white shirt. I turned and sat down on his grey comforter to pull on the socks I'd also stolen.

"I am glad you took what I said to heart. No woman has worn my underwear before."

Brass sat down next to me, but it was more of a plop making the mattress on the four-poster bed bounce. I crossed my legs on the edge of the bed and saw just how exhausted he was.

"Do you mind if I crash here?" I asked and reached over to his waist.

He shook his head. "I expected you to," I nodded and grabbed the hem of his red stained shirt.

His amber eyes swung to mine beneath his thick masculine brows. "Everyone always helps me. Let me take care of you," I asked softly offering him a small reassuring smile.

The fight had left him. He lifted his arms, and I pulled his shirt over his head letting his hair fall with a click of beads. Sliding off the bed, I knelt before him and pulled off his boots and he fell back in the bed.

This was my fault. Any man that hung out with me, like Slate, and Jett ended up being exhausted by me. I stood up and unbuckled his belt and unbuttoned his pants before tugging them down over his hips. He was awake enough to lift his hips, but by the time I'd climbed back into bed, he had fallen asleep.

I called pulling him up the bed and positioned myself, so his head rested on my stomach while I laid on my back. I started unbraiding his hair and taking out his beads as he laid on his stomach. His dark honey arms curled to my sides, and I smiled down at him. It felt good to take care of him for a change, to reciprocate all that had been for me.

Brass was a rare, good man and I was lucky to have him. I called again and sent the beads onto the coffee table on the other side of the couch. Scooting down, I comforted myself by holding Brass. I'd been in a fight to the death. I'd had the man in my arm's life in my hands and his friend's.

No one saved me, I saved myself. That felt good. Really good.

"Good morning," I told Brass, stretching.

He slept like a rock; I'd woken up ten minutes earlier and let him rest until he stirred on his own. His dark honey brow furrowed when he lifted his head. He had moved up little, but he was now using my chest as his own personal pillow. Worse things had happened to them lately, so pillow was an acceptable job position.

I stretched my arms up arching my back and he sat up further between my legs. He shook his head making his hair fly around and he touched it with his hands.

"I figured when you showered this morning, you'd take them out anyway, so I did it last night. Did you sleep well?" I asked, pulling my legs up and resting my chin on my knees.

He looked down at himself, "You undressed me?"

I knit my brows but smiled, "Yes. Don't you remember?"

"No. I was so tired last night I hardly remember walking back to the room," he mumbled.

Why did I feel like I'd done something wrong? I had overstepped my bounds and now he was uncomfortable. I slid off the bed.

"I'll see you tomorrow. Thanks for helping me back last night and letting me crash here."

Brass lifted his head and amber eyes peered up at me. "You do not have to leave," he shook his head again like he was trying to clear it.

"No, that's alright. I can see you need some time," I walked to the door picking my cloak up off the couch as I went and flashed him a smile at the door, "Your beads are on the table. I will leave your clothes in your cubby for the laundress."

"Scarlett —"

I held up my hand. "Don't worry about it," I waved my hand and shut the door behind me.

I couldn't stand in the hall; Brass would still pick up my thoughts, and I was barefoot — in his underwear. The prep room was at the lowest floor of the building scolding myself the entire way. I should've gone home or slept on the couch. Maybe I shouldn't have taken off his pants. I shook my head ruefully; I was engaged. Other men's beds were off limits.

I never would have done this in Chicago. Mostly because I didn't have any friends to do it with, I wasn't sure I would've done it if I had. Brass was different. He wonderfully combined deadly sexy and incredibly sweet. The two, once thought mutually exclusive, had made me comfortable around him. Too comfortable, if this morning was any sign.

Trust was huge to me, and I trusted Brass. When Slate wasn't around, I knew Brass oversaw my safety. He didn't leave me last night. When they told him he could go free and leave me, he stuck by my side. I'd been afraid for his life, but I'd also felt something when he was willing to die to help me get away. I didn't think dying was noble, living was harder. Since my mom died, I knew that better.

No one needed to tell me I was letting my lockbox of emotions get too cramped. Not enough release and too many additions. Training would have released some steam, but I couldn't face Brass after taking such liberties with him and seeing the uncomfortable look on his face this morning. I'd have to find another way to work through my sugarfoot.

There were a dozen other people in the prep room who were getting ready to train, none of them were walking around in men's underwear and socks, unless they were men. I got my fair share of looks, but no one spoke up. It was a small concession. It was obvious I'd stayed with a man last night and there was only one man it could've been, that they didn't leer, or jeer told me they had already known we slept together.

I had moved my cubby next to the others and when I reached my aisle, my stomach flip-flopped. The morning couldn't have gotten any worse. Slate and Quick were sitting on the black marble bench in front of black metal cubbies in different stages of undress. I tried to sidle up next to them, but the second I stepped into the aisle both men's heads turned.

Quick narrowed his dark eyes at me, and I spun to face my cubby, "Are you wearing my brother's underwear?"

I shoved my entire head inside my black metal cubby to hide my face. Did Quick have to always seek answers, couldn't he use some context clues? I felt Slate's electricity, and I sucked in a deep breath before straightening. He was right behind me, so close I couldn't take a step back. This was going to be bad.

"Scarlett," he rumbled.

I pivoted since turning was impossible and craned my head back. He used my name. My real name, "Yes?"

His grey eyes framed in his long lashes were full of concern, "How are you?"

My eyes widened. How was I? No yelling? No slamming? No low and dangerous tone? What was going on with the men in my life?

"Um, okay?"

I wanted to look at the surrounding Breakers to see if they were watching our interaction, Quick would be. The pads of his fingers ran along my jaw and tucked a strand of hair that had come loose from my bun behind my ear.

"Lera filled me in. I had to drop Amber off otherwise I would have been there. When Quick and I were on our way back, you were already out of danger."

My brow furrowed and a few biting remarks came to mind about him mentioning two women he'd slept with. But he was holding my face as if I was made of glass. Tender Slate got me every time.

"I didn't get them to drop the contract on you," I whispered.

His lips curled, but it wasn't a salacious smile, "I know. I am sorry you had to go through that."

I blinked at him, "Are you feeling, okay?"

He chuckled warmly making my brows climb, "I am."

"Why aren't you calling me Torch? Or yelling at me?" I asked cautiously, by all rights, he should, *er*, could be.

Slate was wearing his snug black shorts, and that was all. His midnight hair fell over his muscled shoulders with their narrow braids and beads. My mind went rogue when acknowledging every detail about the confusing man.

"Do you like when I call you Torch?"

My brows twitched together. "I was just curious; you rarely use my name," his fingers slid to the side of my neck where his thumb was tracing along my tendon.

"You will have to take that off," he rumbled low, and my skin prickled.

"Excuse me?" my brows shot ever higher.

"To train."

"Oh!" I laughed nervously and tried to look away, but he filled my eyes with all his — Slateness. "Yes, shoes would be nice."

"There you are. Scarlett, I am sorry about earlier," Brass walked down the aisle freshly showered, hair wet and free of beads.

Slate didn't turn away from me, but he let his hand fall. My cheeks heated, and I pivoted to Brass making my side brush up against Slate's bare chest. He had no concept of personal space.

"I said it was fine," I wouldn't be having a discussion, vulnerable, in his underwear with Slate and his brother watching.

Brass gave me a dry smile, "I can read minds, in case you forgot."

I pivoted around until I faced my cubby and bent at the knees to pull out my freshly laundered clothes from yesterday. Brass would turn around if I removed my top, so I did, careful to keep myself angled towards the cubby and heard the shuffling of feet and a sharp inhale.

Good. Served them right for...

Slate had shifted blocking me with his powerful body from all other eyes. I frowned up at him as I clasped my bra. His eyes narrowed and made no pretense of staring me down. It made me smile; I liked him better this way. Still, he should close his eyes while I dressed. I yanked my shirt over my head and moved under his arm to sit on the bench and pull out my belongings.

"Girl. Lera wants to see you," I leaned past Slate to see Chafer.

A much cleaner, much more deadly looking Chafer wearing long seax blades sticking up over his shoulders, his sharp features undoubtedly as sharp as those blades. Large brown almond eyes appraised me in such a condescending manner it made my lips want to turn down into a scowl.

"As soon as I change, I'll be up," I told him, pulling the hair tie from my hair and turned it over to shake out the tangles.

I flipped my hair back over; Chafer hadn't moved a muscle, "Where were you last night? What is the point of bonding the girl if you do not answer her summons? Sick of her already?" Chafer flashed a razor-sharp smile.

"Summons? I didn't summon anyone," I took advantage of Slate standing there and changed into my pants.

Chafer laughed, but it wasn't a warm merry sound. It was cold and cruel, and I tugged my pants over my clean underwear before grabbing my boots with all my weapons in them.

"She does not know. That must have taken a great effort."

"Shut your mouth if you value your teeth, Chafer," Slate growled.

"Do not waste your threats on me," Chafer said to Slate with a mocking smile, and he looked down at me, "Why did you think I told you to bite your lip? You have been bonded, girl. For life." His lips spread back into that wicked smile, and I stood up temporarily forgetting my boots.

"Bonded? Like the tracker? I have the Breaker tracker."

Brass sighed, "No, not the tracker." Slate shifted so I could see Brass.

He felt apologetic, worried, and sad. I shook my head.

"What —"

Slate interrupted me, "I had you bonded after our fight with the bauk. I knew I had to keep track of you. You would not have allowed it, I did it for your safety."

I made a face, "I —"

Quick had enough, he came around Slate's side, so I felt dwarfed by dark-haired men over six feet tall. Trapped. I felt trapped. Caged.

"The tattoo on your lip. Slate can track you with it, it is a bond like the one family gets. Brass, Coyote, and I share them," Quick held up his hand pointing his index finger, and I saw Brass hesitantly meet his finger with his own on the inside.

I sucked in a scant breath that was filled with cloves, cinnamon, metal, sandalwood, and earth mangled with spring rain, "They tattooed me while unconscious? In January?"

My mind scanned my memories. Me, in my bed and Slate having a discussion with someone with a gruff voice — Brass — it was Dhole. That was my first week in Tidings and he'd had me branded without my knowledge. My head swam, and I sucked in a shallow breath.

"So, you could find me?" I asked tonelessly and Slate gave a curt nod, "Bond implies more than tracking."

"She has a brain in that pretty little head," Chafer sneered.

"Watch your mouth," Brass barked.

"When activated, I can feel your emotions. Like an empath, but only yours," Slate rumbled.

I gasped, "When I went to Dhole, whatever he added to my lip. It changed it, didn't it? That's why I could feel you."

He nodded, and I ducked my head hoping my hair would cover my face. I'd never been so betrayed.

"Wait. You knew you had another mark aside from the tracker?" I nodded and Chafer's condescending laugh resounded in my mind, "I take it back. You are dense."

"Jett lied."

Some part of me knew his reason for how they'd found me in the Valla U prep room was a lie, but I'd been in denial. My denial had run even deeper when my brother had explained it away. I swallowed convulsively before trying to blink away the tears.

"He did what he thought necessary," Quick explained.

"Lies. The four of you. I'm not dense," With fire in my eyes, I raised my head to Chafer, "I'm a trusting fool." I snatched my boots off the bench and tried ducking away.

Slate grabbed my arm, and I burned, my elemental powers making my skin glow red until his skin burned. He gritted his teeth, and I yanked away my arm.

"How much did you think I could tolerate from you?" I whispered harshly and looked at amber eyes, "I trusted you," A traitorous tear fell, and it was as good as slapping him the way he flinched as it fell from my chin. "I quit. Tell Cordillera she doesn't have to concern herself with me any longer," I said facing Chafer with my chin tilted up with as much pride as I could muster.

"Do not be rash, Scar. It was for —"

"Shut up, Silver Regn!" I snapped, "You, with all your talk of honesty. Fiddlesticking sugarfoot!"

I shoved past Brass and continued down the aisle in only my socks on the white marble with grey skein. Sure, footsteps sounded behind me, and I knew it was not any of my former friends since I felt amusement.

"Go away," I ground out as I called slamming open the metal doors that led to the stone steps.

I needed air, lots of it before I started sobbing in front of all those murderers.

"Quit your whining. Lera still wants to see you. You have a contract. You come now. On your own, or I will drag you there," he promised darkly, and I gritted my teeth.

In no mood to face Cordillera, but not wanting to be dragged up several flights of stairs like a petulant child. I gave a curt nod and followed Chafer running my hand along the polished wood and wrought-iron balustrade.

Instead of going to her office in the rumpus room, Chafer kept walking past the pinball machines, the card tables, the bar, and to the other stairway on the far end that led to the higher floors. I stopped on the wood floors with the door on my left and the hall to leave headquarters on my right. I could make a run for it, I doubted they would drag me back.

Chafer paused and turned back. He stood under one of the hanging lights in the large loft like room making his sharp features as cruel looking as the man. The bartender called out for someone's breakfast and my stomach rumbled. He shot me a look of impatience; I rolled my eyes starting forth again.

We climbed the stairs to the highest floor; I'd never been on any floor aside from the bedrooms. The heavy wood door from the stairs was locked. It was the only one I knew that was, Chafer put his hand to the door and called. I heard multiple clicks, and the door swung open, Chafer went in first and I followed.

Sconces lit the navy walls of a long hall. Dark wood floors reflected the warm light of the sconces, Chafer's boots were soundless against it as he walked.

"You will only have access to this room with those of us in Cordillera's inner circle. She keeps Shadow Breaker's records here, and it is where she meets her — private clients."

Chafer didn't look to me as he spoke. He didn't even check to see if I was still with him. He turned towards an intricately carved gold door and Chafer opened it and went through; I did not know why he was wasting his breath; I didn't give a fig about Shadow Breaker workings. Didn't he hear what I said? I'd quit. I could no longer be around liars.

In the room hung a gold chandelier which reflected off the gold damask wallpaper. There wasn't much furniture in the room, she wouldn't need much to see her clients. An intricately sculpted gold desk sat in the center of the room in front of black velvet upholstered chairs and love seat. A large Persian rug in black and gold laid underneath it all.

Unsurprisingly, a laptop sat on the desk. Shadow Breaker's headquarters was more modern than anywhere else I'd been in Tidings. Cordillera stood gesturing to the couch then sat at a high-backed black velvet chair behind the desk, the gold painted wood around it intricately carved.

She sat smoothly crossing her legs and placing her arms on the rests, her red nails prominently displayed matching her red lips. Her brown eyes glittered.

"I earned my Grand Mistress title. Inherited a clientele base and expanded it with the competitions. I have been outside of Tidings and recognized the potential earnings something like a sport would bring here."

I tried not to look surprised to match as cavalier as she did. I hadn't expected a background on the Breakers; it kept me enraptured. The black velvet couch I sat on was softer than it looked, but firm enough so I wasn't sinking into it.

"I choose my contracts at will, not because I must for the income. It makes the Shadow Breakers more flexible, and better, more elite than others," she continued, obviously proud of her accomplishments.

I interrupted. "Elite?" I asked.

She didn't seem perturbed, "Yes, our equipment is state-of-the-art, nothing like it anywhere else. My Shadow Breakers are the best of the best. But I did not bring you here for a history lesson."

She reached into a drawer and drew out a neat pile of papers placing them on the desk so I could reach them. I leaned forward and took them.

"They are standard contracts. I want you to familiarize yourself with them, so you may be of use in the future. I do not need to tell you to keep these to yourself, do I?" she arched a perfect dark eyebrow at me, and I shook my head.

"Why are you doing this?" I asked finally, it was better than, *what's in it for you.*

Her tongue rested against her teeth before one end of her mouth curled. "I knew a girl like you. Underestimated and angry. They showed her how to channel what she had into power."

"What if I don't want power?" I asked, and I put on my weapons and boots needing a distraction.

Cordillera laughed; it wasn't a pretty laugh, "That is the ideal person to have it. You might find you need it even if you do not want it."

She saw the confusion on my face and leaned across her desk, "I usurped my predecessor. I know the Breakers have come to admire you, I keep my friends close and enemies closer."

She thought I would usurp her. I shook my head and looked at the contracts. Chafer was cleaning his nails with a wicked looking knife.

"These are binding... through magic?" I asked.

They hated the 'M' word in Tidings. Chafer laughed, his wide mouth spreading cruelly.

"No, not magic. Leshy's enchantment. Each of our contracts is bound like a blood oath without speaking the words, you should know. You signed one yourself, if I am not mistaken. They are worth more than your life," he said pointedly.

I doubted that, but they would be close. Leshys hadn't been seen in ages, who knew how they would keep getting contracts once they ran out. I suspected there was a black market for Leshy items. My fingers found my seax sheath, Slate paid a fortune for it.

The contracts were typical, nothing I couldn't follow easily. Guarding people, merchandise, finding missing people, object recovery...probably stealing, and the last, assassination. It was such a short contract; it made my stomach turn. No details like the others. Only client and subject, then the promise from the Shadow Breakers that they wouldn't stop until they succeeded by any means necessary and the signature of the person too chicken to do it themselves.

I put the contracts down disgusted, "What is all this? Why are you showing me all of this? What position of power? Honestly, I want nothing more than to go home and see none of you again."

Cordillera's red lips tightened. "I would like to offer you a more permanent position among the Shadow Breakers. You did well with the Stygians. It was most likely your fault that my nephew would have died. They painted a target on your back. There is strength in numbers," she sounded almost resentful.

Was this her version of an olive branch?

"What kind of position?" I asked skeptically, she always had an end game.

"I do not have anyone belonging to a greater family with my Shadow Breakers. It is a rule I keep avoiding bias. I would break that rule for you," she was obviously trying to flatter me, but I wasn't biting.

She continued, "You could start your own team, small to start, or join one of the already formed teams. I would like you to train under me, work the contracts with me."

I laughed aloud, and she narrowed her eyes, "What is in it for you, Lera? Why would you make me... what?"

"Delegate. I underestimated you. I mean to rectify it. Your marriage has limitless influence, if it proceeds. You would compete, you still answer to me. I can use your talents with negotiating contracts, and you obviously work well for the competition. Challenge yourself further. Perhaps grow enough to challenge the Stygians further and retract a certain contract." Cordillera hinted.

I grit my teeth. She knew just how to play me. I hated Slate, but who knew if in a few months if I'd forgive him. I couldn't run away from him like I could the Regn brothers, he lived with me. All that and if the Stygians wanted Slate dead, I could not knowingly walk away if I thought there was even a sliver of a chance, I could stop it.

"I'll be your right hand, Lera. I'll help with contracts, train, and compete for you. Nothing that goes against my morals. I'll leave that to you. I won't be subject to any obscure rules and no more restrictions on my training."

She narrowed her eyes. "You may want to stop bedding your trainer in order to continue learning," she spat it out.

My lips curled ignoring her jibe, "Delegate Tio has a certain ring to it, Grand Mistress."

Cordillera's red lips spread into a smile that was not kind, "Agreed, Delegate."

Lera put a new contract on the table. She sliced her thumb and pressed it to the paper. I read it through and smiled. It was cut and dry. She was making me answerable only to her. I sliced my thumb and pressed it to the paper.

Her red lips parted into a secret smile. "I was not sure you would agree after our less than amicable start. I am glad you are a better woman than I gave you credit for."

She plucked the contract from the desk and handed the paper to Chafer so he could file it away.

"I need a new trainer," I said meeting her dark eyes.

Her high arched eyebrow quirked further as she leaned back in her chair, "Few women can turn down a Regn once she has had him. Best of luck trying. Chafer can when he is not busy. He may train with you today if you wish."

I nodded and rose to my feet.

"I'm done here," I said looking to Chafer.

He only nodded and hopped to his feet sheathing his knife.

The door was closed behind me. I followed Chafer as we left the long hall; I didn't even care what was behind those other doors. I wanted to get out and punch something. My pent-up emotions were brimming dangerously, my few fallen tears were not nearly enough release.

On a different day, I wouldn't have accepted Lera's contract. I was going to be Ash's wife; I didn't have any need for the Shadow Breakers. Still, maybe, I would have enough strength and influence to do something about the Stygians. I hoped I wouldn't be too late to save Slate before then. Why Lera hadn't done it herself crossed my mind, but she wasn't a woman who would jeopardize what she built for one man's life even if that man was her lover.

Chafer opened the door to the stairs and walked beside me as we headed back to the rumpus room.

"Why do you waste your time?" Chafer asked.

Did he expect an answer, or did he only want to irritate me?

"I think I can help. Make the Shadow Breakers, I don't know, more honorable," I told him.

He snorted, "Silly little girl wants to fix us. That is not what I meant, I meant with the Grand Mistress's pet. He has no loyalties to women, less than a dog. She knows well why you agreed."

I stopped in my tracks balancing on one foot on the stairs. It wasn't just what he said, it was how he said it. If Slate was a dog, he thought of me as less than one. I fixed my gaze on Chafer. He was tall and not an ounce of fat on him. His straight eyebrows over his dark narrow eyes made him look like a predator always scanning for prey, right now he was looking at me. People were always underestimating me. If it wasn't my strength, it was my mind, but that wasn't why I was so upset.

"My time. I do with it what I will," I said low.

I wanted him to hear it as a warning. He was treading in dangerous waters. If nothing else, Slate was family, and I couldn't tolerate him talking about Slate like he was inferior or like I was some dumb girl.

"Waste it, apparently. You think he will care about you in a month, two months now that he has had a taste. You are his toy, the way he is hers."

He had me all wrong. My tone had obviously not warned him enough.

"Watch what you say around me about my loved ones."

Chafer laughed darkly stepping closer to me. My back was to the rail of the stairs.

"I wonder which ones you refer to. You accumulate many. Does the

Prime's nephew know you have been fucking a lesser son? That your brother bonded you for life?"

My cheeks heated at his comment. "My lovers are no one's business, but my own," a thought sparked in my mind, and I curled my lips, "My so-called brother is a better man than you'll ever be. I'm sure Lera knows that very well."

Getting people to hate me was a talent. As much as I hated the fact that Cordillera had carnal knowledge of Slate, Chafer had some sort of attraction to her and he was jealous of Slate.

Chafer's jaw flexed just before his hand sprang out and clasped around my throat. My toes lifted from the floor as he pushed me against the railing, so my top half hung over the flights below. My hand clasped around his wrist.

"You're making a big mistake," I ground out as he squeezed.

"You are the mistake. Lera is wrong about you."

"You are the one who's wrong."

The skin on my throat flared so flames licked his hands. He dropped his grip, and my hands gripped the railing at my back, keeping me from toppling over the edge. Calling against him could get dirty, but I'd resigned myself to the fact that it was about to get physical.

He shook out his blistered hand and cocked his arm. My leg shot out and caught him in the midsection leveraging my weight off the balustrade. He slammed into the stone wall. His hands were quick, he pulled a knife and suddenly it was in my thigh.

Things were escalating rapidly.

I resisted the urge to grip the wound as I yanked it out. He was already in front of me aiming for an uppercut. I moved my head back just in time to feel the breeze of his fist whizzing past my jaw. Off balance, our legs tangled, so we both went sprawling down the stone steps to the next landing. We panted for a moment before scrambling to our feet. I winced as blood poured down my thigh.

He sneered and my hand shot out to knock it off his face. His sneer spread into a sickly smile and my thoughts scattered. I had no idea what happened. I didn't know who I was, where I was, or what I was doing. Chafer walked down the stairs casually as I laid half on the stairs and half on the landing.

Freya's burly boar, that was terrible.

I got to my feet, and he snickered. Every single part of me hurt.

"Mind blasting, my talent. Not giving up?" he said, spitting blood out.

"Not fighting fair?" I countered, readying myself.

"All is fair in love and —"

"War, yeah, yeah, I got the memo," I said, bored.

I was starting to hate the expression; it was like a mantra to justify their actions. Brass had said it to me once, but where Brass was referring to love, Chafer referred to war.

His eyes darkened at my interruption. He came at me in a blink, his fists finding their way to my kidneys, mine found his throat. I pulled my seax, and he clamped his hand over my wrist while pushing his thumb into my thigh wound.

I screamed in pain and lost my balance but held onto him as I fell over the stairs. The weight of him crashing into me knocked the air out of me and I was pretty sure it broke at least one rib. We tumbled down to the next landing.

Only three more flights till the rumpus room, I thought ruefully.

Chafer rolled off me, and he caught his breath again. I rolled onto my knees and picked myself up. Blood pumped anew from my thigh wound.

I nudged him with a toe, "Get up."

I saw then that my seax had gone into his shoulder to the hilt as we'd tumbled. I leaned over him placing a boot next to it and pulled it out, not yanking it, but not being delicate either. He winced and his other hand went over the wound.

"Get up," I said, beckoning him on.

He grinned at me still filled with evil intentions, but there was something else there.

Respect?

I felt something trickling down my neck and I knew I had cracked my head at some point, probably down all the Gods' cursed stairs. He rolled onto his feet wincing again and pulled a dagger. I ducked low and pulled a boot knife before he could stop me; I threw it into his booted foot. He let out a yell and let his knife fly. It lodged in my shoulder, right where I had gotten him. I ignored it as I came at him again kicking his good leg, so he bent in front of the next flight down. He jabbed with the force of a kangaroo kick, hitting me just below my belly button. I doubled over clutching my stomach.

He rose; I knew I couldn't take another punch, so I threw myself at him hoping I could stay on top while we fell down the stairs. It didn't quite pan out. He hit the back of the stairs with a sick crunch, and we slid down slowly, our feet pointed towards the top.

I couldn't help but check his injuries. I called and saw his eyes widen. He had a spinal fracture, and he had cracked his skull. He moved his hands up to push me away, but I slapped them down.

"Don't move," I told him.

I closed my eyes and let my calling carefully move his nerves around so I could repair the fracture causing no other damage. Then I worked on healing his skull. I opened my eyes, and he was staring at me almost wide eyed, and then suspicious.

"You forgot my foot and shoulder," he said with his breathing hard.

I was on top of him, probably crushing his lungs. "So, you can be healed and kick my fanny pack while I'm injured? I don't think so," I said, narrowing my eyes.

Chafer grinned, teeth covered in his own blood, and it was almost pleasant. He lifted his hand, and I nodded. His hand rested on my injured shoulder, and I felt him heal me. Warmth flooded my system, and I sighed in relief. I didn't realize how much pain the wound on my head was causing. I healed him the rest of the way and rolled off him, so I sat on the stairs.

He pulled his legs off the stairway and sat next to me. He wanted to say something, but one thing Shadow Breakers were not, was good with words.

"No need," I said to him as we exchanged our blades, and I tucked mine away.

Chafer nodded, and we heard multiple footsteps running up the stairs. Brass led the charge, followed by Quick, Slate, Ama, and Shale. They stopped so suddenly when they saw us, Ama bounced off Slate's back to fall onto the floor. She glared up at him until she spotted Chafer and me.

Chafer had blood covering his chin and down his neck, there was blood soaking the sleeve of his shirt and down his skin. My hair matted to the back of my head from the blood, and it drenched my pant leg in it as well as my white shirt sleeve and down to my chest on the one side he'd stabbed my shoulder. My lips weren't swollen anymore, but I probably had blood on my face.

We slowly stood facing them. Chafer's eyes raised and Brass stepped up and hit him square in the jaw before he could react. I jumped up to get between them.

"Stop it! We worked it out."

I should have known Brass would find me in my mind at some point and know I was fighting Chafer; I should've expected him to deck Chafer. If not Brass finding me with his mind, then Slate with his bond. I'd almost forgotten I'd activated it last night, and it hadn't deactivated.

Brass was a solid wall of angry. It took both my hands to push him away enough so I could heal Chafer again and bring him back into consciousness. His eyes met mine, and he grinned again. I couldn't help, but grin back.

"Quite the calvary," Chafer said, rising to his feet.

Brass growled, and I blinked. Slate was being held back by Quick I realized, and Quick's eyes were wide at his brother. Shale had helped Ama back to her feet and she was gawking.

"Crawl back to my aunt, Chafer, before I tell her what is in your mind," Brass said, threatening Chafer.

Chafer guffawed, "Grudging admiration, is all."

I looked to Brass, but his eyes were on Chafer. "Get out of here," he ground out.

"No," I said firmly, and they turned to me as one, "Chafer is my new trainer. I'm Cordillera's delegate. None of you have any say in what I do or who I do it with anymore."

Chafer sniggered behind me.

"Truth," Quick cursed and released Slate.

"If you touch her again, you will not walk away from it," Slate promised in a growl.

"Don't threaten him. Come on, Chafer. I've got a Crash Course to beat. Shale, Ama, I welcome you two to come, as always, and thank you for all your help."

Chafer crossed from behind me shooting me an angled glance that reeked of cockiness and shouldered past the men. Ama and Shale looked at one another and shrugged.

I gave my most regal look despite my condition. "How do we deactivate the bond?" I asked with all the coldness I could manage.

Slate jumped all over my willingness to talk to him, "Cordillera has a plan for everything. What did you sign, Torch?"

"None of your business. Are you going to deactivate the bond or not?" I nocked my chin higher.

Slate's temper frayed and he charged me, but before he reached me, I went full elemental. He stopped abruptly and noticed I hadn't burned off my clothes. I'd learned it the night Brass had stayed in my room. I was getting good at controlling it, it almost never flared when I didn't want it to.

"I need to touch you to deactivate the bond," Slate growled, silver eyes flashing at me.

"How? I want answers. No more surprises," I said in a disembodied voice.

The fire did strange things to my vocal cords, but Slate would never touch me again if I had anything to say about it.

"Same way you saw Quick and Brass deactivate theirs," he rumbled.

I winked out and felt my hair fall down my back, "By pressing my mark to yours? Where's yours?"

I narrowed my eyes. If he put it somewhere inappropriate, I would cut his skin off myself.

Brass turned around and looked to be coughing through a laugh despite himself. Quick whirled around to his brother.

"Why are you laughing? What was she thinking?" Quick queried with a smile already on his face knowing it must have been something bad if Brass could laugh at such a serious time.

"No. Not there," Brass choked out between laughs.

"Ooh!" Quick said, chuckling and I grit my teeth.

"It's hard for me to believe you would find a line you would not cross."

That shut them up.

"Scarlett," Slate lifted his arm, and I flared again.

He sighed and pulled down his full lower lip. The same vertical line with the tilted intersecting line made by Celtic ropes. I was mad all over again. I'd have to press my lip to his to deactivate it.

I couldn't believe I hadn't seen it sooner. I could let Slate kiss me again, or I could force him to live with me in his head. Gods, if I slept with Ash he would've felt all of it.

"What is it, Torch? Are you going to deactivate it or not?" Slate growled, likely following my line of thinking.

"No. You wanted it; you can keep it. I make no apologies for living my life how I see fit. You should have thought about my betrothed before you put a bond on an unknowing woman," I said frostily before skirting him.

"Perhaps I should have thought of Brass too. I am astonished you did not lay with him again last night from how wanton you were," Slate snapped at my back.

I didn't meet Brass or Quick's eyes as I left. I wanted nothing to do with any of them. I'd fix the contract with the Stygians and then Slate could go back to his womanizing and I'd never pay him another thought.

Yes. That's exactly what I'd do.

CHAPTER
EIGHTEEN

I programmed the mp3 player and put on my black leather two-piece that Cordillera had left in my cubby to wear for the competition. I hadn't done the course in it yet, better to get in the practice. Ama and Shale waited at the dock to cheer me on with Chafer watching over me from the sides just in case.

I stood in my black leather boy shorts and a cropped halter vest that barely contained my chest, looking through the bladed Guillotine to the end of the Crash Course. My competition outfit was little more than a leather bathing suit. I strapped my arm band tighter making sure my mp3 was secured and pushed in my ear buds.

I stretched my muscles. A little more wouldn't hurt, I was already feeling unwound from my battle. I'd washed off my blood and got ready, not bothering to take a shower when I'd probably get bloody anyway and need another.

I scrolled to my playlist Crashing that Course and took a deep breath; I pressed play. The slow heavy base steadied my breaths as the lyrics washed over me.

I was running, jumping, and sliding by blades. I was pure instinct. Nothing else existed, but the next few steps and the goal.

The music filled me. My actions were a blur to my own eyes, but my mind knew. My mind had memorized every move it needed to make.

I neared the end of the bladed gauntlet. My adrenaline had kicked in, but I was the picture of calm control.

I reached the end of the Guillotine, but I didn't pause to break. I had to keep going. The next song on the playlist was faster paced, no more soulful cries streamed into my ears, but a rougher, raspier more desperate man crooned to my soul.

My momentum drove me forward to the trees. After watching Shale, Ama, and Brass tackle the trees countless times, I knew what to do. I pushed from tree trunks with my feet launching me to the next one.

When I couldn't hit the trunk with my feet, I knew to aim for the branches so I wouldn't risk my body whacking against the thick tree trunks. I flew almost gracefully from tree to tree.

I neared the end of the trees and felt an exhilaration I'd not felt while doing the Crash Course. It was fun.

The song about a man's willingness to let a woman he wants hurt him was still going when I hit the ground in front of the ground quaking section. I didn't even stop for a breath before moving onto it. I was rolling and jumping all while maintaining my balance.

A new song started on my playlist. This higher male voice told his woman he doesn't care if she hurts him. I needed to be more like him. Boulders fell in slow motion, and I move with inhuman speed to avoid them.

I leapt over the fissure opening in the ground in front of me. That was it. I was through. It was time for the lava.

My heart was pumping in my chest as I readied myself to leap to the first rock floating by the lava pit. I inhaled deeply. The next song began and the only line that stuck out in my mind was, "I don't know what I want."

But I knew what I wanted. I wanted to train so I never have to use another bodyguard. I wanted to be proven tried and true, and show my mom, that I could do it.

A geyser sprung up as I leapt past, I wondered idly if it just burned off the hair trailing behind me as I'd jumped. I was at the end of the lava pit, faster than I'd ever done it before. The water was roiling as I faced the whirlpool of rafts. I'd never completed it.

I clicked through my playlist and hit play on the only female vocalist whose ethereal voice told me my hardest days were behind me. I hoped she was right.

Ama and Shale were standing at the dock with Chafer. The girls' smiles told me all I needed to know. I could do it; I was doing it. No one had to save me, I'd be strong enough to do things on my own if I was smart. No more distractions.

My goal was to reach that dock. I had to be better, faster, stronger, than I'd ever been. I couldn't give up; failure was not an option.

I vaulted from one raft to another, my legs absorbing the lands with ease.

I was only two rafts away from the dock. The whirlpool was as much about balance as it was about timing. I was nearly there, but I've failed close before. I hurdled to the next raft.

One more left.

The girls' arms were open beckoning me forward, their smiles bright. They were some of the strongest women I'd ever met, and they were welcoming me with open arms as one of them. I flashed my very best smile, bent my long legs, and leapt again.

I jumped, my feet hit the dock in unison and Shale and Ama's arms took me in. They were congratulating me, I thought, my earbuds were still in. I bounced off my toes after I landed on the dock, and they caught me in unison. Their arms embraced me, welcoming me.

To think that under a year ago I had only just come to Tidings from Chicago. If you had told me then that I could run the course, I would've called you crazy.

Chafer was talking. I pulled him with a hand despite the scowl he shot me and gave him a hug. I removed the earbuds to hear what he was saying.

My arm was around him and the girls were still smiling, but he was looking above, I followed his gaze. Cordillera sat in her glass suite with Slate, Brass, and Quick. Lera knew I'd passed the Crash Course, as did the others. She must've known about my fight with Chafer and the argument I was having with the men. Fantastic.

"Three weeks. That is a record!" Ama beamed.

Shale patted me on the back, and I gave her a smile. I didn't think I would ever grow to like Shale after believing she was Slate's girlfriend, but I did. I even liked her dry humor and cocky attitude.

Chafer crossed his arms and looked down his nose at me.

"This calls for a celebration. I will not be the one to give you your massage, but I will get the drinks ready," Chafer said with glittering dark eyes.

I felt grudging admiration and almost laughed. He'd warm up to me yet. "Don't worry about it. There is no need for a massage. I am starving though so lunch and a few drinks sounds terrific," I said with a smile.

"Nonsense! We can do the massage, right Shale?" Ama said, nudging the petite girl with her hip.

Shale smirked and tossed her sheen of black hair over her shoulder, "We certainly can, Ama."

CHAPTER NINETEEN
JETT

Jett

Not only did Jett find Slate's plan morbid, but he doubted she'd be speaking to either Slate or Brass if she found out. After Scarlett had come home more than a little tipsy the day after her birthday, Jett didn't think he had anything to worry about. Not as far as Slate's plan coming into fruition anyway.

Scarlett wasn't speaking to Slate, Quick, or Brass. Jett thought he'd only gotten out of his sister's wrath because she had a soft spot for him. She'd told him everything that had happened the night of her party and heard the rest from Slate after dinner.

Jett hadn't been mad at Brass, if Brass didn't take Scarlett and she found out about the Stygians, she would've gone herself and who knew what would have happened then.

That bastard Chafer had revealed the bond and Scarlett had been livid, as they'd expected. They hadn't expected for Cordillera to sneak in while she was vulnerable and give her a contract as her delegate. Just what game was Lera playing at? There was always an ulterior motive with that woman.

Worst came to worst he'd go see her himself, but he hadn't spoken to Lera in three years and had no intention of doing so unless he absolutely had to. There were worse things for Scarlett to be doing then focusing on training and learning how to deal with the Grand Mistress's array of clientele.

After Scarlett's birthday, Jett had gone to Alder and asked him to revisit her marriage contract with Ash. She wasn't ready. It seemed everyone knew it but her. Jett was nervous that she was only pushing it forward because she was afraid of the feelings she might experience for someone else. Alder said without either Scarlett or Ash having excellent reasons for voiding the contract, his hands were tied.

Jett was spending more time with his father and Indigo now that Scarlett was in her little Ash bubble. She was making time for Alder and Indigo. They were the only two she was making time for as she pretended everything was fine when nothing was.

It had been a month and if Jett thought it had been bad before, he'd been wrong. It was December and Slate was downright volatile. He was training harder than he had in years and his already short temper had a hair trigger. All horrible things in the way of Slate. Quick had made some comment after a particularly nasty bar brawl in Ostara that had made Slate snarl. Jett wondered what would crack first.

Brass was right there with Slate. Jett had never seen Brass brood as he did when they were out.

Jett gleaned from Quick that the only woman Brass had been with was Scarlett for the last four months and it was only two nights.

Watching Ash and Scar certainly didn't help. Their engagement party was in three weeks, and it would be the first celebration of their union. It was going to be a rough month with Jett and the other first years having to go through the Wild Hunt, Amethyst having to do the Ragnarök pregnant, and then the Yuletide masquerade and the engagement party.

One of the rare nights Scarlett had brought Ash home for dinner on the weekend, Jett had announced Amethyst's pregnancy. Scarlett and Indigo had cried and hugged them. Amethyst dutifully tolerated it though she didn't like to be touched. She warmed up slowly to others and always came across snotty. Jett and Cherry were working on it. She didn't need any warming up from Jett these days; she was a little sex kitten in her pregnant state and Jett knew he had much to repay after the first few weeks of his mother's death.

That was the good thing about having another spouse, when Jett had been busy seeing to his adopted brother, Cherry had been more than willing to see to the needs of their pregnant spouse. Jett's marriage was perfect. Everyone should have two spouses in his eyes. If Slate had his way, Scarlett might find herself in his position.

After Scarlett had cried out of happiness, the tears didn't stop. Sparrow's hadn't either. His aunt had not been the same since his mother's death. No one really had, but it was most evident in them. Ash had taken the crying Scarlett from Jett's arms and soothed her admirably and Jett thought Slate's teeth would crack the way he clenched them.

Ash with his piercing light green eyes had sat across from them kissing his sister and talked about their future children making even Jett fight the grimace that was forcing its way onto his face. Scarlett had smiled up at him. Marriage, babies, stability — Scarlett's dream come true.

While Scarlett was his most current problem, Indigo wasn't a far cry away. If Indigo wasn't careful, others would find out about her little boyfriend and things would get bad fast. Yes, two introverted sisters would have been nice, maybe even a little pudgy to keep the shallow men away.

CHAPTER TWENTY

I hadn't been near Slate, Brass, or Quick since the day after my birthday party. I wasn't as upset anymore, not with Quick anyway. Brass had been the one to bring Slate's blood to Dhole, and I finally understood why he had apologized so cryptically the night he'd stayed over. Slate was another story all together. If he didn't think I understood the significance of the rune EH he was wrong. Ash would find it eventually.

"Brass can stay with you during the competition," Chafer said, snapping me away from my thoughts.

Chafer had met me at the entrance and was escorting me in.

"Why not Shale and Amalgam?" I asked, "I'd prefer a girl or you."

Blunt honesty worked best with Chafer; he didn't do sugar coating.

"They are competing as well," Chafer informed me, "Lera wants to introduce you to the crowd tonight to draw more patrons to next month's competitions."

Cordillera was there and ready for the night when we entered the rumpus room that was more crowded than ever. She wore a shimmering red floor length dress that clung in all the right places, her dark chin length hair in elegant waves. She saw us come in and sauntered over.

"Slate and Silver are the main event tonight," she told us, "They will go on last." Her eyes met mine. "Time to put those gifts to work. You will be in my suite; I will introduce you to some major patrons," her eyes raked me in, "Let us hope the girls can make you look more appealing."

I rolled my eyes. Some things never changed. Except for one, I had accidentally walked in on Cordillera laying atop her deep cherry wood with none other than Chafer gripping her thighs in the air. I was the most embarrassed person there that day.

"Brass will bring you to my suite once you are ready. I know how much you enjoy spending time together. He is waiting at the bar," Cordillera strode away, Chafer in her wake and I sighed.

How uncomfortable I was didn't seem to matter. Someday I'd have enough influence to do what I wanted; no more being pushed around. My eyes slid to the polished wood bar, and I found Brass immediately, he was the only man there looking like he was going to his own execution. I sucked it up and crossed under the hanging overhead lights to where Brass sat.

I bellied up to the bar next to him unsure of what to say.

"You look like you could use a drink," Brass said casually without looking at me.

"Looks like you started without me."

He had a three empty glasses in front of him. Brass wore black leather pants and boots with a dark brown waistcoat over a black linen shirt and a matching ascot. He even looked to have put something in his hair, so it shone with his usual ebony and bronze beads threaded through his braids.

"My last one. I oversee your protection tonight — must keep my head about me."

He ordered another whiskey for himself and a glass of white wine for me. I sat next to him ruing Lera for putting us together.

Brass's mouth spread into a reluctant grin. "If you think about it, her intentions are in the right place. I am not competing; I should be the one watching over you," he said with his amber eyes glittering.

I glanced away. I hated knowing he was reading my mind at that he knew my heart had leapt when our eyes met and even though I'd been furious with him, I'd missed him. That morning he'd been so uncomfortable with me stood out in my memories; I wouldn't soon forget it.

"Bring your glass, I have to take you to get you prepped."

Brass slid off the bar stool and held his arm out like a gentleman. Problem was, I knew he had access to my memories when I touched him, and I didn't want him to know how I'd been feeling as of late.

"Please don't be offended. I think I'll walk on my own, thanks," I said, avoiding his eye contact, but I wasn't unable to ignore the spike of hurt that shot through his melancholy emotions.

His tall frame stiffened, and I gnawed he inside of my cheek as I started forth feeling plain awful. If I was spending the night with him, it would only make it harder if I was being a brat, I'd lighten the mood a bit.

"You clean up nice," I said in an amicable tone, and he arched an eyebrow at me in my peripheral as we walked down the stone steps to the prep room. "Why do you do the competitions?" I asked.

"It brings in new customers. Not everyone is as skilled as the few you know. They need the work, they are our people, we provide. I do not mind. I race, sometimes I win, I get most of the earnings and sometimes we get another client. It works well for everyone."

"It sounds reasonable when you say it like that," I admitted.

"It is reasonable. They hired us for our skills, what better way to show them off than with a competition?" he said, pointedly.

"Okay, you've sold me. I guess I don't enjoy being objectified, or people I care about being objectified."

We stopped in front of the metal door leading to the prep room and he laid his big dark honey hand on my forearm, "Scarlett. I understand why you are angry. I am truly sorry, but if I did not think Slate made a good point, I would never have gotten in contact with Dhole for him."

He should have stopped while he was ahead. I gave him a lopsided smile as I met his imploring amber eyes. I wouldn't stay mad if we spoke — that was why I had been hiding from them all month.

"I know, Brass. I'm sorry too, for overstepping the night of my party," he tucked a finger under my chin to raise my eyes after I bit my upper lip.

"It is very cliché of me to say, but it was not you. It was me. You took care of me. I appreciated it, know that," he appeared to want to say more, but one Breaker opened the door and started up the stairs.

He gave me a wry smile, "Come. Katydid, Bronze, and Cricket are waiting."

The prep room was bustling with more activity than I'd ever seen it. Shadow Breakers, I didn't recognize were getting prepared as well as Shale and Ama.

"Hey! We heard you were coming. Checking out the competition?" Ama joked as Bronze applied her makeup.

"You two look beautiful," I told them.

Even Shale had makeup on, which was a first for the naturally striking woman.

She gave me a wry smile, "How else will they know how skilled we are at what we do without all this?"

Shale gestured to herself. She was wearing a black satin robe, but I could see a hint of the black leather bra underneath. Ama gave her hand a squeeze. Ama mouthed period, to me and Brass laughed.

Katydid came over to me and Brass. He gave her a kiss on the cheek.

"Scarlett, I did not expect to see you again so soon. Hi, Brass," she said shyly. I could only imagine what Brass saw in her mind.

Katydid had been there prepping me for my mother's funeral. The blonde, younger sister of Cricket had a crush on Brass!

I didn't know why I was so surprised; Tawny thought Brass was gorgeous, too. It was more than that, Katydid gazed up through her blunt cut bangs at Brass with expectation. When he smiled at her smile grew brighter. She was pretty in a cute way, slim with soft curves and blonde hair that fell past her shoulders. It was apparent something was between them.

I knit my brow feeling something inexplicable and nasty. If Brass was happy, that would be awesome, I should be happy for him.

"Work your magic. I will be right back."

Brass flashed me a warm smile with his plump defined lips, and I ducked my head hoping he hadn't read all that in my mind. He probably had his hands full with what Katydid was thinking.

Someone handed me a gold satin robe, and I stripped off my clothes in the shower section then tied the half robe before taking a seat in front of Katydid. They had three brightly lit vanities set up where the massage tables were, and Katydid set to work.

"I would normally ask what you want, but Cordillera made it clear how she wants you to look," Katydid gave me an apologetic look.

"I assumed as much," I told her reassuringly.

My heart skipped when I heard a familiar rumble, and I cursed myself. I had to stop doing that. It would be the closest I'd been to Slate in a month, and I wasn't sure how I would react. Now I knew. I was no longer Torch; I was a Rabbit again. My heart was beating in my ears and my cheeks had a flush to them as I stared back at myself in the mirror.

Brass came around the corner first as Katydid dusted my face with her brushes. He flashed me a smile I tried to return and hoped the mirror was a fiddlesticking liar and I wasn't all wide eyed.

Slate and Quick came behind him and I quickly averted my eyes. They were wearing black leather briefs with leather bracers and their black leather boots and that's all. Slate's hair had dozens of tiny braids with his silver etched beads in them and the little white carved fetishes threaded through his wavy midnight mane that spilled down to his shoulder blades. Quick's hair was combed like a gentleman, as usual. The only difference between the two men was Quick's extensive body art that covered his left side.

Quick moved behind me and ducked his handsome olive face into the mirror next to Katydid. He flashed me a dazzling panty dropping smile, and I pursed my lips together fighting a smile in return. The bright lights reflected in his deep chocolate eyes that always glittered. There was some indescribable quality to Quick that hinted at how amazing he'd be in bed, and he knew it.

"You missed me. Admit it," he purred.

I gave a grudging smile. "Depends on the context." I said playfully, and he kissed the top of my head.

"Well, I missed your disapproving looks and all the compromising situations you get into. Busy month?" Quick walked over to the side and I followed his moves in the mirror while Katydid did my makeup.

"Not really. I've been boring, no one to get me into trouble," I flashed him my very best smile.

Quick grabbed his bare chest, "Oh! I have missed that smile of yours."

"Do you want to put these back in your hair?" Katydid asked, and I shifted in my seat.

She held up the ivory pearl with the jade canine. I nodded and caught Slate's silver eyes in the mirror. Freya's burly boar! He shouldn't go around casting those kinds of looks at taken women, he'd get arrested. Slate always dripped an innate sexuality, but that look! If looks could fiddlestick, I would've been clenching in my seat.

Cricket came into view by the men and Brass came to sit next to me on the bench next to the one Ama and Shale sat upon. Cricket took up a bottle and poured the liquid into her hands. Her hands slid over Quick's calves where his boots ended and his greaves exposed skin, she oiled his olive muscles. My cheeks were on fire. The oil brought their muscled bodies an inhuman glow and accentuated their every hard ridge of their sculpted muscles.

I couldn't stop my rogue thoughts remembering what Brass and I had done in that very room with that very oil.

"Close your mouth, Scarlett," Quick teased, and I ducked my head making Katydid pull my hair.

I could not get any more embarrassed until Katydid apologized.

Slate and Quick finished being oiled by the time Katydid had finished with me leaving me to change into my dress. The two men sat next to Brass, and I took my dress further into the aisle.

Strapless with a sweetheart neckline, the beige barely opaque fabric reached the floor. Diamonds glittered over my essential parts, giving the illusion of nudity. They loaded me up with bronzer and shimmering highlights on my cheekbones. My make up just as glittering as my dress. My hair was pulled back and curled so it hung over my shoulder in big ringlets.

I checked behind me and saw no one was looking my way so I slid my satin robe off my shoulder and let it billow to the marble floor. I guided the dress off the hanger and stepped into it, pulling it over my hips.

I jolted when big, calloused hands closed over mine and I yanked away. Slate pulled the dress higher than began zipping the back of the dress. His hands moved over my shimmering shoulders; I had makeup there as well. I turned around to face him and his reaction was all the affirmation I'd ever need.

Fierce silver eyes flashed down at me full of carnal desire and a base primordial need. Heat, hot and intense was rolling from him. My eyes flickered to his hard body, his scent mingling with the oils; a heady, intoxicating scent. A silky trail of midnight hair began below his navel that led into the leather briefs. A little gasp pulled from me, and I swung my eyes back up to his. A faint smile played on his lips.

"How are you, Torch? You look — positively irresistible," Slate said in his low growling purr.

My heart thudded, and I felt lightheaded. It must have been that glass of wine I'd had earlier. I wished I had it then, my mouth had gone as dry as the red hills.

"Good. You?" I temporarily forgot how mad I was, reminding him would take many words I wasn't sure I knew anymore.

"Very well now," his full lips curled further.

The pull to him was a constant tug, his skin touching mine made my entire body thrum scattering my thoughts like dandelion seeds caught in a breeze, "Good."

"You said that already," he purred, and my cheeks heated.

I remembered why I had gone through great pains to stay away from this man. It was like he was several men crammed into one; he took up too much space. Standing next to him overwhelmed you, bent you to his will. I could feel him permeate my skin with his heat infusing me with what he wanted me to feel. He'd never give up; he wasn't the giving up kind. What didn't come willingly, he took. Might was right.

Would he try to take me tonight? Right now?

I licked my lips self-consciously and his eyes followed my tongue, "Was that an invitation, Torch?"

"No," I said breathlessly.

Slate's bronze sculpted body, countless oiled muscles moving, stepped closer. My chest was against his and my neck craned back.

"Are you sure?" he said huskily, and I swallowed.

"Fuck me," Quick said, loquacious as ever.

Quick had turned around on the bench looking back at us. The spell broke, and I straightened my dress over my hips as Slate's hands fell from my shoulders.

Slate only smiled at me, but I heard Quick grunt as Brass elbowed his stomach.

"I'm not sure that's a compliment, Silver," I told Quick as I skirted Slate to go by the bench.

I felt like a little girl playing dress up with Quick drinking me in and Brass doing a better job of not gaping while he did it. Slate emerged from the aisle and leaned against the cubby behind the men.

"You change before you see the patrons, right?" I said, looking at Quick and Slate again.

No one could keep their hands off them, it would be impossible.

Quick laughed wholeheartedly, his boots slapping against the marble.

Slate smiled. "Yes. Worried, are you?" he purred.

"I have more clothes on than you all for once, and that's not saying much, so yeah."

Brass chuckled, Quick responded, "You have not looked in the mirror, have you? We might be near naked, but you look like all your fun parts glitter. I know however, that they do not."

Ama laughed from the bench next to them, "That is because you have only seen her full of blood. When Shale and I gave her a massage after she finished the Crash Course, we used the shimmering oils. All the fun parts glittered."

Quick's head turned slowly and looked at my dress as if he could see what she was describing. I knew there was something strange about that oil, until I took a shower the next day, I felt like someone had dipped me in glitter.

"You had to be mad at us, right? Gods, all the fun parts?" Quick reiterated and Ama nodded bouncing her blonde curls.

"She would never have let you, Quick," Shale said crossing her toned legs out in front of her.

Quick snorted, "I suppose not. She is a freak of nature. An anomaly immune to my wiles."

I laughed, "I'm not immune, Quick. You're just not my type."

"Yeah? What type is that? Smooth as silk, devilishly handsome, and able to make you scream out in —"

"Where are we headed?" I interrupted Quick's boasting.

Brass stood up to collect me, "They stay here until the last round. We are to go to Cordillera's suite so she can parade you around as her newest treasure." He shot me a dry grin.

Slate came around the bench to sit, and his scent wafted up to fill my nostrils.

Quick was chuckling, "Are you all right over there, Scar?"

I nodded without looking, "Good luck. I don't want to choose favorites, so it's a general kind of luck."

Brass took my hand, and we exited the prep room.

The stands around the Crash Course were packed. Brass pulled me aside and pulled out a golden shimmering lace mask, he slid it over my eyes and tucked the thin elastic into my curls.

"Breathtaking," he said, smiling warmly.

My breath hitched as his eyes drew me in. Would that compliment from him ever not remind me of the morning we made love?

I couldn't help but notice how we looked like a couple. I wondered if Cordillera had picked his deep brown waistcoat whose gold threads matched mine so well.

"I did not know what you were wearing, this one is my own," he said amusedly.

...Speaking of breathtaking...

Brass chuckled, and warmth bloomed inside me. The last month had more of a punishment for myself then I cared to admit.

I pushed closer to him as we navigated through the crowded stone stands that lined the top of the Crash Course. All walks a life were there for the competition. Every day Guardians sat in the stands as if it were a sport to watch. I half expected to see signs with GO QUICK painted across them.

Loud music played with a heavy bass played in the background, it matched the adrenaline amped crowd's mood perfectly. The arena was brightly lit with iron wrought chandeliers that matched the wrought-iron railings that lined the wall keeping the crowd from falling onto the Crash Course.

The Guardian upper crust had seats at the end of the arena, you could tell by how well they dressed and some of them wore masks as if they didn't particularly want to be recognized.

We attracted more than our fair share of attention as we walked three quarters of the arena. I arched an eyebrow at Brass that he couldn't see, but he could read the amusement from my mind.

"She asked that I show you off. All I need to do is walk beside you, hardly seems a challenge," he said jokingly.

"You had better not be enjoying yourself too much," I chided.

"Escorting the most beautiful woman here? Never," he said sarcastically.

Despite myself, it flattered me.

We had to go into a hall to reach Cordillera's elite suite. I grew more nervous with each step, I would be on display tonight, under everyone's scrutiny. I licked my lips before Brass opened the door.

He turned to me and lifted my chin to meet his eyes through the mask, "Be yourself, I will not leave the room. If you need rescuing, you know how to reach me."

He tapped his temple with a finger. I nodded nervously, the butterflies in my stomach growing into 747s. I searched his eyes and the corner of his mouth quirked. He knew what I wanted and waited for me to ask for it. I needed to melt.

"Don't make me beg," I breathed.

"I thought you might be over needing my kisses since you went back to Ash," he pivoted so my back was against the wall and his body shielded me.

"Are you through with mine?" I asked, swallowing and my fingers caught the ends of his jacket.

Brass bent down sliding his hand into my hair at my jaw and his eyes slid to slits as he rubbed his nose against mine, "Not a chance."

Breathing him in just before our lips met felt like the most natural thing in my life. It required no effort at all. Our bodies pressed and I parted my lips for more. Brass's hold grew firmer, and my quick breath sucked in sharply.

I was the one to break the kiss. The path I was headed down was more of a slope and I couldn't go any further without slipping down it.

The music was altogether different in Lera's suite. There were two different levels, one where a food and drink spread was set up and the second level carpeted in deep red with plush seats spread out before the glass to see the entire arena. It certainly gave quite a view.

The room was dimly lit with gold sconces along the walls, reflecting off the glittering dresses of the women gathered, and the satin embroidered waistcoats of the men. Here was the real Guardian upper crust, I realized. Only about fifty people gathered in the room, all wearing masks. Chafer was there alongside Cordillera in her red shimmering gown. It surprised me to see he cleaned up so well. His short dark hair combed stylishly to the side reminiscent of a playboy. He stood sipping from a glass as Cordillera spoke with two men much taller than she was.

Her eyes passed over us. "She beckons," Brass said sardonically.

Brass grabbed champagne from a nearby table and passed me a glass. His kiss in the hall had been just the ticket. I secretly wondered if I had deep seated feelings about the middle Regn brother and had wanted him to kiss me because I hadn't liked how he and Katydid were looking at one another.

We went to Cordillera's side as she stood in front of the two taller men. One had chestnut brown hair also side swept stylishly that matched his brown carefully trimmed beard. I couldn't see anything past his brown eyes since he was wearing a simple black half mask. He was as tall as Brass with a swimmer's body shape; I placed him in his early thirties.

The other man was older with white hair and blue hooded eyes, I thought I recognized him, but the masks most of the patrons wore obstructed his face. His eyes twinkled before he turned to address another guest. I turned my empath abilities up and he seemed amused. The brown-haired man was taking his time drinking me in. Brass was not happy about it, but helpless to it.

"Let me introduce my newest recruit. She will compete next month. She shows great promise," Cordillera said, schmoozing.

She hated complimenting me to my face; I tried not to appear too satisfied but offered my hand to the brown-haired man. He bent down to kiss it letting his lips linger.

"Cordillera, they seem to get younger and younger. I for one, am not complaining. What will you call this one?" he asked still holding my hand as he ran his finger along my palm. I tried not to stiffen; he was only holding my hand.

"Wildfire," she said knowingly. "She shall wear white for her first night," Brass's emotions raged as Cordillera and Chafer's seemed as smug as ever.

"White?" the brown-haired man's smile was ribald. I blushed on cue which only deepened his smile, "She is young enough."

"Stop fondling my Breakers, you know the rules. If you want her time, come back next month," Cordillera said in a smokey teasing voice.

She turned me around removing his hand from mine, and I never thought I'd be happy if Cordillera touched me. This was the first time she had laid a finger on me, even though she was saving me, it was for her own gains.

Brass was at my side; he turned his hard gaze on Cordillera, "You are offering her up like a dish to be tasted. They presume too much."

Cordillera's eyes narrowed at him. Brass was the only one who I'd seen challenge Cordillera.

"She is a grown woman. You are training her, no? In more way than one. She can fend off their advances, or not. It does not matter to me. She might even enjoy herself. Or are you jealous, Brass?" she said bitingly.

Brass fumed. I wanted to grip his hand, but something told me if I did Cordillera would be furious.

Her eyes softened. "I am sorry, nephew. You know how dear you are to me. The girl will make her own decisions," she told him.

He stared at her and shook his head before letting her lead us to another group of people. They introduced me as Wildfire to men and women alike, most of which did not offer their own names and wore masks. The men, and a few women gawked at me, I recognized two or three of them. Which was bad, because I knew pretty much no one in Tidings, and if I knew them, they undoubtedly knew me. I was thankful for my mask.

A few women rubbed against Brass, addressing him as Heat. I wanted to roll my eyes so badly it hurt. The women were blatant with their intentions even though he was obviously escorting me. My frustration redoubled when I realized these were the same women who would bid for Slate.

I jumped when a booming voice filled the room. The music faded, and the voice told us the first match was about to begin. We were Cordillera's honored guests, so I sat at her right, Brass to mine. He gave me a reassuring smile. I was drinking my fair share of wine; I was going to need it to get through this night.

The voice came back on, "Guardians! May I introduce the opening match of the night!" The people in the stands stomped their feet making the arena rumble, "Our first competitor, standing in at five foot eleven, and two hundred pounds... JOLT!"

The crowd cheered and Jolt came out of the prep room doors that were thrown wide. He wore his own pair of leather briefs and leather bracers. He smiled at the crowd and sauntered over to the Guillotine waving with both hands.

The announcer started up again, "Our second competitor stands at six feet and weighs in at one hundred and two hundred and ten pounds... HAVOC!"

The man called Havoc came out of the prep room, dressed identically to Jolt, he didn't play to the crowd at all, but marched right out to the Guillotine next to Jolt. They were running it side by side all the way through. I'd only ever done it one after the other, never side by side.

"All ready, men?" the announcer asked.

They both gave a thumbs up and a boom sounded that made me jump again.

Brass patted my hand that gripped the armrest.

The men were neck and neck for a while, but then Jolt had gotten his foot caught in a crack during the earthquake portion and that gave Havoc a lead that never faltered. Havoc had won. He raised his arms to the crowd smiling. The crowd loved it. Havoc waited for Jolt to finish, and they shook hands and trotted back to the prep room together. The whole thing lasted about fifteen minutes.

People around us moved, nearly all women. There was a man taking pieces of paper from each of the patrons and I saw a screen behind him give an amount. More and more papers flooded the man, he kept upping the amount on the screen.

"There is a screen inside the arena and the prep room as well. You will see your room number after the bidding has ended on the screen in the prep room, so you know where to go," Brass explained.

Havoc's company went for a hundred and twenty solid gold Daymarks, the highest coin they had in Tidings. From everyone's reaction it was a decent bid. I squirmed in my seat and a server brought around another round of drinks. I was already motioning for another one as he walked away. Brass arched an eyebrow at me.

...*Liquid courage*...

"I do not think you would like it if I had to carry you out of Cordillera's suite," Brass whispered.

... *True. How do you all stand it? Doesn't it make you feel dirty?*...

Brass smiled and shook his head at me. It was apparent that most men would not mind being bought be a rich, probably attractive, woman. Nor would they shy away from her attention. There was that weird feeling again, envy or something I couldn't explain. I didn't want to sit next to Brass; I didn't even want to be in the same room with him. By the minute, I grew angrier with him.

Slate or Quick would be in a room with a woman for an hour and a half and I knew either of them would welcome the attention. Ama would too. I couldn't imagine Shale welcoming anyone's attention that she didn't chase herself. I wondered how her patrons felt about that.

Havoc came from the preparation rooms again and was all cleaned up, looking rather handsome. He climbed through the stands greeting his fans and making his way up to the door that led to the hall outside of the Grand Mistress's suite.

The announcer came back on, "For our second match, our first competitor the unflappable, stunning… WIDOW MAKER!"

Shale ran out in her black leather bra top and leather shorts like the ones I wore. Her small muscular body flexed for the crowd, and they ate it up, she didn't smile, but shared a smirk.

"Our second competitor is everyone's favorite bouncing blonde… RISK!"

Ama came trotting out giving the crowd an eyeful of bounce in her leather bandeau top and shorts. I thought my outfit was downright modest compared to theirs. Her blonde curls were extra springy and cherub mouth smiled for her fans; she even blew kisses. It was clear she was a favorite to win.

Shale was watching her with the same smirk she'd given the crowd.

"Are the ladies ready?" the announcer asked.

Ama and Shale gave thumbs up and the boom sounded. They were off. I'd seen them do it so many times before, that I knew what to expect. Then Ama beat Shale, and I was stunned. Shale was faster than Ama. Every time we practiced Shale always beat Ama.

Brass leaned in close, so his lips were touching my ear, "The crowd likes Ama to win, sometimes the other competitor lets her since she gets higher bids."

I guessed if people weren't betting on them to win that would be okay. It's not like anyone was keeping score. It still seemed deceptive. Ama and Shale hugged at the dock and ran back to the prep room together. The same process went on with the bidders and the screens. Ama went for two hundred gold Daymarks, I judged it was high, but not unusual for her.

Next up was Slate and Quick, and I was trembling. "Um, where's the ladies' room?" I asked, I didn't care who answered, but I needed some air.

"I will take you."

Brass stood and offered me his arm. I took it gratefully as my previous drinks went straight to my head as I stood.

"You are very drunk," he noted.

...Am I?...

My stomach was in knots and I was lightheaded.

The bathroom was just outside Cordillera's room. Once I was relieved, I scolded myself for my stupidity for being so short with Brass. Imagining him with Katydid. Imagining him with countless other women in the suite. And while I was being honest — imagining Slate.

Gods, I was a mess.

Things were going so well with Ash, why I still was attracted to other men was beyond me. It was physical, despite that, shouldn't my brain kick in at some point and say, "Gee Scar, these guys are mind numbingly hot, but you're coming between them and their lifelong friendship." or even, "They are not meant for you!".

Stupid heart, stupid mute brain, thank goodness I had Ash, or I would've been a goner. He prevented me from doing the most insane of my urges, like moving into Slate's room as he'd asked, or willingly submitting to him whenever he beckoned. If I didn't get it together soon, I'd have to move into the Straumr palace. I'd gone over the marriage contract with my father recently and I'd found an option to move in before the wedding after we'd signed our contracts. It was right next to the stipulation that both partners be physically able to conceive. Not very romantic, but we had both passed our physical exams. I never knew having children would be so important to me, but it had become a priority now that I had a timetable.

My ruddy cheeks complimented me well, I didn't look so washed out in the skin toned dress.

I pulled it together and headed back out of the bathroom. Brass was waiting, but a blonde had joined him and was leaning against his chest speaking to him oozing lust. Even masked, I could tell she was gorgeous and with her high heels, she was only an inch or two shorter than he was. Her legs were long, super long. She was statuesque with a swan-like neck and a model physique. I felt like a frumpy little troll.

I skirted them and went back into the room double fisting wine glasses before I sat back down. Cordillera gave me a side glance and smirked. My palms were sweating, and my heart was racing. It was much harder than I anticipated.

"For our last match we have two of our favorite competitors of the crash course," there were spotlights swinging wildly around the room, all other lights had gone out, "Everyone's favorite bad boy... QUICK!"

I guffawed. I should have known. Brass sat down next to me, and I ignored him. I could feel him want to explain, but I was not supposed to care, and he didn't owe me any explanation.

Quick sauntered out of the prep room every bit the bad boy they proclaimed him to be. His dazzling smile even more so in the spotlights. He gave the crowd a wink, and I heard at least half a hundred women swoon. Gods, no wonder he was so darn cocky. His body was sculpted to perfection, his tattoos only stressed his tight corded muscles.

"Our second competitor and undefeated champion of the Crash Course... SAVAGE STORM!"

The crowd went crazy. Slate's body moved with fluid like grace, every single muscle in his carved body pronounced with the oils and spotlights. Grey eyes roamed through the crowds as if he could meet every single person's eyes. His wavy mane of hair spilled down his back, pieces of silver catching the light. He entered the arena like a bronzed god and had every right to be that arrogant.

He let his eyes rest on Cordillera's box, and he let his lips curl. I wanted to think it was for me, but so did half a hundred other women in the surrounding section judging from the screams that ignited.

I slammed my wine and started in on the other glass plucked from the tray of a passing servant, "Ready men?"

They both gave a thumbs up and the boom sounded. I jumped again even though I'd expected it.

Quick was as good as his name implied. He rolled through the swinging knives within a hair's breadth. Slate was just as nimble, his leg muscles working visibly like I'd never seen them before. I squeezed my eyes shut. I was sharing this intimate view of him with a thousand other people.

Quick darted and jumped, but Slate was all brute force, he pushed aside falling boulders with inhuman strength giving him another second on Quick. They both did well over the lava, and the whirlpool, but Quick had never gained backed those precious seconds. Slate had won or Savage Storm his alter ego.

Slate grasped Quick's forearm, and Quick patted him on the back. Slate gave Cordillera's suite another look before following Quick to the prep room.

Now the bidding would begin. My stomach twisted, and I sipped more wine. My face was burning, and it wasn't from my fire.

Cordillera leaned close to me so her dark hair tickled my cheek, "I hope you are as good as you think."

She wanted me to increase the bid for Slate. I clenched my jaw, as if he'd need my help.

I opened myself up to everyone's feelings, and there was an overwhelming lust for Savage Storm. I couldn't blame them, but that didn't mean I liked it. Higher, spend, treasure, more, more... It became my mantra as the bid climbed higher and higher. I kept my eyes closed; I couldn't wait to leave.

Slate topped out at eight hundred daymarks. Cordillera was beaming, and the crowd cheered his highest bid. The winner was in the room, and I didn't want to see her. Lust and desire rolled off whoever she was that left nothing to my imagination.

"I fulfilled my part. Goodnight," I told Cordillera and rose.

Cordillera placed her hand on mine, "Now we go to the party. You knew that already, delegate." I vaguely remembered some mention of an after party.

"Fine. I want to go now though," before Slate walked up the hall.

"I will take her," Brass offered.

Cordillera smirked and nodded, dismissing us with a flick of her red painted nails.

Brass led me by the arm out of the room. "I need to sit somewhere. I probably need water too. Gods, I think I drank too much." I told him nearly breathless. My near nude dress felt like it was strangling me.

Brass led me the way we came originally, the opposite of the way they'd be going, "You have drunk a lot, are you sure you are up to this?"

"I can still feel, I haven't drunk enough, but water would be nice."

Brass steered me as much as walked with me through the crowds in the stands.

I heard a few people call out HEAT and Brass would wave and keep going.

He took me up two floors and we exited into a dark hall; I could hear thumping music coming from the room ahead of us. Brass opened the door, and it was a nightclub. My jaw dropped. It was an ultra-chic night club in Shadow Breaker headquarters, complete with purple velvet V.I.P. area and black tiled dance floor. More purple velvet couches lined the walls with free standing tables. A man stood behind what I could only describe as a DJ booth. I was in shock at how modern it all was.

"Not what you expected?" he asked smiling, nearly yelling, so I could hear him.

"Drinks first, then we'll find a seat. Make it two."

He rubbed his lips together, and I reached up and pulled his chin smiling. His eyes widened ever so slightly but he quickly recovered. I really enjoyed surprising him. It was easy when I was too drunk to think before I acted. I made a shooing motion with my hands, and he gave me a lopsided grin before heading over to the sleek black bar. I wandered over to a purple couch and fell onto it.

... *Crap these are soft. I could fall asleep right here...*

"You are better not. Lera would kill me if her prized recruit passed out when it came time to show off your moves," Brass yelled over the music.

... *My moves?...*

"Dance moves. This is where she likes to show you off more than in the Grand Mistress's private suite," Brass told me dryly.

I groaned, and he laughed.

I sipped on my wine and watched as the crowd flooded the club. Within a half hour I'd had three more glasses of wine, and the place was packed.

Cordillera came up to us and sat down between us on the velvet couch, "We need to get you onto the dance floor. I hope you know how."

She stood up quickly before I could answer. I knew she was pleased with my performance with the bids since she came over to tell me to move it instead of telling Brass telepathically.

I rolled my eyes.

... I'm going to go talk to the DJ...

Brass nodded but watched me warily. I walked up to the booth and my mouth dropped open.

"Haarder? You work here?"

He beamed me a smile that crinkled his slanted dark eyes, "I DJ here once a month as a side gig. It is an exclusive club. I like to be in with the in crowd."

Haarder looked at home behind the array of technology with his dark spiky hair catching the multicolored laser lights every so often. I'd never seen a DJ mix with wrist blades on though. Chicago was a far cry away.

"Do you have anything from the U.S.? Like mainstream pop?" I shouted over the music trying not to sound too drunk. Haarder smiled and nodded, "Would you mind playing a few songs for me? I've got to go shake it and something familiar would help."

"Say no more. It is good to see you again," Haarder shot me another face splitting smile.

"You are too."

A masked Quick came out of nowhere and swept me away. He was laughing at me, "He must think you are stalking him. My, you are drunk. Come on. My brother will never work up the nerve to get you to dance. Looks like it falls to me." He seemed more than willing to bear the burden and I laughed with my head thrown back.

To my surprise, Haarder had some of my most favorite tunes. I stopped myself before obnoxiously telling Quick it was my jam. I pulled him out onto the dance floor and was happy my equilibrium was still stable. Quick was an amazing dancer, he kept his hands on my hips as I moved to the heavy bass, my whole body thrumming from the beat. How well I danced surprised him, it annoyed me, so I amped it up.

Dancing for me did what therapy did for others — catharsis.

I turned around to face Quick, and he gave me a patented dazzling smile. We bounced and stomped to the beats. As it grew slower, Quick pulled me to him and our bodies matched rhythms. It picked back up, and I bounced away shaking my hips. Quick laughed. I was glowing.

It was a world away from college.

The song ended, and we went back up to the bar. Quick ordered us a round and turned to me.

"I saw you dance at your birthday but being on the receiving end is quite another thing."

"Try not to look so shocked, it's insulting. Before I came to Tidings, I had gone to a few parties. Here, all I ever do is fight and get beat nearly to death," we clinked glasses, and I took a sip.

I pulled Shale onto the dance floor while she was sitting with Brass. She shimmied in my face inches away from my own and she bent forward to plant one on my lips. I spun away laughing. Shale kept moving on the dance floor and I moved back to her. I couldn't stop smiling. I couldn't remember why I'd gotten so drunk, but it didn't matter.

I walked with Shale back to the couch where Brass was alone. Quick was dancing with a group of fans who were basically stripping him on the dance floor.

... *Want to dance?...*

"You are very drunk," Brass said plainly.

... *Please don't make me beg...*

I flashed him my very best smile.

He couldn't see it well under my mask, but he got the idea. He smiled reluctantly and stood up taking my hand in his and bringing me back onto the dance floor; I swayed my hips the entire way.

The Guardians were loving the mainstream pop. I bit my lip in excitement as another familiar tune played. I wrapped my arms around Brass's neck and serenaded him with my drunken singing, his leg was between mine as we swung our hips. It reminded me of our last night together when we danced after dinner and then made love until we fell asleep. An unexpected pang shot through me that felt an awful lot like longing and I shoved it into my lockbox of emotions.

The beat picked up, and I bounced away moving my whole body screaming, "I love it!".

Brass was laughing, and I was smiling again.

The music changed then, Arctic Monkeys came on and Brass stopped and looked at me. It was the song we had started off dancing to, and it had progressed into something much more intimate. I turned around and guided his hands to my hips and wrapped my hands around his neck. We moved slow; our movements sensuous as I rolled my body along his.

Brass took my hands down and turned me around and pulled me close so I could feel his muscles along his stomach move as we swayed. The song ended, and I took a step back with a hard swallow.

... Hope we gave them a good show....

His big dark eyes were heavy; It was a look I knew well. I grabbed his hand and led him to the bar where I ordered us drinks. I gave a thumbs up to Haarder who seemed happy to have obliged. Brass recovered after I sipped my wine.

He couldn't give me that look. It had crossed my wires all night, and it felt unfinished between us.

He shook his head, "I want to leave, are you ready?" I guzzled my drink and nodded.

"Wait here, I am telling Lera we are leaving."

... Okay...

I waited by the door until he came back.

Quick came by, "Leaving so soon? Slate should be done."

Done not down. My stomach twisted.

"There will be plenty of other parties."

Quick walked away having made eye contact with a voluptuous blonde. I rolled my eyes. Brass didn't break stride as he grabbed my hand and hurried me away. We walked to the rumpus room.

"We can go to my room," he said as we headed to the other staircase.

I stumbled after him, so he stopped and wrapped an arm around my waist, "Why are you being so strange?"

He ignored me and opened the door to his room once we got there, turning on the lights for us. I walked to his bed none too gracefully and tossed myself onto it.

Brass disappeared into his closet. He came out shirtless in a pair of low slung green linen pants. He walked over to the bed and tossed down a shirt and pants.

My head lifted, and I looked at them. "I'm going to need help to get out of this thing." I told him pinching the fabric of my dress between my fingers and pulling it away from my skin before letting it fall back.

Brass's muscled chest rose and fell as he looked at me with those deep amber eyes. I pushed myself up on my elbows and knit my brow.

"Gods, Tidings is so bad for my moral compass," I pushed myself up into a sitting position and grabbed the clothes he'd brought. I planned to go into the closet to change.

Brass stopped me with a hand at my waist, "I will unzip it for you."

I nodded and pulled my hair over my shoulder giving him access to my dress, "Not all the way, I don't have any —"

Too late.

I blushed to my toes and let the dress fall in a puddle on the floor. I looked up to him over my shoulder. Brass stood behind me too good looking for my questionable morals. His chest rose and fell heavily as his eyes roamed over my skin.

He lifted his hands and ran his fingers along my collar bones. My eyes fluttered as I exposed my throat to him. His arms wound around me, and I wrapped my arms around his neck arching my back.

His palms slid up my stomach running over my ribs and over my breasts. I tilted my face to him as he rocked his hips against me.

Yes. Again. One more night with him to close the book for good was what I needed. Closure.

A very thin layer of material existed between us.

"Curse the Gods," Brass whispered, his hands making a slow descent south. I moaned with a heavy breath leaning my head against him, and he stilled his hands. "You cannot stay here," he said gruffly and took a step back.

I blinked drunkenly.

"Where are the guest rooms?" I asked in a squeak as I fumbled with his shirt as I pulled it over my head.

Brass slid his feet into slippers before placing his hand on my back and leading me from the room. He guided me down the hall to a room on the end and opened the door but embraced me before I entered. Cinnamon and spring rain filled my nostrils. I looked up at him and he pulled pins from my hair letting my curls fall around my shoulders. He gave a faint smile once they were all out and placed them in my hand.

"Goodnight, Scarlett," he said before turning around and walking away.

His back was a series of sculpted muscles that led to the hard curve of his backside. I sighed. Brass would have been perfect for me if it weren't for Slate. I didn't care about money or family names; I chose Ash because he was guaranteed forever. He made the right promises, said all the right things, my life would be how I'd envisioned it in my head when I'd imagined a husband. *But* with Brass he was the commitment and the heart. Slate was a variable for which there was no factoring. A woman could not be attracted to Slate and make a life with his best friend.

To maintain my healing free streak, I suffered through my hangover bravely as I ate breakfast with Shale, Ama, Quick, Brass, and Slate. I couldn't meet Slate's too intense silver eyes after knowing he had been with a woman last night while I'd slept alone with only my dreams to comfort me.

"What did you think? Did you have fun? I heard you were dancing again," Ama giggled as she ate her sausage.

I shrugged wearing the clothes from yesterday morning, "Fine, other than being fondled. I'm kind of terrified to win. I might lose on purpose just so I won't have to go to Vegas."

Quick guffawed, "Vegas?"

My lips curled puckishly, "The patron's rooms. What happens there, stays there. It's like Vegas. You guys have never given me a straight answer as to what really goes on. I can only assume the worst most debauched actions consequently." I smiled, but inside I was hoping someone would speak up. They didn't.

"After compromising my brother's virtue, how did last night go?" Quick asked making me blush.

Brass shot him a semi-irritated look, and I forced a laugh, "I hardly think I would compromise Brass. I saw him with a stunning blonde in the hall outside the suite. Besides, I stayed in a guest room last night. No dishonor done."

Slate arched an eyebrow at Brass who had gone back to eating his meal.

"Gharial," Brass said, and Slate's eyes slid to mine.

The blonde had a name. She could've had dark honey arms to hold her last night, and that's why he dismissed me.

I was a cheater. There was no other way around it. *Passion.* I had it by the boatload, but not for my future husband.

I carried my plate back to the bar and said my thanks to the tender before returning to the table placing my hands on the back of my chair.

"A little reminder. You're all invited to the engagement party at the Straumr palace, so I expect to see you there," I told them with a smile.

Shale snorted, and Ama elbowed her in the ribs.

Quick crossed his arms across his chest displaying his olive muscles, "We are always there, you just never noticed us before."

I gave him a lopsided smile, "Not true. I've noticed you all from the very beginning, I just didn't realize the extent of your presence."

Brass shot him a look only intriguing me further, but Quick either didn't see it or ignored it, "When you went to the cottages in Valla."

"You mean last December with Ash?" I asked.

Quick nodded and popped the last piece of his bacon into his mouth and chewed, "We were there."

My stomach twisted, "When you say there…"

"Making sure you were safe."

"You followed me?"

Not that it was surprising, but I had the feeling Ash had meant to seduce me that night. I had fallen asleep on him, so nothing had happened, but still.

"To make sure they did not hurt you," Slate said inflectionless, and I looked to Quick who shrugged.

"You do not need me to tell you the truth of that."

"New rule. When I am with my fiancée, it does not matter where, no watching. Go somewhere else out of sight and wait if you must, but I want privacy," I tried for a no-nonsense tone daring them to argue.

"You will get no argument from me," Brass reassured me, but I was ignoring him.

"Why do you need the privacy? Do you plan on fucking him, Torch?" Slate asked brusquely and Quick looked at me with raised brows.

I pinched my lips together narrowing my eyes at Slate. I leaned forward digging my fingers into the chair back.

"I fully intend to," I said low and carefully never breaking contact with those steely eyes and Quick sucked in a sharp breath before rising.

Slate's big hand snapped out catching Quick's wrist. Brass shook his head and Slate slowly turned his head to Quick.

"Do not make me say it," Quick said in a hushed tone.

"Truth," I said for him crossing my arms across my chest.

It happened in a blink. It'd been months since Slate manhandled me. I thought maybe since Brass and I had had our weird thing that we'd moved past it and he wanted to do a different type of manhandling now. How wrong I was.

Still, he'd sent Shale and Ama sprawling since they were sitting next to where I stood. Luckily, Quick was standing or he would have been trampled too. Slate's eyes were flashing silver, his full lips pulled back in a snarl as he pinned me to the floor. One night he wanted to bed me, the next morning he wanted to tear my throat out. I saw all that in his eyes, a brutally savage violence that lurked just beneath the surface.

He grabbed me by the back of the neck simultaneously fisting his hand in my hair making me hiss and bare my teeth as he dragged me towards the stairs, my feet stumbled to keep up all the way.

"Slate..." Brass reached for him, but Slate shrugged him off.

"Slow down before you rip the hair from my scalp," I hissed again.

"You should have thought about that before," Slate growled.

"Before what! I did nothing," I cried, and his fingers pinched harder into my neck.

Gods, the man had a grip like a vise. I debated going elemental half a hundred times already, but it would only prolong his ire. He walked me down a single flight of stairs to the landing and spun me around. Slate shoved my shoulders, so I flew into the stone wall. I gritted my teeth.

I looked through lowered lids at him with as calm a face as I could manage.

His eyes were terrifying. He'd never been so unleashed with me. His lips pulled back in that snarl exposing his straight white teeth. A low growl was pulling from the depths of his powerful chest.

"You are not afraid," he growled as he brushed my ear with his lips.

"I know you won't hurt me. I've already yielded to you. You win, Slate," I said in a low calm voice.

As calmly as I could manage because I was irate, but letting out that anger would do nothing for me.

He chuckled darkly and nuzzled my throat. "No, you have never yielded to me. Allow me into your den, let me visit for a while, and then destroy my scent. You do not yield; you make others yield before you. I can smell your anger," he ran his nose along my jaw, "and your lust."

He was already on me though, his hands tangled in my hair forcing my face up as I stood on my tiptoes, "Do you want me to deactivate the bond, Torch? You will have privacy then. The ultimate privacy. I cannot find you unless you activate it yourself or use the Breaker tracker."

The bond. If Brass had given in last night, Slate would've felt everything.

His body crushed mine against the wall as his lips brushed mine; featherlight. When I sucked in a breath, his spicy scent filled my lungs and his eyes flared again, but this was something more recognizable. Raw carnal lust. I knew this Slate.

"Do you want to?" I retorted, lids heavy, my voice coming out throaty from the pressure he put on my chest.

He smiled, but it was all teeth, and nothing particularly nice about it. "Did you lay with him?"

I wanted to scoff, to ask who, but this wasn't the time for my renowned wit, "No. Can't you feel that with the bond?"

We were nose to nose; my toes were barely touching the floor.

"I can feel your pleasure. Perhaps it was one sided?" he growled.

I did sniff then since I couldn't scoff, and his eyes tightened. As if whom he thought I would have slept with would leave me hanging. It would be a matter of pride for Ash, and if he was referring to whom I thought, there was no way he wouldn't, *er*, finish.

"Do you need a little ego stroke? I can't provide that for you. Have one of your countless disgruntled married women help you," I taunted.

"You could help me," he said, searching my eyes.

"Is it always about sex with you?" I asked earnestly, sensing the change in mood.

He let me slide down the wall until my heels hit the floor, but that was all he gave me. His silver eyes didn't move from mine for an instant as if he was waiting for some facade to crack. My head craned against the cool stone behind my head as He peered up at him trying not to look as angry as I felt.

The corner of his mouth quirked, "Your scent will always be that of spicy citrus and vanilla, but when you are with me, I can smell your lust as well. There is no need to act as if you do not feel it. I *want* to take care of you. Do not lay with the Straumr. Swear it," his gray eyes darted between mine.

"I'm not promising you that," I spat, and he growled.

"Why must you be so infuriating? Give me until the Wild Hunt."

I narrowed my eyes and felt his calling still my stomach, "Why —"

"I swear to you, I will not have a woman," I laughed, and his face hardened, "You afford Brass trust. I am asking for an imperceptible amount of the same."

I opened my mouth and shut it. Slate's lips curled, but it wasn't his usual mocking smile, it was a rare cheek creasing smile that transformed his face.

"My thanks," he rumbled before rushing off without so much as a goodbye.

I went to lunch with Alder, Indigo, and Jett in Thrimilci the following weekend. Alder and Jett seemed on better terms than ever before. The sun was bright in the clear blue cloudless sky as we sat at the tiled table outside after we finished our meal. Jett's long legs stretched out in front of him and crossed at the ankles. His corded muscled arms crossed his chest. Every time something happened, it felt like Slate went back and told Jett. It seemed my brother knew every detail of my life without having to say a word. For whatever reason, Jett seemed blissfully unaware of Slate's supposed plan.

Jett was happy. Ever since Amethyst announced her pregnancy, he and Alder had been toeing the line between them. It was cute in a dysfunctional way. Jett had taken brief trips to Ostara with Alder, not to the Var castle, but to the town itself and getting to know the people. Letting the people get to know him. He had traveled on a scouting mission with Alder one weekend and came back excited. Jett excited was like a little boy. Turquoise eyes bright, tan chiseled cheeks flushed, full lips moving a hundred miles a minute. My brother was even more handsome when passionate.

"Have you begun planning the wedding?" Alder asked me.

I twisted my finger in the lightened end of my hair. "Some. Sparrow still isn't doing very well and if I go without her, Dahlia railroads me. I know she means well, but it can be frustrating," I admitted.

Meant well. Snort. She spoke over me like I was an idiot whenever we started talking about the wedding. The best part for me was that I knew, like, twenty people. That was my entire guest list of friends, the rest was all family or friends of Pearl's and Dahlia's. Guest lists. Gods, no one tells you how bad mothers-in-law can be.

"Bring Amethyst. She knows how to deal with Dahlia. She grew up in the same palace as her. If she persists, Amethyst will tell Moon," Jett said as if it was the simplest thing in the world.

Indigo gave me a sympathetic smile. She'd been coming with me to Dahlia's for wedding planning. My sister had withdrawn, but with my mother's death, who could blame her. I was thinking Tawny might get jealous though; she was spending more time with Cherry. That led me to finding out that Jett had stolen Cherry from Quick the night they'd met, and Jett had taken both girls home that night. Not exactly a story you tell your grandkids about, but still a happy ending.

"I don't want to bother Amethyst. She's got so much on her plate right now," I ran my fingers through my long wavy tresses and pulled them over my shoulder.

Alder's hard face's only soft feature were his full lips. It was where

Jett and I got ours from. Indigo was much more proportioned, classically beautiful, she would be just as lovely at a hundred as she was now. Alder's sun kissed skin held a hint of sheen from the scorching sun as he sat across from me.

"Do not be afraid to ask me for help. I know the Straumrs can be difficult to deal with. How are things with the Straumr boy?" Alder rumbled.

The Straumr boy. The men in my life were not huge fans of Ash.

"Good," I nodded, replacing my glass on the tiled tabletop.

"Are you sure? If you are unhappy, it is not too late to petition an annulment of your marriage contract."

His cold eyes had softened some with the time he'd been living with us, but years of sorrow had taken their toll on our father. I wondered idly if he would look years younger if he had told his father and uncle to shove it.

I bet he would.

I bet he'd be more like Jett, have that warmth that made all those hard angles softer. My mother would have been a different person as well. If we had all gone to Chicago, Jett and Indigo would have the same memories I had. Ones where my mom had baked cookies every Christmas Eve with me even after I found out that she doubled as Santa Claus. Or that she'd come to every one of my soccer games and brought fresh oranges for the for a post-game energy boost. I bet Jett would've played football and Indigo would've joined me on the volleyball team. I never would've pushed through school, never would have crushed on Chris. Jett would've kicked whatever boy's fanny pack who was crazy enough to cross one of the Tio twins.

I smiled at my alternate reality before facing my current one.

"Things are good, dad. Why? Have you heard something?"

I kept waiting to hear that Ash had cheated. That they had seen him. I hoped he wouldn't; it was hard enough for me to fight for myself with Slate tempting me with his weird promise, but I couldn't worry about him too. At least Slate was leaving me alone for the moment. That went double for Brass, I was officially a pariah of men.

Alder grunted. "No. Only checking. How about you Indigo? No suitors come calling. Do you need me to contact some people to get them started?" Alder asked, grasping her slender tan hand and giving it a paternal squeeze.

She smiled shyly at him. "I'm fine, dad. I might not get married," she said, leaning forward to pick the glass off the tiled table.

Alder's brow furrowed, "Indi, get married. You do not want to spend your life alone. Is there anyone... special?" Alder fumbled over the sentence, you'd have to be blind and deaf not to see how uncomfortable he was with the conversation. He was trying to fill the gap my mother left and I truly loved him for trying.

"Fox is still single," I offered with a smile.

Indigo flashed me a smile, and Jett rolled his eyes. Half the girls at Valla U thought Fox was a fox. Those baby blues got you every time.

"Fox Straumr is a good choice. He may court someone, though I am not sure if it is very serious," Alder rumbled.

"Too bad Sterling is betrothed," Jett interjected.

"Who is Fox seeing?" I asked, intrigued.

"Novaculite Natt," Alder rumbled, and I snorted.

Indigo's face was bright red, "Gosh, when did that start?"

"It is fairly recent," Alder told her.

"We should find someone for Gypsum before the cats get their claws in him," Indigo said.

"You may be a bit late for that on many levels," Jett murmured, and I whacked his knee.

"He'll meet someone when he attends Valla U," I told them.

Gypsum was too deep in his Diamond thing. Cherry had told me she walked in on them in the bathroom stall at POP in a very compromising position. I would never understand the appeal of public bathroom sex. Suffice it to say, Gypsum was temporarily lost.

"What about Silver Regn, Indigo? He's handsome," I offered.

She made a face, and I chuckled. Apparently, we Tio/Var women were immune to Quick. Alder raised his brows with interest.

"Regn? I have met him. Some things change in a man when he meets the right woman. Regn is a lesser family name, it would be a good marriage for you."

I admired my father's phrasing of Quick's penchant for bed hopping,

"I thought we were talking about Gypsum. Silver is handsome enough, but he's so..."

"Promiscuous?" I offered.

"Indiscriminate?" Jett countered.

"Frolicsome," I said, laughing.

"Impish?" Jett chuckled.

"Hubristic," Indigo said.

"Oh, good word," Jett chuckled, his chest bouncing with his tapering laugh.

Alder's light eyes glittered as he watched us, "Men change. Do they not, Jett?"

Jett jutted his chin and shone an arrogant smile, "For the right woman or two."

A belly laugh bubbled up and soon we were all laughing.

CHAPTER
TWENTY-ONE

Tawny sat on the edge of my bed while I got ready. The Wild Hunt was happening. I was a wreck. I hadn't gone to Shadow Breaker Headquarters all week because I'd been practicing calling and making last-minute preparations for my engagement party in three days. Tomorrow we would all sit and fret about Amethyst and the baby while she ran the Ragnarök at twelve weeks pregnant.

Slate's big secret or plan — or confession was eating me from the inside out. Whatever it was, Brass had taken a big step back from me which left me frustrated more than anything.

I tucked my stone pendant into my corset and patted my Yggdrasil necklace. Hopefully, I'd be adding a silver torque to my array of jewelry. I slid off my rings, both the amethyst teardrop and the emerald, then I strung them on to my stone pendant chain. My seax was on my thigh, and blades around my belt. I was as ready as I was going to be. I rubbed my fingers on the two fetishes in my hair. They were my good luck charms.

I got to my feet and turned to Tawny. "Now or never," I said, flexing my fingers.

The morning was thick with tension. Everyone made an appearance. We ate mostly in silence with Gypsum trying to lighten the mood. Hawk filled the silence with tips, while Alder sat in stony silence. Amethyst was the most relaxed. She thought we'd all be fine once it had started and the most nerve wrecking part was the wait beforehand.

After breakfast we headed to the portal room to go to Ostara. Alder led the way, he was going to be on the stage being a Var. Delta would be there too, as would the rest of my father's estranged family.

The normally unflappable Jett was tight-lipped and broody. The challenge would be on our own, he couldn't help Cherry, Tawny, or his sisters. His natural inclination to protect us was in overdrive and he was helpless to do it. Steel had taken a different approach. After bolstering Tawny's spirits, as soon as she wasn't paying attention, his brows knit in worry.

It was the first time we could wear our real fighting gear if we wanted. I did. I wore my armored corset with its gold and black skirt. The cloak my mother gave me for my hike with Ash last winter clasped at my throat. I had added black greaves with gold trim that I strapped over the boots Hawk had given me. I had found the greaves in my mother's room when we'd cleaned it out in November. She meant them for my birthday. That had been a terrible day, but between Indigo, Sparrow, and I, we kept most of her stuff.

Tawny's choice of armor was simple, a corset tank top that cropped at her waist and fitted leather pants. Her archery bracers went from her fingers to her elbows. It was all blood red. Indigo had a corset top with skirts that hung to her booted ankles, the front of the skirt exposed her brown shorts. The entire outfit was earthy browns and creams.

Jett and Slate were head to toe black leather. The only color on Jett was the silver damask on his bracers and sheaths. Black pauldrons with neck guards rested on the guys' shoulders. Slate's chest was crossed with belts of small, wicked knives, the ones he always wore while out and about. They were an intimidating wall of muscle over six feet tall striding towards us as the men entered the portal room showering them with blue starry light.

Slate's black wavy mane was all pulled back in a leather throng. It was the first time I'd seen him wear his hair that way. Jett's fluid like walk had a bit of swagger to it, but Jett wouldn't be Jett without a little attitude. Turquoise eyes identical to mine twinkled as his smug smile reached his lips. Nothing to do but smile back. Even Alder looked impressed by his son's appearance. It felt like I'd just found out that the playful dog I'd had around the house was really a wolf. Slate clasped a cloak around his shoulders as we stood in front of the door, it reflected blue of the room in his eyes the like twin mirrors.

"Time to go," Alder told us, taking one last look at our faces.

We stood on a cliff that was home to its town portal. A sleek white stone bridge started at the portal and spanned the water below it to the castle that rose straight up from a piece of land that stood narrow and tall high above the water. A second bridge spanned the other side to reach another cliff face. Mirrored spheres nestled in the bridge rails reflected the blue sky.

In the clear water below the castle, I could make up forms swimming or slithering in the water.

"Anguillan," Alder said over my shoulder.

Their scaled bodies moved unnaturally through the water.

"Eel hybrids. Below the castle is a cove they live in. A river passage inside it lets out where their homelands are," Alder explained.

I suppressed a shiver. Seriously, what was wrong with bunny people?

Alder guided us away from the bustling town. It was the first town made of wood. Despite the warm feel of the wood, it was still opulent. Intricate lace carved trim lined the storefronts and homes. Floral scents assaulted us even from where we stood, flowers bloomed everywhere. A riot of colors so many flowers I couldn't believe someone had taken the time to name them all.

Signs directed us to the challenge course. We passed through hanging willow branches and entered a clearing. Many of the women wore lightweight caftans with thick colorful trim and wide belts. The town was vivid with color.

Moon and Reed stood in the clearing with Dahlia and Boa Sunna, tyros stood in groups as they waited for their wave to begin.

Alder walked up to Moon and Reed with Sparrow, Hawk, and Pearl. Amethyst and Gypsum hung back, and Steel didn't leave Tawny's side.

I saw Ash in a circle with Sage and Sterling and made my way forth with Indigo. "Good morning, my love," Ash said, slanting his mouth over mine.

"Good morning," I told him, kissing him back.

Ash's long seaxes handles stuck out over his left shoulder. He dressed similarly him to Jett, but his jerkin and pauldrons were a deep brown over his black leather.

"Do not be nervous," Ash said, kissing my cheek.

"I can't help it," I confided.

Ash's eyes slid lower to my corset, and he met my eyes with a cocky smile. Gods, it had been hard to keep his hands off me lately, but in a few days all that would change. I'd met Slate's deadline and finally felt ready.

He slid his arms around me, so our bodies pressed together, as if over a hundred other people weren't around. "Everything is ready for our stay. Two nights, just you and I," Ash whispered into my ear and my cheeks heated as a grin grew over my face.

Our trip to the cottages had not gone as planned last year, but this year we were both in on the plan. I could make sure neither Quick nor Brass would show up to spy because it was my time with Ash.

Movement at the back of the group of tyros drew my eye, and I saw Quick with his arm on Slate's shoulder glaring our way. My brow furrowed, what was his problem?

Moon stood on a low dais to address the crowd of tyros. "Good morning, future Guardians! Today is the first of two challenges to prove you tried and true," Moon was in rare form. He was smiling, "I will send the second wave a half hour after the first, and so on and so forth. Each wave has two hours from their start time to complete twenty feats. Good luck to you all!"

Moon turned back to Reed who was pulling out stone saucers that emanated a faint red glow.

Alder and the others came back and hugged us, he even grasped forearms with Slate and Quick. I smiled wondering if my father was going to push Indigo and Quick together.

They headed to the finish line. Moon continued once all the family members were gone, Steel being the last after giving Tawny a deeply passionate kiss.

"Each wave will activate their stone. You have a two-minute head start. During your two hours you must finish the challenges, if not, you fail. If you reach the end before the challenges are complete, you fail. If they strike you down, you fail. It is not a team exercise, but it is also not a competition. It is an individual challenge, any fighting within the challenge will cause expulsion and you will forfeit all chances to be proven tried and true."

Reed stepped forth and read off the names of those in the first wave, it was half the Embala course. I wasn't in it, but Ash, Sage, and Tawny were. I gave Tawny a hug as she headed to Reed who gave her a glowing stone saucer and I gave Ash one last kiss.

"Once you have completed your obstacles, it will recall the creature into the stone. Once you activate your stone with fire, drop it and run. That signals the beginning of the challenge. If you are in grave peril, fatally so, send a fire signal and we shall retrieve you from the challenge. You must have all twenty obstacles finished before your two hours are up. Your family will wait at the finish line and offer healing, which most of you will need."

"Good luck and have courage," Moon said.

A small smile lined his ebony face. Tawny's group walked to the edge of the forest, she looked back and gave a wave. Her stone was growing brighter. She called fire, and the stone fell from her hands; it looked blazing hot.

One minute there was a fiery stone on the ground, the next, a dark shadow pulled forth from the stone expanding and took form. I wished I had been in the first wave. Tawny yelped and ran. The shadow found a form. It looked like something that had crawled out of the bowels of hell.

"Barghest," someone whispered, and my breath caught.

The barghest was twice the size of a man, so pitch it seemed to suck the light out of the sun. There was one for each student. They looked like demon wolves with red glowing eyes, but I'd never mistake those three sets of horns for anything other than barghest. After the allotted two minutes, the barghest gave a howl that made me want to retreat into myself and gave chase.

The barghests were hunting down the students who had activated their stones. I was terrified. Mostly, I was afraid for Tawny; I couldn't imagine one of her little arrows being able to do any damage to it. I hoped I was wrong.

These were not my barghest hybrid. My barghest was big and dangerous, but these were devoid of conscience. Their only thoughts were to kill. The half hour passed achingly slow. I huddled between Jett and Quick with Slate standing off to the side. Jett had an arm around Cherry's shoulder, but no one spoke. I kept catching Slate watching me in the most unnerving way.

Reed and Boa were the only two universities officials left. They had collected the stones and prepared to hand more out. Reed spoke, "The rest of the Embala course is the second round." Reed rattled off another twenty-five names.

I was one of them, Quick was another.

Quick flashed me a dazzling smile, and for the first time, it warmed me from the inside. I slid my hand into his and gave it a squeeze. After his initial surprise, he smiled warmly in a way that made me think of Brass. Brass would wait for Quick at the finish line.

Jett pulled me in for a hug, as did Indigo and Cherry. "You're going to be good, baby sis," Jett winked.

I nodded and turned around running smack dab into a wall of man. I rubbed my nose, "Gods, Slate."

"I need to speak with you," Slate said with an impassive face.

"Right now? You've been avoiding me for weeks, can't it wait?"

I couldn't have a talk now, if it was demoralizing who knew how it would affect my performance during the challenge.

He glanced around him to see if anyone was paying attention, and I made a face. Slate caring who listened, I did not know who that man was. He grabbed my hand and led me into the tree line; he kept his hand over mine as he faced me.

Slate's straight black brows knit making a little crease between them as he hesitated.

I sucked in a deep breath, "You told me to wait until today. Out with it!"

There was a protracted silence where he only stared at me looking like he was struggling to find the right words. I groaned with frustration and I walked away, but Slate grabbed my wrist and yanked me against his body where he wrapped his hands tightly around me.

"I have little time left, but what I have is yours, if you wish it. I give it all to you. Whatever you wish. I am yours," he rumbled, and my body felt heavy.

The fight had gone right out of me. Slate had just proposed. Hell must have been freezing. I closed my eyes and dropped my head.

I pushed limply from him, and he let me go, "No. For so many reasons. No."

"Meet me tonight. I must show you why I have waited. I believe it may change your mind."

I knit my brows, "I'm not —"

"Please," he pleaded.

I walked back to the group, and he didn't stop me again. I gave Jett and the others a smile. Jett's face was dark, and he gave me a strained smile. I shoved everything I felt into a lockbox that could not take another single bottled emotion and mentally prepared myself for the task at hand.

I walked to my group gathered at the forest's edge. I wasn't friends with any of the other challengers in my group so there weren't any warm smiles except for Quick at my side. Crimson Rot was in our group, she met my eyes and glanced away. She'd also avoided me for weeks.

Slate had proposed. The bastard. The knuckle dragging, womanizing, Neanderthal, fiddlesticking cache hole! Slate wasn't a one-woman

man. He'd probably only been with one woman for maybe as much as a month or two *and* it was probably Lera!

We were up.

Reed handed me the stone, and it felt warm to the touch. Its faint red glow was ominous. I called fire; it came to life in my hands, and I dropped it. It was happening so fast! The other people in my group had run. I chased after them, Quick had already disappeared into the fray.

There were several paths to take. I chose blindly and kept running. That was when I heard the howl. It was terrifying when the barghest had done it to Tawny, but when it was after me, it turned my legs to noodles. I saw other students running along, but I didn't want to spend two hours on the defensive.

I found myself in a magenta filled wood. Magenta moss, magenta trees with magenta petals everywhere on the wood's pale ground. I used air to help me climb into one of the magenta trees. I was going to wait for the barghest to find me so I could be done with it.

It didn't take long; I had gotten comfortable when I saw bushes rustling. The black beast erupted from them, eyes glowing red. Its body was misty as if they made it from black smoke, but its teeth and claws looked very solid.

Then it did something I didn't expect, "Scarlett".

I heard it call my name in my head. I almost fell out of the tree. Its voice was raspy like my hybrid and sent a shiver down my spine. It bared its sharp teeth; they must have been if my hand. It came to the tree I sat perched in and dug its clawed paws into it, climbed one paw at a time a low growl sounding in its throat. I didn't panic; I needed it gone. I grabbed a knife and threw it hard right between its eyes. The black smoke evaporated into the air. I couldn't believe it had been so easy.

I looked around waiting for it to reappear, but it didn't. I jumped down from the tree and landed smoothly on my feet. Another challenger ran right past me, a barghest hot on his heels. The barghest didn't give me a second glance. The man charred it with fire as he flipped into the petal strewn pond. It went against the very fiber of my being not to help him; it was against the rules, so I followed along the path to see where it went.

There were only two ways. The way you came and the way you needed to go; it was simple enough. I pulled my hood up and absorbed the beauty of the magenta woods. Shrubs covered in red berries and purple wildflowers grew along the narrow pond. Under different circumstances, it would have been one of the most beautiful places in the world.

I walked along for a few minutes disbelieving my good fortune until I heard the howl. Something about this howl let me know it was for me. I found a large boulder and crouched atop it, poised at the ready. It burst at full speed from the shrubs to my right; I threw my knife, but it had no effect the second time. It soared right through its head as it pounced. It landed on my chest pushing me into the milky pond.

I swallowed gulps of water before I realized it was in the water with me and determined to rip my face off. I called more water and had it push the barghest deeper into the pond as I floated to the surface. It struggled against it, its eyes burning red. I didn't know if it breathed, but I was going to drown it. It stopped struggling and faded into black mist.

I broke through the surface and looked around. Not a single witness to me hacking up a lung. I called to dry myself off enough to keep going. Two down, eighteen to go. I knew from throwing my knife that I wouldn't be able to kill it the same way twice, I'd have to get creative. Morbidly creative.

I trotted out of the magenta woods and into a gulch. Purple leafed trees on grey rocks lined either side of a crystal blue river. I broke in my gloves and climbed along the rock wall.

A rock the size of my fist knocked me in the head, and I almost lost my grip. I shifted my fingers one at a time and looked up. The barghest was on a ledge about thirty feet above me. I tried not to scream when its legs crouched to pounce down at me. It could squish me flat. I called. The purple leafed tree on the ledge with the barghest grew branches that wrapped around it squeezing it closer and tighter as it growled and struggled.

Its smoky mist evaporated. I let out a breath and looked down into the river. It looked peaceful enough, but I didn't want to find out what was beneath those calm waters.

Fifty yards from the edge of the gulch, I heard a growl. Waiting for me at the end of the rock wall was the barghest. I could either fight it from where I sat or climb up and hope I could beat it to the top.

It started howling. Fire was supposed to be for when I really needed it, but it trapped me. I blasted it and it blew apart. I reached where it had been standing moments before. No proof it had even been there. I had been on the course for half an hour, but only defeated it four times. I had to step up my game.

The river turned green, arches of vines hung over it, paths to either side of the river. I took the right path.

I tripped sideways; my feet tangled in the vines that made the arches. Good thing, since where my head had landed before I swung down, the barghest lunged. I called so the ground under it opened right where I had been; the barghest jumped right into the crack in the earth. I closed it quickly.

I took a knife and freed my tangled feet. I was a quarter of the way through. My gut told me it was regenerating faster. Less than five minutes passed before I struck it with lightning.

When I was halfway done, I was feeling disgusting. Killing held no interest for me, and even though I knew it wasn't, it still reminded of my barghest hybrid. I had sliced it with razor sharp air, tossed seeds into it and then grew trees in its throat, it surprised me once, but I got the best of it and broke its thick neck. The tenth time I defeated it was especially grizzly. I kept shoving air into its mouth until it exploded.

I hoped everyone else was being as horribly creative and I wasn't some special kind of evil. The one reprieve was that it didn't seem to feel, it didn't bleed; it existed only to attack me. It eased my conscience, if only slightly.

When I came out of the archway vines, the water had gone underground. I stood in a forest with trees that grew at a sharp curve. Large moss-covered stones lay scattered everywhere. I could see someone had recently had a skirmish there. Loud sounds came from every direction where other challengers were battling their way through the course. It had been an hour since I'd gone in already. Everyone would be on the paths and the people in the first wave would start reaching the finish line.

Before I came to the end of the curved tree woods, I had fought the barghest five times; it was taking about two minutes to regenerate, and it could come from any direction. I crushed it with rocks, strangled it with a vine, and sent spikes of earth through it. Then I beat it to death with the curved trees and threw it high into the air, so it landed on its head. I was panting from the effort. I was on the run. There was time to defeat it five more times in the next forty-five minutes, but my macabre ideas were running low.

I came out of the woods and into a swamp. I had no experience with swamps and my boots sucked at each sinking step. The barghest came up from the swamp water with rivers of murky water running its face; I fell back but sprung my wrist blade as it landed on me gutting it. I squeezed my eyes against the sight of its death, but it evaporated into mist before its weight could settle. It appeared in front of me but facing the opposite direction; I didn't think. I jumped on its back and shoved my blade through layers of flesh. It tore through muscle and slit its throat. It evaporated again, and I fell face first into the muck.

I felt it bite into my thigh and cried out catching the musky slime into my mouth. It was regenerating almost immediately; I hadn't even picked myself out of the swamp water and got my boots back when it was on me. I froze the swamp water and sent spikes of it into the barghest.

I winced as I got to my feet and spit up as much of the swamp as I could. Blood poured out of my leg where it had bitten me. My cloak dragged through the swamp water as I got back on the path.

I looked for the barghest, but didn't see it. Only twice more and the hunt was over.

I didn't understand how you could kill a creature nearly twenty times and not feel something, even if it was out for blood. My stomach was sick with it. I felt weak and staggered along. Anytime I put weight on the leg, I winced from the pain. I was plum out of ideas. I felt miserable for coming up with the ones I had conjured.

It materialized in front of me; it didn't rush me. I was being stalked. I shook seeds from the nearby trees and used my calling to grow them into the barghest's path. Roots circled its ankles as it struggled, but I only grew the trees faster until they completely encompassed the barghest inside and had wrapped gently around it. Dirt tumbled down from the rapidly grown roots. I didn't hate myself as much when it faded into mist.

I limped, filthy from head to toe, down the path. A low growl curled behind me, and I was batted back into the swamp; it had swatted me with a massive paw and knocked the air from my lungs. I wanted to cry in frustration, but the action might break my ribs is they weren't broken already. There were no new ideas on how to kill the mist beast. I probed its mind, and it snarled. I couldn't access it without contact. It came right for me. I wrapped it in air, knowing it wouldn't kill it but hold it placing my hands on it and put it to sleep like Slate had done so many times to me.

It worked. The barghest burst into mist, but this time it was red. I had completed all twenty obstacles and felt like a monster for having killed it in so many ways.

I sat in the swamp not caring about the gross muck. There was over a half hour to finish the challenge. I could take my time.

I cried. Not a lot, but a little my ribs would allow. Tears of frustration mingled with tears of relief and sadness, always sadness.

I hadn't needed to kill it. I only needed to stop it. My already heavy heart felt even worse, and I wondered how long it took for people to die from a broken heart. I should have been dead by now. I was sure of it.

Eventually, I climbed to my feet and trudged through the swamp as it sucked at my boots and back to a path. I found it easily enough since twenty or so other people had recently come that way. Muck dripped off me as I limped down the path that curved reentering a thicker jungle of towering angelim vermelho. There were others walking as I was bloody and slinking along, a few looked like they were going to cut it close and were still battling their barghests.

I took a shuddering breath and limped slowly towards the wall of willow branches blocking our view of the finish line. There was a girl a hundred feet ahead of me, a man about thirty feet ahead of me on the path and two more merging onto the path we walked. My wave was all finishing about now.

"Scar!"

I stopped and pivoted to look down the path. Jett was running towards me, blood came from a cut above his brow. Otherwise, my brother looked as handsome as ever. Letting a man go past, I waited for him. I didn't care about timing; I would rather cross the finish line with my brother.

I offered him a smile when he reached me, but we were careful not to touch one another. Physical contact would disqualify us.

"Where's Indi and Cherry?" I asked, knowing my brother finished his challenge if he had run to meet me.

Jett's turquoise green eyes scanned my body and settled on my bleeding thigh, "Cherry finished her challenge, she's a little way back. Indigo is in the next wave with Slate. How's the leg?"

I gave him a small smile and shrugged my shoulders. "Not terrible. How about you?" I lied.

He nodded once, his chiseled face still looking hard under the patterns of shadows the leaves played on his tanned skin. Jett sighed and ran his hand over his close-cropped hair.

"Good. Let's finish this crap," he huffed out a breath and walked slowly next to me as we walked towards the curtain of green leaves.

Jett gave me a wry smile as his corded arm swept back the branches and we walked into the clearing. A crowd of nearly a thousand people gathered in a curved stadium. Wildflowers lined the sides of the willows that butterflies had made a home in. Butterflies, almost as many that were in my stomach, flew willy nilly in the clearing.

Ash turned from where he stood on the dais and smiled at me. My lips quirked as he hopped off and started towards me.

Jett was still by my side, and we'd crossed the finish line once we'd passed through the willow. Reed Tio clapped from the side grinning at us with a basket full of normal stone saucers and another basket full of still glowing stones.

"Congratulations, tyros. You are one step closer to being proven tried and true Guardians," Reed said, his coppery hair catching the sunlight to show the gold streaks that peppered it.

Jett turned me around and hugged me so fiercely my lungs couldn't expand. He held me against his hard chest for a moment longer after he healed me.

"Scarlett!"

I turned in a whirl. Ash scooped me up in his arms and swung me around before pulling me in for a kiss laughing.

"How did you do?" I asked.

"First one finished," he said with a cocky smile.

I forced a smile back at him, "I knew you would be. Are you already healed?"

His celadon eyes glittered, "I did not need healing. You?"

"It bit my leg, but they healed it already."

"Come, then," Ash laced his fingers through mine and led me to the dais where the Vars waited with Moon Straumr.

I cast a last glance at Jett who watched me go with hard turquoise eyes. It was an eerie sight. I hadn't even healed him back. I was walking up the stairs to Moon before I turned back around. My father was standing next to him, with Pearl and the others waiting next to the stands smiling and waving. I waved and Tawny's wide mouth beamed me a smile.

"Scarlett Tio," Moon drew my attention.

I turned to face his ebony face and deep dark eyes. "Congratulations, tyro. While victorious, keep your humility," he said and held out his hand.

I gave him my hand, and he slid a silver torque over my wrist, and I felt a little thrill shot through me. It shifted in size right before my eyes to fit me and I looked up in astonishment. Moon's eyes glittered and Alder let out a chuckle. I crossed the dais to my father and threw my arms around him not caring who saw, or his father, uncle, and Delta sitting to the side on the dais. Only Ruby, my grandmother, looked thoughtful.

Alder's big hand stroked my hair as he murmured. "It is over, daughter," he soothed, but I could feel his relief and joy.

I cleared my throat fighting the tears. Oh, the tears were coming all right. A slew of them.

CHAPTER
TWENTY-TWO
JETT

Jett

Jett stood just outside the willow trees watching Scarlett and Alder hug. Scarlett's tears were falling freely, and Jett knew she was crying for many reasons. He was waiting for Cherry as he promised he would when he left her.

What a bastard.

Jett had seen Scarlett run off and Slate follow her. He had thought Slate had gone and pissed her off again and meant to intercede until the Wild Hunt completed but ended up eavesdropping when he heard them speaking. Then he'd heard him propose and nearly ran in to stop it.

Gods, what a fucking train wreck. Jett had hurried back after Scarlett gave Slate her big fat N-O. Scarlett would have freaked out worse yet if she knew Jett had overheard. *Great timing Slate, honestly, fucking fantastic*, he'd thought.

Scarlett moved with Ash's arm around her waist down to the stands. At least he had waited for her — one point to Ash. The rest of the family was waiting before the wooden stands amidst the fluttering butterflies and hugged Scarlett.

Ostara was beautiful.

As soon as Scarlett had gone into the woods with Quick, Jett had rounded on Slate. His anger had quickly evaporated when he'd seen his adopted brother's face. Slate pressed his lips into a firm line, hard face like granite. It reminded Jett of his father and his sorrow that his beneath his stony exterior. Perhaps in private Slate would find a release, otherwise the next time they went out some poor unsuspecting jerk would get the beating of a lifetime once they inevitably pissed Slate off. Either that or he'd find comfort in the arm of another woman.

Jett had moved up next to where Slate had stood at the back of his group and gazed off into the distance. "She's just shocked," Jett had said, and Slate's shoulders had bunched as if he wanted Jett to goad him into a fight.

Slate had moved away from him making it clear he had no desire to speak about it.

"Jett, baby!" Cherry burst through the willow and Jett spun towards her.

Jett picked her up immediately and healed her not wanting to see where his wife was injured. Her cobalt eyes glittered at him as her red stained lips puckered. Jett smirked and slanted his mouth over hers, she deepened the kiss, ever eager his Cherry.

Reed cleared his throat and Cherry giggled unwrapping her legs from Jett's waist. Jett set her down and wrapped his arm around her waist.

"A-okay?" Jett asked her.

"Sure am, babe," she slid her hand into his back pocket, palming his hard ass and he arched an eyebrow down at her.

She waggled her delicate brow back at him as they started towards the dais. There'd be quite the scene once Amethyst met up with them. He could already see her freeing herself from her brothers.

Jett and Cherry got their torques from Moon and grasped forearms with Alder. Cherry hugged Alder in a way that made Jett chuckle when Alder's eyes widened slightly. What were you going to do? The girl had passion.

"Congratulations, son. So far, you have completed the course in record time. We are only waiting for the rest of the Ask course to give out the award," Alder had said with a proud smile.

Jett allowed the affirmation to boost his ego a bit. The only reason Jett had gone through so quickly was for Scarlett.

Cherry had hopped off the dais and her and Amethyst were kissing, much to the Straumr brothers' dismay, right in front of everyone. Jett met the girls and Amethyst embraced him, slanting her mouth over his.

"I knew you two would do wonderfully. I am glad it went quick," she said, her big brown eyes looked watery.

He kissed the top of her head and pulled Cherry under his other arm as they walked towards his family.

The Regn were there and Brass and Quick were by Scarlett now that Ash had wandered away. Scarlett was stiff as she spoke to them, visibly trying to conceal her mind from Brass. Jett sighed. Slate should never have gone after Scarlett.

Pearl reached Jett and the girls first and he embraced her, her musky floral scent filled his nostrils. "Darling," was all she said, but he understood.

"We're all okay. Slate is watching over Indigo. They'll be fine," Jett told her as he embraced his grandmother who didn't look a day over fifty.

She turned her head and her emerald cat eyes took him in. Technically, they weren't supposed to have teams, but the actual rules were that you had to incapacitate your own barghest, and you couldn't receive healing before the finish line or touch. There's nothing against say, holding out a vine for someone to climb, or a sudden burst of air to make someone swim faster. Quick had overseen Scarlett, she hadn't known of course. Life would be much easier if she'd accept their help instead of getting indignant about it.

Jett had beat every previous record of tyros. Alder had been all puffed up, and Jett grudgingly accepted more of his praise. He'd need his father's help with Scarlett soon, and if you were twisting his arm, he'd say Alder wasn't as bad as he'd first suspected. Alder had not taken Amethyst's pregnancy lightly; the man had pushed ever harder to insert himself into Jett's life until it was easier to give in than to fight him. The girls adored Alder, so that was enough for Jett.

Slate had taken his sweet time as he always had, he had nothing to prove to these people. He wanted to be a Guardian of course, they all did, but Slate did what he wanted when he wanted, and how he wanted. It was how he'd always been. He'd not made any pretense of arriving at the same time as Indigo either, the two had walked from the willows together.

Jett had rushed to her side and healed her. He embraced until she started crying. Wren's death was still fresh in their minds, and with big milestones it was like rubbing their noses in the loss. Once Indigo and Slate were through, they had all gone back to the Sumar palace leaving Ash behind.

"She is upstairs," Slate had rumbled after he opened his bedroom door and turned around to throw himself on the tufted leather couch.

Two empty carafes of wine sat on the coffee table with two more waiting for Slate to fill up on. Jett sat on one of the tufted leather sofa chairs and looked at the man who laid shirtless, with his muddy pants and boots still on as he drank straight from a fifth carafe he'd placed on the floor.

"It's harder to control when you're drunk. I don't need to remind you of that," Jett said in a low, careful tone.

Slate drank deep, Adam's apple working as he chugged the red wine. "Then why bother?" he rumbled.

Jett used both hands to rub over his short hair. "Frigga's sweet grass, Slate," Jett cursed.

He had a point. Two introverted sisters that never left the palace. That's what would have been better. Jett had thought Indigo had been the bigger problem for so long.

"Why don't we hit the town? Get some fresh air? On me," Jett said trying to cheer him up.

Slate arched an eyebrow at him. He didn't care about currency; they had oodles of it, "No, I will end up hurting some innocent man or fucking some faceless woman. She may still show."

Jett bit back the anger at that and inhaled deeply before a knock sounded on the bathroom door and Gypsum came in. "I thought I heard the devil himself laughing in here. I came to make sure you hadn't sold your soul just yet," Gypsum's dimples shown when he smirked at Slate.

Slate laughed and gestured to the sofa chair opposite Jett, "What brings you in, chief?"

Slate asked, feigning a good mood, but it did not fool Gypsum. Gypsum crossed the room and sat meeting Jett's eyes before he started.

"The oddest thing happened earlier. I was sitting in the stands with the rest of the family when a Gods be damned squirrel walked up to me and spoke. It said, the one who smells of fire is not right of mind. Deductive reasoning tells me one of two things; I may be crazy if squirrels are talking to me, or I'm a zoolinguist and can talk to Freya's burly boar myself. If I am a zoolinguist, the squirrel meant Scarlett. Anyone care to explain for me why my cousin is letting off serious power disturbances, so much so that nature is coming to warn me?"

Jett's eyes widened, and he looked at Slate who was no longer pretending to be drunk or aloof. Gypsum saw their reactions and nodded to himself. His copper beads threaded through his hair catching the light.

"I pray you remember there are brains behind all this beauty," Gyps flashed them both a smile and Jett found his own smile.

Gods, they were a bad influence on their younger cousin. The ladies had better watch out for that one once Diamond was finally married. Train wrecks. They surrounded Jett. Gods damn it all, one at a time.

CHAPTER
TWENTY-THREE

Slate answered the door looking miserable and drunk, but immediately straightened when he saw it was me.

"*Behold a woman!*

She looks out from her quaker cap—
her face is clearer and more beautiful than the sky.

She sits in an armchair, under the shaded porch of the farmhouse, The sun just shines on her old white head.

Her ample gown is of cream-hued linen,
Her grandsons raised the flax, and her granddaughters spun it with the distaff and the wheel.
The melodious character of the earth,
The finish beyond which philosophy cannot go, and does not wish to go,
The justified mother of men."

I narrowed my eyes, "If you're going to be a cache hole, I'll leave."

The only reason I was there at the ungodly hour was because Indigo convinced me that if I didn't close the door on Slate for good, I'd always wonder what if. Slate offered his hand palm up displaying his array of calloused. Those calloused had scratched my skin on many occasions.

I lifted my cool gaze, "If this is a ploy to get me into bed…"

His smile mocked me, "Only if you wish to bed me, Rabbit."

I sniffed derisively and took his hand. His emotions swelled over the carefully crafted walls, and I felt triumph. Goodness, it was just a hand.

From what he'd said, I'd assumed we were going out, so it surprised me to find him leading me higher into the palace. I'd chosen my matching bra and panties with care for a reason that escaped me. Blush pink with ivory lace under a clinging pale pink sweater dress. My golden waves were carefully coifed, and I had painstakingly applied my makeup. I felt silly I was so dressed up and he looked like he was in for the night.

He stopped before a set of carved double doors and turned to me, "It is not finished —"

"Why did you give me your mother's ring?" I interrupted.

Slate's chest rose as he inhaled.

"Whoever you are, holding me now in hand, Without one thing, all will be useless,

I give you fair warning, before you attempt me further, I am not what you supposed, but far different."

He acted as if this explained everything, but it only confused me more. "It is your ring now. My mother would have wanted you to have it. She had a prophecy about your mother, about one of her daughters. I do not want the ring back," he said with finality.

"I didn't get you anything. You took such good care of me," I told him, and he chuckled.

"Selfishly, everything I do for or with you, is for me. No good will come of our union. I admit it, but it does not stop me from wanting it."

I scoffed. That was honesty for you.

"Do you love him?" he asked, placing his hands on the doorknobs, and opening the doors behind his back.

"Who?" I asked moronically, following him into the room.

"Ash."

I shook my head. Brass had been quick enough to point that out.

"I know you think you will marry him, but I know the prophecy, and it tells me that something will prevent it. Only one of you will walk away from this, that is why I have had men watching you since you arrived. I know much more, but it will have to wait until you are ready to admit it, at least to yourself," Slate's confidence in his words chilled me to my core.

Gods, what it must be like to know what was going to happen and unable to affect it enough to prevent it. I wouldn't want that talent.

"What about the barghest?" he asked next.

My breath caught, and I blinked up at him. "I don't know," I swallowed hard, not what Slate wanted to hear, but it was the truth. "He could kill me just as well as love me if I let him," I breathed.

"Some beasts mate for life. If you mated with a barghest, it would never take another."

"Barghests mate for life?" I asked. I shook my head to clear it, "Don't bother asking about Brass. He's not a topic I'm willing to discuss with you."

"Because you are falling for him, Torch," he rumbled.

I wouldn't dignify his comment with a response.

His hands rested lightly on my shoulders, and I craned my neck to look up at him, "What do you think?"

"I don't know what I'm looking at," I said swiveling my head around the expansive room painted a pretty dusky blue.

"Our wing."

I opened my mouth and shut it thinking I must have heard him wrong, "When you say ours…"

"For you and me and whatever children we may have," he rumbled.

My world tilted, and I stepped back from him trying to process what he said. Under a white sheet I lifted I saw a plush beige couch very unlike Slate, but very like me and modern.

"You were serious?" I asked bewildered.

"About making you mine? Yes," he said, watching me wander around the room, "It is a full wing as all married couples inherit."

"I think I need to sit down," I murmured dizzily.

"I will get you water. Come."

Slate didn't seem daunted by my lack of response. We walked through the tiled halls of the Sumar palace hand in hand.

"You went back in there and fought him, didn't you?" I asked, needing to change the subject so I could think. "The night we went to the movies," I'd seen the blood on his knuckles when he'd come out from the theater.

"It was a fair fight. I did not call, and his four friends helped him. He is still alive. What more could you ask of me?" he said, unabashed, as we walked down the stairs to our rooms.

I had hoped Chris had been on his way out, not on his way into the theater so they would have been long gone by the end of our kiss, but no such luck, Slate had found him and pummeled him.

"You didn't break anything serious, did you?" I asked.

"He was smarter than he looked. Football must offer limited physical training."

I smiled at Slate, "Did the myopic, hurt big bad Slate?" I teased, he only sniffed.

Myopic was the derogatory term for those who lived outside of Tidings who had no ability to call. Gypsum had been called myopic and had gotten into a scuffle for it on his first night in Tidings.

I could feel Slate's rapt attention as he gazed down at me running his thumb over my knuckles to encourage me to open, "Chris was my friend. I'd never been drunk before. Chris asked me to go get air with him. I was so blissfully happy. He coaxed me back into the limo and —" I broke off and cleared my throat, "We had drunk so much... It was over in a matter of minutes, but I didn't go back to the dance. Chris was very drunk and passed out; I don't think he had experience either. It's all kind of a blur," I said feeling shaky.

I might have slept with Chris in time, I had really liked him. I'd given in thinking it would get better and we would become a real couple. Instead, I felt such consuming shame, I didn't want to see Chris again. Ash was the first person I'd dated since I was sixteen.

Slate sucked in a deep breath, and I swung my gaze back up to him and panicked. He probably thought I was stupid now. I *knew* I was stupid.

His midnight hair fell in a sheet in front of his eyes so I couldn't see his expression and his walls were up like eight feet of cinderblock guarding me from them.

He whispered harshly stopping on the stairs. "I should have killed that boy instead of bloodying him. When we were on the raft and you were on the rousen, that was the first time you had touched a man," he said silver eyes flashing, intense, demanding.

I nodded, and he let out a breath.

"I had not realized," he breathed.

Slate could have done anything he wanted to me that day, but it had focused him on restraining me.

"That was also the first time you —" he continued, but I placed a finger over his lips and nodded. He pulled my hand away from his face and kissed the inside of my wrist. "I did not know, Torch. I would never have let you, or have...," he trailed off.

Maybe that was true. I didn't think he knew if it was. "I forgive you. It's not like you could have known. I can think of people I wouldn't have wanted to experience a few firsts with," I said nibbling my lip.

Slate slid his fingers into my hair pulling it over my shoulder. My heart drummed thunderously in my chest. He had so many expressions. Who knew such a hard face could contort in so many ways? He was showing me a new one, respect, awe, frustration, and hope. What was the word to describe that?

My eyes flitted between his as I contemplated my next words making sure I knew I meant them beyond a shadow of a doubt. I turned and tugged his hand as we started walking again.

"I wouldn't have wanted it to be with anyone else," my words were barely audible, but Slate heard them.

I started panicking again; I had to keep some walls up with Slate or I'd drown. Slate wasn't a life raft; he was the Kraken pulling me into watery depths from which I would never return.

"If I had known what happened before I would not have been so forward those first weeks," he smiled ruefully, "I understand much better why you were so fearful of me."

"Who says I'm not still afraid of you?" I pondered aloud and my eyes widened when realized I'd said it out loud.

I was on his floor. We'd walked right past mine.

There he was, the savage predator stalking his prey, and it caught her out in the open. Guards down, emotions high, and around the corner from his lair.

Slate moved so fast I only had time to gasp as he slammed into me taking my mouth with his. His hands picked me up as if I was weightless and I wrapped my legs around his waist as my tongue danced with his.

We were in his room. We'd knocked over every other vase in the hall and crashed into each wall multiple times, but we made it in.

I slid my hands over his shoulders as he watched while we stood next to his big black leather bed. My fingers gripped the hem of his shirt, and he lifted his arms, so I had to step up onto the bed to pull it over his head revealing the countless bronze muscles beneath. I ran my fingers through his hair to smooth it back down and fell to my knees sitting back on my heels to admire one of the most perfect bodies ever created. I thanked the Gods for blessing the earth with such spectacular forms.

He stepped closer so his legs were up against the bed, and I craned back my head to look at him.

"I have no idea what I'm doing here right now."

"Why did you follow me here, Torch?" he asked, looking down at me.

I blushed squeezing my eyes shut.

"I came in here because…"

"Tell me," he asked, standing before me.

"I'm thinking." I copped out, and he laughed.

I imagined if I scanned a dictionary, a picture of Slate with a rare cheek creasing, white straight teeth flashing, full lips stretched in a smile displayed prominently next to *temptation*. He wasn't smiling now though. He was gazing at me, thinking impossible thoughts through dreamy silver eyes.

He kicked off his boots, so he only wore his black pants from earlier and prowled up the bed, countless hard bronze muscles flexing like a sleek beast. He clamped his powerful hands on my booted ankles making my back hit the bed. I gasped when I felt the cool satin sheets against my backside; I was wearing a pink and ivory thong I'd chosen especially for tonight.

Slate made a noise low and deep in his throat that was in no part human, making my body thrum and want to purr to him. It made my eyes widen, my mind may have been confused, but my body was making things perfectly clear. I tried to pull my legs up, but Slate held them firmly as he lowered his mouth. His eyes on mine, he placed his first kiss to the side of my knee, slow and openmouthed as he bent my leg up, the trail his tongue along the inside of my knee next, with my booted foot in the air. He kissed languorously up my thighs to skim over my apex and come down my other thigh. Wet kisses that sizzled my skin as he worked pulling my legs over his broad muscled shoulders and my breaths came in short pants.

Slate was the master of his domain, his domain being a woman's body, my body. I wriggled unable to stop myself, but he kept his hands on me at all times, so I didn't squirm away. My soft moans drove him ever onward until his hot breath hovered between my thighs, puffing at the slip of lace.

Oh, my Gods. It was really happening. I was finally giving in after a year of fighting him. I knew going in that I wouldn't be the same coming out.

That was how I felt with Brass. It changed me. *He* had changed me.

"Tell me to stop, Torch and I will, but once I start, I will not. No matter how much you beg," the deep timbre of his voice nearly vibrated the soft, sensitive spot between my legs and my hips tilted of their own volition up to his mouth.

He chuckled darkly, and I felt a wicked smile twist my lips until his full mouth brushed against me. I jumped. I balled my hands into fists at my sides unable to keep them open. I knew I shouldn't be doing it, that I should run for the hills and never look back, but the man was too much man. Certainly too much man for me and I enjoyed feeling small and feminine under his big capable body.

I knew Slate liked poetry, so I favored him with one of my own favorites.

"*Out of your whole life give but a moment! All your life that has gone before,*

All to come after it, — so you ignore

So, you make perfect the present, — condense,

In a rapture of rage, for perfection's endowment, Thought and feeling and soul and sense — Merged in a moment which gives me at last

You around me for once, you beneath me, above me — Me — sure that despite of time future, time past,

This tick of our lifetime's one moment you love me! How long such suspension may linger? Ah, Sweet—The moment eternal—just that and no more—When ecstasy's utmost we clutch at the core

While cheeks burn, arms open, eyes shut and lips meet!"

His eyes glittered and my voice came out much throatier than I intended.

"Don't stop."

My cheeks heated. I could play a little hard to get. My goodness. A token objection wouldn't have hurt. I shook my head at my nagging inner voice whom I'd listened to for too long.

I wanted Slate; I had since I'd seen his dark, dangerous form half hidden in the shadows moments after I'd met Ash. If I'd been a more experienced woman, I would have read what Slate's look meant then and it would have been me with Slate in the powder room and not Lera. Me in the arboretum at the Tio palace, me at the induction ceremony, never anyone else.

Slate's teeth grazed my hip as he caught the thin material of the lace, and he pulled slowly down as I raised my hips. He took his sweet time running his tongue and teeth down my legs gently tugging my thong along until I growled in frustration.

"Fiddlesticks! Just take it off!"

I was aroused to the point of hostility. My skin ached to be touched, and none too gently, the ache between my legs was almost painful. I'd never felt the like, and it was making me lose my sanity.

Passion. I had oodles of it.

Slate laughed loud and rich only adding to the tight pull in the pit of my belly. Was he trying to torture me? I didn't see what was so funny. Why were the men I tried to bed always laughing at me?

"So eager, Torch," he purred as he slid my panties over my boots with his hands.

FINALLY!

Slate bent my legs over his shoulders as he laid on his stomach, the curve of his tight hard backside was all I could see when he ducked his head between my legs. His midnight hair spilled over my thigh and my head bent into the mattress. I'd fantasized about his black mane between my legs and it was happening. I couldn't watch or it'd be over before it started. I cried out when his tongue flicked against me sending a pulse deep inside me, squeezing and flexing compulsively and completely out of my control.

"Oh, Gods!" I arched my back.

He'd barely touched me with that velvety tongue, and I was coming apart. "Not yet, Torch," he whispered against my skin only intensifying the waves of pleasure crashing around me.

His tongue swirled against me, and my hands flew to his head, fingers twining in his hair driving my hips hard against his mouth. I shouldn't be allowed access to my limbs when being intimate, I was much too forceful. Someone could get hurt.

Slate growled and that deep timbre vibrated against my skin as his tongue dipped into me. It pulled me taut, and my breath hitched as my insides clenched.

My fingers curled in Slate's hair as I cried out, my back bowing on the black bed. Slate's mouth had stopped moving, and he kissed my sex before lifting his head once my fingers had loosened, slack in his hair. He lifted himself to his hands and knees between my legs.

His mouth glistened with parted lips, his midnight hair was wild around his gorgeous face, but his eyes. By the Mother! Those eyes. Silver and fierce, full of something primitive and carnal that made me whimper. He dripped an erotic intensity I couldn't hope to meet on even footing — but I'd try.

Before he wiped his mouth, I lunged up at him pulling his mouth to mine licking his lips, tasting myself on them, slick and sweet as I devoured him whole. I'd wanted to kiss Slate like this, of my own free will, for ages and *fiddlestick*, did it feel good. Too good.

Slate's hips lowered to mine, and he pulled my thighs up again, his hand cupped my breast roughly as he ran his thumb over my hard pearl that pushed through the fabric of my bra and the sweater dress. He found the clasp in the front and my breasts were free. He pulled the low scoop neck even lower as he moved against me. My hands roamed freely over his hard back relishing in the movements he made as he ground against me with delicious friction.

Slate ran open-mouthed kisses along my throat to the swell of my breasts until he found my nipples, sucking and nipping until they were full and hard against his tongue. Soft moans pulled from my throat in bursts, my body was begging to be taken. The rub of the seam of his pants and the hard ridge of him through them was enough to drive a girl mad. I demanded satisfaction.

I had shoved my dress up to my waist, and down around my elbows. Slate tore himself away from my breasts as I pulled on his hair to bring him back to my mouth. He growled ferociously as he stretched his body on top of mine and met my lips again.

"I need you, Scarlett," he breathed harshly against my open mouth.

"I want you, Slate," I responded and opened my eyes enough to see the flash of teeth in his smile before I smiled myself.

"I would do a great deal for that smile," he purred in that growly way of his.

I said two words I never thought I'd say to a man, but Slate's answering growl of laughter made it worth it.

"Torch, you do turn into an animal," he purred while he laughed.

I called, flipping him onto his back and climbed on top of him. *Yes, that was better.* I straddled his hips with my bare bottom and bent my head down to take his mouth possessively, if I could claim a man with my body, I would have done just that. I would have made it so any woman who came close enough to smell his scent would find mine buried deep within his skin, a scent he'd never be able to wash clean — bone deep.

He was mine, he wanted to only be mine. I could give myself to him and he would give himself to me in balance.

Slate's hands cupped my bottom as I caressed his tongue with my own, sucking and nipping on his lower lip. I pulled back his hair, so he looked into my eyes, and I slid my hand between my legs to grip him over his pants.

"Mine," I breathed out roughly, not having the slightest idea where it come from.

I had gone feral. A mindless creature interested in only possessing the man under her, if he'd tried to deny me, I might have attacked him.

Slate's eyes flashed as he looked up at me through thick black lashes. He was not a man who had been dominated — ever. The struggle in his eyes was clear and then the slow curl of his lips as he rocked his hips against my hand. I had my answer. I lowered my mouth to his in a slow kiss, savoring his heady scent mingled with my own before letting go of his hair and kissing down his throat.

I licked his Adam's apple and one of my many fantasies had come true. I tasted every ridge, every silken curve of sculpted muscle on his rippling chest and stomach. A girl could get used to this; therein laid the danger of a man like Slate. One night, yes. More than that? Absolutely not... but he wanted to be mine.

Now, I didn't care as my tongue swirled around one perfect dark pink nipple watching the stomach muscles below flex with his shallow breaths as I moved ever south and down the happy trail of soft black hair to the waistband of his pants. I didn't fumble as I unbuttoned them and pushed down his black underwear to pull the hard length of him out.

I made a noise in my throat that rose at the end as I peered up at Slate whose face looked both strained and relaxed at the same time. My fist was unable to meet my fingers when I gripped him and he inhaled sharply before I pulled him into my mouth. The man was a treasure trove of delectable tastes and velvety feels.

"Scarlett," he whispered fiercely as I sheathed my teeth to take him fully, sucking and stroking with my tongue.

I wanted him to take his pleasure with my mouth; I wanted to give it to him. I'd never done it, not even with Brass, and I wanted it to be with Slate. His hands tangled in my hair as he rocked his hips into my mouth with soft pants as he growled and stiffened. He filled the back of my throat in warm spurts until his hands loosened from my hair to run through it to the ends in a stroke. I held my mouth there for another moment before drawing back to sit on my booted heels.

I ran my fingertips along the corded 'V' at his hips careful not to touch what was surely sensitive, but still enjoyed the feel of him. My eyes lifted to his face, and I smirked. He was nowhere near being finished and the dark promises in his eyes did something delicious to me. I lifted to my knees and grabbed the hem of my dress and pulled it over my head in a slow seductive show for the man that was mine.

He gave an animalistic growl as I held it out in my hand and let the dress fall to the floor. He sat up to grip me just under my breasts before pulling one pink nipple into his mouth.

"I knew this woman was inside you," he whispered against my soft skin, "You have perfect, succulent breasts, Scarlett." He palmed them both as I arched my back letting my head lull lazily.

I was feeling incredibly sexy, and he only fueled the fire. Sexy? Me? He spoke like I was exquisite and made me feel like I was special.

"And your ass," his hands slid over my ticklish ribs to cup my bottom again, "Gods, I have wanted to bury myself in these soft supple curves from the moment I saw you." He ran his teeth over the sensitive underside of my breast.

Well, what does a girl say to something like that?

"What are you waiting for?" I purred, looking down at him and his eyes snapped up to mine as a wicked grin spread across that full, lush mouth.

I laid down on my belly with my arms folded under my head as I watched him shift to his knees, still hard, and hanging out of those black pants. Slate's eyes raked down the length of me as I bent my legs and crossed them at the ankle. He slid off the bed and I watched him push his pants and black boxer briefs off with a quick flick of his wrists.

He was back on the bed, his hand cupping my backside yet again, his other hand pushed my hair over my shoulder, and he planted a searing kiss at the nape of my neck.

Abruptly, he made it a bite that made me suck in air hard and I felt him straddle my thighs as he ran his tongue down my spine giving me shivers. When he came to the curve of my backside, he palmed my sex roughly and licked with a flick of his slick tongue, kissing it before continuing down to nip at my soft curves.

I moaned as he pushed my thighs apart, and the subsequent anticipation built anew. His tongue surprised me with a jolt between my legs and he rested a soothing hand against my curves as his fingers slid inside me, my body already pulsing around them. Slate moaned as I clenched, inhaling sharply, and heard him groan as he pulled it out.

"Mouthwatering, Scarlett," he purred as I heard him pop a finger audibly from his mouth and felt him shifting behind me.

He leaned forward and brushed against me. Slate raised my hips and slid a pillow beneath me, making me lift to my elbows as I trembled. I felt his tip dip inside as he thrust again, and I gasped as lust shot through my body. He ran it along me teasing, torturing me until I arched my back and bent to shift on my knees. He chuckled deeply sending my stomach into convulsions. His laugh did spectacular things to me.

Slate cursed in Wemic as he pushed deeper into me, "By the Mother, Torch."

I didn't trust my voice, so I tried to unclench all my contracting muscles which was impossible in my current state. Slate was mind-numbingly skilled at reducing me to urges and sensations. He breathed roughly as he fed himself into me inch by spine tingling inch until he filled me to the hilt.

I felt as his hard muscled body unfurl over me, and he ran his hands along my ribs to my arms pulling them over my head as he leaned on his elbows to either side of me. He grabbed my wrists in one hand as he slid his other to my face and turned it to his mouth. He took his time, thoroughly kissing me, claiming my mouth as his tongue slid against mine, his hair fell around his face like a dark halo. Then, he rocked his hips.

My wildest imaginings were nothing like the real thing. If I thought my vocabulary dwindled down to four-letter words before, now I was down to uttering monosyllables.

Slate filled me to the brim with himself, with a boatload of unwelcome feels, and the man could have asked me for the sun and the stars, and I would have given him all he wanted. I knew why women came back to him even though he promised them nothing. Nothing, but a mind-blowing experience — the like in which they'd never know ever after with someone less.

I turned my mouth away from his to gulp air. My head was swimming, and his slow torturous movements were permanently damaging the stability of my mind if I didn't get release soon. I bucked against him, and he slowed me down with a palm slid under my hips. I couldn't move unless he allowed me to, and he wasn't letting me.

"Easy, Torch. Let me feel you," he purred, and I moaned.

Did the man have to be sexy all the fiddlesticking time?

If his mission was to get my body to not clench in response to his animalistic growls, then he failed. I felt the strongest pull in my loins like a super-sized magnet drawing powdered steel spread through my body and like a light switch; the magnet was on, and everything pulled inward. My muscles clenched around Slate.

"Ahh!" I cried as my skin tingled alive with sensations, aftershocks rocked my system, and he moved even faster inside me.

He shoved apart my legs with a knee and pulled my hips up, lifting himself onto his knees as his hand gripped my hip, the other slid around me to rub above the bud between my legs. It was a different pace entirely, and instead of spluttering out as I'd expected, the pulsing inside me kept tightening deliciously as he moved.

"I need to fuck you. Hard and fast, let me know if it is too much," he growled, and I made an unintelligible noise of ascent.

When his hand left my hip and he wrapped my hair around his fist, waves of pleasure crashed over me again. He made good on his promise, and I arched my back as he slammed audibly against me. I made noises I didn't know my throat could make and was surprised to hear them pull forth from my mouth. His fingers moved faster against me until I stiffened.

"Come for me, Torch. Let me hear your torch song," he growled, and he plunged deep into me as he shuddered with a deep rumbling moan.

My muscles contracted around him in hard clenches cradling him snugly inside me and I muffled a cry as my toes curled. He used an arm to sweep my hands out from under me and gently laid me on my stomach before turning me on my side with him still inside me. My eyes shut, and my muscles ached while I tried to catch my breath. Slate kissed along my shoulder and my neck and the sensitive spot behind my ear.

"I have decided how I want to die," he said after a moment.

I laughed. My insides moved against him, and he thrust his hips deeper, "Okay?"

"After coming inside you, just like this, Torch," he purred, and his hand snaked around to cup my heavy breast.

"If that was supposed to be romantic, I think you failed. Having you die after we have sex sounds traumatizing," I told him, and I knew my wits scattered.

Was I having a conversation with Slate — who was inside me—after we had sex— and he was playing with my nipple — Gods.

"How do you feel?" he asked, propping himself up on an elbow to look down at me.

I wasn't ready to look at him though, oddly enough, I was embarrassed. It was Slate we were talking about. The man whose advances I'd been dodging for a year.

"Good," I told him.

Honestly, how could he expect me to have a conversation with him still inside me?

He must have read my mind and called, a hand towel flew from outside the bedroom, and he shifted gently placing the towel between my legs. I blushed and I could see that it colored me down to my chest.

"Come now, Torch. Do not be shy. We have a long night ahead of us, and I have you at least until the morning, or until you pass out. Whichever comes first," he purred as he turned me onto my back and tilted my face to kiss him.

All night? Until I passed out? Somewhere my debauched inner voice squealed in delight, while my common sense shook her head reprovingly and pointed to my ring finger.

Slate rolled over me bearing his weight on his arms and took off my emerald ring and slid it in my engagement ring's place. My cheeks heated again; that man was dangerous.

"Never take it off," he said with a rare cheek creasing smile and I stared at the white straight teeth I so seldom saw, "It is as it should be."

I just had sex with this... being. I felt like someone should pinch me, even just lying there his bronze muscles were prominently chiseled.

"Stop thinking, Torch. Time for a shower," he pushed off the bed and landed on his feet next to the bed.

Fighting the urge to cover myself up, I pushed up on my elbows. "But what about Gypsum?" I protested.

Slate was magnificently naked and pulled off my first boot, then my sock, and then repeated the procedure on my other foot, "This is not a debate. We are taking a shower. I thought I was going to bend you over at headquarters. I plan to, but in my shower. Up. Now."

I bit my lip. After my meltdown, he turned away from me and

banned me from showering at headquarters, I'd wondered why. I felt a surge of triumph that I could do that to him.

I moved too slowly for Slate's taste, and he grabbed my ankles until he pulled me off the bed then tossed me over his shoulder and smacked my bottom with a loud whack.

Slate delighted in washing me, I stood there as he sudsed up his hands and ran them languorously over my body. After I was thoroughly washed, courtesy of a meticulous Slate, I'd wrapped my long legs around his waist, and he plunged into me with my back against the wall with the water spilling over us. Wet, flexing, bronze muscle against my body.

Oh. My. Gods.

The man was insatiable, and I was his willing pupil. He made good on his promise to bend me over in his sprawling shower much to my delight.

He dried my hair and wrapped me in a big fluffy black towel after he ran creamy lotion over every inch of my skin, only then did he lead me back to his bed.

We climbed back into bed, and he refused to lend me a shirt forcing me to lay propped up on a mountain of black pillows with him between my legs. He sat with his legs undermine with the sheet piled around our bottoms. Every time I pulled it up to my chest, he tugged it hard and arched a black eyebrow at me, daring me to try again. Which I did when I thought he wasn't looking, but he always was.

He braided in my jade and pearl fetishes and, after he'd had a staff member passing in the hall bring up a midnight snack, I'd straddled his back and braided back in his silver Celtic etched beads and the white fetishes — he told me were ivory. He had four in his hair about the size of copper skolls; a sun, a solar cross, a starburst, and a jumis which reminded me of two hockey sticks crossing one another.

He'd pulled an ivory carving out of his end table and called it into his palm before showing me a starburst identical to his, but smaller. It was the Tio sigil, and he threaded it through the end of my braid adding it to the jade canine and pearl.

"Thanks," I said running my thumb along it wondering if he'd planned on giving it to me whenever he finally got me into his bed. The thought made me pull the black satin sheet up and he tugged it back down.

"I have seen you with your clothes on every day. Give me something to bank in my memory of our first night together. I am a man dying of thirst on a desert island, would you deny me water?"

First?

I scoffed, "With all the bodies thrown in your path to quench your thirst on?" I pulled another red grape off the plate and popped it into my mouth. I was thankful for it since he didn't seem to want to let me get some sleep.

Slate narrowed his grey eyes at me as he sipped from a goblet of wine. I leaned back on the feather pillows feeling like a goddess out an epic poem, eating grapes naked across from a gloriously equally naked man.

"Bodies that are not yours will never sate my thirst," he rumbled as he leaned back on an elbow. Powerful legs peeked out from under the folds of sheets, his black hair was tossed over the side of his head, "I understand why Brass took you to his bed a second time even though I threatened his life. He could not live with himself if he turned you down. I am regretting my anger towards him."

"You have to say that if you expect to spread my thighs again," I teased, giving him a slow seductive smile and ignored his Brass comment completely.

I couldn't figure out where he fit into in the scenario playing out.

He chuckled, and I watched his muscles move in his abs. Slate overloaded my senses, that was a fact.

"No, I should not say such things," he said so low I wasn't sure if I heard him right, "But things have changed. You are mine."

Pain lanced through me. A glimmer of a dark-haired woman with chin length hair falling shot through my mind and I felt stretched taut until it snapped, and the pain was gone. I gripped my inguz tattoo.

"Did a Shadow Breaker just..."

"Die? Yes," his eyes hardened, and I thought he would leave, but he stayed.

He watched me eat another grape, and I was glad he had trained me so hard in previous months and made a mental note to get Fox a gift basket.

"How are you feeling, Torch?" he asked for the umpteenth time, and I rolled my eyes, but was glad for the subject change.

"Good, I was good two hours ago, good an hour ago, good a half hour ago, and I'm good now. Honestly, stop worrying. I'm smiling, see.," I beamed him a megawatt smile and his lips curled.

"I would do a great deal for that smile," Slate purred, and I shifted under his intense predatory gaze.

The entire night had been surreal, and it wasn't over yet. "Yeah? Like what?" I asked, waggling my brows.

Slate rewarded me with a deep chuckle and a heart-stopping smile. He downed the rest of his wine and called, floated his crystal goblet back to the nightstand as his hands disappeared under the blankets. His hand latched around my ankle, and he yanked up my foot. I pulled my lips between my teeth as I tried to wriggle free.

"Easy, Torch. You are going to hurt yourself," he said with a lip curling smile as he lifted my foot to his mouth.

"Ah! Slate!" I squealed when he grazed the pad of my big toe with his teeth and ran his tongue along it.

"I will never tire of hearing you scream my name. Let us see how many times you can do it in a single night," his eyes glinted silver as his full lips puckered to kiss my instep and his tongue slithered out sending me writhing on the bed.

The bowl of grapes fell off the bed as I tried to kick Slate with my other foot while laughing hysterically as he tickled me, "Oh Gods! Stop, Slate! I'm ticklish!"

He laughed but didn't let go, "I have eyes."

I pulled the pillow out from behind my head and whacked him in the face with it. "I can see that since I have eyes of my own," I giggled helplessly under his onslaught.

I widened my eyes when his hand slowly reached up for the pillow on his face, his eyes were glittering. "You are going to pay for that," he growled and flipped onto his knees.

I squealed as he whacked me with it, my hands outstretched to rip it from his hands. I grabbed another pillow from behind me and beat him back, belly laughs bubbled up. Slate was smiling, the creases in his cheeks deepened while he smiled broadly laughing — rich and throaty. The pillow I held tore and feathers flew; they floated down around us. I grabbed for his wrists as he knelt above me the pillow still in hand and it flung free landing on the floor.

Slate knelt between my bent legs his wrists clasped in my hands as I laid back on the bed my giggling tapering off as my chest heaved from laughing so hard. His sculpted chest rose and fell heavily as feathers fell all around us; they were in his hair.

Oh.

His eyes were hooded, and glittering and I knew he mirrored my expression. Our lips parted, cheeks flushed, our eyes covetous. Slate looked so young and tremendously happy; he looked like a completely different person.

I couldn't tear my eyes from him. He didn't seem to mind. "You are breathtaking," he whispered.

It was the same thing Brass had said to me.

Brass.

I blew feathers from around my face and laughed again. My ribs hurt from laughing so hard.

"I'm sorry for ripping your pillow and making such a mess."

My eyes met his again and if I wasn't already sitting down, I would have stumbled. They nearly glowed silver against his bronze skin, and I could see how aroused he'd grown during our play. Just the sight of him getting excited did the same to me. I loosened my grip on his wrists, not that it was doing much anyway, and he launched himself at me.

Kissing me passionately, his hands pulled me into his lap, and he lifted my hips angling himself to plunge deeply. I moaned wrapping my arms around his neck as I returned his fervent kisses. My breasts smashed against him as he held me tight, our bodies moving together.

The position was so intimate I tried looking away only to have Slate grab my chin and force me to meet all that lurked behind those silver eyes. Primitive yet brilliant, beautiful yet savage, aggressive yet tender. The man was a paradox. He laid me on my back and rose above me running his calloused palms over my skin.

"Your skin is so soft. Gods, Scarlett, I want this," he said breathlessly as he covered my body with his, "I will never get enough of you."

I knit my brow as he ran his thumb over my lips. "There's a lot to consider.. You haven't even been with one woman for an extended amount of time."

Slate lowered himself to me, not shifting outside of me for an instant. He kissed my lips softly as he rocked into me.

"You could handle me, Torch," Slate said as he kissed me again.

I scoffed.

"You only want me for my body?" he asked, thrusting deep inside me.

My lips curled up at him, "I thoroughly enjoy everything about your body, but I won't lie, I think you're witty, and secretly brilliant."

"It is a secret? Well, you discovered my hidden genius, so I suppose the secret is out," Slate said, and he rocked his hips a little quicker. "Tell me more, Torch," he said gruffly, and I fancied I could feel my body's fluids flow south.

"You're funny. You make me laugh," I kissed him threading my hands into his hair sprinkled with feather bits. "Is your ego inflated enough now?" I teased and Slate chuckled and rolled over, bringing me with him so I straddled his lap.

His hands moved from my hips up my ribs to my breasts which he cupped and kneaded with his hands. "I was not saying things I thought you wished to hear. I meant them," he said, and I watched his neck strain with cords of muscle as I moved with him inside me, "Give me your mouth. I will not last long watching you."

I smiled and brought my mouth down to his, my hair fell like a shimmering curtain shielding our little bubble. My palms on his chest rocking myself faster and harder against him. I took his hand and sucked his finger into my mouth.

Slate let out a Wemic curse and gripped my hips tight. He slammed into me, thrusting deep and hard. My fingers curled and my nails bit into the hard flesh of his pecs and I cried out. Slate's hips fell back to the bed, and he moved deep in me.

"Scarlett," he whispered harshly as he spilled into me.

I fell against his chest feeling spent and sated, relishing in the feel of my pulses that gripped him inside me. He stroked my hair and cupped my face and I smiled lazily at him. I didn't think I could climax again, but I knew Slate would want to find that out for himself. I felt alive and happy.

Doubts tore through me in an instant. Had Slate painstakingly tortured my sanity away as I'd feared?

He pushed on my lower lip and a tinge of blood activated my bond by the way he sucked in a deep breath. Gods, what could he feel in me?

"Scarlett. Wear this ring every day. I meant what I said. Stay with me. Do not —" a knock at the door came and my heart pounded, "GO AWAY!" Slate roared.

It was in the wee hours of the morning, two or three at least. Who would come to his room at this hour? Perhaps the staff bringing more wine.

I heard the click of the knob turning and scrambled off Slate pulling the sheet with me, and without fail, I fell off the bed falling to the floor with a thump and did the only logical thing I could think of.

I crawled under the bed.

Slate was way too angry. No, angry was putting it mildly. Irrationally enraged. Wrathful. I saw his feet hit the floor, and he pulled on his pants. He stormed from the bedroom section and into the sitting room and I wriggled my way deeper under the bed pulling my boots, dress, panties, and bra from the floor and wriggled back under when I heard a woman's voice.

"I would not have come unless it was an emergency."

No.

She could wait until tomorrow and then things would have to change.

"What?" Slate barked peevishly and I could feel her emotions, she was taken aback.

Slate must not speak to her that way; a vicious smile curved my lips.

Cordillera walked deeper into the room despite Slate trying to block her with his body. Her black heels came into sight at the foot of his bed.

"Lera, you know I do not want you in my bedroom. Do not make me ask you to leave."

He was practically growling at her, and my inner voice had shut up tight. "I thought you did not allow any women in your room," she said carefully and sauntered from the bedroom.

I heard the closet door open and then saw her cross the room to the bathroom. Sugarfoot! She was looking for me!

"I do not allow lovers in my home. Ever. Hence, my confusion as to why you think it would be okay to come here now."

I winced. She was his lover; I didn't want to be reminded.

"What happened here? I see two goblets and scratches down your chest. Fresh ones, still bleeding," Lera cooed.

"Get to it Lera, this is not a social visit," he spat.

Her feet disappeared as she sat on his bed, feathers fell from the blankets to float where his bare feet stood before the bed, too close for my comfort to where she just sat. Something tightened in my chest that felt an awful lot like heartache.

"You know you will only break the myopic's heart. She cannot possibly fulfill all your needs as inexperienced as she is. Keep your pet if you must, just do not complain to me when you are done with your little toy, and she follows you around as the other one does. I suppose if you grow tired though, Brass has an affection for her. I wonder what he will make of you sullying his devoted flower."

"Are you jealous, Lera?" Slate purred. "*Women sit, or move to and fro —some old, some young; The young are beautiful—but the old are more beautiful than the young.*"

My breath caught. He quoted her Walt Whitman too. I bit hard on my wobbly lower lip until I tasted blood.

"Are you still dressed from your challenge?" she teased playfully, and I seethed, "Come. Take them off, my pet. Freshen up, we need to talk."

I slowly let out a breath through my mouth getting madder by the minute. Why was I hiding under the bed and she lazing about on top of it? When his pants hit the floor, I was going to crawl out from under the bed nude. I squeezed my eyes shut. I must have imagined it.

No. No way. I opened my eyes, and his feet were gone, and his pants were there.

I slithered around under the bed like a snake, not caring that my bare skin felt like it was being torn as it stuck to the floor. I heard murmuring and I couldn't tell where it was coming from, but what I could feel was her lust.

Their feet came back into the room, and I saw Slate's hand grab his knife belts from the floor.

"Let us go now then."

He didn't sound half as irritated with her as he had been. What did they do while they were in the closet? Did he kiss her? Did she press her petite body, more mature and daintier than mine, against him?

I heard his door shut and shimmied out from under the bed still clutching my clothes in my hands. I slumped against the floor with my back to his bed; we covered the floor in feathers and grapes. Luckily, the glass bowl hadn't broken. I sat there debating, with feathers in my hair and stuck to various parts of my body, whether to clean it.

Indigo told me to only plan on one night. To not spend the rest of my life wondering what if and instead say, "I tried, but we wanted different things." To have gotten a little taste of what it would be like if he were mine. Well, I'd gotten it. It felt exactly as I'd expected. I felt dirty and disgusted with myself. The second his lover appeared he ran off with her leaving me aching, cold and feeling stupid on the grandest possible level.

Nope, not cleaning it.

I sighed and chalked it up to a life experience I cared not to repeat but let it go. Slate couldn't help to do what was his nature, and I had been the one to step out of character letting myself get sucked into his vortex of savage sexuality and cheated. I was a cheater.

Served me right.

"Scar?"

CHAPTER
TWENTY-FOUR
GYPSUM

She was closing the door to Slate's room when I caught her. She turned and gave a shrug. Bits of white feather clung to her tangled hair. Beard burn covered her from jaw to the neckline of her sweater dress. I hid my sympathetic look before she could catch it. Whatever she thought was going to happen by spending the night with Slate obviously didn't end how she'd imagined.

"What's up, chief? Late-night snack?" she asked, pointing to his slice of chocolate cake.

I gave her my dimpled smile mischievously, "It's a big slice. I could use some help chowing it down."

It was three thirty in the morning. A fact we were both ignoring before we had to answer unwanted questions. Like, where we were both were and who was with us. Diamond had begged me to come over. She'd start Valla U with Sterling in the coming year, and they were getting married at the end of next year. She was feeling trapped. There was nothing I could do but give her as much as myself that would placate her. She wanted all of me.

"Did you say cake?" she said playfully as she crossed the hall with a grateful smile.

She followed me in and closed the door behind me. I had the room below Indigo's with the same layout in brown tufted leathers styled as Slate's room.

My hair fell over my shoulder when I placed the cake on my coffee table. It was getting very long and I'd started braiding it and threading copper beads on it like Slate's because I thought it looked cool. Imitation was the sincerest form of flattery after all.

I looked up at her furrowing my straight thick brows and flashing her that dimpled smile she loved so much which reminded her that I was her quasi-little brother.

She sighed as she plopped down on the couch next to me and picked up the fork before taking a big bite of triple fudge cake.

I stood up and crossed to my closet and grabbed a tank top and sweats before tossing them at her. "It'll be hard to crash in that... dress. It's more of a shirt," I teased.

Scar had always been gorgeous and totally oblivious to it. Everyone at our high school had thought she only dated college guys until rumors of her and Chris at prom got around. They forgot she was only sixteen when she was a senior. Wren had pushed her so hard back then. Her reserved quiet wasn't because she thought she was better than the other students. It was because she had no socialization skills and stuck with Tawny who had the same upbringing as she had. They dubbed them untouchable and snooty before they gave them a chance.

She bit her lip from either crying or smiling. I didn't know which. I knew with one look she was down in the dumps, and I didn't want her to go back to her room to cry.

"Thanks, chief," she said trying not to strangle the words and went into the bathroom.

She'd just been in the bathroom an hour ago with Slate. Slate never brought back women. Ever. I knew it had to be Scarlett.

I went into the closet and changed. We similarly dressed as I plopped down next to her and took a bite of cake.

"Gyps, why are all men crazy?" she asked, trying not to let her last bite of cake fall out of her mouth.

I scoffed, "Men? You're crazy. Maybe you attract crazies."

She gave me a lopsided smile, "You might be on to something there."

After I brushed my teeth, I crawled over Scar and stole the blankets. "Just don't touch me with your cold feet," I joked.

She laughed, "I don't even want to know how you know about women and cold feet."

"Diamond has cold feet in more ways than one." I said, turning towards her, and tucked my hair under my head.

"Gypsum, I don't have to tell you you're playing with fire, do I? If someone found out it'd ruin your reputation. You're going to be the patriarch of the Sumar line, the ruler of Thrimilci. You know you need a good partner in life for that. Diamond is Sterling's partner," her breath exhaled gustily as she offered him an apologetic smile.

It was my turn to sigh, "Don't marry Ash."

She chuckled, and it wasn't a pleasant sound, "You too? He's smart, wealthy, charming, ambitious, and he cares about me. Wait, did I mention that he's drop dead gorgeous?" She paused, "I don't know if he'll still want to after tonight." She snapped her mouth shut and pulled a hair that stuck to her lips.

I rolled my eyes dismissing her admission, "He's also full of himself, and you don't love him. I haven't been awake all night for my health."

"Love will come with time. We respect one another — care about each other. He'll be a good husband after the wedding," she blushed and ignored my comment.

"So, you say, but I've seen the way you and Slate look each other. When you look at Ash that way, then marry him. Then there's Brass. I like Brass. You have options."

She knit her brows. "Gyps, that's lust not love. Slate doesn't love me. Slate isn't built that way. He doesn't love, he possesses. Brass," she sighed his name. She was so in love with that guy, "Maybe if we were different people, I could have had a life with Brass."

I widened my dark eyes, "Clearly the wrong time to talk to you about this. I will say this though. You're wrong. Slate loves like a man. Sure, he struggles with it, but I've seen him with other women, and I've seen him with you."

After a protracted silence, she grew frustrated, "And?"

I smiled, and my dimples poked, "And he acts like you hang the moon."

She scoffed, "Oh, chief. He must be looking his own reflection in my eyes when you see that expression."

"Whatever you say crazy attracter," I smirked before I turned around and I felt her do the same.

A squirrel had overheard Quick and Brass discussing a brawl that broke out and a scandalous agreement between Slate and Brass was struck. Brass wouldn't be as upset as she thought. I knew exactly what was going on. Part of the plan anyway, if the squirrel was to be believed.

Gods, I lived a weird life.

CHAPTER
TWENTY-FIVE

I was still reeling from my night with Slate and had no desire to be anywhere near him. I didn't want to be on the same island — the same planet. Maybe I could call enough air to jet myself into space and live on the moon. I'd save that for Plan B. For now, I would look for a gift for Amethyst.

The bond tattoo had made me feel betrayed. Me finally giving into him and him running off with Lera was worse. So, so much worse. A hot mix of devastation and low self-worth with a garnish of guilt. It massively sucked.

I'd readied and ventured out into the town's heart and wandered the white shimmering stone roads until the shops opened. I didn't have a specific thing in mind, just a bit of window shopping.

I entered the Armored Armoire and greeted by a luscious smile courtesy of Solder, "Hey, gorgeous!"

A girl could get used to being greeted like that, "How's it going, Solder?"

He gave me a burly hug and smiled at me again. "I hope I did not cause too much of a fuss the other night. I could not resist antagonizing Brass a bit," he admitted, and we walked through the aisles of armor together.

I ran my fingers on random items, not really paying attention. "I noticed. What's that about? Brass doesn't rile easily, but you seem to irritate him with ease," I shot him a playful smile, and he laughed.

The store smelled like leather and cool metal, most places in Tidings did because of all the weapons and armor. "Brass and I... dated a girl at the same time," he flashed me a wicked grin, and I shook my head.

"Naughty. No wonder he despises you. How long ago was this?" I asked curious to hear more about Brass's love life.

Solder thought about it, "About two years ago."

I nodded, and we walked over to curio cabinets where little carvings were lit and I peered inside. Little carved fetishes in ivory, jade, ebony, and just about any material you could fathom displayed. My eyes held covetously on a turquoise piece that must've been carved by magic, the details were so intricate. It was the tree of life, the sigil of the Var.

Solder leaned next to the cabinet with his lush lips parted in a knowing smile. "That is right, you are a Var as well. That is a lot of heritage in one little woman," he said the light from the cabinet making his cobalt eyes glitter.

I ran my teeth along my lower lip, "It's gorgeous."

"Like you."

Solder shifted and pressed his finger to the glass, and I heard something click as it unlocked, and he opened the glass door and lifted the little copper skoll sized carving and held it in front of me.

My fingers itched to touch it, and he chuckled. He placed a hand on the small of my back and led me to a mirror sitting on top of a glass case. He stood behind me taking my braid of fetishes in his fingers and carefully braided the turquoise tree of life into the end and put it over my shoulder. I ran my thumbs over it.

"Okay," I sighed, "You've sold me. What's the damage?"

"It is a birthday present. Happy twentieth birthday, Scarlett," he ducked his head and pressed his lush lips to my cheek, and I beamed a smile at him in the mirror. "There we go. Try not to frown so much, your smile puts the sun to shame," Solder said casually, and I turned and gave him a hug.

"Thank you, Solder. You've just made my day."

I spent a little while longer with Solder making small talk before leaving and continuing my mission to find Amethyst a gift.

"You should be glad it is me watching you today rather than my brother. I do not think he would have liked all the hugging and kissing going on in there," Quick said from behind me and I stiffened.

I knew Slate would send someone to watch me.

Quick walked with an arrogant swagger to where I stood and looped his arm through mine. "Whatever you did to him has him profoundly confused. I do not think I have ever seen him so distracted," he flashed me a dazzling smile, and I tried to remember it was not Quick's fault, but Slate's for my inner turmoil.

"Okay, but today is for quiet introspection not for ogling women and flirting. Understood?"

He started forth taking me with him. "You wound me, Ms. Scarlett. I do not ogle, I appreciate," he corrected as we walked arm in arm together.

I found Amethyst's gift at a jewelry store. It was a charm to place on her new torque once she earned it. I had liked it so much; I bought one for myself when Quick wasn't paying attention too busy flirting with one girl behind the counter. The charm was the silhouette of a mother holding a baby. I got mine in silver and Amethyst's in gold. I didn't know what I was thinking — a feeling had warmed me as I looked at the little charm.

The worst-case scenario was Ash dumped me on my fanny pack. The silver baby was a reminder of what was most important in my life. Marriage, a family, and stability. Slate's moment of matrimonial delusions would be forgotten in a fortnight.

"Slate did not answer his summons last night," Quick said, leaning into my ear.

"Summons?" I asked.

Quick gave me a knowing grin. "You were in his room last night," Quick said pointedly and my eyes widened at him. He shrugged a tattooed shoulder, "They were still arguing about her showing up unannounced when they got in. I was there and Lera asked if he'd had a girl in his room and he lied. Slate does not lie about women. If he did, there was a bigger reason behind him not wanting Lera to find out. He does not want her taking it out on you. So, where were you when she came in? Give me the dirty details."

I ran my teeth along my lower lip, "I was under the bed." As he laughed, I blushed and averted my eyes, "Brass knows?"

"Brass always knows. He never should have gotten involved with you. From the moment he met you, Slate asked us to monitor you. You were a mission. Seen from a distance only," Quick said as his laughter tapered off.,

"I care about Brass. I wouldn't have — done, *um*, been with him if I didn't."

Quick shrugged. "Slate's never gone after a woman as he has with you. Brass knows that. He got in the way. No offense, but once you walked into Slate's crosshairs you did not stand a chance. Brass snuck in there and deflowered Slate's coveted dream woman. He is the envy of every man who knows, but me. I prefer blondes," he said lightening the mood as I grimaced.

"I am sorry about your teammate," I said, offering a sympathetic smile.

"We will get to the bottom of her death. Do you need to replace any of your blades?" Quick asked as we strolled.

He was an excellent escort. Since it was crystal clear, I would never ever sleep with him, he'd started treating me like a younger sister... well, an adopted distant cousin. Quick's scent was as seductive as the man, even under the growing heat of the day he smelled sinful.

"I do. Thanks for reminding me."

Quick led us up the road towards the portal gate and into their favorite weapons shop. It was significantly cooler the moment we entered the long narrow shop. Two burly salesmen stood behind the glass cases that lined the room.

The one with a blonde ponytail and tattoos smirked at us when we walked in. "Quick, sweetheart — morning," Hopper said, placing his rough hands on the top of the case in front of him.

I recognized the other employee and waved; he was a Shadow

Breaker they called Jolt. I'd watched him compete on the Crash Course but didn't know his real name. He gave me a nod and continued to help his customer. Quick smirked back and told Hopper what we needed.

"Are you a Shadow Breaker too?" I asked in a whisper and Hopper grunted.

Quick turned to me with a lazy smile, "Grasshopper here, is one of our elite captains, like our Slate."

"Slate? Quick, how dare you come in here without my lover."

My stomach twisted and bile rose quickly to the back of my mouth before I could swallow it down. Skipping breakfast had been a terrible idea. A tall, leggy blonde dressed in a snug pair of khakis and a low-cut white tank top smirked with a wide mouth at Quick. Her straight hair fell around her sun kissed, toned shoulders framing a round face. A pair of big bright blue eyes judged me before I had a chance to make a first impression. A sliver of her stomach peeked from her tank top, and as toned as the rest of her. She was a Guardian; she wore both torques and the Yggdrasil necklace. A short seax buckled to her thigh completed her self-possessed look.

I was regretting wearing flats that day now that I was face to face with yet another one of Slate's lovers, this one with legs that went up to my belly button. She stood a good four inches taller than me when she moved past Hopper to cock out her hip and shoot Quick a steamy look. Slate must not have been the only one she'd had those long legs wrapped around.

"Anthias, this is Scarlett. Scarlett, this is Anthias, Hopper's sister," Quick said, introducing us.

The tall, smirking blonde ran her eyes from head to floor and back again with a seriously unimpressed look and I was ready to claw her eyes out. Hopper stood next to her, and I could see a small resemblance. His hair and blue eyes were darker, but they had the same crude arrogance.

"This is the Grand Mistress's delegate. Try not to completely piss her off," Hopper said, and I almost blushed.

Hopper had heard about me enough to know who I was and how far I'd risen in such a short time. How the Shadow Breakers would figure in with my dysfunctional relationship with Slate, or how Cordillera would take it — I would cross that bridge when I got there I supposed.

"How did you make that happen?" she asked with distaste.

"Anthias has been trying to get recruited into the Shadow Breakers for a few years now," Quick explained.

A different day would have been better for the conversation or meeting that woman. As it was, standing there after my night with Slate in front of yet another one of his lovers was doing nothing for my mood.

"I didn't think Lera let women who'd slept with Slate hang around headquarters?" I asked feigning innocence.

Her eyes narrowed at me, and Quick chuckled, "She is tougher than she looks."

I didn't know if he meant me or her.

"Jealous?" Anthias purred.

Quick still held my arm, and he gave it a little reassuring squeeze, as if her words would hurt me. They did fiddlesticking hurt for more reasons than Quick could fathom.

Hopper cleared his throat, "Sweetheart, do not take it personally; she is like this with everyone. If Lera was recruiting, I would consider it as a personal favor if you put in a good word for her."

Anthias' eyes glittered. "I can show you my talent," she widened her eyes slightly and then shrank.

I gasped when I was looking back at myself. She was projecting an image of me, from my long light brown waves to my bronze chiffon strapless dress, and plump lips. She was me and she blew a kiss at me. If Quick hadn't been holding me in place, I would have jumped.

"Gods," Quick whispered and held out his had to grope her, *er*, my breast.

My hand snapped out as I slapped his hand away. I didn't care if I wouldn't feel it, those were my breasts he was trying to grab.

"Oh, Quick. I have missed that look in your eyes. Any time you wish, I can wear her for you," Anthias purred in her own voice.

I crinkled my nose, "I'll consider it Hopper, if she never projects me again."

"Do not make that promise," Quick said, and I shot him a look of death.

"It is only a mirage, that is what they call me, Mirage. I will not feel as you do. It is only a projection," Anthias grew back to her height and her body.

"Hopper, thank you for the blades. Good day."

I'd had enough. My pleasant morning stroll was turning sour in a hurry.

Quick was on my heels and looped his arm through mine again, "Truth. Gods, could you imagine? She has never done that with me before, but now that I know she can..."

I stopped. "You would never. Joke all you want, but you know seeing a naked projection of me while feeling her is wrong," I started walking again. "Besides, nothing is ever as good as the original," I muttered and Quick laughed.

"Truth. I wonder if my brother would agree," he watched me out of the corner of his eye.

My stomach twisted. Brass never would.

"I'm sorry, Quick. You can go ahead with your day. Thanks for keeping me company," I flashed him a smile and he couldn't help but return and shake his head.

"Truth. Makes my job easier when you let me do it, Ms. Scarlett." Quick said, releasing my arm.

Elivagar was never over forty degrees Fahrenheit. I went back to my room and pulled out the few outfits Tawny had bought me when she found out she would rule Elivagar. The style there was heavier fabrics and instead the Grecian look Thrimilci leaned towards, or the caftans of Ostara, it was a Victorian style. Which meant corsets and bustles, but none of that puffy sleeve business. The outfit I chose was a snug navy wool double-breasted jacket over an ivory shirt. The wool skirt that kicked as I walked which I liked.

I felt like I needed some sort of fancy hat to complete the ensemble but opted instead to braid my hair around my face pinning it to my head with loose strands hanging to give me a softer look. I clasped my cloak after a few swipes of mascara and lip gloss and hurried to the portal pulling my gloves on as I went.

My boots rang out on the tiled floors as I reached the blue lit portal room and skidded to a halt. Slate was leaning against the wall next to the door and I clenched my jaw determined to ignore him.

"That is it? You are going to pretend it did not happen?" his tone was cavalier, but I knew better.

"I'm late. We can discuss this when I get back from my trip in five days. Surely five days is long enough for you to realize you've gone twenty years without wanting a wife, so this need not make any difference in the grand scheme of things."

Slate's eyes flared as he straightened from the wall.

"I hurt you. I suppose I deserve it, but a man has limits," he warned, the blue light from the room casted demonic shadows over his hard planed face.

He was head to toe black with his cloak on and hands gloved. He plaited his mane of hair away from his face to spill down his broad back. Slate looked every bit the assassin even without the dozens of blades hidden about his body — and there I was with a measly three.

Several caustic comments came to mind about Slate's supposed limits, but I bit them back. I walked forward and stood before him with surprise flickering through his thick-lashed eyes.

"I don't want to fight. It is what it is. I don't want you breathing down my neck bullying me," I paused and rubbed my lips together. "You were an indulgence. A chocolate ganache trifle. I only wanted a few bites, but the whole thing every day would make me sick. For now, leave me be," I exhaled gustily.

"Not good enough," he pushed off the wall and towered above me, "I wrapped your dessert up in a black bow — just for you."

"It's going to have to be. I have nothing else to say to you," I crossed my arms, and his eyes went to the braid that was threaded into my hair, new fetish attached.

His big hand shot out and ran the pad of his thumb on it, "Torch?"

"A birthday present," the bastard trainer voiced me, and I answered lightening quick.

"From?" his silver eyes swung to mine, his tone low and dangerous.

"Solder," I sighed, and his nostrils flared.

"Scarlett Tio, I am going to claim you one day soon. It will be so complete that you can never look at another man without thinking of me. When I walk into a room, your breaths will sharpen, and sex dampen. No one will come close; you will forever be mine."

It would have done just that except it wasn't a promise, it was a threat, and I took it as such. I pinched my lips together and glared up at him.

"Don't hold your breath," I bit off and his lips curled mockingly.

"Do you want to deactivate the bond, Torch?"

I nodded then added. "No funny business, just get the job done."

Slate's chuckle was wicked, "Here or would you like more privacy?"

I shifted uncomfortably and swallowed. "It would be difficult to explain if someone walked in on us. There's a utility closet around the corner," I said, thinking aloud.

Before I could say another word, Slate had gripped my hand and was pulling me back to the entrance. He turned left and walked seven steps until he reached the nearest door and flung it open dragging me in after him.

"Gods, you don't have to be so rough," I cursed, straightening my jacket.

I looked up and froze. Slate filled the tiny room of cleaning implements; I wondered how long we could breathe in there with him gulping up all our air. The constant charge his body emitted was more powerful than ever in confined places. I shifted trying to look unimpressed, even bored.

It was ineffectual. Slate wasted no time closing the distance between us, he moved so quickly; I jolted back running into the shelves behind me. Slate caught two bottles that fell before they hit the floor and leaned past me to return them while I blushed.

"Relax, Torch. We have done this many times," he purred adding to my embarrassment and irritation.

He was so close I could feel the heat of his body even through my clothes. He started removing his gloves, one finger at a time before pulling them off.

"Why do you need to take off your clothes? It's just a kiss," I said craning my neck, breathing in his seductive scent.

"You want it done properly, do you not?" he said, tucking his gloves into his belt.

I narrowed my eyes, "Tell me exactly how it works."

"We have to press them together firmly," he said cocking his head, "I have it on good esteem that you are quite talented at this."

For a brain-dead minute, my lips quirked at his playful tone. "Okay let's get this over with," my tone was all business even if the rest of me wasn't.

Slate smiled, and it was one of his rare cheek creasing smiles that smarter women wouldn't have melted over. I tilted my chin up and met his long-lashed silver eyes. Slate's lids were low as he gazed down at me. I licked my lips, and he brought his mouth a hair's breadth from mine and kept it there.

"Kiss me, Torch," he breathed.

I kept my eyes open and pressed forward planting a quick kiss, hard and fast before stepping back and folding my arms, "Okay, now move. We're missing Amethyst's challenge."

Slate laughed, making me bite down hard on my lower lip before I smiled with him, "Bond is still there, Torch. That was hardly a peck. I have seen you kiss Keen deeper than that."

"Keen and I are great friends, whereas you and I are hardly friends on a good day," I huffed. Slate's eyes flared, and he gripped me tightly around the waist made extra tiny by the corset, "Why do you need to —"

"Shut your mouth," Slate growled, and I clicked my mouth shut.

He brought his mouth down to mine again and this time he moved his other hand to my nape before bringing his lips down. He brushed lightly against my lips with his; I watched wide eyed until his slid closed and his lashes fanned across his cheeks. His tongue slid out as he ran it across my lower lip just before he pulled it between his teeth. My eyes snapped open, and I opened my mouth to protest. The second I parted my lips; Slate slanted his mouth over mine.

It started out harmless enough as my lips molded to his, but then his hand tightened on the back of my neck and his soft tongue probed into my mouth. Slate deepened the kiss with no resistance. My hands lifted of their own accord, and I had no control over the way one wound its way into his hair while the other slid around his hips to that delicious hard fanny pack of his groping at will.

He sucked in air at a hiss when I bit his lower lip then chuckled against my mouth when I felt the bond shoot through me then rapidly evaporate. His hands roamed over my body as he growled in frustration at the many layers of clothing I didn't normally wear. My jacket was open as he gripped my shirt in his fists and tore it. I gasped at the sudden exposure, but my corset covered me while Slate buried his face in my cleavage. My head fell back as I moaned wrapping my fingers in his mane.

Slate growled, "Why do you have so much fucking clothing on?"

I may or may not have uttered something unintelligible that sounded like, "Stand back so I can burn it off."

A light shown on us like a beacon in the darkened room and a startled woman in a royal blue gown dropped her supplies with a loud clatter, "Oh! Oh my! I am very sorry, sir. Miss."

The poor woman's cheeks reddened when Slate turned around and it was obvious what we'd been up to. He adjusted himself looking down at the woman while wincing and I buttoned my jacket.

"Don't worry about it. We were just leaving," I told her, offering the young woman a smile.

I grabbed Slate's hand as he growled and led him back to the portal room. As we went a million thoughts hit me in an instant, I straightened myself. I stopped before the door and faced him. His face was dark with displeasure, and it crammed his pants full. I wanted to laugh again, but I settled for a nervous smile.

"We needed to go, anyway; we're being selfish."

"It would not have taken very long," he said, a small smile curling his lips, and I leveled my eyes at him.

"I need time. There isn't much because you waited until the last possible second to lose your Gods' cursed mind, but the engagement party is the day after tomorrow and I promise I will let you know my decision by tomorrow night. I have a few things I need to think about," I bit my lip and prayed he understood.

"So, we are perfectly clear, what are you thinking about, Torch?" Slate asked, arching an eyebrow.

My insides heated as my stomach lurched, "Um, what you asked me before the Wild Hunt. If the offer still stands of course, if it doesn't, I understand. I wasn't very receptive at the time to anything you had to say really, I am still struggling with —"

Slate was smiling arrogantly at me, and I shut my mouth tight, "A little retribution. I meant what I said. I would not have left you last night if a Breaker had not died. It was the only time Lera has been in my bedroom."

"If I thought maybe, it could work, we could take it slow like… there's no rush. If. Big If," I rambled, and he took another step forward and slid his hands around my waist.

"I want you, Scarlett. Think about it if you must but promise me you will not lay with the Straumr boy until you tell me your choice."

I knit my brow. "Gods, Slate. Please. How I am with you is completely different from when I am with other men. Pretend you think I have a little moral fiber left," I crossed my arms, and he bent his head to mine.

"If you did not, we would not be going to Elivagar right now and you certainly would not be about to tell me you want to spend the night alone. Sleep on it, Torch."

He was so darn arrogant. Still, I tilted my chin, and we kissed again. I didn't think we'd had such a wonderfully normal kiss before. There's something to be said for sweet simple kisses that wouldn't lead to something else.

Slate drew back and rested his forehead against mine. "Careful. A man could get used to that," he growled, sending a thrill through me.

"What have you done to me?" I whispered, more to myself than him.

Slate grunted, "Reading my mind, Torch?"

CHAPTER
TWENTY-SIX
JETT

Jett didn't think they could be any more transparent. When Slate had volunteered to wait for Scarlett Jett couldn't hide his astonishment. The man a glutton for punishment.

Scarlett and Slate had walked into the clearing at Elivagar together and they'd smiled at one another when she went to greet Ash who was networking since so many great families gathered in one place. Scarlett then came over to where they sat and greeted everyone before nonchalantly sitting next to Slate.

Jett was glad he had someone to make a face at. Gypsum met his eyes over Indigo's head and mouthed, *what the —* Jett's sentiments exactly.

Ragnarök lasted for hours, Wren had taken nearly eight hours to complete the trek last year. Jett was trying very hard and failing not to think about his mother.

The town center in Elivagar was a snowy mountain town nestled in a valley below the castle Vetr. The town's buildings comprised a variety of different colored red bricks. Chimney smoke blended in the air above the town. If the North Pole had a city, this would have been it.

Elivagar's portal gate was a free-standing iron gate with square pillars on either side. You could see through the iron bars, but every time a person would cross, it would light up. Portal doors came from a time when Guardians were also elementals, the bright white light made you think you were traveling at the speed of light.

Slate and Scarlett reached the stadium at the top of the mountain as the competitors had run into the tree line, managing a wave to Amethyst before she joined her team in the thick forest. It was half a stadium, one half being completely open to the forest before it. It was heated, the seating warm. Nervous parents waiting for their children to come out the other end filled the seats.

The Ragnarök challenge threw everything you had learned at you in real life form. It had been deadly in some rare cases. More often than not, people got hurt. They claimed it still wasn't as bad as being unprepared for what could happen out in the world.

The start was also the end. You traversed the mountain and back again using the tracking skills learned in at Valla U. There were twenty obstacles you had to collect flags from to complete the course. The good part was if you took the challenge with your class then you could team up to four. You weren't competing with the other course runners; they designed it for you to utilize every skill you could muster however you could. If it was easy for you, excellent. If not, then you didn't learn enough at Valla U and you'd have to wait to retake the challenge. The public knowledge of your failure was enough to cause future Guardians to do the damnedest not to fail.

Tawny sat on Orion Vetr's right with Steel since she was the heir to Elivagar. She looked at home on the platform. Cassiopeia Natt sat there out of sheer stubbornness. The Vetrs were estranged, or she disapproved of Tawny. The frosty old blonde gazed haughtily out at the crowd.

The Hausts were there too, Quartz and Nova were doing their Ragnarök with Amethyst. They sat on the other side of the stadium where Ash was currently schmoozing. The rest of the Straumrs sat in the seats below them, Fox kept turning around and chatting with a dazzling

Scarlett. Slate didn't seem to mind not being the center of her attention either, something big must have happened and he missed it.

"I'll see you all at the end of the challenge," Indigo got to her feet and crossed the stadium to where the Hausts sat.

When she stood, the spot next to Gypsum was vacant so Diamond got up from the Straumrs sitting next to him. Gods, it was like musical chairs. Jett thanked the Mother for his wives, he'd never have to bother with all those games ever again. He pulled Cherry closer to his side, and she leaned her head against his shoulder.

Six hours they'd waited before Amethyst came through the tree line and Jett had been clenching his jaw so hard his teeth hurt. Scarlett and Slate had been quiet, but the heat coming off those two... By the Mother, how would Fox sit in front of them? Things got weird when Gypsum went to relieve himself and came back trying not to be too obvious about talking to a fawn, but when a fawn was walking alongside you and you're trying to talk like a ventriloquist, it sticks out.

Cherry and Jett ran down the stairs to the clearing and started towards Amethyst. She had minor wounds and went straight into the healing tent before getting her golden torque, but Jett had barged into the tent and delved into Amethyst while she smiled at him wryly. That was fine. She could act like he was overreacting, but that was his kid in there and he was going to make damn sure it was okay.

The Straumrs had held a big party for Amethyst at their palace and that was when the coolness returned between Scarlett and Slate. Ash had taken Scarlett's arm the minute she walked through the ballroom door and had not left her side. Slate brooded in stony silence as he followed them from the shadows with his silvery eyes.

Gods, he hoped Scarlett knew what she was doing.

CHAPTER
TWENTY-SEVEN

The after party at the Straumr's had been touchy. I'd been with Slate all day and then Ash all night. Gods, what was I doing? Slate could have left the party early, no one would have noticed, but a part of me knew he wouldn't leave until I did. I wished he trusted me more; I wouldn't stay the night even though Ash had pressed me to.

Tawny had been right. Ash was a sure thing. I knew exactly what I was getting with him, and Slate was completely unknown. It terrified me. What Slate and I had was what Ash, and I lacked, and vice versa. Ash meant stability. I'd be provided for the rest of my life, that my children would be provided for, and Ash would never ever leave me. He might have an affair. I'd thought of that already, but I could deal with that because he'd keep it very covert.

Slate was all heat. Sure, he was making promises now, but he'd never been in a relationship. My head hurt from thinking.

There was always Brass at the back of my mind. Stable *and* hot. He would never want me since I slept with his best friend, besides, we were friends. We weren't romantic. Right?

I'd gone back to the palace and was only mildly annoyed that Slate walked me to the bedroom door and stole a goodnight kiss. So, I fell asleep thinking about him, he'd said. As if there was something else on my mind.

Guilt would have been suffocating if I wasn't positive that Ash didn't love me in the way I needed to be loved. He didn't and if I broke things off he'd be angry. Furious, but not hurt. He'd get over it and the girls would clamber over themselves for him.

The inside of Myriads of Muhrad was all a glitter. Dazzling gowns hung everywhere, the newest designs from New York's fashion week hung along one wall, Tawny informed me, eyes as big as saucers. She dragged us back there. Amethyst hung back, she wasn't showing very much, but they might have been worse for her. Instead, she had a little potbelly on her normally svelte form. She always kept a hand on her belly.

We'd waited until the last minute to buy our dresses. I'd have to splurge and get one for the induction ceremony as well. I wouldn't need one for tomorrow, I thought gleefully and bit down on my lip to keep from smiling.

I stood before a brightly lit mirror with Tawny as we tried on dresses, "What do you think about Ash?"

She whirled around and her hazel eyes were wide, "Why? What happened?"

I hadn't asked her opinion on him since the first week we met. "Nothing. I'm having doubts is all," I looked at her from my peripheral and she was gaping at me.

"Leave him. End it. Do it now. Fiddlestick! I wished they had cell phones here so we could do it now," it split her wide mouth into a smile.

"Jeez... try to act less enthusiastic," I said dryly as I looked at the back of the dress.

"Don't marry him, Scar. You'll be content, but you'll never be happy. Truly happy."

Things were getting deep.

I chewed my lip, "I don't think I'm going to." She hopped onto me and knocked me to the floor as she squealed.

I rolled away from her and got up with much difficulty in the snug dress, "Freya's burly boar, Tawny. You just tackled me!"

She was giggly and not listening to a word I said, "Who is it? Dish. Which guy stole away the allusive heart of Scarlett Tio? Brass? It's Brass isn't it! By the Mother, I live vicariously through you. Tell me."

I rolled my eyes, "Who are all these men you speak of?"

Tawny gave me a look like she thought I was an idiot and started ticking off names, "Oh, I dunno. Brass, Solder, Slate. Those are the top contenders, aren't they?"

I made a face. "Dude, you are seriously deprived of reality television. Solder... no way. He is a onetime guy and then after that only when it's convenient for him. Brass..." I smiled moronically at myself in the mirror, "Brass is special. I love Brass, but he doesn't look at me like that. Not really."

Tawny was practically bouncing on her toes. "So, it's Slate?" she beamed, and I nodded. She squealed again, "Oh, thank the Gods you two idiots finally got it together. I know how scary he must be for you Scar but take it slow. You'd have to be blind not to see how crazy you two are for each other."

Slow. Right.

"Tawny, he asked me to marry him," I said in a low voice and her jaw dropped, "I told him I need time, and like you said, to take it slow. It's all happening so fast."

Tawny snorted, "You move at a snail's pace, but yeah, I agree. Slow would be good. Don't jump right in blind with both feet, you'll find yourself with a bun in the oven and you'll have to drop out of Valla U then you'll be miserable. I'm going to try on the wine-colored dress."

She hopped off the little platform and went back into the dressing room and I sighed.

Cherry grabbed a few dresses and hurried back into the dressing room. Indigo gravitated towards pastels and blues; they suited her. She picked two, either would be gorgeous, or went into the dressing room. As soon as I saw the dresses, I knew which I wanted. I hoped I'd feel the same way about my wedding dress. The thought snuck up on me.

I hurriedly grabbed the dresses and headed to the saleslady. For their dresses, they kept a list of who had bought it recently so you wouldn't wear it to the same event. I held my breath as she checked until I got the go ahead.

Tawny chose wine colored dress in sequined lace and satin. Indigo chose an aqua blue dress that's neckline went across her collarbone in a sheer aqua panel. Everyone was lucky with their dresses except for Cherry, who had to go with her third dress choice. She left with a glittering backless blue gown.

Tawny was looking pensive as we strolled to the Tearrific Cafe. "What's up?" I asked her as I fell back from Indigo.

"I'm nervous about Orion."

"It'll be fine, Tawns. Orion won't let her evil witch of a wife do anything to you," I told her as we walked along the shimmering white roads.

"There's that, but he's hinted at some sin in his past that — I might not like. Bad things," she was whispering.

"What do you mean?" I thought about when we watched my mother do the Ragnarök course in Elivagar and Jett told me they put criminals on pikes outside their castle.

"I don't want to jump to any conclusions, I just feel like there's a lot he isn't telling me because it will scare me off. Which makes me more afraid because, he's my grandfather. I've grown to care about him," she chewed her lip. "If he thinks that whatever he isn't telling me is bad enough to make me not want him around, then it must be bad. *Terrible*," her eyebrows had climbed halfway to her hairline.

"He's willing to change his family lineage from a male line to a female line, just to have you be a part of his family. He could have done that with the evil twins before now, instead he's chosen you. That's a lot to deal with," I was nervous about what she was saying, but I wanted her to be wrong too.

She nodded, but she didn't look convinced.

We were crossing in front of Hopper's shop when an enormous arm slid around my middle pulling me away from the rest of the group. Tawny turned her head startled, but then a smile grew on her face, and she looped her arm through a gaping Indigo's and followed behind Cherry and Amethyst.

"I was hoping to run into you," Slate rumbled against my ear and butterflies beat in my stomach as I turned around to face him, "That is not the smile of a woman who is about to turn down a man, Torch." His silver eyes flashed, and I pulled my lips between my teeth.

"Ash has to be told before —"

My words couldn't come out fast enough before Slate had picked me up under my arms and spun me around forcing several passersby to dodge us, but our smiles were infectious, so they didn't stay mad long. He set me on my feet, my head spinning and closed his mouth over mine. I'd lost my mind.

"Slate, we're in the middle of the road," I muttered when he got grabby, deepening the kiss.

"I do not care. Let them watch," he closed his mouth over mine again and I pushed him away laughing.

"I have to meet up with the girls. I don't want to put Amethyst in an awkward position. Tonight," I shot him my very best megawatt smile, "It's been exactly one year since I met you."

Slate grabbed me again. "Happy anniversary, Torch," he kissed me sweetly before letting me go and stood on the doorstep of Hopper's shop as I walked away watching me.

Flirting with disaster, I knew I was, but I couldn't help myself. The man made my brain turn into mashed potatoes.

Bronze, Cricket, and Katydid met Indigo, Tawny, and me in our bathroom. We showered, dried, teased, curled, pinned, and pampered. Every superfluous hair was incinerated from our bodies and our makeup applied to perfection. I was feeling a little crazy, so I forewent my usual pale pink polishes for O.P.I.'s The Best Silver Ever on my fingers and toes so they glittered under the lights. Tawny approved.

The busty brunette helped me step into my sea foam green satin gown. My favorite part of the flowing dress was the illusion sleeves that looked like I had painted glittering ivy along my arms to my wrists, it matched my half mask. My eyes looked greener than ever, my hair hung in loose curls with a plait across the front and pinned in place.

Tawny touched her sequined wine mask and smiled at Indigo and I in the mirror. "I won't offer to get your guys' phone numbers this year, but seriously you three. I love you," Tawny beamed.

Even the professional Cricket seemed to preen from the compliment. She tossed her coifed curls over a shoulder and finished packing up their array of items and left to help Cherry and Amethyst ready.

I ran my fingers along my braid, and the delicate fetishes threaded through it. I understood now why Slate had not liked Solder giving me the little turquoise fetish, but it wasn't a romantic gift, just a token and I seriously loved it.

I was nervous about tonight. Nervous wasn't a good enough word though, apprehensive to the point of trembling was more like, but I had gotten myself into this mess and I would get myself out of it. Mentally, I was already making plans to send messengers out in the morning to cancel the party. I knew my family would support me no matter what my decision, none of the men in my family had warmed up to Ash. Alder was always gently probing to see if I was still determined to marry him. Pearl seemed wary as well, though I didn't know why.

Despite the inner turmoil, there was a center of calm, I felt better about this decision than I had a few questionable ones I'd made since arriving in Tidings. Oddly enough, I thought my mother would approve.

Hawk, Gypsum, and Steel waited in the informal dining room for us. They sat at the carved light wood table lit only by the lanterns that hung above the table giving it a soft feel. Gypsum whistled when we walked in making us laugh, Steel got to his feet and walked to Tawny with a bright smile that belonged in a magazine model.

He kissed her chastely and smiled, "Slate and Jett said they'd meet us there."

A little thrill shot through me. I knew where I would find Slate and bit down on my lip to hide my smile. I was wearing both engagement rings; it wouldn't be right to take off Ash's until I could officially end things. He would not take it well and I knew I'd have to do it in a public place, or he would freak out, maybe this way he'd only storm off. I hoped I would be that lucky.

Steel wore a wine-colored waistcoat over his long white sleeve shirt that matched Tawny's dress, and a half mask half of it the wine, the other half black. Gypsum still couldn't attend until next year, but Thrimilci would have a party of its own and he dressed for it.

Hawk had on a burgundy satin waistcoat, a white under tunic and a burgundy ascot. His pants were also black and tucked into black boots that went up to his mid-calf. His mask was black with trimmed in gold with horses at the top in front of his silver hair. I'd never get used seeing my silver fox of an uncle dressed this way.

Hawk gave us each a hug and a kiss as Alder walked through the archway, his tall, powerful frame taking measured strides towards us. His short blonde hair peeked from behind his golden sun mask that matched his waistcoat. I smirked. It was a definite slap in the face to the Vars. He returned my smirk with a knowing quirk of his lips.

Hawk laughed out right and slapped a hand to his massive shoulder. The two men had been spending a lot of time together since Alder had moved into the pal- ace and they looked like friends. Alder said something in his low guttural tone making Hawk laugh again. I missed my mother so bad it hurt.

Pearl and Sparrow walked into the room together, Pearl in a flowing rose gown and Sparrow in burgundy. Her and Tawny's dresses were so similar Gypsum teased them. I slid my arm through Indigo's after bidding Gypsum goodbye and we walked to the starry portal room.

It was just as I remembered. The yellowed stone portal room of Valla U was unrecognizable with all the beautifully dressed, masked people milling about. Tawny and Steel set out right away promising to meet us later, but I had a feeling they were going to relive their first night together in the conservatory.

Indigo rolled her eyes at me with a smile. I'd be doing the same myself in a few minutes. Hawk and Sparrow smiled and went their own way, Sparrow's eyes still looking a bit lost. No one would fault her if she was never the same. I doubted you bounced back after your closest confidant and sister dying. I knew the feeling with painful intimacy.

Pearl hugged us both. "I cannot tell you how happy seeing the two of you together makes me, darlings," she slid her slender hands into ours and held them firmly, her emerald eyes moistening, "If there is anything either of you want to talk about, please come see me. I have been giving you your space, know that my door is always open for you both. I have raised five children and though I may seem busy, I am never too busy for either of you."

I swallowed hard, and Indigo took a step forward and hugged our grandmother. While fighting back tears, I did as well. The constant sorrow from my family and being an empath had been too much for me to be present. I should have drawn them all closer instead of pushing away, I had needed them more than ever.

Pearl lifted the edge of her mask and wiped a long-nailed fingers under her eyes, "My, I will make a mess of Cricket's hard work." She smiled, "Have fun girls, I shall see you in the morning. We have another big day ahead of us tomorrow."

She flashed me a smile, and my stomach flipped. "About that, I am having some issues," Indigo and Pearl looked at me questioningly and I offered a small smile, "I don't think Ash and I are going to work out."

Indigo gasped, but Pearl nodded, "Speak with Ash. Let us know what comes of it, it only takes a moment to summon messengers to cancel a party, darling."

I nodded and Indigo led us deeper into Valla University. The cavernous, seldom-used ballroom so seeing it again in all its glory was stunning. Huge, tiered chandeliers hung from the high ceiling; tiny, mirrored pieces nestled into the stone walls reflecting the light from the chandeliers like starlight. Guardians mingled on the marbled floor and a band was playing ethereal music with instruments I'd never seen before, aside from a drum. Which, even in my limited experience, was recognizable.

It was a sensory overload, at some point I thought I'd get accustomed to the beauty and erotic mysticism that was a running undercurrent of Guardian culture, but nope, never had. The rich scents of the people gathered, and the decadent foods completed the scene, so you felt as if you been transported to another planet or at least another time.

Swirling dresses, jeweled masks, powerfully built men, and leather. Gods, it was good to be a Guardian. As I took in the room, I spotted my shadow man. Leaning against a marble column with bits of mirror in it was a towering shadow. A tall man with a horned black half mask made to look like the classic depiction of Lucifer leaned with corded muscular arms folded in front of his chest. I wondered how I ever walked away that first night.

"I'll meet you in the water pipe room," I said distractedly to Indigo.

"Are you really going to end things with Ash?" she asked abruptly, and I turned to her loathing to break eye contact with the God like being waiting for me.

"I'll give you details tomorrow. It will not work out. My fault, not his. See you later," I couldn't wait another nanosecond.

I glided over to the column as Slate retreated deeper into the shadows of the incandescent room. I bit my lower lip and followed; sea foam dress trailing behind me.

Slate was walking down the stone hall and had turned the corner. I looked both ways to make sure I wasn't being watched, but I couldn't recognize anyone with all the masks on, so I tossed caution to the wind and picked up my skirts to chase after Slate.

The hall ended, and I furrowed my brows. I'd lost him. I thought the whole point of cat and mouse was so the cat could play with the mouse. Wait, was I the mouse or the cat?

A big arm slid around my waist from behind, and I was moving sideways. Slate pulled me into a darkened alcove and pressed my back against the door as he lowered his mouth to mine. He smiled that rare smile, just for me.

"A second chance at what should have happened last year?" I breathed and his eyes flashed silver behind his demon mask.

"I do not think I would have made it out of the ballroom," he growled and kissed me deeply, making my toes curl in my gold heels.

I gasped as he pushed his hips against me, "Gods, Slate do you walk around like that all day?"

He chuckled kissing me again, "Only for you, Torch." I made a contented sound in my throat, and he smiled.

"World, take good notice, silver stars fading, Milky hue ript, weft of white detaching, Coals thirty-eight, baleful and burning, Scarlet, significant, hands-off warning, Now and henceforth flaunt from these shores."

I wound my arms around his neck. I was happier than I had a right to be.

"Have I ever told you how unbearably sexy it is that you know any type of poetry at all? You could quote Dr. Seuss and I would swoon, so I suppose I'm not the best judge."

Slate chuckled, and I captured his mouth with mine.

He moaned against me, "I need you, Scarlett."

"Tell me this isn't just physical. Let your walls down. Let me feel you," I breathed.

His silver eyes studied me for a moment, "See for yourself. Activate the bond."

I licked my lips and grabbed a fistful of his black waves roughly making him growl as I kissed him with little nips until I tugged on his lip with my teeth. His emotion sprung up in my mind and I sucked in air sharply, Gods how could he stand having me in his head all the time?

His emotions were so strong I could easily mistake them for my own. He watched me intently as I processed everything I felt. Darn it all, I was going to cry.

Those full lips of his quirked as he bent down to kiss me again. "Seeing things clearer?" he breathed against my lips.

Our foreheads were touching as I nodded. "I still have to tell Ash, Slate," I pulled back so I could face him, "I'll move into your room until the wing is finished. Tonight, if you wish it."

He had a dizzying effect on me, maybe that wasn't the right thing to say, but it was the first thing that came to mind. Yes, I would spend every night sleeping in the arms of this man and would relish waking up next to him.

"The bar is higher these days, Torch. For now, I plan on seeing this lovely dress in a pile next to my bed in an hour. Go finish up with the Straumr boy," he pressed a kiss to my forehead so I could still feel his bond and walked away.,

Now the hard part.

I walked to the water pipe room that adjoined the ballroom certain I would find Ash there. Featherlight red curtains shielded the room. Wall to wall fabric draped in oranges, reds and yellows surrounded the rest of the room. Pillows lined the walls and the low tables. People lounged about splayed on the colorful pillows. Water pipes sat on each table with people passing around the hoses to inhale the flavored mixes.

The crowd was all younger, first years, second years, and recently made Guardians gathered in the side room to escape their families and provosts. I strolled deeper into the room passing by few people who were drinking and more people who seemed to enjoy the other recreational items such as the small plates of boomers that laid on the tables.

Indigo spotted me and waved me over. Gods, it was last year all over again. I smiled and walked over to her; she stood when I approached and whispered into my ear.

"Ash knows something is up, he's been looking for you. He's not here right now, but please don't leave yet. They're driving me crazy," she begged, and I smiled and sat next to her.

Sage, Quartz, Nova, and Jonquil sat on one side, while Sterling, Diamond and Indigo had been sitting on the other. I placed a cushion between Indigo and Nova.

"Evening, all," I said amicably.

Jonquil and I were ignoring one another which was just fine with me. She'd get what was coming to her soon enough. Diamond beamed me a smile looking almost as relieved as Indigo had.

"Ash just left. He went to find you," her eyes, just like her brother's, sparkled.

"I'm sure he'll be back soon," I reassured her.

"Where's your drink?" Indigo asked, "I can go get you one."

"No thanks. I'm taking it slow tonight," I told her.

"Why don't you two come sit by the cool kids?" Jett whispered into my ear as he passed, and I laughed.

Cherry and Amethyst stood behind him looking as glamorous as ever and Jett slid his arms around their waists and led them over to the back table. He wore head to toe black with a Guy Fawkes mask that made me shake my head. Two shadows leaned forward from the corner, and I grabbed Indigo's hand.

"Diamond," I nodded to her, and she looked nervous, so I added, "Come see me, we're going to sit by my brother."

Sterling had his arm around her casually and she nodded.

Brass and Quick were both wearing half masks. Quick's eyes were drinking in Indigo as we came closer. I smiled internally, Quick would be a great escort for her tonight and shower her with the attention she deserved, and hopefully kept it to that or I would castrate him.

"Indigo, I don't think we have formally introduced you to the Regn brothers. Brass and Silver. Indigo," I introduced them and sat between Brass and Quick knowing she'd have to choose to sit either beside Brass or Quick.

It would dictate what happened next. She reached down and shook Brass's hand as she flashed him a bright smile.

"Nice to finally be introduced," she said before taking Quick's outstretched hand.

Tidings' hierarchy of greater and lesser families was archaic. They wouldn't approach a greater family daughter being lesser family sons. It was doubly worse for the Regn because their reputations for stealing women preceded them. I had finally heard what *they* said about those Regn boys and my firsthand experience proved it was true and then some.

Quick dazzled her with a smile and her cheeks reddened even though she didn't appear nervous at all, "I have seen you around for years."

Before she could pull away, Quick gave her hand a slight tug and patted the seat next to him. She flushed again and took the seat. Quick didn't let go of her hand.

"My reputation proceeds me. Lies. All of it," Quick dazzled her again with his panty dropping smile and Indigo looked down and away.

I doubted my idea of setting the two of them up. Jett looked at me like I'd lost my mind and Brass scoffed. Never a good sign. Diamond and Sterling were looking at our table and Brass shifted his head to meet their eyes, making them look away.

Quick had found a topic of conversation that engaged Indigo after a little while I talked Shadow Breaker competitions with Brass, he'd be competing in a couple weeks the same night as I would.

Jett grimaced at Quick and Indigo almost comically which deepened when Indigo laughed. She had an ultra-feminine laugh. It made her entire face light up, the beauty mark on her right cheek lifted on her high cheekbones. Quick shifted his body nonchalantly to devote all his attention to her.

"Quick, don't you have a date or something?" Jett asked abruptly, making Cherry giggle.

Quick and Indigo looked at Jett as if just realizing he was there, "Not at all. Indigo, I do not suppose you came with a date, did you? I would have to steal you away if you had. I do not want to part from your company," another smile, Indigo returned it with a gentle pat of her slender hand on his knee.

"I came alone," she said with soft, sparkling eyes.

The subtle hint was masked, but Jett's face darkened as mine reddened. I had no idea Indigo was so capable.

Quick got to his feet, "Jett, I am taking your lovely sister to dance. Who knew your sisters would be so ravishing?" Quick didn't take his eyes off Indi as he pulled her to her feet and looped his arm through his and left the room.

Sterling, Diamond, and Sage's eyes followed them out. Jett huffed.

"By the Mother, Scar, you are going to send the lamb to the slaughter?" Jett pulled up his mask and dry washed his chiseled tan face.

"It is not as bad as all that. Give Indigo some credit," I chastised Jett, "Besides, everyone deserves a little fun every now and again. Quick is nothing if not a good time."

Brass made a choked sound, and he put his goblet of wassail down. "I hope to never hear you utter those words again," Brass muttered to me, and I nudged him with my shoulder.

Things felt tense between us. We needed to talk.

"Why? It's true," Cherry said with gleaming cobalt eyes.

Amethyst leaned over and placed a finger to Cherry's lips, "Not now, love."

Jett sighed. "Two awkward..." he muttered and trailed off.

I frowned at him, but soon lost myself in a conversation with Brass again. "So, I know, you know," I said in a low voice.

Brass gave a slight nod.

"I think we may need a little space," I said with a sigh.

Brass looked at me for the first time that night and I averted my eyes. "Do you regret being with me, Scarlett?" he asked sounding wounded.

"Gods, no," I said in a rush, "That's the problem." Under his scrutiny, I licked my lips, "Whomever I was with first was taking a sizeable piece of me." My hand found his and gave it a squeeze, "You're compassionate, sweet, kind, and we both know I can't stop thinking about how attractive I find you." He was hiding a smirk behind his goblet in an effort not to draw the others' attention, "I think... I enjoyed myself more than I should have. If I'm coming between you, say the word, Brass. I kept thinking there was more to us than there was, and that night Slate and you fought —"

"We both did," he interjected, and our eyes briefly met.

"Brass, I have feelings for you," I blurted, and he stealthily found my hand between us.

"I would not have let you in my bed if you did not," he said, casting me a quick glance. "I understand the need for time. I am not angry, Scarlett. Only wistful," he said, and I turned giving him a quick kiss on the cheek.

I was feeling better already.

Having Slate in my head would take some getting used to, but I enjoyed knowing how he felt and where he was. I might come to forgive him for tattooing me without me knowing. I was seeing the benefits of it. For instance, I knew he was near the ballroom and happy. I hoped I was the reason for that happiness.

Then I felt that presence in my mind move closer and it became hard to pay attention to my conversation with Brass. Brass smiled at me from beneath his black leather mask, his defined lips curling in a knowing way as the scent of blueberry and strawberry wafted through the air in the pipe smoke.

I felt him. My heart skipped a beat before I even saw him, his own heart rate increasing as if I held a stethoscope directly to his sculpted chest. Slate stalked into the room that grew ten times smaller just from having him in it and he stood before us.

"I ran into Quick," he said simply before taking the seat next to me and I fought the urge to lean into him.

"We're not talking about it," Cherry said pointedly and rolled her eyes.

Slate's lips curled mockingly at Jett who was sucking on his teeth, "How many women do you suppose are in Tidings? Ten thousand? Twelve? I don't know, math was never my forte, but let me ask you this. Why out of all these women, do you think the most degenerate come calling on my sisters?"

Cherry, Brass, and Slate chuckled, and I scowled at him.

"Because they're smoking hot. They are your sisters, babe, and we all know you're the most gorgeous man ever born to be a Guardian. No offense, fellas," Cherry said giving Jett a kiss.

He smiled impishly down at her, "Well, when you say it like that..."

Someone speaking with Diamond caught my eye, and I went rigid. Sugarfoot, it was Ash. He must not have been able to see me sandwiched between the two mountains. I sucked in a fortifying breath and got to my feet.

"I've got to go do something. See you all later," I turned around giving them all a smile and let my eyes linger on Slate's silver eyes debating whether to activate my bond.

I waited until the hard part was over; I didn't want him knowing how bad it was going to get, or that I cared about Ash. It just wasn't enough.

When I started towards him, Diamond gestured to me, and I flashed a smile. His lips tugged into a smile, but I knew he was pissed. He lowered his head to greet me with a kiss and I turned my head, so we kissed one another's cheeks.

"Let's go someplace private," I said to him, and he scanned my face.

"Lead the way, my love," Ash said, offering his most charming smile and looped his arm through mine.

His mask was a golden lion that looked beautiful with his caramel skin and light green eyes. He dressed in all greens and golds and looked like he belonged at a costume ball in Venice.

He said I could lead the way, but he led me into the ballroom. "We should go somewhere in quiet," I told him not meeting his eyes.

"We will. First, I want to dance with my betrothed," Ash led me onto the dance floor and my stomach twisted.

A minor concession, I decided. Ash was a superb dancer, and he reminded me why I saw him again to begin with.

I lost track of time dancing with Ash, guiltily enjoying myself before I persuaded him to go get some air with me out on the balcony. It was freezing on the stone ledge, but my stomach was roiling, and my nerves were shot. I had to end things. No more procrastinating.

Ash sipped from his goblet looking out over the distance, the moon hung high in the dark blue sky that glittered with star light.

"You have been acting strange," he said without inflection.

"I know. I'm sorry. Fiddlestick, I'm sorry for so much, Ash," bile splashed in the back of my throat and I gagged.

He straightened, "How much have you had to drink? Perhaps we should get you home? We have a big day tomorrow."

I swallowed hard. "Give me a moment. I'm going to powder my nose and grab water," I told him feeling oddly hot.

Gods, what was Slate doing? He knew I had to talk to Ash, he shouldn't be getting me, or himself all worked up. Ash might've thought he aroused me!

My feet stumbled across the hall and into the nearest restroom and cursed when I passed a flustered-looking man. I couldn't retreat now; I was going to puke, and the men's room was empty. As I leaned over the stall, I held my hair back.

Slate's emotions in my head were rising and it was seriously pissing me off. He must have gotten sick of waiting for me and was trying to tempt me back to him. Gods, just give me fifteen minutes and I'd be all his!

Bodies slammed in the stall next to mine, so hard I fell back. A female set of hands gripped the top of the stall side and a man's set slid up over the woman's hands. My eyes widened when I realized what was happening.

EW!

I wanted to plug my ears, but I had to puke again. An odd combination if there ever was one, my body wanting to climax while it forced out puke. What a glamorous life I led. The woman moaned, and I heard things abruptly stop.

I had to get out of there before they knew I was in the bathroom with them. I thanked the Gods Slate had granted me a reprieve as I opened the stall door and went to the sink swishing water in my mouth and spitting it out getting the foul taste out of my mouth.

"Torch?"

I froze, washing my hands when the stall behind me opened. A blonde woman reversed wearing a black dress with her underwear in her hand, her arms were up in a placating manner.

"We are having fun, yes?"

I stiffened when my eyes met silver thickly framed by long lashes that went wide at the sight of me. I thought I was going to faint. His shirt was open down to his pants that weren't buttoned. My eyes met big blue eyes. Anthias shot me a little smile, and I sucked in a rattling breath.

"You used to be fun," Anthias purred.

My limbs felt weak, and my heart felt torn asunder. I wished the pain would stop, that my heart would give out already! No one should be alive after feeling so much pain!

Slate had gone terribly still as he watched me. Anthias was stepping into her underwear leaning back on the stall to pull her them back up under her dress.

The bathroom door banged in the powder room and Brass crashed into the stalls at the end when he skidded to a stop.

"Scarlett, no!" he shouted, but it was too late.

I hadn't realized what I was doing. The air in the room was being sucked away, I stole the energy from the lights as they flickered, and watched morbidly as Anthias went wide eyed. With a twist of my wrists, my palms splayed up, I blasted Anthias and Slate with the energy I'd been building. They flew into the wall above the toilets in a spray of plaster and fell against the stalls.

My hands balled into fists, and I raised them both up by their throats. Brass tackled me and we went flying into the far wall, but he didn't stop.

He picked me up and cradled me as he ran back to the hall. "Everything is going to be okay, love," he pressed a kiss to my brow.

Jett was there waiting, and he took me before Brass went back in. "Sleep tight, baby sis," Jett said as placed a hand to my forehead.

CHAPTER
TWENTY-EIGHT
JETT

"She says you're not to come to the party tonight," Jett stood, leaning against the wall of Slate's room.

Brass had shot up like a rocket from his cushion and darted out of the room. As a rule, everyone knew when Brass ran, you ran. Jett hadn't even thought, he had sprinted after him and stopped outside the door when Brass went into the bathroom.

Maybe the guy had to really piss.

Then he heard Brass shout and itched to go in, but something told him that would be a bad idea. He'd been right. Not thirty seconds later Brass had shoved a semiconscious Scarlett into his arms.

Jett had put her to sleep because she probably would've wanted to walk back herself or worse, go back into the bathroom and finish the job. Jett didn't blame her. Brass had come to the palace and found where Jett had tucked Scarlett into their mother's old bed and told him what happened.

Scarlett had called an enormous amount of power and had knocked Anthias unconscious by throwing her against the wall, then she'd gripped them both by the throat. Brass said he wasn't sure if she had wanted to kill them, or just strangle the shit out of them, but he had stopped her before she could hate herself.

That bitch Anthias was always getting into trouble, it's why she didn't have any Gods be damned friends.

Slate was still in his clothes from last night with his head in his hands. "She plans to go through with it?" he rumbled.

Jett shrugged, "Don't know. Ash showed up this morning to check on her, they were in the middle of talking when she ran off, he said. She says it's too late to cancel the party, so she must go. Who knows what will happen after."

Jett gripped the doorknob. If he stayed in Slate's presence any longer, he was likely to punch him.

Slate tilted his head enough so he could look at Jett from under his brows, "You have not tried to attack me yourself."

His brother knew him well. "She made me promise not to," Slate leaned back and ran both his hands over his hair. "She said it's between you two and she doesn't want to come between us. You don't fucking deserve her," Jett cursed.

Slate laughed, making Jett's hackles rise. "You do not think I know that? She has always been too good for me. I want her anyway. I will not be there. She can rest assured," Slate rumbled at his back and Jett nodded.

Scarlett had woken up late this morning and started sobbing uncontrollably in Jett's arms. He'd stayed the night with her after making sure the girls had gotten back all right. Ash had shown up shortly after, and Jett had eaten breakfast and brought some up for Scarlett until Ash left.

Whatever Ash had said had calmed her down a bit and, man, did that gall. Jett had been helpless as she bawled. Brass had told Jett about being in the bathroom while Slate and Anthias had gone at it, in the very next stall. Brass had picked up the images in her mind. After Brass healed Anthias and Slate, Slate had stormed from the room without speaking to either of them.

Brass had looked down at Scarlett with sorrow in his eyes. "Is the baby, okay? I delved it was fine. I did not know..." he trailed off.

"Yes," Jett had told him, and Brass had smiled warmly down at her stroking her hair away from her face, "I don't think she knew. I don't think he knows. It's a flicker. She must have inherited our mother's fertility." It wasn't the time for jokes, but what else was he supposed to do?

"Do not let her marry Ash," Brass had said, and Jett scoffed.

"I don't think she planned to until Slate hooked up with Anthias. Now we're back to square one," Jett sighed, "I'll have our father speak to her, Pearl too. He fucked it up beyond repair this time."

Brass nodded. "He recognized her voice and stopped before... Slate did not sleep with her," he had stroked her head again before leaving, "She has other options. Be sure she knows that."

Scarlett had gone up to her room after Ash left and finished breakfast. Jett had embraced her tightly, and she'd started crying again. Damn Slate for hurting her.

The pregnancy was the frosting on the crap cake.

BIBLIOGRAPHY

"A Boundless Moment" by Robert Frost
"A Woman Waits For Me" by Walt Whitman
"To The Garden of The World" by Walt Whitman
"A Clear Midnight" by Walt Whitman
"Beautiful Women" by Walt Whitman
"Whoever You Are, Holding Me Now In Hand" by Walt Whitman
"World, Take Good Notice" by Walt Whitman

Made in the USA
Middletown, DE
27 December 2023